What readers are saying about the PJ Sugar series

"PJ's adventures . . . are hilarious and the resolution of the fast-paced mystery is thoroughly satisfying as well. Think of this series as a more wholesome version of Janet Evanovich's Stephanie Plum series."
—*Booklist*

"Warren does it again with an excellent blend of humor, romance, [and] mystery. . . ."
—*Romantic Times*, Top Pick

"With an enchanting heroine, witty dialogue, and a puzzling mystery, *Nothing but Trouble* is a satisfying start to the PJ Sugar series."
—Rel Mollet at Titletrakk.com

"[*Double Trouble*] is filled with all the things I loved about the first book. . . . Romance, mystery, and lots of laugh-out-loud humor make this yet another of my favorite Susan May Warren books."
—Melody at Kids, Cakes, Dishes, and Laundry

"I had the pleasure of reading this gem, and PJ is a kick. I think a lot of us out there could relate to her more than we want to admit."
—Julie at The Surrendered Scribe

a PJ Sugar novel

Susan May
WARREN

One good lead could close this case . . .

Licensed for Trouble

Tyndale House Publishers, Inc.
Carol Stream, Illinois

Visit Tyndale's exciting Web site at www.tyndale.com.

Visit Susan May Warren's Web site at www.susanmaywarren.com.

TYNDALE and Tyndale's quill logo are registered trademarks of Tyndale House Publishers, Inc.

Licensed for Trouble

Designed by Jacqueline L. Nuñez

Edited by Sarah Mason

Scripture quotations are taken from the *Holy Bible*, New Living Translation, copyright © 1996, 2004, 2007 by Tyndale House Foundation. Used by permission of Tyndale House Publishers, Inc., Carol Stream, Illinois 60188. All rights reserved.

Library of Congress Cataloging-in-Publication Data

Warren, Susan May, date.
    Licensed for trouble / Susan May Warren.
        p. cm.
    ISBN 978-1-4143-1314-6 (pbk.)
    1. Women private investigators—Fiction. 2. Minnesota—Fiction. I. Title.
    PS3623.A865L53 2010
    813'.6—dc22   2010005975

Printed in the United States of America

16 15 14 13 12 11 10
 7   6   5   4   3   2   1

For Your glory, Lord

Acknowledgments

The more I write, the more I'm aware of how the input of others is key to writing a great book. And I've been blessed with a team who partners with me on every level—from idea to polish—to craft books that I pray touch lives. Thank you for your gift of encouragement and wisdom to me:

Rachel Hauck, who works through every single scene, asking me the right questions, giving her opinion, and always being on the other end of the phone when I need her. Hey—I think you need to fix up that spare room because I'm moving in.

Ellen Tarver, who continues to amaze me with her ability to find holes in my stories and reads manuscripts two and three times into the wee hours of the night to help me get it right. You're such a gift to me.

Karen Watson, who understands PJ and partners with me in vision and concept, who is on my team in every way to help me get the story right. Your wisdom and friendship bless me beyond words.

Sarah Mason, who is such an amazing editor—I'm so grateful she gets her hands on these stories! You take what I think is pretty good and make it amazing. (Who knew it needed so much polish!) Thank you for your talents and the way you encourage me even as you cut huge sections of "brilliant" prose from my manuscripts. In the end, you're right.

The Tyndale art, editorial, marketing, and sales teams—I'm so grateful for all your hard work in selling SMW books and especially PJ. Thank you.

My friend Cindy Kalinin and her family for saying "YES!" when I suggested going skydiving. I know you don't really mean it when you say "come back to California," but thanks for saying it anyway.

Lee and Renaud at Adventure Center Skydiving in Hollister, California, who made flying amazing and not in the least scary! Cool!

Steve Laube, because you keep me calm. Thanks for always answering the phone and acting like I'm the only person in the world.

Curt and MaryAnn Lund, who brought me into their home and their hearts. I am blessed to have been a Lund.

Andrew Warren, my Jeremy, who makes me believe I am more than I am. I love you, baby.

David, Sarah, Peter, and Noah, who remind me that now there are others like me.

And to my Father in heaven, who adopted me and gave me an amazing name: Beloved.

Chapter ONE

PJ Sugar knew how to spot a criminal. Even when that criminal might be dressed as a two-hundred-pound raccoon, complete with bandit eyes and a ringed tail, toting a ten-pound pumpkin toward the apple dunking and hot cider station near the cherry red Kellogg Farms barn.

PJ simply possessed those kinds of gumshoe instincts, the sort that could spot a murderer or a car thief or even a cheating husband at first glance. Maybe she'd been born with them. Maybe they were simply honed after years of toting around the nickname "NBT"—Nothing but Trouble.

Whatever the case, it didn't take more than one look to recognize Meredith "Bix" Bixby—despite the fifty or so pounds she'd put on since senior year of high school or the fact that she'd cut her long blonde hair to within two inches of her head, dyed it black, and crowned it with a pair of knobby black ears.

Gotcha, you little bail jumper.

However, nabbing said bail jumper might be a different bushel of apples, thanks to Jeremy Kane's brilliant costume idea. Really, sometimes she wondered if her boss actually wanted her to succeed at her job. Especially when Jeremy pulled the foamed construction of a six-foot hot dog, once used to advertise Tony's Footlongs in Dinkytown, Minneapolis, out of his tiny office closet.

A hot dog. Yes, she had arms, and her face protruded through an oval opening in the front, but she could only manage a lurching wobble, and forget about seeing anything in her peripheral vision. She had to turn her entire . . . uh, *bun* . . . to follow Bix's movements as she plopped her pumpkin near the Kellogg Farms sign and moved toward the hot cider station.

And of course, Jeremy had vanished. At least he wouldn't be easy to miss, not with his foot-high nozzle hat and bright red foam tube marked *Ketchup.*

"C'mon, Auntie PJ." Davy gripped her hand with his two grubby ones and turned his full attention to yanking her through the coarse grass toward a hay maze. As if she could resist the charms of a four-foot policeman, complete with blue uniform, utility belt, and what looked like a shiny pair of working handcuffs.

Local Detective Boone Buckam's influence, no doubt. His way of reminding PJ that she may have broken up with him, but she'd never quite be free of the imprint he'd made on her life. Like his name tattooed on her shoulder.

"Just a second, Davy." PJ shot another glance at the cider

table, where Bix stood now next to a Tinker Bell dressed in green with wide, glittery wings. Perfect. Bix had brought her daughter.

"Davy, why don't you go get Sergei—maybe he'll do the maze with you." She even shot a look toward Connie, Davy's mother, where she stood with her husband. Sergei seemed to be trying to explain to his parents, in broken English and begrudgingly translated Russian, just why people might dunk their heads into a corrugated metal bucket full of chilly water in an attempt to snag an apple with their teeth.

Admittedly, it didn't make sense to PJ, either.

Along with things that didn't make sense—why would Meredith show up here, at a community event? even dressed as a raccoon? Surely Bix knew that her fourth shoplifting charge, along with her three prior misdemeanors and one ancient domestic assault against a former boyfriend, would net her a stint in the community jail. Right?

Probably. Which was why she'd failed to show up for her court date a week ago and had been playing hide-and-seek with PJ ever since. PJ had missed her by seconds at her house, the country club, her favorite salon, and even at Fellows Academy, where her daughter attended class with Davy, PJ's nephew. In fact, PJ had started to believe that Meredith might be onto her and her assignment to bring the bail jumper back into the system.

Hey, PJ wanted to tell her, she was better than the knee-cap breakers that Liberty Bondsmen usually sent out. Bix should be counting her blessings that Kane Investigations had landed her bounty-hunting contract.

Around them, little hobbits and superheroes searched for the perfect pumpkin to go with the perfect Sunday afternoon, fragranced by the rich redolence of decaying loam, the crisp musk of hay. Laughter spilled into the afternoon, and near the front of the farm, a bluegrass band warmed up with a whine of fiddle.

Yes, PJ could understand the pull to attend the annual Kellogg Harvest Days event, even for a wanted criminal. And the raccoon costume might have stymied a PI and bail-recovery agent of lesser caliber.

Now it seemed that Davy might be in league with Bix as he yanked PJ's arm. "Noooo, I want you, Auntie PJ. Come into the maze whif me."

Davy's little bottom lip quivered, and her heart gave a painful lurch. She missed waking up to him bouncing on her stomach and the flying leaps he did into her open arms. Connie's words this morning at church, in passing—*"PJ, I hope to see you at the festival this afternoon. . . . I need to talk to you"*—had stirred all the ache she'd steeled herself against since her sister threw her out, one armful of clothes at a time into the purpling night. She didn't really blame her sister for the deep freeze out of her life over the past month. Her sleuthing skills *had* inadvertently threatened Davy's life— twice. But deep inside she was hoping Connie's casual invitation was about a second chance. She couldn't camp out on Jeremy's office sofa much longer.

And if she captured Bix, the bounty might be enough for a tidy rent deposit.

"Okay, little man. Hang on—let me find Jeremy." PJ slid

out of Davy's grip and did a wobbly three-sixty. No sign of the deserter. And Bix had finished her cider and was edging toward the dessert table. Shoot.

"I'll meet you in there!" Davy had given up on trying to manhandle her inside the maze. PJ turned just in time to spot the little law enforcer running around the first corner, his dark, curly hair bouncing as his cop gear jingled.

"Davy!" One more scan for Jeremy, a pleading look in Connie's direction, a glimpse of Bix . . . "Wait for me!"

She took off after Davy, her legs straining against the foam in a sort of half-drunken lurch as she wobbled into the maze. "Davy!" She slowed to a speed-walk, rounded a corner—

"Boo!" Davy jumped out at her, holding his toy .45. "Hands up!"

PJ put up her hands. "Don't shoot; I'm an unarmed frankfurter!"

"Don't believe her, partner." The voice came from behind her—low and laughing—and accompanied the dangerous swagger of Boone Buckam, six feet two inches of lean trouble, with lethal blue eyes and a too-familiar I-caught-you-now expression on his face that made PJ tremble just a bit. More than once she'd wondered at her decision to cut him loose and declare herself a free agent.

Especially since it didn't exactly seem like Jeremy might be snatching her up anytime soon. Six weeks since the kiss that had seemed more desperation than a romantic move, she'd started to wonder if she'd hallucinated what she considered interest on his part.

"Boone!" Davy bounded toward him, wrapping his arms around one of Boone's legs. "I love the handcuffs."

PJ met Boone's smirk with a withering look. "I thought so. You haven't learned how dangerous it is to arm a Sugar?"

"I'm hoping he redeems the family. Maybe he leans toward a different side of the law."

"Hah. I'm on the right side of the law." Speaking of—she tried to jump, get a glimpse of Bix over the top of the hay mounds, but she couldn't quite get high enough.

"Oh, sure. By cheating?" He patted Davy on the head. "I think she needs a lesson in what happens to lawbreakers, don't you, Davy?"

As if on cue, Davy whipped out his handcuffs. "I have to take you in, Auntie PJ," he said, with such a serious look on his pudgy face that PJ couldn't help but hold out her hands.

He snapped the cuffs on, put his hands on his hips as if to survey his handiwork, and took off.

Leaving her handcuffed in front of Boone like a criminal, while the *real* criminal downed apple fritters and pumpkin bread at the Girl Scout fund-raiser booth.

"Davy, come back here!" She held up her hands to Boone. "Please?"

He gave her a lopsided smile. Thankfully, it didn't hold the same power it once did. "I don't know. I think it's safer for mankind to keep you a little handicapped."

"Oh, whatever." She turned and waddled around the hay bales. "Davy!"

"I've been meaning to talk to you, PJ." Boone edged up behind her.

"Get me out of these cuffs, Boone." She whirled, held out her hands.

"Do I look like I have a key on me? And anyway . . ." He jutted out his chin, shook it a little, then lowered his voice. "I can't take sides against the family, you know."

Oh, good grief. "Brando? Seriously?"

"I'm hurt." He stepped back as if taking a bow. "Don't I look like the Godfather?"

"You're wearing a tux. I thought you were a groom or something."

His smile deflated. "No, I'm not a groom, PJ."

Then he turned and strode away.

Not a groom. Oh, that's right. He'd asked her to marry him. Twice.

Why did her mouth run out ahead to ambush her? Wow, she knew how to destroy a Sunday afternoon. "Davy! Get over here with that handcuff key!"

She ran through the maze, into dead zones and out again, finally emerging on the other side.

Davy crouched below a model cow, spraying dyed "milk" into a metal bucket. "Look, Auntie PJ, I'm milking a cow."

"I'm going to milk you, little man, if you don't come over here and uncuff me." She held out her hands.

"Davy, did you handcuff your aunt?" Sergei strode toward them, carrying two cups of steaming cider.

Davy glanced up at his six-foot, muscle-cut Russian stepfather and went white for a moment, long enough for PJ to remember that he and Sergei still treaded on new soil.

"It's okay. We were just playing." PJ crouched next to Davy. "Hand me the key, kiddo."

Davy fished around in his pocket and gave her the key. PJ unlocked herself as Connie swished up in her elegant Maid Marian dress—a complement to Sergei's dashing Robin Hood costume. Sergei handed Connie the other cider cup.

"PJ, do you have a second?" Connie tugged on her elbow. "I have to talk to you about something."

Connie was grinning, the old warmth in her eyes. Maybe Connie had begun to forgive her. PJ shot a look toward the apple-dunking bin, the band, then spotted Bix near the Girl Scout booth, buying a cookie. That probably meant she would stick around for a moment.

"Sure, Connie." PJ followed her sister, tucking the hand-cuffs into a handy, concealed front pocket between bun and dog.

Connie had changed over the past six weeks—maybe the way she left her brown hair down to blow in the slight wind, or the shine in her green eyes. PJ could attribute it to any of the things that suddenly felt acutely absent from her life. Newlyweds. Marriage. A life on track.

"Thanks for coming today. Davy has really missed you," Connie said, blowing into her cider. "And I have too."

PJ smiled at her. "I can't say I miss the fried fish."

Connie's gaze tracked over to Sergei. "We've gotten the fish eating down to once a week. And his parents' visas have been extended another year." She said the words without any malice in her eyes. Yes, perhaps things had smoothed out at the Sukarov household. Without PJ's troublemaking.

A knot began to tighten in her stomach.

"Great costume, by the way." Connie wore amusement at the corners of her mouth.

"Please. Jeremy worked as a street advertisement in Dinkytown. He inherited his costumes."

"You two seeing each other now?" Connie had the good taste not to glance at Boone, currently hauling a pumpkin from the patch.

"Besides work every day?"

"You know what I mean."

"I don't know. We haven't exactly progressed past our one impulsive kiss. I'm not sure he even remembers it."

"But you do." Connie's eyes twinkled.

PJ didn't answer her. But yes, she well remembered being in his arms, the way he kissed her as if suddenly something sweet had unhinged inside him.

"Yes," she finally said quietly.

"Where are you staying these days? Please tell me you're not in your car." Connie bore genuine concern in her eyes.

"Hey, the Crown Vic has enough room for the entire family."

Connie didn't smile.

"Jeremy's office. On the sofa."

Connie stared into her cup.

The sun had started to slip into the dusky October horizon, the heat of the day moving with it. A slip of crisp breath dried the sweat around PJ's face. How she longed to remove her sauna dog.

Still, Connie didn't move.

PJ had sort of expected something like "Well, those days are over. Please move back in." Or at least "That has to be awkward."

But nothing. Until . . .

"I'm pregnant, Peej." Connie brought her gaze up, wearing a hesitant smile. "I'm pregnant."

Oh. *Oh.* Well. "That's great!" PJ's voice sounded strange, though. Too high, too happy.

Connie didn't seem to notice. "Yes, I think so." She again glanced past PJ. "*We* think so."

We. As in Sergei and Davy and Boris and Vera, and probably also their mother, Elizabeth Sugar, strangely absent from today's activities.

"Congratulations." There. Now her voice sounded normal. She leaned forward and wrapped Connie in a one-armed hug. "That's wonderful."

Connie returned the hug, but when she stepped back, she still didn't meet PJ's eyes.

"Okay, what's the deal?"

Connie shrugged as she looked out into the fields of pumpkins. "You can't move back in, Peej. We need the room for the baby, and besides, it's time for you to set up your own home."

"Oh, I . . . I knew that, Connie." Except there went that strange voice again. Happy, happy PJ. "Of course you need the room."

Connie glanced at her fast as if testing PJ's words.

PJ took her hand. "Really. I need to find my own place anyway. I'll be fine." Really. Fine. Just. *Fine.* "In fact, we need to celebrate the good news with some pumpkin cookies, don't you think?"

"Well, I am eating for two." Connie slid her hand over her stomach.

Right. Cookies, pronto.

A crowd had formed around the dunking-for-apples trough, and as PJ approached the cookie stand, a cheer went up from the ensemble. Boris broke through the crowd a moment later, an apple clutched in his golden teeth, water dripping down his wide, grizzled face and onto his sopping shirt.

Vera applauded behind him, dressed as . . . well, a Russian babushka, in her curly lamb's-wool jacket, a blue polyester housedress from the early seventies, and a pair of flat boots. She took the apple from her husband and handed him his leather jacket. *"Maladyets!"* she said, taking a bite of apple.

And right behind them appeared Bix the Raccoon, laughing at Boris's heroic performance, clutching her pumpkin with one hand, her six-year-old Tinker Bell with the other.

She locked eyes with PJ. For a moment, everything went silent as PJ read Bix's face, those conniving eyes, those tight, budded lips, and deciphered two things.

Bix knew PJ had been hunting her.

And after today, PJ wouldn't have a prayer of capturing her.

"Meredith," PJ said, and that's all it took.

Bix whirled, dropped her daughter's hand, and took off as fast as her paws would carry her.

Which turned out to be considerably faster than PJ, who sort of half ran, half bounced after Bix. "Stop! Stop, Bix!"

But Bix wasn't having any part of *stop*. She shoved past the gawkers in front of the Great Pumpkin cutouts, past the bluegrass band, and through the split-rail fence out into the parking lot. Then she turned and hurled her pumpkin at PJ.

And PJ, encased in a giant foam pillow, couldn't dodge it. It thumped her hard in the thighs and she went down like a bowling pin, spinning out on the dirt.

"What in the world?"

Jeremy. All seven feet of ketchup, looming over her and then peering after her prey.

"It's Bix!" PJ said, pointing above her head. "Help me up."

Jeremy tossed his cup of hot cider and held out both hands. "Who?"

"Meredith Bixby!"

Recognition registered on his face as PJ bounded to her feet. But she didn't wait for him to catch up, just turned and watched as Bix skidded to a stop beside a shiny yellow Vespa scooter, threw a furry leg over, and inserted a key.

She wasn't getting away—not on PJ's watch.

PJ heard ripping as she threw herself at the raccoon in an all-out tackle. She took her out just as the bike lurched forward. They flew off together, rolling into the ditch with a bell-ringing landing that huffed the breath out of her.

Ow.

"Get off me!" Bix slammed an elbow at PJ's face. It landed on the bun.

PJ wrapped her arms around Bix, trying to roll on top of her. "Meredith, you jumped bail—"

"Of course I did, PJ. I'm not going to jail!"

PJ finally got ahold of Bix's wrist, both hands fighting for control. "You . . . should . . . have . . . thought . . ." She groped for the cuffs, curling her fingers around them just as Bix rolled out from under her.

Then, in a move that both Boone and Jeremy should have been cheering, she whipped out Davy's handcuffs and managed to snap one cuff on Bix's wrist.

But instead of giving the snarl PJ expected, Bix looked at PJ with an expression of horror, her black-rimmed eyes filling. Her voice dropped, low, desperate. "You have to listen to me. I'm not the person they're saying. I'm not a thief. It was an accident. I meant to pay for the wallet. I just slipped it into my pocket while I was looking at a pair of earrings. I swear it was an accident. My lawyer is trying to sort it out, but until he does, I can't go to jail."

PJ hovered above her, her hand searching for Bix's other wrist. "What about the other three charges?"

"Years ago, when I was a mess. I'm not that person anymore. I swear it. Please." A tear rolled into Bix's ear. "My kid is watching, PJ."

Her expression whisked PJ back a decade, to the humiliating moment when the Kellogg police hauled her away in her grass-stained prom dress, the smoke from the country club kitchen inferno blotting out the starry night. The false arrest had driven her out of Kellogg, put her on the run for nearly ten years, and kept her under suspicion until Boone had come clean and cleared her name.

PJ found the woman's eyes, pinned hers to them. "I don't

want a scene either. If I take off the cuffs, do you promise to come in quietly? You can even call your lawyer on the way, and he can meet you there. And then neither one of us will make the papers." She gestured toward the crowd behind them.

"Really?" Bix wiped her eyes with the back of her free paw, smearing makeup into her ear.

PJ nodded. "Promise?"

Bix nodded.

PJ rolled off her, and Bix offered a paw to help her to her feet. PJ handed Bix the key to the handcuff.

"Sorry. It's just a misunderstanding," she said to the crowd. She searched for Jeremy, but he seemed conspicuously absent.

Tinker Bell ran and embraced her mother, who crouched beside her and whispered in her ear. The little girl skipped away, her thin legs barely able to stretch out, thanks to the slim green skirt. She must have hiked it up past her knees to ride behind her mother on the small . . . one-person . . . Vespa. Wait—Bix couldn't have ridden here with Tinker Bell. Which meant someone else was taking care of her daughter. Which meant she probably wasn't going home. . . .

Oh no.

And then, as all her instincts fired off like little explosions in her head, Bix slapped a cuff around PJ's left wrist. She had the other wrist caught and the cuff snapped on before PJ could turn.

"Bix! Don't—"

"Stop following me, PJ, or you're going to get hurt!" Bix snarled as she pushed her, hard, into the dirt.

PJ rolled onto her back, trapped, her eyes closed, listening as the Vespa roared to life and whizzed away with a high-pitched *whee!*

And from somewhere beyond her periphery, she heard a camera click. Oh, perfect.

"Problems, PJ?" Boone said, his voice over her. He grabbed her by both sides of her bun and pulled her to her feet. "What was that?"

She'd torn a hole through the costume at the knees, and her dirty legs poked through between bun and dog. "She jumped bail. Were you serious—you don't have a handcuff key?"

Boone's silence made her look up.

"What?"

"Jeremy has you skip tracing now? A couple solved crimes and suddenly you're tracking down fugitives?" A quiet anger simmered in his expression.

"Listen, I know you're still worried about me, but you can stop now. I'm fine. I just need to get out of these cuffs."

"You think just because you don't want me in your life that I'm going to suddenly stop caring? that I'll stop waking up in the middle of the night in a cold sweat, afraid that someday you're going to get yourself hurt—really hurt?"

Oh. "I *do* want you in my life. Just not . . . as my boyfriend."

He took a long breath.

"Please, Boone, I miss your friendship." And the cuffs had begun to pinch.

He shook his head slowly, then turned away. "Boone!"

As if she might really be in some sort of B movie, Jeremy swaggered up, a convenient entrance, wearing a black baseball cap backward, and minus his ketchup costume. "You okay, babe? What's with the cuffs?"

Boone stopped. Rounded. One second too late, PJ recognized his expression.

"Boone, don't—"

"You're going to get her hurt," he said, advancing on Jeremy, who took a breath. PJ winced at the cold, calm look in his eyes.

Boone's voice stayed low and lethal as he stopped just in front of Jeremy. "You don't deserve her, and worse, you're going to get her hurt."

"You're overreacting. I'm fine. I just . . . I shouldn't have believed Bix."

Boone shook his head, his eyes hard on hers. "People don't change, PJ. You should know that by now. Just try and stay alive."

He strode away, his tails flapping as he loosened his tie and dumped it in a garbage barrel.

PJ watched him go, her throat burning. She turned to Jeremy, scraping up her voice, any voice. "And where were you, Mr. Ketchup? Did you not hear me? Meredith Bixby, bail jumper, remember?" She indicted her still-cuffed hands. "A little help would have been appreciated."

But Jeremy's gaze had trailed after Boone. "I knew you

could handle it. Besides, I wasn't going to do you any good trapped inside a tube of tomato paste." Finally his eyes met hers. "Why'd you let her go?"

"Because she had a hair appointment. I didn't let her go! Clearly, because I'm wearing handcuffs. Do you happen to have a key?"

He gave her a small smile. "Somewhere inside that hot dog beats a heart of compassion. Don't worry; you'll get her next time." Jeremy ran a hand down her arm. "I'll track down a key. And then I need something to eat. Seeing you in that hot dog costume is making me hungry."

Chapter *TWO*

"You're very photogenic. This is the second shot of you in handcuffs in four months."

Jeremy folded the Monday edition of the *Kellogg Gazette* in half and tossed it toward PJ, who sat on his black leather sofa. It landed with a plop at her feet. She didn't even glance at it. Not again. She'd already scanned every last grainy detail in this morning's mail delivery, read every last jot and tittle about the fiasco at Kellogg Farms over the weekend.

"Thanks for bringing that up. I feel so much better." She'd have to track down—she leaned over and read the photo credits—*Lindy Halston* and strangle her for the fabulous shot of PJ as she stood, scuffed-up and alone in the parking lot with the setting sun behind her, a torn, unhappy, handcuffed hot dog, while Jeremy tracked down the handcuff key.

"I can't wait for my mother to see it. She'll probably have it framed."

Jeremy leaned back in his desk chair and smirked at her. "Have you heard from her yet?"

"No. I left a number of messages at her house and a few on her cell, although she barely knows how to turn it on. My mother has the technical acuity of a gecko. Still, she should be able to answer her phone. I might need to do a drive-by today."

"She's probably just out playing Bunco or something."

"For three unaccounted-for days?"

"She's single. Give her a break."

"My mother is not single. She's widowed. There's a big difference." In fact, in many ways, Carl Sugar was still very much a presence in her mother's life: his clothes still hanging on his side of the closet, his golf clubs on the hook, even his green Jag taking up space on his side of the garage. Not that her mother lived in the past—she simply felt it disrespectful to erase him from the life he'd worked so hard to build.

"She's probably lonely, PJ. Give her some room to fill her life with friends."

The morning sun pressed into the windows, gilding the wooden floor into a sea of amber. Downstairs, the smell of freshly baking sub sandwiches ribboned through the paned front door of Kane Investigations and found her stomach. A half-eaten sesame bagel, the two halves glued together by cream cheese, lay wrapped in a napkin and balanced on the arm of the sofa.

PJ nudged the paper away from her with her toe and

finished off her latte. "I should give up on finding Bix. I'll never see her again. She's probably over the state line by now, halfway to some spa in Brazil."

Jeremy got up and walked over to the sofa. She loved how he looked in the mornings after his workout—freshly showered, his dark hair cut close to his head, neatly shaven, smelling like clean laundry and soap, and today in a button-down dress shirt over a gray Navy tee and blue jeans. It appeared like he eased into every day without effort and expected it to be glad to see him.

Not PJ, who had wrestled herself off the sofa at 6 a.m. and eked out of her body two miles on the treadmill at the gym while trying to ferret from the crevices of her foggy brain an idea as to where Bix might be hiding. Think like a criminal. Where would PJ go if she were a fugitive?

Uh, South Dakota. Or at least that's where she'd headed ten years ago. Today? She hadn't a clue where she might lie low while ducking from the law. Nor would she want to. She'd gotten painfully used to having her family—Davy, Connie, even the crazy, fish-frying, vodka-consuming Russian federation—in her life.

Connie's pregnancy news throbbed inside her like the ugly scrape down her arm. She hated when her longings snuck up on her and pounced, filleting open old wounds.

She was happy for Connie. Really.

Jeremy sat on the end of the sofa. She was still barefoot, and he surprised her by picking up her foot, setting it on his lap.

"Listen, Princess. Stop beating yourself up over Bix. A

good PI doesn't give up. You have to have confidence and a positive attitude. But you have to be empathetic, too. In order to think like your subject, you need to understand her. And although you usually have pretty good instincts, you may have let your heart sympathize just a little too much with Bix. In hindsight, it might not have been the most savvy of moves."

PJ couldn't take her eyes off the way his thumb moved over her foot, sweetly, almost absently.

"The truth is, I'm not sure I would have done any differently. It's not like she murdered anyone. She stole an expensive wallet. She's not exactly a menace to society."

"Mmm-hmm." His touch tickled a little, but she wasn't pulling away.

Just like she hadn't last night when he'd bandaged the scrape on her elbow.

The stiffness in their relationship seemed to crack at the harvest event, a freshness to his demeanor that spilled over into the evening, when he'd rented an old Gregory Peck movie and watched it on the sofa, popping microwave popcorn long after his bedtime. As if he hadn't . . . wanted to leave?

Or maybe he just felt guilty about trapping her inside a large, puffy advertisement while the entire town convulsed into hysterics. Another spectacular moment for her wannabe-PI scrapbook.

"So you said you talked to Connie. You didn't tell me what it was about."

PJ pulled her foot away and stood, collecting her uneaten bagel, his empty cup. "She's pregnant."

She didn't know what she expected, certainly not the way his eyes twitched as he watched her throw away the garbage.

"Really. That's . . . very exciting news. Isn't it?"

She'd let the conversation simmer inside her since yesterday and had emerged with two truths. First, she might really have to start living in her loft-size Crown Vic, especially if Jeremy took on any more cases and his horizontal filing system started engulfing the rest of the office. More than that, though, Connie's news screamed the glaring truth. At least *one* of the Sugars was moving on with her life.

"I'm thrilled for her. She and Sergei will make great parents, and Davy needs a sibling."

Jeremy still wore that strange look, as if he might be trying to peel back her words, searching for a hidden meaning.

Okay, fine—"I can't move back in."

He nodded, real slow.

"They need a room for the baby, and I have to find a place to live."

"You don't like my sofa?" He smiled finally, something teasing in his dark eyes.

"I can't live on your sofa forever, boss. Besides, I know how you like to work late. I'm throwing you off your game."

"I'm not sure I'd put it *quite* that way." He pushed one arm out along the top of the sofa. "But you've certainly changed the rules."

His smile had vanished, and with it went any words she might have conjured. So he hadn't forgotten their kiss.

Then he sighed. "Listen, I can advance you some money, if you need it, for rent."

"I do your books. You don't have any money to advance me."

"Ouch. Not everything is on the books. I might have a few personal resources."

It was the way he said it, dark and husky, that reminded her that she knew very little about Jeremy Kane. Other than the fact that he always seemed to appear when she needed him, like the first time—dressed as a pizza deliveryman, hiding in the garage in just the right place to save her skin. He also had more faith in her than she deserved.

But she couldn't take his money, and she met his hard look with one of her own. "We need clients, and now."

She crouched next to the pile of fugitive recovery subjects messengered to them by Liberty Bondsmen and picked up the top file. "Bruno Dirkman."

"I'll take care of that one, PJ."

She glanced at him, then opened the front cover. Attempted murder. Bruno glared into the camera as if hoping to take out her heart and chew on it. "Right." She'd let the guy who'd done time as a Navy SEAL handle Bruno. She closed the file and picked up the next one. "Brad Knightly. Armed robbery."

"Him too. Just put him in my pile."

PJ put the file aside. "Keith Dennis. Assault—"

"Mine."

She closed the file, angled a look at him. "Excuse me, but what are all those self-defense lessons for if not to apprehend fugitives?"

Jeremy's past gathered in his eyes for a moment; then he pasted his mouth into a grim line. "Self-defense is just that—*defense*. There's a difference between defending your-self and apprehending someone. You need to be ready to follow through when you're on the offense. You've walked into the fight with the goal of finishing it. Defense is about getting away to fight another day."

She opened her mouth, *case in point* already forming in her throat—

"And I definitely want you alive to fight another day. You're not going anywhere near those kinds of people."

"So let me get this straight. I can do fugitive recovery, but only the *nice* criminals."

One side of his mouth quirked up. "That about sums it up."

"I'm going to start calling you Boone."

His smile disappeared. "I'm not Boone, PJ." He said it so softly it made her heart skitter. "I'm far from Boone."

Oh yes, that couldn't be truer. Jeremy, with his steely demeanor, a man of few but poignant words, a tightly knot-ted control about him that she'd seen unravel only when he'd thought she might be hurt. Jeremy had a mysterious, breath-taking allure about him, the feel of autumn, like riding down a leaf-strewn road, churning up the fragrance of tomorrow in her wake. Yes, Jeremy was a dangerous mix of something sweetly familiar and the enticing scent of change. Boone, however, his presence woven into every high school memory, entwined with every future she'd envisioned, was a Saturday afternoon in the summer, the husky remnant of a sun-baked day still lazy in the wind. Easy, expected, comforting.

In a way, she loved them both, needed them both. And in that, perhaps, she saw their alikeness.

"His warning got to you. That bit about me getting hurt and his suggestion that you don't deserve me."

"Oh," Jeremy said, his eyes softening along with his voice, "I know I don't deserve you." He took a breath, and his tone contained an edge when he continued. "And Boone's words were more to the tune of *I'm* going to get you hurt."

She wasn't sure what sentence to address first. He didn't deserve her? His whispered words, spoken before the first time he'd ever kissed her, chanted in the back of her brain. *"I'm not ready for this."* And now he didn't deserve her? It didn't take her PI instincts to recognize a man fleeing the scene of the relationship, and fast.

That settled it. She'd move her gear to the Vic starting tonight. She swallowed back the pain rushing into her throat. Wow, she had really duped herself this time.

She managed an easy shrug. "I'm a private investigator. Getting hurt comes with the job."

"Not necessarily."

"Not necessarily? Do you mean the not-getting-hurt part or the fact that I haven't gotten my license yet?"

"Both, Sugar. The last thing I need is you getting hurt on my watch and having the Minnesota board yank my license. You still need hours of weapons, self-defense, legal, and first-responder training."

PJ tossed the files onto his lap. So that's what all the babysitting was for . . . safeguarding his license.

She got up and shuffled to the window, staring down at the college students hiking to class at the University of Minnesota campus, their messenger bags thumping against their backs. She'd never actually made it all the way to college.

"Maybe I shouldn't even be here." She closed one eye in a cringe, wanting to pull back the leak of self-pity.

She heard rustling behind her and jumped a little when Jeremy slid his hands over her shoulders. "Give it time, PJ. You can't be a PI overnight."

She didn't lean against him, but he didn't remove his hands, either. She swallowed, palmed her hand against the cool glass, seeing her fingerprints as she pulled it away. "I just want to solve one amazing case without the answer sneaking up on me."

"You did."

She turned, expecting him to move away. But he didn't. Just looked at her with those dark eyes, his strong hands now moving down to catch her wrists.

She couldn't meet his eyes. "Fine. Name one."

"You found Gabby's so-called stolen jewelry."

Gabby? The next-door neighbor of her previous client? "Oh, brother. You can hardly call that a case. Her cat was pushing her jewelry behind the furniture. Any housekeeper would have discovered the truth."

"You still solved it. And if you hadn't, Gabby's daughter would have convicted the old woman of losing her mind, and poor Gabby would be in an old folks' home today."

"Jeremy, open your eyes!" She twisted her hands from his grip. "I nearly got her and myself and about four other people killed. Not to mention pushing my sister's father-in-law into the middle of a carjacking ring, and let's not forget nearly getting my nephew murdered by an assassin."

He hadn't moved and now slid his hand around her neck, rubbed his thumb along her face. "Don't you think you're overreacting just a smidge?"

She met his eyes. "Name one real crime I solved. *Really* solved. Me."

And then maybe it didn't matter, because he kissed her. Sweetly, with nothing of the reluctant, desperate urgency of before—first her top lip, then her bottom, finally kissing both of them, gently nudging them open. She sighed and let herself curl toward him.

See, she wasn't much of a PI.

Because she hadn't seen that coming at all.

Jeremy slid his other arm around her waist, pulling her closer to his chest.

"Hello?"

Jeremy moved her away from him so fast she thought she might fall over. He whirled around, holding her behind him, and she had to peek out at a . . . lawyer?

The interloper standing in the open doorway *looked* like a lawyer, anyway. Tall and pinched, blond, and belly-white pale, as if he hadn't seen the sun in over a decade, he wore a black suit and blue tie and clutched a briefcase. He approached them, his bony hand stretched out in greeting.

"Michael Finch. I'm with Tyler and Finch, Attorneys." He had to pick his way around Jeremy's filing system—manila folders positioned like a mocked-up battlefield on the wooden floor.

Jeremy met his hand. "Jeremy Kane. What can I do for you?"

"Actually, I'm here to see Miss Sugar." He nodded toward her, and PJ emerged from behind Jeremy.

Finch shook her hand. His was cool and felt freshly lotioned. "Can I talk to you privately?"

"Uh . . ." PJ shot a look at Jeremy, who raised an eyebrow. Clearly, he wasn't budging. "I think we can talk in front of my boss."

"Fine. I represent the estate of Agatha Kellogg."

"Kellogg? As in the *town* of Kellogg?" Jeremy asked. He motioned for Finch to sit down. The lawyer negotiated his way to a blank space on the sofa. Jeremy leaned against the desk, his arms folded over his chest. PJ joined him, moving a cup of coffee to slide onto the desk.

"Yes, that's right."

"Wow." PJ turned to Jeremy. "I did a report in school on the Kellogg family. They were wealthy beyond imagination. Owned half the town, lived in this huge estate on the lake near Maximilian Bay. It sat on a hill above the lake and had this rolling thatched roof, right out of one of Grimms' fairy tales. I used to imagine what it would be like to be a princess in that amazing house . . ."

Finch wore a strange expression as he stared at her.

"Agatha was one of the oldest surviving family members," she finished quickly. "Boone mentioned something about her passing this summer."

"Six months ago, actually," said Finch, who continued to regard PJ with a look that made her feel as if she might still be wearing the hot dog. "It took us a while to sort through the paperwork, and then we tried to track you down. . . ." Finch's gaze trekked over to the *Gazette* lying on the floor. "I should have noticed you the first time you made the rounds in the paper. Thankfully, I noticed this today."

"Find me? Why?" Oh no. "I'm not being sued, am I? I mean, you're not here because of the Kellogg Harvest Days incident? Listen, I was doing my job—Bix *was* bail jumping."

"No, actually, I'm not here in that capacity." Finch seemed to study her one final moment, a question in his eyes. Then finally he sighed and opened the briefcase on his lap. He handed her a sheaf of papers. "I'm here because you are the lone beneficiary of the personal estate of Agatha Kellogg."

PJ scanned the top page of the ream of papers, her gaze focused on the photocopied handwritten letter. To . . . *her*?

She looked up at Finch, over to Jeremy, again to the letter. "I . . . don't . . ."

"You, PJ Sugar, have inherited the Kellogg family fortune."

Chapter *THREE*

"You inherited the mushroom house? I can't believe it. I always loved that house." Connie sat at the center island of her kitchen, smoothing the papers onto the recently redone black granite counter.

PJ couldn't quite wrap her mind around her sister in a pair of green striped pajama pants and a pink T-shirt in the middle of a Monday afternoon. Connie usually packed in five hours of work by this hour of the day but today had answered her cell phone at home when PJ called at lunchtime. "Sick day," Connie had explained and invited PJ and her Big News over. If the newly pregnant woman wasn't sick now, at the rate she was foraging through the kitchen, she would be by dinner.

"The mushroom house?" PJ opened a can of diet soda and sat down next to her sister on a tall leather stool in the middle of Connie's restored Craftsman home, with its polished oak, soft leathers, and jewel tones. The furnishings of a well-honed life. "Please tell me why you named that beautiful Tudor after a fungus."

Connie picked up the eight-by-ten black-and-white glossy of the home included in PJ's file. "The way the thatched roof rolls over it, curling over the edges—it reminded me of a mushroom."

"I thought it looked like the dwarfs' house."

"As in the seven dwarfs? And who were you, Snow White?"

PJ sipped her drink, reaching for a bowl of yogurt pretzels in the center of the table. "Sometimes. Other times, I was Cinderella."

"Of course you were." Connie set her tea beside the file, picking up the handwritten letter. "Do you even remember this woman? Because she obviously remembers you."

PJ had spent all morning digging into the vast history of the Kellogg family, finally focusing on ninety-eight-year-old Agatha, belle of Kellogg, philanthropist, railroad baroness, and PJ's benefactor. "Vaguely."

Outside, the wind stirred the piled leaves in Connie's backyard, tossing them against the screens of her enclosed porch. The few chrysanthemums that had survived Boris's potato-planting crusade bloomed a fall palette in the cold garden. The gardener worked silently outside, covering the flowers one by one with Styrofoam forms. He occasionally glanced at the house, meeting PJ's eyes once with a smile.

Boris's snores buzzed from under the closed door just

beyond the kitchen, and Baba Vera sat at the table reading a Russian magazine, her orange hair tied up in a scarf.

"Agatha Kellogg used to sit in the front row of the theater," PJ said. "I remember her hats most of all. They had feathers and velvet bows, looked like something out of a Chanel millinery on the Champs-Élysées. She would peer at us through cat-eye glasses, wearing a ratty mink stole. She went to nearly every rehearsal that I can remember, would say nothing, and then leave without a word. I think she might have been the benefactor of the Kellogg theater scholarship. She reminded me of the old woman searching in that Christopher Reeve movie . . . what was it called?"

"*Somewhere in Time?*"

"Yeah. She always seemed to be looking for something, waiting for it to appear."

"She used to watch you on stage?"

"Well, I was only in that one play. But yes, she was there most of the time."

"Did she ever talk to you?"

PJ shook her head.

"So you had no contact with her?"

"What is this, *Law & Order*? Should I get a lawyer?"

"You came to me, remember?"

"Okay, well, I've been racking my brain, and I remember something—I was in her house once."

"You're kidding. Wow, I can't believe you got to see the big house." Connie reached for the bowl and began collecting all the broken pretzels.

"No, actually, I only dreamed of going inside that one.

I have to admit, I longed to explore it. All those tiny windows, the nooks and crannies. It had to have a million secret passageways, probably hidden doorways."

"Seriously, PJ, you read too much."

"C'mon, don't tell me you never imagined what it was like inside."

Connie had created a small pile of broken pretzels and now began to nibble each one. "Nope."

"What it might be like to live in that family?"

"Nope."

"You never wondered what your life would be like if you were somebody else?"

Connie finished off the last of the cashews mixed in with the pretzels. "Never. I'm a Sugar—or at least, was a Sugar. I'll always be a Sugar at heart. How could I ever be anyone else?" She pushed the closed file toward PJ. "I like my life. Why would I want a different one?"

PJ reached for the file, flipping it open to the eight-by-ten. "The carriage house gave me a little glimpse into their world. The floorboards creaked with every step, and it smelled like one of Dad's old books, the kind with parchment pages. It had these cedar beams running the length of the ceiling, and white walls, like that wattle-and-daub look in old historical Williamsburg."

Connie gave her a blank look.

"You know, the place where they dress up and pretend they're from Colonial times? Remember our school trip to Washington, D.C., my junior year?"

"I didn't go to D.C., remember? I went skiing with the

Carlisles in Vail. Please tell me you didn't break into the Kelloggs'—"

"C'mon—I wasn't always in trouble. Mom insisted I raise half my ticket for the trip to D.C., which I did through the school fund-raiser. People bid for students to help them with home projects, and I got the Kellogg mushroom house."

Connie smiled at her.

"Okay, it does sort of resemble a mushroom."

"And now it's *your* mushroom."

Her mushroom.

Her mushroom.

Connie tilted her head down and spoke the words that had pricked PJ's brain since the lawyer's visit that morning. "Are there no living Kellogg relatives? That's really hard to believe."

"I know. Or at least, if there are, Mrs. Kellogg didn't want them to have her house."

"Why would socialite Agatha Kellogg give you her house?"

"I . . . don't know." She reached for the letter, reading it again.

> *To Miss PJ Sugar:*
> *Among all my assets, the Kellogg name has*
> *been the most treasured. I carried it with*
> *pride after my beloved Ort shared it with me.*
> *But it has come to ruin and is without rescue.*
> *So I must turn to my next best hope. Carry*

*on, Miss Sugar, and know that the blessings
of your inheritance are also your destiny.
Regards,
Mrs. Orton (Agatha Brooks) Kellogg*

"Your inheritance is also your destiny?"

Connie took a sip of her tea. "They say a woman loses a thousand brain cells with every pregnancy."

"I think that's ten thousand."

"I'd need a lot more than that to figure out what she means." She set down her cup. "Have you even seen the house yet?"

"Nope."

"I think it's been empty for a while."

"She only died six months ago."

"I've driven by there. The place is a wreck—overgrown yard, and I think there might even be a hole in the roof. Don't tell me you're going to keep it."

PJ put the letter back in the file. "I don't know. There's only enough money left in escrow to pay the property taxes for the rest of the year. I have to decide by January if I'm going to dump the place. But the will says that if I keep it, I have to live in it."

"Sounds like a money pit to me. What are you going to do with an eight-thousand-square-foot house?"

PJ glanced at her. "The old me might have said, 'Hold the world's largest kegger'?"

Connie wrinkled her nose at her. "And the new you?"

PJ lifted a shoulder. "Move in with the Vic?"

"I'm sure you and Vic will be very happy. Until it snows and you need to heat the place. And you probably need a handyman. On retainer. Hey, there's a guy who does that at our church—I saw his ad on the bulletin board."

"I've got just enough to pay for gas and maybe a few pizzas, Connie. What would I pay him with? my witty banter?"

"I think *you'd* owe *him*." Connie got up and opened the fridge, apparently not done with her binge.

PJ drummed her fingers on the manila folder, the words in her chest fighting their way to her mouth. She took a breath. "What if she—the Kellogg family—was related to me? After all, I'm adopted. They could be my real family."

Connie didn't react, at least from behind. She simply reached in for a packaged piece of cheese, turned, and slowly unwrapped it, then broke the cheese into tiny squares. Finally she looked at PJ.

Everything inside PJ tightened. She took another sip of soda, then cleared her throat. "What? You know something, don't you?"

Connie put a square into her mouth.

"Connie?"

"It's probably nothing. . . ."

"Connie?"

"Okay, fine." She put the cheese wrapper on the counter. "First, I'm going to let your comment slide because you know who your *real family* is. But not long after you left town—"

"Ten years ago? After graduation?"

"Yes. A couple weeks later, I was at the country club, playing tennis."

PJ tried to ignore the jab of pain, realizing how Connie's evenly knit life had carried on in Kellogg while PJ's unraveled mile by mile as she headed west.

"I was coming up from the courts when I heard Mom. She was in the parking lot, on her way to lunch, I think, and she was having a fight. With Agatha Kellogg."

"Are you sure it was Mrs. Kellogg?"

"Positive. You're not the only one who remembers her. Only in my head she was the woman with the silk scarf wrapped around her head, smoking cigarettes with one of those long cigarette holders like she was Rita Hayworth."

PJ had to smile. "Yep, I remember that now. She had a convertible Karmann Ghia."

"Of course you'd remember her car."

"I miss my Bug; what can I say? But she certainly did like to live out loud."

"That wasn't the only thing out loud. She was livid that day—one finger in Mom's face, the other hand resting on her cane, wearing one of those looks Mom used to give us when she wanted to threaten us with something dire for whispering in church but couldn't in front of the deaconesses. Only Mrs. Kellogg wasn't biting back her nasty words."

"Did you happen to hear what she said?"

"Something about letting people down or not showing up for something—maybe a committee meeting? You know how Mom seemed to be on every club board.

I remember thinking with your recent disappearance, maybe people should cut her some slack if she wanted to stay at home and pull the curtains."

"Mom stayed at home and pulled the curtains? Over my leaving?"

Connie stared at her a long moment, eyes squinting, as if trying to see something inside PJ. "You're seriously surprised by that?"

PJ raised a shoulder.

"Wow. Okay, well, Mrs. Kellogg pulled herself together in a blinding moment of society poise the second she saw me. But Mom had turned white. I don't think I've ever seen her so unraveled."

"No?"

Connie grinned and finished off her cheese. "Well, maybe after our prom when the cops showed up at our door in the middle of the night."

"Are you sure it wasn't the day I came back to Kellogg?"

"Oh no, PJ. That was the first day in years she wasn't white. I think she'd finally stopped holding her breath."

"I don't know, Connie. I think she probably went into a full-scale panic. Trouble's back in town." PJ offered her sister a good-natured grin.

Connie didn't return the smile. She pursed her lips, then slowly turned and pulled a glass from the cupboard, opened the fridge, and retrieved a carton of milk.

"Okay, what?"

Connie regarded the milk for a long moment. "At some point you're going to actually have to figure out what else to label yourself. Because no one is calling you Nothing but Trouble anymore but you."

Oh. She hadn't noticed that exactly, but a girl could hope, right? "So what does that have to do with me being adopted?"

"I don't know. At the time, I couldn't believe that Mrs. Kellogg could be so cruel. And then I wondered how Mom and Agatha knew each other. They weren't exactly peers. Mrs. Kellogg was about fifty years older than Mom and ran with the Pillsburys, the Fairmonts, and the Hills. Way above our set. So what did she have to do with Mom?" Connie shrugged. "I think I have too much of your PI curiosity. It probably had to do with a blood drive or something."

PJ caught her smile. "Yeah, probably. But I'll ask Mom about it."

Connie's smile fell. "How about you let me ask, okay?"

"Speaking of Mom, she hasn't checked in with you lately, has she?"

Connie poured her milk, shaking her head.

"You're not even worried?"

"She's a grown-up, Peej. She gets to be busy if she wants. She'll call if she needs me."

"Connie, you don't work for a PI. You don't know the darkness out there, what people do to each—"

"I'm a DA. I think I know. But Mom's lived her own life for years. It might actually surprise you to know that Mom and I don't talk every day. In fact—" she leaned over the counter, lowered her voice—"sometimes we go for an entire week and don't call each other." She widened her eyes, nodding.

"Funny. Okay. It's just that . . . it feels strange to have her so close and not check in."

"She'll check in when she wants to. She's not a child."

Vera got up, greeted PJ in Russian, and disappeared into the room with Boris.

"How's your Russian coming?" PJ asked as Connie watched her mother-in-law leave.

"By the time the baby gets here, I hope I can say things like, 'Please don't feed the baby caviar.'"

"I'll bet Sergei is excited."

A sweet smile edged up Connie's face. "I admit, he's surprised me. He already has names. We're in negotiations."

"Negotiations?"

"I want Emily; he wants Luba. Marriage, children—it's all about negotiation. I have to admit, although I've been married before, this time around I'm more careful. I see my words before I say them. Still, it's been harder."

"You're walking into the marriage fully formed, Connie. You already have your child, your home, your life. And you have to bend that identity around Sergei and his parents to find the new you together. And now the baby? I think you're doing great." PJ flicked her gaze to Connie as she spoke, moving her hand over to her sister's arm.

Connie's eyes glistened. "I'm sorry I threw you out."

PJ lifted a shoulder, her words webbed in the knot in her throat.

"I miss you."

PJ nodded. "Ditto. But it had to happen sometime. You have to start your own life."

Connie palmed the file. "And you, yours. Although I have to say, I'm not thrilled about the chinchilla you gave Davy. Did you know it screams? and spits?"

PJ grinned. "Just wanted to leave my mark, Connie. Be grateful you didn't get two. I think Dally has more she's trying to get rid of."

"No thank you. I don't need any more reminders of your crazy past mysteries. In fact, maybe you need some company. It's an awfully big house to be alone in."

Alone?

Connie must have read her face. "Or . . . not alone?"

PJ considered her a moment. Then, "Okay, I admit, men confuse me."

"Boone?"

"Jeremy. He kissed me."

Connie set down her tea. "Really. You're just full of big news today, aren't you?"

PJ dragged her finger through the condensation from her glass, drawing a circle on the granite. "Something happened Sunday. He's going all protective on me. He's pulling a Boone."

"Speaking of, did you see *him* at the festival?"

"Yes. We talked. Or rather, he snarled. We have a long way to go before we're friends."

Connie got up and set her glass in the sink. "I have to admit, it's hard to imagine a world without you and Boone together. It's always been that way in my head."

PJ's too. In her mind, sometimes she still saw herself on the back of Boone's motorcycle, arms wrapped around his waist, heading into the sunset. And it didn't feel quite right to clip him out of the photo and put Jeremy in his place. The cutout lines didn't quite match up.

"I'm hoping we can be friends."

"Friends. Let's see. Friends. Like, him telling you about his dates? You calling him up after kissing Jeremy? That kind of friends?"

"Funny, Connie. But yes, maybe we can get past what we were to something new."

Connie shook her head. "That would nice, but he's been waiting for you for a long time. It's not going to be easy for either of you."

"I hope so. Boone's been my best friend . . . well, at least he knows me better than almost anyone. I can't imagine not being friends with him." Even as she said it, the words ground into her heart.

Connie touched PJ's arm, her hand warm. "I can't imagine it either. A PJ Sugar world without Boone."

PJ stared out the window as the gardener covered the remains of the once-beautiful garden with a dark mulch of dirt and leaves and clippings, leaving behind only the memory of the summer glory.

Chapter FOUR

If a gal had inherited a house, it wouldn't hurt to look around the place, would it?

PJ tapped her brakes as she drove up to the mushroom house on the hill, past the ivy-laced stone walls. The house overlooked the glistening waters of Lake Minnetonka, and the afternoon sun poured over the rolling thatched roof, throwing thick fairy-tale shadows into the overgrown yard. The place could have been read aloud into existence straight from the storybook pages, the ones with witches and goblins and ogres prowling through dark forests.

Maybe she should just keep driving. Maybe, in fact, she should turn the car around and head over to her mother's house. After all, Elizabeth Sugar had bypassed two more calls—if indeed she was at the house and was simply playing hard to get.

But the Vic clearly wanted to check out its new digs. It coasted to a stop just beyond the gate, in a pocket of overgrown weeds on the other side of the road, next to the tiny gardener's cottage PJ had cleaned.

PJ got out. Closed the door. Scrutinized the big fairy-tale house. *Her* big fairy-tale house.

Which meant she wasn't trespassing. Going over to the gate, she gave it a nudge. To her shock, it whined open as if waiting for her to enter the world it guarded. She slipped through the opening and hiked up the long driveway. Fall had littered the yard with scraps of brown cottonwood leaves, pieces of orange oak foliage. A row of overgrown pine dropped grenade-size pinecones on the broken paved drive. Spindly arms shot from the wild and woolly shrubbery near the house, waving at her as if she might be the first surge of storm troopers, here to rescue the villagers.

Ivy had consumed one entire end of the stucco house, hanging down over wooden garage doors, the red paint wrinkled and crackling. Hanging baskets on either side of the colonnaded front entry swung in the breeze, the deceased flowers brown and netted. The roof, made up of millions of ash-gray cedar shakes, flowed over the house like . . . well, a giant mushroom cap that curled under the eaves of the house. The leaded-glass windows, crossed with thick iron bars, winked at her, blinking awake as she trekked over the grass. She stopped in front of a dry, leaf-poured fountain, the standing water in the bottom of the stone bath black with sludge.

Snow White and her dwarfs had obviously abandoned

ship, maybe a decade ago. But it was nothing a smidge of Cinderella grease couldn't whip into shape.

Besides, the smell of fall perfumed the air, the leaves crisp and shiny, culling the hues of evening. If she listened closely, she might hear the sounds of children playing in the yard, the smell of barbecue on the porch. Or maybe it would have a terrace? a giant flagstone patio leading out to the lake?

The Realtor had slipped her the key in her package of papers. Now she dug it out of her pocket, approaching the massive front entrance under the overhanging colonnade. The house even had an appropriate castle door, complete with rounded top, crossed with giant iron blades and a doorknob and lock set precisely in the center. She inserted her key, heard it click, and the door eased open.

A hundred years of history haunted the darkened foyer in the smells of age, the creak of the door, the moan of the wind as it snuck in behind her.

"Anyone here?" PJ wasn't sure why she called out—perhaps to alert the spirits that lingered in the nooks of the ornate oak beams partitioning the ceiling and buttressing the doorframes. A wide, dusty staircase ran up to the left. The room before her opened all the way through to the far side of the house and a wall of windows facing the lake. Square panes of leaded glass fractured the light, checkerboarding the dusty tiled floor with pink and amber.

She wandered farther into the murky front room. Dust cloths covered the leftover furniture—a sofa, a highboy, a coffee table—adding to the ghostly aura. A fireplace yawned in one of the walls of the long room, tongues of black soot licking the whitewashed brick. The cloying smell of mouse droppings nested in corners, and an underlying odor of mildew, or perhaps decay, laced every breath.

At the other end of the room, she found the kitchen, in sore need of updating, from the 1970s apple green stove to the matching refrigerator. A butler's pantry contained the cookware and heirloom dishes of a family accustomed to entertaining. Shelves covered all the walls but one, at the far end of the pantry. PJ closed the door and paused in front of the fridge, noted the rust pooling on the peeling linoleum floor.

How had elderly Agatha lived here?

PJ wandered through the rest of the house, past what looked like servant's quarters just off the kitchen, then out through the screened porch to the flagstone terrace with the rusty iron furniture and ancient grill, and finally meandered down the shaggy lawn, admiring the view. The lake spewed the debris of summer onto the shore—sticks and seaweed, trash from careless boaters. From the looks of it, the beach hadn't been raked since Carter was in office. But beyond it, on the indigo blue, white sailboards bobbed in the rolling waves, their farewell nod to summer.

Back in the house, behind the kitchen, she found another staircase, took it up, and landed in a long hall covered by a formerly pink or perhaps mauve carpet, with empty rooms she guessed had been bedrooms. The French doors at the end of the hall—the ones she supposed might lead into the master bedroom—remained locked. She tried the key. Nothing.

But it didn't matter because she'd found the jackpot. Yes, suddenly, she had become Cinderella and probably Snow White, definitely Belle, and every other fairy-tale character swept into a story line beyond their belief.

A library.

PJ stood at the door; her breath caught. Floor-to-ceiling shelves. Filled with books. Old books with fraying bindings. A stack of *National Geographic* magazines. A pile of what looked like romances. Thousands of books.

All hers. Along with eight thousand square feet of lake-shore and history and prestige.

She was . . . rich. Wealthy.

A Kellogg.

At least for the next two months.

She reached for her phone and the number rang once before she stopped herself. Closed the phone. No, she couldn't call Boone.

Not anymore.

She dialed Jeremy instead. Of course, it flipped to voice mail. She didn't bother leaving a message. She didn't want to interrupt him taking down a vicious criminal.

She ran her finger along the bindings of a row of books, ratty volumes worn by age. She pulled one out, blew off the dust. *Ragtime* by E. L. Doctorow. She wiped off the cover and replaced it on the shelf next to a hardback yellowed copy of *Robinson Crusoe*.

Scuffing to the window, she peered out over the driveway. She spotted her Vic, waiting patiently for her in the weeds below.

Maybe she could live here. She had to admit, her thoughts had immediately run toward selling this "money pit," as Connie put it. But what would it be like to sit on the terrace sipping lemonade as the sun dipped into the lake? or sink into a leather chair and bury herself in a book in her very own library?

She bounded down the far stairs, her feet falling hard on the risers. She couldn't wait to show—

The step cracked even as she came down on it, and she reached out, grabbing the rail before she went through. Her heart wedged into her throat. "Yeah, that would be good. Get trapped in the house on your first night, only to perish in the basement." Her voice was thin in the layers of age and expanse of the house.

She laughed. Okay, maybe she would call Boone. Because, well, he'd also had a fascination with this house when they'd been teenagers. More than once they'd driven by it, and PJ whispered her dreams into his ear.

Yes, she'd call him. Just for old times' sake.

She walked out the front door, toward the fountain of sludge, her phone to her ear. Boone's voice mail picked up. "Hey . . . it's me. PJ. You'll never guess where I am—the old Kellogg house! You're not going to believe this, but I inherited—"

The ground beneath her sagged, groaning, and then, as if it yawned beneath her, waking from slumber, it gulped her whole.

She screamed as she fell into open space and landed fast, jarred by the earth. Her hand planted in what felt like fresh, sucking cement.

Ow. She fought to catch her breath as her landing shuddered through her. She'd bruised her arm, and her leg burned—probably a wicked scrape up the side. But otherwise, she felt intact. In a moment her eyes adjusted to the wan dusky light streaming from eight feet above. From the torn patch where she'd caved through, she guessed she'd stepped on a rotted door.

A storm cellar? She remembered the stories of tornadoes ripping through the Minnesota prairie. In the early 1900s when the Kellogg home had been built, they would have added protection from the storms. It reminded her of her parents' apple cellar, built into the basement of the house, where her mother stored summer apples and potatoes.

But this seemed less of a cellar and more of a . . . tunnel.

Oh, this couldn't be good. Not from the pungent swamp smell or the texture of goo under her. *Please don't let me have fallen into an old sewer drain.*

"Help!" She patted the . . . mud? . . . around her, searching for her phone, but came up empty. "Help!" Not that anyone would hear her. Or if her phone was still on, somewhere—"Help! Boone!"

Oh, she hated to admit that, again, she needed him. *Come and rescue me, Boone.* The child's voice rang in her head, and she shook it away. Maybe Connie had figured her right— she didn't know how to live a life without Boone in it.

She got up and searched the walls for steps or perhaps a ladder, but nothing remained from the past to rescue her.

She trekked to the end of the fading light, peering into blackness.

Uh, no.

Finding a dry place, she sat down, staring at the ragged square of twilight. Perfect. No, she wouldn't spend her first night in her new home. She'd bed down thirty feet outside it. Maybe never to be found again. She drew her knees tight to herself and wrapped her arms around them.

Breathing slowly through her mouth, she mentally made a list of the things she wouldn't think about. Her stomach growled. Like pad thai from the cute little restaurant *To Thai For* in Dinkytown. Or an Italian sub sandwich from the sub shop. Or a pizza—oh, a pizza—with lots of pepperoni, delivered by one broad-shouldered former Navy SEAL.

And speaking of, she certainly wouldn't think about Jeremy and the way he had pulled her into his arms this morning, the taste of him lingering on her lips. And especially not the fact that after the lawyer left, Jeremy had grabbed his stack of manila files and glued himself in front of the computer, tracking down suspects.

She'd strike off her list the desire for a warm shower, even a dip in the lake. Which meant she also wouldn't think about the many late-night dips in the bay just outside the house, nor the memory of Boone, his hair glistening wet in the moonlight.

Clearly, she couldn't think about Boone's face when he'd walked away from her Sunday. Right after the words, *"People don't change, PJ. You should know that by now."*

They left a burn there, his words. Because *she* could change, would change.

"No one is calling you Nothing but Trouble anymore but you."

PJ sank her head onto her knees. Definitely, she wouldn't think about Connie's words and the fear that she might be right. Because if she wasn't trouble . . . who was she?

✳ ✳ ✳

"PJ?"

She lifted her head. Darkness had swept over the mouth of her prison, engulfing her in soupy shadow. She pushed her hands against the sides of the cellar. "Here! I'm down here!"

"PJ?" A light whisked across the opening.

"I'm down here in the cellar!" Yes! Someone had gotten her call, tracked her down, hadn't left her to rot in a hole outside her new mansion. "Over here!"

The light poured into the hole, and she wanted to chortle with glee when she spotted her phone in the muck.

"Are you okay?"

She peered around the light, smiling at the hero on the other end. He moved the light off her face and it reflected just enough for her to recognize Boone, staring down at her, wearing an expression of horror, as if he'd just found her buried alive.

"I'm not even sure where to start with the questions." Boone lay on the ground, his arm extended, and PJ took a jump for it, finally grabbing his hand.

"Get me out and I'll come clean; I promise." She clamped her other hand onto his as he growled, pulling her from the hole. She kicked at the dirt, trying to assist him.

"Just let me pull you out—stop trying to help," he grunted. He pulled her up to head level. "Now grab my neck; climb out over me."

PJ wrapped her hands around his neck.

"Try not to knee me in the face—*ow*!"

"Sorry." She scrabbled over him, Boone pulling her up by her waistband as she kneed him again—"Sorry!"—and then finally rolled onto the grass beside the opening.

"You smell like you slept under a bridge. So much for coming clean." He wanted to smile, she saw it, but fought the urge with a grimace that had any warmth locked tight.

"Thanks for that. I'm not sure what I fell into."

"You okay?"

"I think so. Just a few bruises."

"Good. I'd help you up, but you're covered in muck."

"Oh, you're a real hero." She climbed to her feet and got her first good look at her rescuer. In a pair of jeans and a leather jacket, he looked a little like he might be going out. On a date? "How'd you know I was in trouble?"

She waited for him to say it, hearing her own voice provoking him. *You're always in trouble, PJ.*

"I used all my detective techniques . . . and the little scream on the end of your voice mail was a slight hint. Thanks for that. Now, what were you saying about inheriting something?"

"Aggie Kellogg left me this place. Her entire estate." PJ

faced her house, eerie in the wan light of his flashlight. "It's mine. The Grimms' fairy-tale house is mine."

Boone stood speechless for what seemed too long a time, so long that PJ turned to him. "Did you hear me?"

"I'm not sure what to say."

"How about congratulations. Or even, wow. Do you not remember the way I fawned over this place every time we drove by it?"

"Oh, believe me, that kind of adoration is hard to forget. But my thoughts run more to . . . escape while you can."

What? "Escape? What on earth are you talking about?"

Boone had picked up his flashlight, was now scanning it into the hole. "Rumor says there was a tunnel leading from the house down to the caretaker's cottage."

"What rumor?"

The light panned her face, and she put a hand up, flinching. He seemed not to hear her as he walked toward the house and then along the front. "Boone? What rumor?"

"The one surrounding Joy Kellogg's murder."

"Murder?"

Boone kept walking, now peering into windows, finally rounding to the back. PJ scrambled behind him, grabbing a few wide leaves from a monstrous hydrangea to wipe the muck from her hands. "Murder?"

Boone ran his light across the patio. Then he flashed it toward the lake, now dark and restless. "You didn't hear about the murder? It happened before we were born, but it's an unsolved case over at the station."

"No one found her killer?"

"There're a few leads, but nothing panned out. And some people said it might have been a suicide. The police didn't have enough evidence to hold the chief suspect, Joy's husband, so they let him go. He left town shortly after that."

He kept walking across the yard, his legs swishing through the long grass. "As the story goes, Joy was a troublemaker, ran away from home when she was sixteen or something. She eventually returned and married a local guy—although I think there was a scandal involved there because years later, they found her floating in this lagoon." He shone his light across a murky cutout of the lake, an inlet with shaggy willows and a covering of algae. "She left behind a teenage daughter."

"That's terrible. What happened?"

"No one knows. She had a terrible fight with her husband apparently. And some say she'd been drinking."

"What happened to the daughter?"

"I don't know. Not much was heard of the Kelloggs after that. Agatha, the matriarch, was still around—I remember seeing her at your play practices occasionally, in those crazy hats."

"I liked them."

"Of course you did." He walked to the door of the screened-in room. Tried the lock. "I guess we need a key."

"Like this one?" She pulled the key from her sodden pocket. He took it, meeting her eyes with a question.

"I told you, I inherited the place. It's mine."

He inserted the key. "You baffle me more every day. Who are you?"

PJ pushed past him. "I guess, a princess." She gave a twirl like she might be at a ball. "I've inherited a castle."

He strode by her, trying the lights by the door. Nothing.

"How do you know all this about the murder?" She bumped up to him as he passed his light into the kitchen.

"When I joined the police force, I looked into some of the cold cases down in the basement. I remembered your fascination with this house . . . that sort of drew me to it, I guess."

He walked over to the sink and tried the faucet. Something rattled deep inside the house, but nothing emerged. "I think the plumbing might be gummed up, too."

"That can be fixed."

He shot her a dubious look. "The place smells as if it's sitting on a swamp. I'll bet the plumbing burst over the winter, and the basement is flooded with sump water."

"So it needs some work. It's old. Built in the early 1900s. It's bound to have a few glitches."

"How about ghosts?"

"If you think Joy Kellogg is roaming the grounds, hunting for her killer—"

"No, I was thinking of Agatha," Boone said.

PJ followed him as he shone his light up the back stairs, but he put an arm out to block her before she could climb them. "What?"

"She died here. Upstairs. In her bedroom."

PJ peered up into the darkness. "Not the one at the end of the hall," she said softly.

"Yep. And quite a while went by before anyone found her. Maybe even a week."

"Okay, that I didn't need to know." PJ backed away from the stairs. No wonder the door to the bedroom was locked. "How'd she die?"

"She got Meals On Wheels delivered once a week. The delivery guy found her. They think it might have been a stroke, but she was so old, she could have died in her sleep. No one ordered an autopsy, if I recall."

PJ said nothing, even when Boone flicked his light on her.

"See, I told you. Run. Put it on the market as is, and get out before you get sucked in. The Kellogg history is rife with trouble and heartache. And that's the last thing you need."

There it was again—the perfect opportunity for him to add *since you already have enough of it.* But no. He just moved toward her, then pulled a handkerchief from his pocket and wiped her cheek. "A little remnant there from your fall."

His touch was too gentle, too familiar. And he smelled good, like a summer night, all husky and sweet. For a terrible second, with everything inside her, she wanted to lean into him, to wrap her arms around him. It hadn't escaped her that he'd come to her rescue.

Again.

"Who knows why she left you this place, PJ. But it's a mess. The electricity is out, the plumbing is probably shot, and the roof could cave in on you at any moment. It should be condemned, not resurrected."

Her thoughts went to the hole in the stairs. "But it's mine."

"Just because you think you want something doesn't mean it's the best thing for you." He put the handkerchief away. Caught her hand. "I just don't want to see you get hurt."

"By the ghosts of Kellogg Manor." She finger quoted her words. "Sounds like a Nancy Drew mystery."

His expression suggested he wasn't amused. "You so want to buy into the fairy tale, don't you?"

"What's wrong with that? Every girl, at some point, dreams that she's a lost princess, forgotten in a faraway land. Can't I want it to be true?"

His blue eyes had turned so soft, sweet, she had to look away.

"PJ?" The voice echoed through the long hallway, bearing an edge of worry. "Are you here?"

Another light, this time wiping across the paned windows, across the dust and cobwebs of the main room. And then footsteps. "PJ?"

Boone's touch dropped away as Jeremy appeared and spotlighted the couple in the kitchen. PJ slipped away from what probably looked like Boone's embrace and saw that scenario flash in Jeremy's eyes.

"Are you okay?" he asked, his gaze going to Boone. "I called Connie, and she told me you . . . were here." A muscle pulled in his jaw. "Am I interrupting something?"

Next to her, Boone stiffened.

"Of course not, Jeremy." She paused there, hoping Boone might fill in the gap, but he brushed past her and began checking the gas fittings over the stove. So much for another rescue. "I fell down a hole outside, and Boone found me."

Alarm crossed Jeremy's face and ignited a curl of sweet emotion inside. "Are you okay?"

"Yes." She rubbed her arms and glanced at Boone. He shot her a quick look, then moved out into the main room, toward the fireplace.

It seemed that Jeremy had the PI instincts not to ask questions, at least not with the way Boone was stalking the room as though he were in the middle of a crime scene. PJ wasn't sure who he considered the criminal here.

Or rather, the dead body?

Jeremy scanned his light over the beams crossing the ceiling, the huddled forms of clothed furniture in the massive room. "So this is it? your new digs?"

"Apparently. Only it has a few glitches—electricity is out; plumbing could be burst." She went to stand in front of the window, staring through it to the lake. "Boone thinks it's too big of a project. Maybe I should just put it on the market."

"Oh, PJ, are you serious? Look at the architecture. And the view. It's incredible." Jeremy came up behind her, not unlike he had this morning, and put a hand on her shoulder, turning her. "Imagine this place cleaned up. The tile scrubbed, the windows washed, the grounds landscaped or even just mowed." In his eyes, alive with something she'd never seen before, yes, she could see the house scrubbed up, free of grime, Vera frying something in the new kitchen, Sergei and Davy playing in the backyard.

Jeremy and PJ sitting on the veranda, drinking lemonade.

Her gaze shot to Boone, now watching them with a stony expression on his face.

Especially when Jeremy hooked her chin with his finger, made her meet his eyes, apparently not caring that Boone hovered a few feet away. "Can't you see the potential in this place?"

"Maybe," she said, her voice a whisper.

"Princess," he said, his voice dipping, "you can't sell this place. You belong here."

"Of course you'd say that," Boone snapped. Then he turned and stalked out of the house.

Chapter FIVE

"You smell like a dog left out in the rain."

"I know you mean that in the nicest way." PJ held up a flashlight as Jeremy stood in the darkness of the utility closet under the stairs. She tilted her light up for a second and located the spot where her foot had punched through. At least she wouldn't have ended up in the basement.

Or perhaps she should refer to it as the swamp, since Boone had been correct in his call about the pipes bursting. The odor that engulfed the house came from a layer of sump water, putrid and containing the fetid remains of a family of rodents, muddying the dirt basement floor. Thankfully only half the house hiccuped brown sludge. The back room, the one that seemed like a maid's quarters, had a small, working bathroom in which the water ran clear.

Even if the electricity didn't seem to work.

"Over here, Princess. Let's get some light on the subject."

Jeremy chuckled at his own joke, even flashing her a smile over his shoulder. He'd been in an oddly jovial mood since Boone marched off the premises, despite the fact that, under the scrutiny of the flashlight, Jeremy sported the makings of a shiner under his eye.

"Are you going to tell me how you got punched?"

His smile faded. "I haven't seen this kind of fuse since my grandmother's house in South Minneapolis." He grabbed PJ's wrist, angling the light over what looked like porcelain drawer tabs, one after another in a giant panel of knobs. Each one contained a glass center, many of them black. After Jeremy unscrewed one, he peered at the metal knob. "I don't even know where we can get a new supply, unless . . ." He reached up, above the metal box attached to the wall, and dragged down a small cardboard box. "I like practical people," he said, sifting through the box to find a fresh—or perhaps fresh from the previous century—fuse.

"Jeremy, really. How did you get hurt?"

"Let's see if we can get any power here." He screwed in the fuse, then scooted past her out into the hall. Looked around. "We should see a light on somewhere. Maybe it's on upstairs."

"I have a feeling it's more than just a fuse," PJ said. "Otherwise, the ones that aren't black would be working."

"See? Natural detective skills." Jeremy brushed by her again.

"But not-so-great interrogation techniques. What do I have to do to get you to come clean?"

"Just a little altercation at work." The smile had vanished from his voice.

"Work? What am I, the answering service? Your work is my work, partner. Should I be worried here?"

Jeremy was reaching above the fuse box again. "Nope. And we're not partners."

PJ flicked off the light.

"What?" He rounded on her, and even in the darkness, she could feel the heat of his expression. "I can't see what I'm doing."

"Neither can I, bub. I'm totally in the dark here. *We're not partners?*" She hated how her voice hitched on the last word. Because this morning, as he'd wrapped his arms around her, tugged her close, it had felt very partnerish. She let her voice find its footing. "When I left you today, you were glued to your computer. How did you go from tracking down the last known addresses on our list of fugitives to getting a shiner?"

He said nothing for a moment. She resisted the urge to reach out to him, touch his chest, maybe just for balance. Or to assure herself that she wasn't dreaming. That something palpable had happened between them.

Still, sometimes being around Jeremy gave her the sense that she might be perched in the open doorway of an airplane, staring down, daring to fling herself into space.

Sure, she'd jumped from heights during her brief career as a stunt girl, but skydiving seemed like a whole different brand of crazy.

"I tracked down Bruno Dirkman. Now turn the light on."

"Alone? He could have killed you."

She heard him sigh, then felt his hand on her wrist, moving up to the flashlight. He pushed the button to turn it on. His expression, however, remained dark. "Give me some credit, will you."

There it went again, that dark tone, the hooded expression that reminded her how little she really knew about Jeremy Kane, former SEAL, current boss, and undercover electrician.

"No, I won't." The words slipped out of her mouth, and she backed them fast with her own steely expression. "Beyond the fact you were a SEAL, well, I barely know you."

"You *barely know* me? Don't you think that's a bit overstated?"

"Fine. I know you have a thing for old movies and popcorn, too." She expected a smile, but she only got the smoldering, intense gaze that brought her back to this morning, in his arms. Yes, okay, she knew a bit more.

"What else do you want to know?"

She swallowed. "Uh . . . well, uh . . ." What did she want to know? What were the important parts? His childhood? His favorite color? Oh, wait, one look at his black leather jacket, dark T-shirt—she could probably answer that one. How about . . . what did he want out of life?

Maybe that was too big a question, too soon, and especially in a caught-in-time electrical closet. "I don't know."

To her surprise, his hand moved to her face, brushing it with his fingertips, a tickle of a caress. His eyes gentled, something that took her breath away, especially from a guy who looked like he'd run face-first into a barroom brawl. "In time, Princess. In time. You'll have everything you need."

For what? she wanted to yell but just stood there, stilled by his touch, her heart tattooing in her chest.

He turned and gathered up the fuses. "I think you're right—your electrical problems may be more than a few blown fuses." He dumped them into their container and placed them on top of the fuse box. "I'll see if I can track down the problem."

"So now you're an electrician?"

He gave her a cryptic smile. Another question to add to her list . . . in time, of course.

Moving past her, he caught her hand. "Are you hungry? I'm starved. I think it's time for a pizza."

See, even if she didn't know his favorite baseball team, his favorite band, or anything significant about his life before the day she met him, they had a deeper bond.

"Pepperoni and mushrooms?"

He gave her hand a warm squeeze in the dark.

An hour later, she emerged from the bathroom of Hal's Pizzeria, not necessarily clean, but smelling like the strawberry-scented liquid soap from the dispenser. They'd hit the fringes of dinner hour, the place still populated by families, a small assembly of grade-schoolers jockeying for space on the stoop outside the kitchen. The victors had their noses pressed up to the glass, watching dough being tossed into the air.

Located in the middle of Kellogg's Main Street, with a dormant volleyball sandpit out back, Hal's appeared to be transitioning from beachside playground to Halloween haunted house with spider netting hanging from the door, a papier-mâché witch dangling from the ceiling, and crepe paper pumpkins taped to the walls. PJ dearly hoped Hal's still hosted their annual Halloween all-you-can-eat pizza buffet.

Jeremy lounged in an orange vinyl booth, perusing the menu, a tall red glass of soda in front of him.

"I thought we were going to get a pizza?"

"We are. But I thought we'd order an appetizer, too. Maybe mozzarella sticks?"

PJ unwrapped her straw. "What's the occasion? Don't tell me you already collected the cash from your FTA collar."

"Nope. Buffalo wings or sticks?"

"Uh . . . wings."

"Attagirl." Jeremy closed the menu, lifted a finger to signal for the waitress. PJ had a mind to ask her if Hal's was hiring. Jeremy might be able to bring in his man, but PJ hadn't the faintest clue where to track down Bix.

"So why the big spender?"

Jeremy placed the order, then shot her a smile. "Oh, you're buyin'."

PJ nearly lunged for the waitress. "What? I barely have enough money for a Happy Meal. I can't buy dinner."

He pulled a folded paper from his inner coat pocket and opened it on the table. "Sure you can. You're an heiress." He said it without blinking.

"Listen, Pizza Man, all I have is a run-down, rather smelly old mansion that may or may not have working electricity and is definitely without adequate plumbing. That hardly qualifies me as an *heiress*. An heiress is someone with a pet Chihuahua, a butler, and a closet full of designer shoes." She lifted her grimy pant leg, exhibiting her Converse tennis shoes. "Unless I'm mistaken, these aren't Jimmy Choos."

He smoothed the paper on the table, sighed, and looked up at her, no amusement on his face. "PJ, whether you want to admit it or not, you received a large gift today. Very large." He turned the paper over and slid it her direction. "I did some homework on you and your house, in between tracking down Bruno, getting punched in the face, and keeping Kane Investigations in the black. The Kellogg home was put up for sale three years ago for—"

"Four million dollars?" PJ picked up the paper to read the listing.

Clearly, someone had done some creative writing—which may have been why the place hadn't sold. Still, *four million* dollars. Even if it had been overpriced, by, say, half . . . that left her with potentially *two* million dollars.

She put the paper down, then looked at Jeremy. "I don't even know what to do with that kind of money. What does this mean? Am I rich?"

Jeremy lifted a shoulder. "Depends on your version of rich. Personally, I think you've always been rich."

"Oh, sure. Which is why I'm homeless, and my earthly belongings total the mass of what fits in my trunk. Frankly, I would be happy with a one-room flat with running water, my own bathroom, and maybe a homely but friendly dog to greet me at the end of the day. I'm not that picky."

He barely gave her a smile. "It's not what you have—or

even your rather eccentric tastes—that make you an heiress, PJ. It's who you are. *You* are an heir."

"I'm *not* an heiress. An heiress has servants and a closet of Prada." She stirred her soda. "I'm worth about a cool grand, if you don't count the Bug and the Vic."

When he said nothing, she looked up at him. He was considering her, frustration on his face.

"What?"

"I just think I've pegged it right all this time, Princess. It's about time someone figured that out."

Before she could answer, he shook his head, then leaned forward, balancing his elbows on the table. "Okay, here's the bottom line. Are you going to live in the house or not? Because if not, then we need to let the lawyer know. It's your decision—you either take the gift or give it away."

"Some gift. It doesn't have electricity, and who knows how badly the plumbing is damaged. I don't have the money to hire a contractor. Most of all, I can't really see myself rattling around that place."

He gave a slight smile. "You don't see yourself in the house? I'm confused. Is this the same girl who told me, and I quote, 'I used to imagine what it would be like to be a princess in that amazing house'?"

PJ took her napkin and folded it into squares.

"I can't believe this. You're afraid."

"What?" She patted the napkin flat. "Hardly."

Something like a dare edged the corners of his mouth. "You're a pansy."

"A pansy?"

"Yes. A coward. A lily-livered jellyfish."

PJ stared at him. "I think you were hit harder than you thought."

He grinned, his eyes warm. "You're afraid of moving off my sofa."

"I think you're giving yourself way too much credit here. I can—and will—move off your sofa anytime I want to."

His smile dimmed. "That might be a good idea."

It was the way he said it, slow, his eyes even with hers, churning in her something warm, even dangerous, that made it hard to exhale.

"I guess I could live in my Vic. I always knew it would come in handy."

He sighed, shook his head. "That's not the point. I have a theory. You won't even consider moving into the house . . . because you don't think you belong. You've longed for this your entire life, yet when it's offered to you, you see yourself as homeless, the girl who lives in her car, with only a ragged duffel bag to call her own. You might consider that there's a reason God gave you this house."

"You think this money pit is from God?"

"I think God could have big plans for you with this house, if you have the courage to say yes. You have always dreamed of living in it—God often gives us our dreams to also show us something we didn't even know we needed."

He smiled, something sweet in his eyes she didn't know how to interpret.

"Stop seeing yourself as a beggar and realize who you are, PJ. You're not that woman who showed up six months ago—"

"Four."

"Fine—four months ago, dragging her past behind her. You're not trouble anymore."

She blinked at him as the waitress returned with their platter of wings and two plates.

Jeremy grabbed the plates, setting one in front of her. "Of course, before you refuse to eat supper, I was just kidding about you picking up the tab." He reached for a celery stick. "For now, of course."

But she was still back on "You're not trouble anymore."

"Even if I do fix up the place, I can hardly afford to keep it." PJ reached for a wing, her stomach roaring to life. "Taxes and insurance . . . it's over my head, if you haven't noticed."

"One hurdle at a time, there, Pollyanna." Jeremy devoured his chicken. "The taxes are paid up until the end of the year, right? Two months. Certainly that would give you time to figure out whether you belong there. And possibly, why God gave it to you."

Was two months enough time? Not likely, since it had taken her ten *years* just to return to Kellogg. And although God had shown her that maybe He liked her exactly the way He'd made her, trouble or not, she wasn't sure if she would ever figure out where she belonged.

Or apparently, to whom she belonged. Sugar . . . or Kellogg.

Boone . . . or Jeremy.

"We'll figure it out."

We'll. She was surprised at how much she liked the sound of that pronoun on his lips.

Still . . . "Maybe Boone's right. Maybe the place should just be razed. Given a new beginning. Maybe it can't be transformed."

"Anything can be transformed." Jeremy took another wing. "And Boone's *not* right."

He said it without rancor, with finality. Boone wasn't right. About the house. About her. About Jeremy.

Oh, she hoped so. But the image of Boone parading around the house, reciting its past, almost with a tenor of worry for her future, swiped at her.

Jeremy discarded the bone and wiped his mouth. "Give the house a chance to become something new and amazing." He grinned at her, winked.

PJ picked up another wing. "Did you know that it's got a mystery surrounding it? A murder. And the crime was never solved."

"Who was this murder victim?"

"One of the Kellogg daughters. Or maybe the only Kellogg daughter. It doesn't matter. That would be horrible—to be killed without anyone knowing who did it. To be forgotten."

Jeremy put down his food. "I can promise you, PJ, you would never be forgotten."

❊ ❊ ❊

"You've heard the saying, if you keep doing what you've always done, you'll always get what you've always got, right?" Jeremy leaned back into the plush cranberry seat of her Crown Vic, his hands laced behind his head, a baseball cap pulled low over his eyes. Light puddled from the street-lamp a half block ahead, although darkness seeped into the car, along with the lick of cool October air. Around them, leaves skittered down the street, the wind a broom.

"I'm sure you have a point," PJ said. The doggie-bag pizza carton sagged on the dash, a reminder that they shouldn't have ordered an appetizer.

"You may want to consider the fact that staking out Bix's place isn't working. Bix isn't here, and she's not liable to show up anytime soon."

PJ curled her hands over the smooth grip of her steering wheel. "I don't know what else to do."

Instead of driving to the mushroom house and retrieving Jeremy's motorcycle, he'd opted for a ride in her Vic, during which, well, yes, she decided to loop around to Bix's house. Just in case.

"C'mon, PJ. You're smart. Think up an angle to find yourself a fresh lead."

Ouch, that hurt, especially the tone. "I've searched the databases for all Bix's past addresses. I even called, pretending to be her daughter's teacher—which made me feel a little slimy—and left a trap phone–number with the woman watching her daughter."

"That'll help if she calls you back, but even then, if she uses a cell phone, the number you get won't necessarily pin-point her location. She could be calling from anywhere. You need to think like Bix—that's why I handed you this job.

You know her. Who would she trust? Who would she go to in a time of need?"

PJ ran her fingers over the steering wheel. Who had she gone to when she needed help? Connie? her best friend from high school, Trudi?

Nope. Boone. She'd gone to . . . well, the person who knew her best.

She glanced at Jeremy, and he must have pinpointed that same truth in her eyes. He blew out a breath. "I guess I'm going to have to face the fact that he's a part of who you are. I just don't have to like it."

PJ started the car.

"Where are you going?"

"To my house. Or my mother's house, to be exact. I have a stash of old high school yearbooks in the bedroom. Maybe I can dig up Bix's friends."

"Now that's what I'm talkin' 'bout."

PJ smiled as they motored through the groomed neighborhoods of Chapel Hills, not far from Connie's Craftsman home, deeper into the stately neighborhoods of old wealth. They passed Tudors, an occasional prairie-style home.

The two-story colonial owned by Elizabeth Sugar lay in quiet slumber under the shaggy hover of towering evergreens planted along the side of their yard in PJ's childhood. PJ eased the car up to the curb.

"Now what?" Jeremy said, his hands folded in his lap as he peered at the house.

"I don't know." PJ picked up her phone and dialed, listening as it rang four, five, eight times. Her mother's machine didn't pick up.

"She doesn't seem to be home." She closed her phone and set it in the cup holder between the seats. "In fact, she hasn't been home all week."

Jeremy didn't seem to buy into her worry. "Maybe she's out for dinner?"

PJ said nothing. Just got out of the car and hiked up the lawn. She tried the front door, then rang the bell.

Jeremy came up behind her, a stealthy shadow. He could probably sneak in and out of a maximum security prison without detection.

Something she'd like to learn to do.

In fact . . .

"The first time I snuck out of the house, I had just turned sixteen," PJ said, lifting the mat to check for a key. "I remember because I was wearing these chunky-heel boots that caught on the drainpipe running along the edge of the screened porch. It tore away from the roof and clattered down onto the stone patio, waking up the entire neighborhood."

"Is there a reason you're telling me this?" Jeremy ran his hand along the top of the doorframe. "Because you know, too much information about a person's past could come back to haunt them."

"Oh, I think you're haunted enough by me." She glanced at him and saw the makings of a grin edge up his whiskered face.

"When I got home, I found my father seated in the

kitchen, nursing his third or fourth cup of coffee. Of course, my ears were still ringing from the concert down at the Motor Junction." She lifted the pot of now-dead geraniums by the door. The sight of them gave her a moment's pause.

Huh.

She put the pot down and stepped off the porch. "I didn't even attempt to sneak back in—the evidence of my crimes being the mangled drainpipe, hanging like a broken tree limb. I planned a sort of ladder from the porch chairs to the roof of the screened porch, to the unlatched bathroom window. And there used to be a trellis that would've helped. But I've always wondered . . ."

"Why don't you have your own key?"

"My mother hasn't quite gotten around to making me one. I'm trying not to take it personally."

Jeremy followed her around the house as she peered in all the windows of the ground floor, hiking through the shrubbery, finally cupping a hand over her eyes as she pressed her nose to the glass and stared through the kitchen window.

Jeremy slipped his arm around her, lifted her slightly, and put her feet on his.

"Do you see anything?"

Uh, no, not with his arm around her waist, holding her tight to himself. Feeling his heartbeat in his chest.

"A drooping bouquet of flowers." Which hinted at PJ's dark fears, accompanied by the dirge of dread.

She sank away from the window. Took a breath. Lowered herself onto a wire porch chair. "I think something terrible has happened to my mother."

Jeremy crouched before her.

"Maybe she hit her head and is lying in a pool of her own blood in her bathroom. Or she was kidnapped while getting the mail."

"I'm sure that's it. A gang of outlaws have tracked her down—"

"Jeremy! Why else wouldn't she answer her phone and especially not show up at her garden club meeting at the country club?"

Jeremy raised an eyebrow.

"Okay, I called."

"Methinks you may be stalking her?"

"I'm not stalking! My mother has vanished from the planet!"

Jeremy stood. "Okay, just stay put. I'll be right back." He jogged back around the house.

Stay put? While her mother gasped her last breath?

PJ stood, measuring the distance from the patio to the screened porch roof.

She must've been some kind of acrobat to think she could scale that, and in a miniskirt and heels, no less. This time, though, she wore a pair of jeans and sturdy, wall-scaling Chuck Taylors.

She pulled the wire chair under the roof edge, near the drain pipe, and climbed onto the seat, then the arms. Maybe she needed the table, because she barely reached the lip of the roof. She recognized the dent in the drainpipe where her father had nailed it back together. One of his last household projects.

A ladder. Her mother kept one in the garage.

Which, of course, was locked.

But Sugars hadn't been designed for defeat. Especially when lives could be at stake. PJ pulled the rusty round table closer, then lifted the chair on top of it.

See, this was probably what her brain had been conjuring, so many years ago. She climbed on the table, then the chair. It wobbled a little, but she righted herself and slowly propped herself onto the chair arms.

She stood a head over the roof edge. Hooking her elbows onto the roof, she pressed up from the chair. Maybe she should start with a little jump . . .

She launched herself forward, catching her weight on her elbows, kicking at the screen—certainly she could swing her leg up. The gutter wobbled as she leaned against it. She kicked her foot around it, searching for a toehold.

With a screech, the gutter unhinged from the wall. It clattered like gunshots against the patio, the sounds sharp in the crisp fall air.

She stilled, listening. Perfect.

But she couldn't stop now. Not with her mother in mortal peril.

Slipping, PJ swung her leg up again and this time hooked it on the roof. Her other foot swept the chair, knocking it sideways, and the entire contraption teetered over, crashing onto the patio.

She hung there, left leg dangling in midair, her right barely hanging on to the porch edge, her elbows digging into the tar of the graveled porch roof. Ow, burning, *ow*.

Okay, so she'd been a lot younger and more spry and, of course, going the opposite direction last time she'd been in this position.

She began to slip.

Ten-plus years ago, Boone had been waiting for her in the darkness, dressed in black from head to toe, ready to catch her as she'd come off the roof, cushioning her landing.

But not today. Today the wind lifted her jean jacket collar and swirled the leaves gathered on the roof, tickling the bare skin at the small of her back. She kicked, swishing the air, putting stock in momentum to propel her over the edge.

No, she wouldn't call for Jeremy. Wouldn't. He'd clearly decided to desert her.

Her elbow slipped and she conked her chin on the roof. "Ow!" Her voice emerged more as a moan as she kicked again.

Her foot went through the screen and caught.

"Help!" She closed her eyes. "Help, Jer—"

"Oh, good grief. Can't you wait one minute for me? I told you I was coming right back. You're going to have the neighbors calling the cops and reporting an intruder. "

PJ craned her head around and caught a glimpse of Jeremy striding up the yard, looking like a hero from some suspense movie as he picked up his speed.

"I'm slipping!"

He broke into a run as her other elbow gave out, her leg swung free, and—

Ooph. She dropped like a stone, clipping her heels on the table, tumbling into space. Jeremy's arms barely closed around her as they both tripped back onto the patio, toppling over, hard. He cushioned her fall, his breath whuffing out of him, arms still tight around her.

"Jeremy, are you okay?" She lifted her head, turned, balancing her hands on his chest. He lay there for a second, staring at the stars, then closed his eyes.

She moved off of him and got to her knees. "Jeremy?"

"I'm fine." He opened his eyes. "Sheesh, PJ. I told you I could probably get us in."

"You did not. You told me to stay put."

He appeared to be processing that information. "Well, I meant . . . I could help."

"'Stay put' and 'I can help' have vastly different meanings."

"I think from now on, we should assume they don't." Jeremy took her hand as she pulled him to his feet. "Are you hurt?"

"I'm okay. But we need to get into the house."

He gauged the distance to the roof, then picked up the gutter. "You do know how to leave destruction in your wake."

"Should I break a window?"

"How about if we, oh, I don't know . . . use the *lock pick* kit I got from your car? After all, if memory serves me correctly, you *can* pick a lock." He held up a lock pick pack— the one she kept in her glove box.

Right. Okay, so she'd panicked and simply defaulted to a previous working MO. PJ moved the patio furniture into place, then followed Jeremy around to the front door. He worked the door lock, but the dead bolt wouldn't budge.

"Let's try the basement door," PJ said.

As he worked the basement lock, she caught sight of a face in the upstairs window of the Lindgrens' blue split-level home next door.

PJ smiled and waved. A curtain fell.

"Think how boring the neighborhood has been without you."

"Just open the door."

Jeremy pushed it open and PJ charged inside. "Mom? Mom?"

She ran up the stairs, hitting the main level and standing in silence—or relative silence, depending on if she counted the thunder of her heartbeat—hearing nothing. She took the stairs to the second level two at a time.

She skidded to a halt in front of her mother's bedroom. Slatted moonlight striped the made bed. It seemed emptier, somehow, as if her mother had decluttered. "Mom?"

Striding through to the bathroom, she passed the neatly closed closet doors, then stood at the edge of the bathroom tile, inhaling the lemon cleanser.

"Mom?"

"She's not in the kitchen," Jeremy said behind her. He pressed a hand to the small of her back. "I'll check the basement again."

PJ headed toward her father's den, expecting to find it still attired as if he'd been working in it the night before, his pencils sharpened in their square holder, pictures dusted on his desk. Instead, the pictures had vanished, his ancient computer cleaned away. Finally. Maybe her mother had begun to move on.

She lingered a moment before she met Jeremy coming up the stairs.

"Nothing. She's not here, PJ."

PJ wandered through the family room into the kitchen, surveying the dried washcloth hooked over the faucet. The wilting flowers now rotten in their pot on the table.

Where . . . ?

Jeremy strode to the garage and opened the door.

Elizabeth's gleaming Lexus sat in her spot.

He closed the door and came over to stand silently in front of her. PJ looked at him, those dark eyes that had, even this morning, seemed so mysterious, so unreadable.

Now she read compassion in them.

He touched her hand. "Don't worry, PJ. We'll find her—"

A crash fractured his words. "Get down! Police!" Two officers, their weapons at the ready, burst into the kitchen.

Jeremy's hold tightened on her arm, and his grim look swept her face for a second before he put her behind him. "Of course you are."

Chapter SIX

"Tell me again why I shouldn't arrest you for B and E?"

Boone stood in the kitchen, leaning against her mother's built-in desk, his arms in a knot as if holding back fury.

Jeremy had his own arms crossed, in a position just behind her.

PJ had the sense that really, she wasn't part of this conversation.

Except for Boone's now nearly livid gaze, pinned again on her.

"I thought she was missing, Boone." Her eyes went to Mrs. Lindgren, dressed in a long overcoat, pulling on her shoes at the door. "Who informs her neighbor that she's going on a cruise but doesn't call her own daughters?"

Boone got up to hold the door open for Mrs. Lindgren. "Thanks again for the call, Judy. I've got it from here."

Smiling at him, Mrs. Lindgren patted Boone's arm. Oh, the Boy Scout. PJ wanted to roll her eyes.

The neighborhood watchdog managed to level another murderous look at PJ before she pushed through the door into the night.

Boone returned to the kitchen. Thankfully, he'd arrived shortly after the night patrol and begrudgingly released PJ and Jeremy from the subduing handcuffs. Not that either of them had put up a fight, but something lethal had flickered in Jeremy's eyes as he watched the officer turn PJ, push her against the counter, and secure her hands behind her back.

And, well, it was a look that went right to the soft, too-vulnerable places in her heart.

"PJ, certainly your wannabe PI brain could list ten solid reasons why your mother might leave the house and not tell you. After all, you made a point of not landing on your mother's doorstep when Connie threw your clothes onto the lawn and barred the door behind you." Boone's attention again traveled to Jeremy, fixing there.

"It's none of my mother's business how and where I live."

"Clearly." Boone's jaw tightened. "And your mother is allowed to return the favor."

Not in a million lifetimes, bub. But she stayed silent.

Boone shook his head. "I think we're done here." He turned and walked out. But his words drummed into her brain like gunshots. *Done. We're done.*

Four hours later, PJ still heard them as she stared at the

darkened ceiling of Jeremy's office, listening to the hum of late-night street traffic, watching the occasional headlight trace across the window. She turned over Boone's words, her mother's sudden itching for a cruise, why God would give her the mushroom house, Connie's pregnancy, Jeremy's kiss . . .

So much for sleep.

Getting up, she clicked on a lamp and pulled the box with her yearbooks close to the sofa. She'd found the box in the garage, and a quick glance inside revealed not only her own yearbooks, but Connie's and her parents' also.

She'd grabbed the entire box, just in case.

"Who would she go to in a time of need?"

Jeremy's words had stirred old memories. Her best friend, Trudi, sitting beside PJ on her front steps, holding in shuddering breaths as she revealed to PJ that she might be pregnant. And Boone, waiting for her every Sunday afternoon with his motorcycle running, just so he wouldn't have to spend the day at home, refilling his mother's bourbon glass.

PJ flipped open her senior yearbook. People who stuck around their hometown usually kept their high school friends. As did, apparently, people who left town for ten years.

Bix might have left clues behind about whom she might turn to today to hide her from her crimes.

PJ's eyes caught, however, on the inscriptions.

To PJ. The woman most likely to drive her car into the lake. We did have fun! Trudi signed her name with a curl and a heart over the *i*. PJ ran her finger over the heart.

To the girl most likely to earn a million dollars (or steal it?). May all your dreams come true. Heather Whitlock, followed by a smiley face. Nope, PJ barely remembered her. Which said, what—that her reputation had earned her more fans than friends?

She turned the page and ran her hand over Connie's neat script. *Most likely to amaze us all.* Why was it that she could never see the person Connie seemed to see?

And then at the bottom of the page, a simple *Love you best, NBT.* Boone.

NBT. Nothing but Trouble.

PJ trapped a tear with her thumb. Flicked it away.

She turned the pages, laughing at remembered snapshots—her at homecoming, with her foam finger and face painted. Boone throwing a pass, another of him in midair, high-fiving one of his wide receivers. The powder-puff football game—the seniors against the juniors. Looking closely, she found her face, Boone's numbers written on her cheeks.

She closed the book and picked up her sophomore annual, the one that listed Bix as a senior. She looked up Meredith Bixby in the index and found her in a powder-puff football shot—messy with faces, smiles, index fingers raised. She tried to read the number on Bix's forehead— Eight? Three? One?

PJ turned to the team shot of the varsity football players and finally settled on Trey Johnson. Number thirty-one. Fullback.

She flipped to the back, found the index listing, and discovered that Trey had numerous cameos. Another football shot, one on the homecoming court. And yet another at a dance—with a dolled-up Bix on his arm.

She found a winter shot with Trey in his hockey gear and another crowd shot. This one included Bix, bundled up, one arm flung around a friend—the same girl as in the football shot. PJ tracked the name to Deena Hayes.

Trey Johnson and Deena Hayes. That gave her *two* fresh leads.

Putting the book away, PJ picked up another.

Age filmed the creases and it cracked as she opened it. Her mother had written her name in a tight, neat hand along the top of the first page, dating it as her junior year of college.

PJ found the index, then located her mother throughout the book. Choir. Drama club. PJ peered close, smiling at her mother in a cheerleading outfit. In a montage in the back, she discovered a black-and-white with her mugging for the camera, her arm around a friend, both of them dressed in leggings and long Wheaton College sweatshirts.

PJ read the identifier. Elizabeth Mulligan and Sunny Barton.

She finally turned to the back and read the curly scrawls. Mostly one-liners, only one caught her eye. *To Lizzy. Thank you for believing in me. PJ.*

PJ? She ran her finger over the letters, then turned back to the index and spent the next hour trolling through names, looking for anything that might condense to a *P* and a *J*. Nothing.

Nor did her mother's senior yearbook give even a hint of the mysterious PJ.

PJ slid the books under the sofa and pulled the comforter Jeremy had brought over from his house up to her nose.

PJ. It throbbed in her head. Her mother had known—gone to college with—someone named PJ.

Pulling the covers over her head, she finally tossed herself into sleep.

* * *

"You look pretty today."

Her toothbrush still in her mouth, PJ turned to see Jeremy in the doorway. He froze for a moment, taking in her Superman pajama pants, her thermal shirt and hoodie, then said, "Maybe I'll go get some coffee."

PJ spit the paste out into the sink of the office's tiny bathroom. She planned on heading over to the gym for a morning shower, but she had no intention of leaving the building with her mouth tasting like the underside of a Dumpster.

"Goo' i'ea," she said, the toothbrush back in her mouth.

Jeremy cracked a small smile and closed the door behind him.

Of course, he looked freshly groomed, a full eight hours of sleep behind him, as opposed to her dismal two.

She ran her fingers through her snarled, almost-shoulder-length red hair. Yep, she'd have to move out, and soon.

She exited for the health club before he returned, and an hour later, she retrieved her coffee and—score!—found three powdered sugar donut holes sitting in a bag on the sofa.

"Did you come up with any leads on Bix?" Jeremy sat at

the computer, searching his data bank for the last known address on Keith Dennis—the FTA whose file lay open on his desk. A half-eaten bismark soaked grease into a napkin beside him.

PJ pulled her sophomore yearbook onto the sofa. "When would I have done that—maybe between the hours of one and three this morning?"

"Someone got up on the wrong side of the sofa."

She popped an entire donut hole into her mouth and gave him a dark look. She'd give him the wrong side of the sofa. . . .

She swallowed, chasing it with a swig of coffee. "Can you do a credit header search on Trey Johnson, see if he's in the area?"

Jeremy gave her a strange look. "Where'd you get that?"

"Well, I did manage to dig up a lead."

"So you *were* up. Please don't tell me you camped out at her house again."

"Calm down, boss. I read my yearbooks."

"What, you discovered the name Trey Johnson scrawled between the pictures of the band concerts and the science project winners?"

"Something like that, yes. I'm thinking that Trey, Meredith's boyfriend, or more likely Deena Hayes, her best friend—see what you can find on her, too—might be helping her now."

"That's a big leap."

"But it is a new lead."

She matched his smile of approval with one of her own.

Jeremy turned his attention to his computer. "I have about three hundred listings for Trey Johnson. Let's start with Deena. Her last name is a bit less common." He sipped his coffee as the trace ran. "She lives in Kellogg. Runs a store—looks like a clothing store."

"Deena lives in Kellogg? What store?"

"Babies and Baubles. Just off Main Street."

PJ got up and pulled her bag over her shoulder.

"I don't suppose you'll be getting another round of coffee while you're out? I'll take a double-shot macchiato—"

"I'm not an heiress!" PJ closed the door behind her, took the stairs down, and climbed into the Vic.

Traffic traveling west, away from downtown Minneapolis toward the burbs, was thin, and PJ sailed toward Kellogg almost on autopilot, noting the backup of cars jockeying their way downtown. PJ smelled a game of toss-the-pigskin in the autumn air. Maybe she could attend a football game if she lived in Kellogg again.

Lived in Kellogg again. In the old Kellogg place. Became a Kellogg. The thought sank into her, along with Jeremy's words. *"You won't even consider moving into the house . . . because you don't think you belong."*

Because, well, a girl like her didn't belong to the fairy tale. No, fairy tales were reserved for real princesses, with real pedigrees. No matter how much she wanted to believe in Cinderella, PJ was a refugee taken in by royalty. She couldn't—or maybe wouldn't—escape her lineage.

Kellogg's Main Street always embodied an old magic that stirred to life whenever PJ turned off the highway and onto the strip that edged the beach. Only a few sailboats beckoned to her from their moors in the harbor of the Kellogg Yacht Club. The beach had yet to be combed—leaves tossed by the nearby oak and poplar trees splotched the sand.

Corn husks tied to lampposts and the occasional pumpkin edging a storefront doorway brought to mind the smell of piled leaves, the nip of morning frost.

She passed the theater, took a left at the corner, and found Babies and Baubles in a tiny three-office building a half block from the beach. She squeezed the Vic between a shiny black Lexus and a white Pontiac GT, wishing her car came in a convenient compact edition.

An elegant script on the door and window betrayed the clientele. Inside the aura of money portioned out in fresh gardenias, the classical music piped through the stereo, the chandeliers dripping from the ceiling and casting spotlights on the displays of designer handbags behind glass, jewelry hanging on glass racks. In the back, a baby section with European-looking prams with shock absorbers, hand-tooled high chairs, racks and racks of high-end baby clothes, lacy layettes. Everything for the well-attired baby and mother. PJ picked up a bear, checked the price tag. Put it back.

A woman dressed in a black baby-doll dress and calf-length leggings looked up at her and gave her a white smile.

Deena?

Time had been generous. Deena wore her blonde hair up, her face as young as it had appeared in the yearbook. "Can I help you?"

And with her greeting, PJ went speechless. What kind

of PI went into a situation cold? She'd walked in without a plan, and now she'd probably have to buy something to get Deena to open up.

She didn't belong here. But . . . an heiress would.

What would a Kellogg do?

PJ smiled, aware that she wore a pair of old jeans and a jean jacket, her red hair down and finger-combed. She affected a lazy browse. "Just looking. My sister is having a baby." She picked up a stuffed sheep.

"That's a sleep sheep. It plays four different soothing sounds to help your baby sleep better." Reaching over, Deena pressed the quilted tummy. A whine sounded from the toy. "That's a whale."

"It sounds more like someone is dying," PJ said, handing her the toy. "Sorry."

"If you prefer, we have a dog that emits a pleasing scent. We just got him in—I'll get one for you." She disappeared into the back.

PJ roamed the store. *Think like an heiress; think like an heiress.* Bix wasn't here, and for the first time in years, PJ hadn't a clue how to blend in, how to act a part.

Deena returned, holding a floppy, long-eared, stuffed hound dog. "Here he is. You just have to push his tummy, and more smell comes out." She gave the belly a little squeeze. The fragrance reminded PJ of something sweet— lavender, maybe, with a hint of baby powder. Oh yes, she already felt soothed.

Deena stopped talking, her cool green eyes running over PJ. "I know you, don't I?"

"I . . . I . . ."

"You look so familiar to me. Oh, I know—I saw your picture in the paper."

"PJ Sugar."

"I met a Sugar just last week." She put the dog down. "What was her name? She bought a bathrobe. It's out being monogrammed."

"It's probably for my sister."

Deena walked over to the counter and typed on her keyboard. "Let's see. Yes, here it is . . . Elizabeth Sugar. Monogrammed initials: EAB."

Elizabeth Ann . . . *B*?

"It came in yesterday. Did you want to pick that up?"

"Uh, no, actually, I'm here on official business. I'm looking for a woman named Meredith Bixby."

Deena's smile vanished. "Why would I know her?"

"I was looking in an old yearbook and I noticed you two were friends."

Deena turned, crossing her arms over her chest. "Now why would I ever be friends with that snake?"

"But you were in high school."

"Oh, honey. People change."

"Like Bix."

Deena fingered her necklace. PJ noticed her bare hand and the strange look that crossed her face. "Oh no, not Bix. People like Bix don't change. *I* changed. I got smart. "

"So you have no idea where Bix might be?"

Deena gave a wry smile. "If she knows what's good for her, a long way from here."

PJ wrote down her number—next on her list would be to get business cards—and handed it over to Deena.

"PJ Sugar . . ." She looked up with a smile. One filled with way too much recognition. "Aren't you the one who burned down the country club a couple years after I graduated?"

PJ smiled at her. Shook her head. "Nope. That was somebody else."

Deena flicked the paper between her fingers, and PJ saw her hold on to it until she got into her car.

Then she crumpled it and dropped it into the trash.

＊ ＊ ＊

Connie stood over her KitchenAid mixer, whipping up a batch of Toll House cookies, as PJ walked in, untied her Converse, and padded into the kitchen. PJ hardly recognized her attorney sister with her hair pulled back in a ponytail, wearing yoga pants and a rumpled Harvard sweatshirt, apparently playing hooky from another day of work. "Who are you?"

"An endlessly hungry pregnant woman." Connie scooted out a stool with her foot. "Tell me about the mushroom house."

"What are you doing home?"

Connie pulled out a cookie sheet. "I'm using my sick time—I probably have a month accumulated. Just until I get over morning sickness."

PJ eyed the bowl of cookie dough. "That's not breakfast, is it?"

"Elevenses." She pulled out a spoon from the drawer. "Are you going to keep the house?"

"I'm not sure—but I came over to tell you that Mom is on a cruise."

Connie put down her spoon. "Come again?"

"She's on a cruise. She told the neighbor, but not us. How do you like them apples?"

"Huh." Connie considered that for a moment, scooping another spoonful of cookie dough. "Weird."

PJ got out a spoon. "Yep."

Finally Connie pulled the bowl toward herself and began to spoon dough onto the pan. "I should attempt to actually cook some of these for Davy."

"That's it? No panic? No indignation?" PJ swiped a fingerful of dough and licked it off. "Mother hasn't been on vacation in ten years. And now she's, what, cruising the Caribbean?"

Connie dropped the final ball of dough onto a pan. "Maybe she'll get a tan."

"Connie. What if something happens to her? Don't you listen to the news? People get thrown overboard, attacked by pirates!"

"Please. Pirates?" Connie slid the cookies into the oven, closed the door, licked the spoon, and then let it clatter into the sink. "Don't worry."

"I am worried. It feels weird—like I suddenly don't know her. And apparently, she's buying bathrobes, only not for you. Sorry."

"Buying bathrobes?"

"One, at least. With the initials *EAB*."

"I don't even know anyone with those initials."

"Yes, you do—Elizabeth Ann . . ."

"Browning? Buckwheat?"

"Funny. Did Mom change her name?"

"It's probably a gift for some friend at the club. Calm down." Connie opened the fridge and pulled out a container of milk.

"Did you know that she had a friend in college named PJ?"

Connie set the milk on the counter. "No, I didn't. I wonder if she named you PJ after her friend."

"She didn't name me PJ, actually."

Connie grinned. "Oh, that's right." She took down two glasses. "Maybe that's why she freaked out when you started calling yourself that. Of course, I always knew you were a PJ."

Connie poured the milk, then turned when the buzzer sounded and moved the pan of cookies to the higher oven rack.

As PJ watched her, Connie's written words from the past slipped back to her. "Why did you write that in my yearbook—about me being amazing?"

Connie looked at her, flicking her hair from her shoulder. "What?"

"My yearbook. You wrote that I was most likely to be amazing."

"Maybe I was being pithy. But to me, you were sort of unbelievable."

"Please tell me that is good."

"Of course. I watched you from the outside of your vortex, always wishing I could be in it. You *did* amaze me."

"But I was always in trouble."

Connie lifted her shoulder. "It looked more like fun to me."

"Do you have significant memory loss? I was grounded for half of high school."

"But the other half, you were out with Boone. Having all the fun."

Maybe she was. She hadn't seen Connie's face in the powder-puff football pictures, the homecoming shots. "Sorry. I should have invited you in."

"It's okay. I couldn't have kept up with you, anyway."

"Stop doing that."

"What?"

"Being so nice. Calling me amazing. Why do you do that?"

"Hey, I'm an attorney. I try to look for the innocent parts of a person."

"Yes, but I was hardly innocent. I remember you standing in the hallway upstairs, watching me sneak out of the house."

"Oh, well, that was pure fun for *me*. I couldn't believe you scaled the porch. Or that Boone caught you. I was so jealous of you and Boone."

"Me and Boone?"

"He was crazy about you. I wished I had a boyfriend." Connie pushed a glass her direction. "It seemed like everything came so easy to you."

"No, you were the one things came easy to. You fit right into the life Mom wanted for you."

Connie took a sip of her milk. "That didn't mean you couldn't fit in. You never saw yourself as a Sugar."

PJ twirled the glass on the counter. "Because I'm not one."

The clock ticked. The fridge gave a moan.

Nothing from Connie. Until, "You've got to be kidding me."

PJ lifted a shoulder. "I'm adopted; let's not forget that. And it's not like we're even remotely alike. You're tall and dark; I'm a redhead—"

"Blonde, actually."

"In my mind, I'm a redhead. And I'm hardly tall."

"You're just right."

"Not for a Sugar."

Okay, really, she hated how pitiful she sounded. She took a drink, then licked her lips. "You know I've always felt different. Strange."

"Like an alien, I know." Connie responded to the buzzer again, taking the cookies out to cool. "But it's not because you weren't accepted." With the spatula she began to scoop the cookies onto the cooling rack. "It's because you didn't really want to be."

Didn't want to . . . "Excuse me, I spent most of my life trying to fit in. Of course I wanted to be accepted."

"No, you didn't. Because then it meant you had to be like us. 'Fit in a box,' I think I remember you saying once. It's why you liked it so much when Boone called you NBT."

"I didn't like it."

"Of course you did. You thrived on it. Because if you were trouble, then no one could expect more from you. No one could make you be a Sugar or anything else. You liked being trouble." Connie handed her a cookie on a napkin.

She liked being trouble. PJ stared at the cookie. Maybe she did. Then. Not necessarily now. "What if I don't want to be trouble anymore?"

"Then don't be." Connie refilled her milk. "But then who are you going to be?"

PJ raised her glass. "I thought I might try on Kellogg for size."

Connie finished unloading the cookies, turned off the oven, and scooped up her car keys. "Show me the house. I want to be a Kellogg too."

The sun had already tipped the scales toward the back half of the day as PJ pulled up to the gate, unlocked it, and then drove up the long, cracked drive to the mushroom house. She noticed the cavern in the lawn where she'd plunged into the ground only the day before, but in the daylight, the house again marched off the pages of a storybook, and for the first time since Boone had declared it uninhabitable, a future panned out before her. Flowers in the boxes hanging below the leaded windows. The ivy cleaned off, the wooden garage doors painted a cherry red. The lawn mowed, and the flower garden reseeded, overflowing with lily of the valley and roses and perhaps a row of variegated hosta.

"Wow. It's pretty rough, isn't it?" Connie said, getting out of her car, parked behind the Vic.

"It'll clean up."

PJ walked to the door, opening it with her key. "Brace yourself."

The house didn't flummox Connie. She wandered the length of it like PJ had yesterday, and PJ watched her catalog the disrepair. Yet, in Connie's eyes—a woman who had taken her Craftsman home and restored it, one fixture at a time—PJ saw the potential, the hope.

Finally Connie came outside and stood on the flagstone with her. "I think you can do this."

Most likely to be amazing.

PJ slipped her hand into her sister's. "Really?"

"Well, you'll always be a Sugar. But live here? Yes. Fix it up?" She turned to PJ. "Of course."

They watched the lake, the way the ripples caught the sunlight. A few fishing boats motored through the water.

"I need to pick up Davy. But tell me . . . when are you moving in?"

"How about now?"

Connie turned to her, and for the first time, her smile dimmed. "Right now? Without electricity? or decent plumbing?"

PJ led the way back through the house. "Connie, trust me, I've lived in worse."

Connie stopped her with a hand on her arm. "I don't want to know. Listen, if you need to move back into my place for a while, until you fix this place up . . ."

"Nope. It's my creepy house. I'm going to live in it."

"Of course you are."

PJ stood in the drive watching Connie pull away, feeling

a surreal ownership. The wind moaned in the slatted cedar boards and rustled the dead foliage clutching the house.

Oh, hush.

Opening her trunk, PJ pulled out a box of memorabilia —mostly mismatched dishware, some bedding. She'd pick up her duffel bag from Jeremy's place tonight. Closing the trunk with her hip, she carried the box inside.

"I'm *home*."

Her voice echoed through the barren rooms. Hiking through to the end, she nudged open the door to the maid's quarters. It overlooked the side yard—and the pond where Joy had died. A slanted roof gave it a cozy lean-to feel. The blue carpet was rutted in places, yet it matched the baby blue–tiled bathroom, with the cracked silver-plated mirror and the claw-foot tub.

A single bed with a bare mattress and a weathered French country frame jutted like a pier into the center of the room. A matching bureau took up the nook in the inside corner.

Home, sweet home.

"Hello?"

PJ dropped the box on the bed. Barely held in a little scream.

"Hello?"

It didn't sound like Jeremy or even Boone. Oh, where was her pepper spray when she needed it? She opened the box and fished around for something heavy, lethal.

Her hands landed on her hardcover Bible. Well, they did call it a sword. She scooped it from the box and held it like a two-by-four over her head.

"Hello? Anybody here?"

Footsteps. PJ tiptoed out of the room, then flattened herself against the doorframe. The steps echoed down the main hall.

She crouched down and slunk across the kitchen, under the counter. Peeked out along the side.

He looked harmless enough.

Wiry, tall, and solid, in a brown canvas jacket and a pair of very faded blue jeans, work boots, a Twins baseball cap that hid the color of his hair, her intruder had shoved his hands into his pockets, as if he had been out for a stroll on the beach and accidentally found his way to her living room. Clean shaven, and about her age, he wore a faraway expression on his face. Especially when he stopped to stare out the bank of windows to the lake, as if, for a moment, he might not actually be in the room.

She pounced out, holding the Bible over her head. "What do you want?"

He whirled around. Emotion flickered in his eyes, not surprise, but something else—a wariness, a reaction she couldn't pinpoint before surrender took its place. His hands went up. "Whoa there. I come in peace."

PJ kept her distance. "Then what are you doing trespassing?"

"Uh . . ." He glanced around, as if searching for her reinforcements.

Sorry, bub; it's just me and the Word of God. Should be enough.

But just in case, "I called 911."

"Aw, you didn't have to do that." He made to lower his hands.

She gave him a look and raised the Bible.

He put them back up. "Fine. Really, I'm not going to hurt you. I'm just looking for someone. PJ Sugar."

"What do you want with her?"

"Are you PJ?"

"Maybe."

This time, he did lower his hands. "My name is Max Smith. And I . . ." He advanced toward her a half step, then stopped and wore an expression so morose, so desperate, she let the Bible fall to her side.

"What?"

"Well . . . I need you to find me."

Chapter SEVEN

Max Smith looked like a guy not easily lost.

"I'm sorry, could you say that again?"

"I need you to find me."

Yes, he definitely looked like he knew his way around . . . life, perhaps. Over six feet tall, he stood with his hands once again pocketed in a demeanor that bespoke casual. But with the hard yet earnest brown eyes and the coiled energy radiating off him, he reminded her of . . . well, Jeremy. The eye inside the storm.

Especially when the sunlight sided against her and crept behind a cloud, shutting off the earnestness in his eyes. The room turned brisk.

PJ stepped back, moving the Bible in front of her again. "I'm not sure I understand what you mean, Mr. Smith."

He closed his eyes, and it was the way he rubbed his

hands down his face, his shoulders rising and falling with a deep sigh, that made her decide to listen.

"Are you lost?"

He breathed again heavily, then took his hands from his face. "I think so. Because after four years of wandering Kellogg, trying to piece my life together, I haven't the faintest idea who I am."

Join the club. Only, she had ten years at that game. But as a beat pulsed between them, PJ measured his face, and every impulse inside her told her he meant his words.

She set the Bible on the counter. "You don't know who you are?"

"I made up Max Smith. I don't know my real name, where I'm from, or who I am." He said it without flinching, his dark eyes holding hers, not a hint of a teasing smile.

Okay. "How'd this happen?"

"Dunno, exactly. Apparently I appeared one day on the Kellogg beach, naked and nameless. First thing I remember is the smell of the hospital and the cops standing at the end of my bed."

PJ narrowed her eyes. "And how, exactly, am I supposed to help you find . . . you?"

"You're a PI, right?"

Yes. *Yes!* "I am." She didn't elaborate.

"Well . . . see, I got a call from someone at the church who said you needed some help with your house." At these words he did a small look-see around the place. "I did a little sniffing and found out you were a PI . . . and I thought we could trade."

"Trade what?"

"Services. It seems I can handle a hammer, and more. And apparently you need someone with . . . uh, various handyman skills to bring life back into this place."

"I . . . Who sent you?" Her thoughts tracked to Jeremy and warmed her. So the Bix failure hadn't derailed him. He still believed in her and her ability to—

"A Connie Sukh—I can't read my own writing." He stared at a crumpled piece of paper. "She left a message on my cell phone, told me something about a mushroom house and how you needed help. Once I figured out what the mushroom house was, I thought I'd swing by. Sorry if I startled you."

PJ tried to imagine Connie leaving a rambling message on this man's phone—probably right after PJ had left her house yesterday. "How do you know my sister?"

"Connie is your sister?"

PJ raised one eyebrow.

"I think she must go to my church—I have a little ad up in the foyer for my handyman services."

Handyman. Yes.

"Please? I've exhausted all my resources."

There was something about a grown man, his voice gentle, his eyes desperate, saying *please* that did strange things to her brain. Like make her nod. And suggest that they get a cup of coffee and talk about his case. And even offer to pay for the coffee.

As if she might be rich or something.

"Listen, how about I get the power running so you don't

have to stock up on candles? Then we'll see about coffee. Or maybe food."

Food. Now there was a thought. She could use a pizza about now.

She followed him out to the car—a red Olds Cutlass that looked surprisingly comfortable next to her Crown Vic. He opened the trunk—in which she noticed a rolled sleeping bag and canvas tote—and reached for a large toolbox the size of a suitcase.

He hauled it out and closed the trunk.

A large furry head rammed itself against a backseat window. Then a fuzzy yellow-brown jaw tried to push through the three-inch opening. A tongue darted out.

PJ jumped away. "What's that?"

Max opened the back door of the car and out bounded what could probably pass for a small pony. A brown and white pony with floppy ears, a short snout, and brown eyes that gave her a split-second warning before the beast launched in her direction.

She caught his front paws. "Oh, oh."

"Dog, get down." Max pushed on the animal's head, grabbed his collar, and pulled him off PJ. "Sorry."

"This is your dog? Or should I say your *lap pony*?"

Max smiled, keeping his hand curled around the dog's collar. "Closest I can figure, he's part Saint Bernard, part Labrador. Friendly, protective, playful. Obsessively afraid of storms. He climbed in with me one night during a summer thunderstorm, and we've been pals ever since."

Climbed in with him . . . in his car? PJ shot a look at the

backseat. It looked clean despite the dog hair. Still, her heart gave a small twist.

PJ crouched before the animal and cupped him around the ears, looking him in his golden brown eyes. "What's your name?"

"Dog."

PJ looked at Max. "Dog? You named your dog *Dog*?"

"I can't settle on anything. I tried Hank. And Rip. Pete, even Ace. Doesn't seem to like any of them. So it's Dog until he can decide what he likes."

PJ rubbed behind Dog's ears. "Dog, you're getting a real name."

Max regarded her with a strange look. "Be my guest. If you can figure out his name, you can name him."

PJ considered him for a moment. "Jack?"

Dog gave her a lick, then bounded away.

"Not Jack."

"Keep trying." Max's toolbox rattled and thumped against his leg as he followed her inside to the electrical closet.

"So how did you come up with Max?"

"I don't know. Felt right. They fished me out of Maximilian Bay. So, Max?"

Again, she found herself beaming a flashlight on the fried electrical panel. Dog explored the house, his paws thundering upstairs, toenails clipping against the tile floor in the great hall.

"Are you an electrician?"

"Sometimes." Max opened the panel, then angled her flashlight at the porcelain knobs. She couldn't help but notice the scars that webbed his hands, his fingers, as if his skin had been taken off, crumpled, and ironed on wrong. Her eyes pinned to them too long.

"I think I was in a fire." Max opened his toolbox and took out what looked like a small meter.

"You think?"

"It happened before I woke up in the hospital. Before I washed up onshore at the Kellogg beach."

"You *washed up* onshore? Like a message in a bottle?"

"Something like that." He shot her a grin. Oh my, he had dimples. Reaching up, he touched one end of the thick wire extending from the inside of the box. "You have power."

"Then why is the house dark?"

"One of the three main fuses is out." He touched the meter to one of the penny-roll shaped fuses at the top of the box.

"Tell me more about the washing-up-onshore part."

"I don't remember it. Someone found me and called the cops. I woke up in the hospital, my memory gone, these scars on my hands." He held out his hand to PJ. "My fingerprints are gone."

"You don't have any fingerprints?"

He tested the next fuse. "That would have helped figure out who I am."

"So you have no memory at all?"

"Snatches—mostly sounds or smells that I know connect to something. But it's like . . . well, like a fuse is out. Something should be working, but there's no connection. I can't help but think if I can recognize something from my past, it might jump-start the entire system. Hey, I found the blown fuse." He crouched and began to search through his toolbox. PJ flashed the light into his box as he moved a tray, picked up first one package, then another.

"You keep a supply of old fuses?"

"You'd be surprised what it pays to hang on to." He unearthed a package and opened it. "I wanted to hire a PI, but since I had no home, no money, no identity, it's been slow going. I wound up at the soup kitchen at Kellogg Presbyterian and the homeless beds at the Lutheran home. Thankfully, people were kind—I helped roof the community center, and my name got around. For a long time, I did whatever job people gave me, lived where I could find a bed."

"Or in your car?"

"It was warm and dry. Makes a person appreciate the important things."

She had to admit, whoever Max Smith was—handyman, fireman, vagabond—he possessed an easy charm that made her want to trust him.

"Didn't the police try and track you down?"

"They gave it some effort—did a missing person's trace, but nothing came up. Try finding the right fish in an ocean. I moved back to Kellogg hoping . . . well, it all started here. But after a while, I sort of gave up. Flash the light up here, please."

PJ guided the light as he replaced the burned fuse.

"So why now? It seems you're making a life for yourself. Why not just start over?"

He paused as if considering her question. "You ever felt like you don't know yourself? like when you look in the mirror, you wonder how you got here, how you became the person you are?"

PJ kept the light on him, caught in his words. Could he see inside her head? She might have nodded.

"Now imagine that happening every day. Like, the other day I was fixing some plumbing—"

"You fix plumbing?"

"I told you, I'm a handyman. I loosen sticky doors, rewire kitchens, unclog plumbing . . ."

"Go on; sorry."

"Well, I was at this house, and this guy comes walking in, and he's talking Arabic to his wife and kids. And I understood him." He fiddled again with the fuse. "Now why would I understand Arabic?"

PJ glanced again at his hands. "Were you a soldier?" That would certainly explain the not-easily-spooked, put-that-down-now expression he wore when she wielded her Bible at him.

"I don't know. But I lay awake every night wondering, *Who am I? Is there anyone out there looking for me?*" He looked at her then, his words in his eyes. "I need you to find me."

She swallowed, the emotion thrumming off him in a way that felt too close, too raw. Her throat tightened. What if she did find him? What if she tracked down his past, solved a *real* mystery?

Max turned back to the fuse box. "Let there be light." He

connected the fuse, and behind her, in the hallway, the daylight seemed brighter. PJ backed out of the closet, and sure enough, the fluted globe of the iron fixture on the wall glowed.

Max climbed out behind her. "Now we just have to replace the burned fuses in the panel, and I think you're in business."

PJ clicked off her light and smiled. She held out her hand. "Max Smith, you have a deal. Help me make this place livable and . . . I will find you."

✴ ✴ ✴

"Who is this guy and what is he doing in your bathroom?"

PJ pressed her hands against Jeremy's chest, pushing him from her bedroom. "Keep your voice down; I don't want to spook him. He's fixing my sink, and I might actually be able to bathe tonight. So pipe down, Mr. Overprotective."

He caught PJ's wrists and held them, clearly debating her request. "What, is he the ghost of Kellogg Manor? or some drifter you tricked into helping you?"

"No, of course not. He's my new handyman."

Jeremy dropped his hold. "I look the other way for a few hours and you've moved out of my office and hired a handyman?"

Looking back over her shoulder, PJ caught Max's glance at Jeremy, and she held up a hand to assure him that yes, this overbearing, loud, rather rude person was actually a friend of hers. Or more, depending on the day. "I didn't exactly hire him."

Max raised a dark eyebrow, then went back to work tightening the pipe under the sink.

After illumination had been restored to her house, Max had done a long walk-through, room by room—excluding the still-locked master bedroom upstairs. Unfortunately, it did include a slimy expedition into her basement—again. Max ran a cursory check on the foundation, inspecting a few cracks, shucking his light into alcoves and recesses PJ preferred not to explore. Especially the one she'd decided to call the crypt—the one with the boat-size metal door. Probably the bodies of the first Kelloggs lay decomposing inside. Or, "Maybe we found a mafia treasure. Al Capone's secret vault."

"Funny," Max said, leaving her in the gloom as he swished his light to another creepy corner.

Max managed to whip up what he called a habitation list. "Two weeks, I can get this place cleaned up. However, I probably need to do more sleuthing for the plumbing leak in the 'dungeon of despair.'" He shot her a smile.

"What would you call it?"

"A basement. But I'm hoping the leak shouldn't be too hard to patch."

So was she.

While Max went to work on her clogged sink, PJ had made a quick trek to the store and purchased a couple boxes of rubber gloves, along with a bag of cleansers. It might take a blowtorch to clean the grime off the fridge, but for now, it could hold the remains of the late-lunch pizza they'd picked up at Hal's.

Dog had found a spot in a pool of sunlight to call home and curled into a ball, lost in blissful slumber, until Jeremy had charged in and seen Max sprawled on the floor of her bathroom.

"What is he doing here, then? Did you pick him up off the street? Did he have a sign—'will work for food'?" Jeremy had apparently forgotten how to whisper. Good grief, he acted like she'd gone out and hired a crew of thirty behind his back. Last time she looked, he *wanted* her to get off his sofa. PJ took him by the hand, pulling him through the kitchen, out to the terrace, and into the yard.

Dog trotted after them.

Jeremy followed the animal with his eyes as if he'd never seen a creature on four legs.

He drew a breath, prepping for another blast, but PJ held up a hand. "Listen, he came to me."

"*He* came to *you*? How on earth did he find you *here*?" He gestured to her enormous, recently acquired mansion. "It's not like you put out a 'PJ Sugar is in the building' banner. . . . Wait. Boone didn't send him, did he?" He shook his head. "That would be rich, coming from a guy who's afraid you might get taken out by an oversize raccoon. I can't believe he sent a stranger knocking at your door."

"Calm down, Jeremy. My sister called Max. He goes to her church. And he came to me because . . . in exchange for helping me fix up this place, I'm going to find him."

That took him back a beat. He narrowed his eyes. "What exactly do you mean by 'find him'?" She detected a definite growl in his voice. Jeremy had an uncanny, special ops way of unraveling her courage with a look when he wanted to, and she had to pull in a long breath, settle herself back into her resolve.

"He has amnesia."

Jeremy raised an eyebrow. "Amnesia. *Really*." He said it in a way that sounded like she might have let the cleaning fumes go to her head. "Seriously, do you know how rare that is?"

"Yes. But he does. *Really*. He washed up on the Kellogg beach four years ago, and no one knows anything about him—what his name is, where he's from. He's lost. And I'm going to find him."

"Stop saying that." He shot a glance at the house like he might want to go in and apply his own method of interrogation.

"It's true. He's a missing person."

Oh, those weren't the right words. Jeremy looked as if he might combust on the spot. Dog bounded up, holding a stick, and PJ threw it across the yard.

Jeremy watched it fly. "Oh, look, and he has a dog, too."

PJ looked back at him, not understanding the expression on his face. "Yes."

"I should have guessed."

"And what, exactly, does that mean?"

He ran his hand around the back of his neck. "Sheesh, PJ, maybe you should give a guy a chance to help."

"I am!"

Jeremy narrowed his eyes at her for a moment, then shook his head.

PJ touched his arm, held on. "The guy has no fingerprints."

"No fingerprints?"

Ah, see, inside that slightly overprotective demeanor, she'd stirred the private eye. "Nope. They were *burned* off."

"Burned off." Jeremy folded his arms over his chest. "*Burned* off."

PJ nodded and lowered her voice even more in case Max could hear her above the swish of the waves on shore, the rush of the breeze in the trees, and all the way inside the house. "That sounds like a mystery, right? The kind that needs solving?"

"No, Princess—"

"It's perfect! I'll solve his past—help him figure out who he is and how he got here—and he'll fix up my house, and you'll be able to give me a legitimate recommendation to the PI board. I'll get my license."

He winced, running a thumb and finger against his clenched eyes. "You have this all figured out, don't you."

"Isn't that what you want?"

His mouth tightened. He sighed and turned away, walking slowly toward the lake.

Wasn't it?

"Jer—?" She started after him, and he rounded on her. She nearly slammed into his chest. He curled his hands around her arms to catch her, left them there. She didn't miss the way her heart hitched, then revved, at the sense of standing so close to him. She couldn't deny that, despite the ease she felt with Max, she'd breathed something akin to relief when Jeremy walked into the house.

And apparently Jeremy could read her mind. "There's something about him that's not right, even dangerous."

"You took one look at him, Jeremy. What are you talking about? He's a handyman. Although, he says he knows Arabic." She made a little face, chasing her words.

"He knows . . . Oh, perfect. See, he's more than a handyman. He's . . . too alert. You didn't notice, but the minute I walked into the room, he knew I was there, was listening to everything I said."

"You were practically shouting. I'd say you were hard to ignore."

"Okay, maybe I overreacted slightly. I mean, yes, I think you should move off my sofa . . ."

PJ raised an eyebrow.

". . . but I guess I thought *I* was going to help you fix the place up. I spent the afternoon tracking down fuses. And then I show up and the electricity is already fixed." He glanced at Dog, now barking at the waves. "And now you have a dog."

"It's not my dog."

He let his hand drop, flicking it out in a sort of helpless gesture.

A second ticked by as she watched him, a different kind of frustration on his face, one she couldn't read. But he closed his eyes again, ever so briefly, and when he opened them, the look had vanished. He cleared his throat.

"The thing is, you have no idea who this guy is. You let him through your front door. He could be a serial killer."

"I highly doubt Max is a murderer."

"You don't know that! He could be a rapist or a strangler, and you let him into your home without a thought. Or what if he's after me?"

"After *you*? Is there something about you I should know? Are you wanted by the mafia?"

"There's a lot of things about me that you should know, or maybe not know."

PJ whisked her hands along her bare arms, gooseflesh rising. Shoot—how quickly the shadow around Jeremy could swoop in, turn her cold. "What don't I know?"

He cupped his hands around her neck, weaving them into her hair. Took a step closer as he gentled his voice. "I'm not wanted by the mafia. But I've made enough enemies over the years to want to be careful about who I let walk through my front door." He attempted a smile; it faded. "Who I let get near . . . someone I care about."

Oh.

He looked away. "Princess, I'm sorry. I'm just . . . It's been a long time since . . ." He closed his mouth as if pulling back the words. Let her go and stepped away.

Oh, how she wanted to chase after him. *A long time since . . . ?*

"But you still don't know anything about him. You can't be too careful."

She stood there, flummoxed, wanting to reach inside him, to pull out whatever it was he kept locked away.

Leaves tiptoed around them. Dog bounded up and dropped a stick at Jeremy's feet. He didn't look at it. Finally he said, "Right. Okay."

Only, she had the sense the words weren't for her.

Then, without another word, he went inside. PJ followed him, still feeling his hands in her hair. "Are you okay?"

But he didn't stop, just went right to the bathroom. Stood at the door.

Max was already on his feet. Face-to-face, the men seemed eerily similar, in stance, in expression. Except Max wore a smidge more wariness on his face. "Max Smith," he said. He held out his hand.

Jeremy took it. "Jeremy Kane." PJ waited for him to add *Kane Investigations*, but he left that out.

In fact, she wasn't sure how to name what transpired, the nonverbal communication that went on between the two men as Jeremy stared at Max with what looked like some sort of promise. And Max took it in, his mouth tight, sighing.

"All right, then," Jeremy said.

All right? PJ opened her mouth, but Jeremy filled in the words.

"She'll take your case, but you'd better make sure this place is award-winning when you're finished."

Max nodded. "I appreciate it."

Dog bounded into the kitchen through the open patio door and dropped the muddy stick on the floor. "Dog!" Max said.

PJ crouched in front of the animal, cupped him beneath his furry jowls, and looked into his amber eyes. "Mud stays outside, okay, Rufus?"

Dog blinked at her.

"Not Rufus."

"You'll get it," Max said, closing his toolbox. "I have faith in you." He smiled down at her. Dimples again.

Max reached into his pocket. "By the way, this was in the pipe. Must have been what was clogging it." He held out a tiny silver locket, a design engraved on the front.

PJ took it, opened it up. A cutout picture with ragged edges lay inside with a nearly washed-out image that looked like a man. She edged out the tiny photo with her thumbnail and held it up to the light. "I think a name is written on the back. Hugh? Who's Hugh?"

She replaced the picture, closed the locket, then turned it over. The letters *P* and *J* were etched on the back. She stared at them. Ran her thumb over them, a churning in her stomach.

Jeremy leaned over her shoulder. "PJ?"

She looked at him. "I don't know. My mother had a friend named PJ in college. But I could never find the matching name in the yearbook. Do you think this could have belonged to a Kellogg?"

"Maybe a maid." Max patted his leg to call Dog. "It was in the servant's bathroom."

"You're just assuming it was for a servant."

Max hauled his toolbox off the counter. "You're right. You're the PI; I'm sure you'll figure it out. See you tomorrow."

Dog scrambled after him.

PJ pocketed the locket and noticed a large plastic bag on the counter. She peeked inside and discovered boxes of fuses. "There are still a few dark rooms in the house," she said to Jeremy. "Thanks."

He lifted a shoulder, watching Max depart. Finally the door closed.

Jeremy turned to her, and she didn't have to be a stellar investigator to recognize a forced smile. "How about I take you out for dinner? Maybe pizza? I think you deserve it after today."

PJ let a swallow pass before she answered. "Would you be angry if I told you I had some already? for lunch?"

Jeremy sighed. "Of course you did." Still, he held out a hand. "How about Chinese?"

Chapter *EIGHT*

Jeremy had hit the red zone on her weird-o-meter. First he pouted all night, long after they'd picked up an order of kung pao chicken, fried wontons, and sticky rice. Then he'd scrubbed her cupboards and the apple green stove with almost-frenetic obsession. PJ thought he might actually be taking off paint.

Then, instead of kissing her good night, he shook her hand.

Shook. Her hand.

Like he might be her *boss* or something.

"It's been a long time since . . ." Oh, how she ached to pry the rest of that sentence from between his clenched teeth.

She'd have to employ her own PI skills, cajole it out of him slowly. Earn it. He never promised her that unveiling his past would be either easy or rewarding.

In fact, he'd practically drawn a line in the sand and ordered her not to cross it.

Maybe, however, he'd trust her for the dark, shadowy parts if he viewed her more as an equal. A partner. Someone he didn't have to always hover over, even rescue. A real PI who could prove that Max had been simply misplaced and wasn't an "escapee from a nearby mental hospital." Something he'd muttered while scrubbing her oven.

Well, whatever egged him to his over-the-top sanitation services, it had resulted in a satisfactory sheen to the apple green appliances and the stained-oak cabinets, and she went to bed in her blue oasis, exhaustion pushing her bones into the mattress. She did slightly miss the hum of traffic and the sound of Jeremy clicking away on his computer. And she would have appreciated Dog at her feet. Just to scare away any lingering ghosts of Kellogg Manor.

How she wished Jeremy hadn't said that. His words had awakened the story of Joy Kellogg in her head. She pondered it long after her body begged her for sleep.

Who had killed Joy? And why hadn't the police ever discovered the killer?

And who belonged to the locket now secreted away in her bag?

"You would never be forgotten." Jeremy's words touched her, and she let them filter through her, just for a moment.

The Kellogg family needed a PI like PJ Sugar on the job. A PI and, like Jeremy said, one good lead.

Maybe she'd see what Boone had on the mysterious death of Joy Kellogg.

Outside, the wind knocked against the glass. PJ pulled her sleeping bag to her chin and stared at the shadows of ivy twining across her ceiling. What must it have been like to grow up in this house? She might have played a little basketball in the great room. Or maybe it had a grand table that held twenty, and she would have had lavish dinners of roast duck and pâté. No, not pâté. Red velvet cake. And beef Wellington.

Why had no one stepped forward to claim this house, the legacy of the Kelloggs?

And why *had* God given her this house? The question did laps in her brain until she finally turned on her light. It bathed the stack of books she'd unpacked—a dog-eared novel she'd been trying to finish, her journal, her Bible, perilously unread in recent weeks.

She picked it up, opening to her bookmark. 1 Peter 2. She scanned down to her last-remembered stopping place.

> *. . . for you are a chosen people. You are*
> *royal priests, a holy nation, God's very own*
> *possession. As a result, you can show others the*
> *goodness of God, for he called you out of the*
> *darkness into his wonderful light.*

Oh, sure, her eyes would wander there, sitting in the middle of the fairy-tale house. *"God often gives us our dreams to also show us something we didn't even know we needed."* She still hadn't worked out what she might need, but it did feel as if God had suddenly turned His full wattage on her. Limelighted her in some fanfare of blessing.

Chosen. Royal.

Heiress.

She'd like to believe that, really she would. As she closed the Bible, she let that thought drift upward, then listened briefly for a reply.

Only the wind, knocking some branch against her window.

She turned off the light. *"You can show others the goodness of God . . . for he called you out of the darkness . . ."*

Darkness . . .

Dark . . .

* * *

"Do I have to smile?" Max had said when she met him at the front door the next morning with Connie's borrowed digital camera and pushed him out into the sunlight of the yard.

"Depends on if people might remember you with a smile."

He'd crossed his arms over his chest and practically glared into the lens.

"That wasn't very happy."

"I thought I'd give people a blank canvas to work from."

A blank canvas. The words reverberated inside her as she left Max to his list, cooed over Dog, then fired up the Vic. It seemed, at times, that she excelled at the blank canvas, reinventing herself over and over. Until she returned to Kellogg and walked into an identity already formed, the brand waiting for her. It had seemed comfortable, at first.

And for the first time, her messy self hadn't seemed as much an eye-rolling horror, but a gift of sorts. Even better, maybe God wanted her to be a little messy. It gave Him all these fabulous opportunities to save her. But . . . well, perhaps she'd been hanging on to that moniker—NBT—just a little too tightly. *"Because if you were trouble, then no one could expect more from you."*

Even herself.

Downtown Minneapolis wasn't made for the freighter-size Crown Vic, and PJ motored through the shadows of the high-rises, down one-way roads to Portland Avenue and the headquarters of the *Star Tribune.*

She docked the Vic in the parking lot across the street, in the shadow of the Dome, and jogged across the road to newspaper central. At the front desk, they directed her to classifieds.

She took out a display ad on Max, big enough to catch attention, and left a number—the trap phone. If anyone called, she'd have a record of their number and a starting place for her search.

Retrieving the boat, she chugged over to St. Paul and placed a matching ad in the *Pioneer Press.* She tooled past the magnificent dome of the capitol glinting in the sun, her local history flooding back to her. Once upon a time, the hub of activity in Minnesota had been St. Paul, the stately manors of Summit Avenue betraying a wealth that even now fostered a girl's wildest dreams. Most of the mansions had been turned into B and Bs. A few, like the James J. Hill home, became historical sites. She knew all about James J.

Hill, railroad magnate, thanks to the railroad station he'd built in the center of Kellogg.

As a favor to his friend and business partner, Paul Kellogg . . . father of Orton Kellogg, husband of Agatha.

She motored back over the bridge spanning the Mississippi River. So what had happened to the magnificent, well-connected Kellogg family? How had they gone from the height of the glittering era of lumber and railroad magnates to bequeathing the last of their possessions to a former vagabond, wannabe PI?

And sheesh, it might have been helpful to discover that answer *before* the plumbing went out and soiled the remains of the wine cellar. She hoped Max would be true to his word and hunt down her leaks. After all, she was certainly returning the favor.

Some sleuthing into the legacy of the Kelloggs might help her figure out where she fit into the picture.

PJ tapped her brakes and took the exit to the central branch of the Hennepin County Library.

A breath of calm swept through her even as she entered through the security turnstile, the reverent hush of knowledge and learning enfolded in the rampart of books that bordered the reception desk. She remembered one of her first meetings with Jeremy, him pressing in behind her to read her computer screen while they researched ancient coins and eventually helped apprehend an international assassin.

Come to think of it, that should count for a reference from the boss, shouldn't it?

Probably she'd just start calling him that. Until he

figured out the difference between a handshake and a good-night kiss.

PJ approached the librarian's desk. A silver-haired, breakable woman who looked more like a professor than a librarian looked up from her computer. Pulling her cat-eye glasses down her nose, she raised one razor eyebrow.

PJ leaned over the counter. "I'm looking for information on the Kellogg family. Specifically, the murder of Joy Kellogg."

The librarian blinked, opened her mouth, shut it, and then pushed her glasses up her nose. "I see. Well, currently, all our historical records are stored off-site. You may be able to retrieve the information in the microfiche file, but since the Kellogg library closed, all those files are still in transition. We'll have to order them—might take a couple weeks." She took out a piece of paper and pen and handed them over to PJ. "Write down your name and number, and I'll call you when it's ready."

"A couple weeks? You're kidding."

Clearly not, from the look she got. PJ scrawled her cell number and handed it to her.

"There's a suggestion box by the front door. Feel free to solve our storage problem for us." She looked at the slip of paper. "PJ Sugar. I've heard that name before, haven't I?"

PJ lifted a shoulder. "I hope not."

She left the librarian, walked back out to the Vic, and surfed the rest of the way to Kellogg.

She swung by her mother's house. Not a hint of life. Cruise, indeed. They probably needed to enter into some sort of binding agreement about communication. She needed at least twenty-four-hours' notice if Elizabeth Sugar wanted to leave town.

Since when did her mother have the right to go gallivanting off to unknown Caribbean locations?

PJ finally ended up in front of the police station.

Boone's red Mustang convertible sat in the lot, the top up. So he hadn't yet replaced his stolen Ford F-150. Which meant, what? That he was holding out for a better answer to his proposal? He'd once told her he'd be willing to use the insurance money to buy them a house.

So they could get married and start a life together.

And she had turned him down, communicating her rejection with a rather unfortunately timed kiss from Jeremy, which Boone had witnessed.

PJ shut the door and made her way inside. Rosie, the desk clerk, glanced at her, a too-familiar expression on her face. Oh, that so wasn't fair—PJ hadn't been inside the police station for nearly two months. And the last time she wasn't wearing any cuffs at all.

"Is Boone in?" PJ asked, swinging her car keys around her finger.

"*Detective* Buckam is in his office. I'll let him know you're here." Rosie picked up the phone.

PJ waited, remembering her night—or should she say nights?—spent in the holding cells downstairs. She folded her arms, bulwarking herself.

"Hey, PJ, what do you need?" All business, just short of frigid. Nice.

She never really got used to this Boone, in a tweed suit coat, wearing a shoulder holster, as if he'd always been on the right side of the law, with his close-cut bronze hair, a no-games look in his blue eyes. A twinge of old pain went through her, as memory swept her up into his arms. She sighed, disentangling herself.

"I'm looking for information on my new handyman. A missing person named Max Smith."

Something sparked in Boone's eyes a second before he touched her elbow. "Come into my office." He glanced at Rosie when he said it. "I'll fill you in."

He closed the door behind her, grabbed a straight-backed chair from against the wall, and set it opposite him as he leaned on the desk.

PJ thumped her bag into it. "My instincts are saying you've heard of him. Who's Max Smith?"

Boone gave a huff, tailing it with a chilly smile. "I thought you were this colossal private investigator. Why come to me?"

"Do you or do you not know him?

Boone held up his hands as if the answer should be obvious. "Okay, yes. I know Max. I looked into his case a while back."

"And you know, then, about his amnesia."

"I know he hasn't shown up on any missing person reports, so if you want to call it amnesia . . ."

"Are you saying it isn't?"

"I'm saying he's got a good reputation around town, and he's never given me trouble. And *you* need help if you want to keep that monstrosity."

"We call it the mushroom house, with affection in our

voices. And don't think for a second that I can't see right through you. You're evading."

"Good grief, PJ. You said you wanted to be a PI, so be a PI."

Oh. His taking her seriously had her at a loss for words.

"Fine. Give me a push off. What do you know?"

He stood, considered her for a moment, then crossed around his desk to sit down. "He came here four years ago, and yes, I tried to help him. But nothing has popped on the radar about this guy." He lifted a shoulder. "He might be telling the truth. We found him washed up on the shore, nearly dead, and not a speck of evidence linking him to a living soul. The Minneapolis police gave it a try, but it's just not a priority. And we haven't a clue where to start looking."

"Did you run an ad in the newspaper?"

"No, but I ran his picture through our database a few dozen times."

"Not one hit?"

"Not even a blip."

"Do you have a report on him I could read? The night he washed up onshore, maybe?"

Boone folded his hands, leaning forward on his desk. She sensed the slightest thaw as one side of his mouth hinted at a smile. "I might."

Uh-oh. "What's that supposed to mean?"

"I think it's going to cost you." There appeared the old, familiar, dangerous twinkle in his blue eyes.

"Boone, do you want me to be a PI or not?"

"Is this an essay question?"

Perfect. And his smirk didn't help because, yes, it made her smile.

Finally he opened his hands on the desk. "As far as the Kellogg police are concerned, it's a cold case."

"But if I find something, shouldn't you reopen it?"

He narrowed his eyes at her just enough to suggest she might know more than she should. "You'd have to convince me."

I could do that nearly made it out past her lips. But she held it in. Because, well, maybe she couldn't, and even didn't want to, anymore.

"Okay, what's it going to cost me?"

"Dinner. With me."

Dinner. Except dinner with Boone was never just dinner. It was a full-out sprint down memory lane, with her trying to shove her heels into the ground, only to be swept up by his lethal charm. There was no guaranteeing that they wouldn't end the evening strolling the leaf-strewn beach under the full scrutiny of the moon, Boone reeling her back into his heart.

She sighed. But she needed her own PI license, her own *life*, if she ever wanted to sort out her feelings about any of the men in it. Including Boone. "When?"

"Tonight. After I get off my shift. I'll pick you up."

Oh, that would be swell. With any luck, Jeremy would be on-site to wish them happy trails.

"I'll meet you. When and where?"

He seemed to be considering her words, and she could nearly see the Jeremy-Boone showdown playing in his eyes.

She was wondering who would win, when he nodded. "Sunsets, 7 p.m."

"Done." She paused for a moment, turning over her next request in her mind. Maybe she shouldn't have agreed so quickly. . . .

"What else do you want?"

Oh, shoot. She had to work on her PI poker face. Especially with Boone.

"Could you bring the cold case file on Joy Kellogg, too?"

He opened his mouth, then closed it in a grim line. "You're not going to find anything."

"Please, Boone. I don't expect to *solve* the crime." She gave a laugh, maybe a bit too high. "Really—I just want to read the file. *Please?*" She gave him a warm, let's-be-friends smile.

He held up a hand. "Don't do that."

"Don't do what?"

"Don't. I'll bring the file."

"Two files. Don't forget."

"Trust me, I won't forget."

✳ ✳ ✳

PJ usually loved a hardworking man. But this one was slimed in mud, from knee to work boots, grime flicked into his short brown hair, along his chin, even ground into his elbows. She wasn't too keen on the smell emanating from said hardworking man, either—an algae pond odor mixed with a trace of sewer? "Please don't tell me that's my basement slathered all over you."

Max peered over his shoulder at her from where he sat on the descending steps off the kitchen. Dog lay in the middle of the linoleum floor, finishing off a piece of driftwood he'd hauled in from the shore. Soggy wood chips soaked in puddles of drool around him. On her way in, PJ had given him a nudge with her foot and tried out Barney. Not a wink of recognition.

"I found the leak," Max said.

"You did? Did you have to dive for it?" She laughed at her own joke.

He didn't. She noticed he was wiping his hands on one of the new rags she'd purchased to dust with. Nice.

"Nope. Sorry." He stood. "If you want, I'll show you."

"Does it involve descending to my creepy, rat-infested, slime-smelling, ghost-ridden basement?"

"Maybe." He gave the word a singsong lilt and grinned. Oh, she'd forgotten about the dimples. She should have mentioned that in her advertisements—definite memory joggers.

"I'll pass. You can describe it to me. Feel free to use adjectives and any other descriptions that will make you feel better."

"How about if I start with a price?"

PJ made a face. "Let's not. How about starting with . . . location? or a time frame?"

Max rolled his eyes and moved past her. She gave him plenty of berth.

He tracked through the kitchen, out along the main room, past the fireplace, and stopped at a place that she calculated fell right beneath the locked bedroom where Agatha Kellogg had breathed her last.

He tapped a wall. What should have been a sharp rap against a hard surface sounded more like a soft, forgiving thud.

"Please don't tell me these walls are soggy."

Max took her hand and placed it on the wall. "Like half-baked bread. Frankly I'm surprised it hasn't come down on you yet."

Now he sounded like Boone, Mr. Doom and Gloom. She ran her hand along the wall, found where the water had saturated it. It seemed like a good ten-foot-wide panel. "So the leak is here?"

"I think it's upstairs in the bathroom. Must have flooded, or a pipe burst, and it flowed down this wall and then into the basement."

"That's a lot of water."

"It wouldn't take much to do this kind of damage. But the amount of leakage in the basement—yes, that's quite a bit of runoff. Do you want my theory?"

"Please."

"I think old lady Kellogg ran herself a bath one night and then snoozed off. The bath overflowed and killed the walls, turned the basement to mud."

"What if that's when she died? She went to take a bath . . . and ended up in heaven?"

He raised an eyebrow. "That's deep and profoundly theological."

"What are you talking about?"

"The idea of cleansing one's soul before departing."

The conversation felt too solemn suddenly. And Max's expression had grown dark, even troubled, as the words settled around them.

PJ resisted the urge to reach out to him, touch his arm. Still, she put kindness in her voice. "We'll figure out who you are, Max Smith. And I doubt you'll have any soul-cleansing to do."

He sighed. "Oh, I think we all have some soul-cleansing to do, but I have to admit, I don't think I could take it if I turned out to be an arsonist or something."

"Arsonist?"

He held up his hands.

She smiled. "I pegged you for a fireman."

"I'll take that." Max met her eyes, gratitude in his. "Now—I hate to ask, but can I use your bathroom to clean up? I have a change of clothes in the car. I don't want to leave a permanent smell in the old Cutlass."

Again the urge to ask him where he lived tipped her lips, but she simply nodded, driven to silence by her own transient addresses.

Twenty minutes later, PJ was finishing off a slice of cold pizza, listening to Max sing "Bye Bye Love" in the shower. She could probably cross off lounge singer from the list of possible identities.

Meanwhile, she paged through a sheaf of papers from Jeremy while she checked her cell phone messages. Twice. Nothing from the boss.

This morning, when she'd stopped by the office, she found that he'd left her a sticky note on a folder, which contained a list of all the forms and continuing classes she'd have to complete before he'd submit her application to the licensing board. Including a first-aid and CPR-training class; Tactics: Baton, ASR, and Handcuffs; a continuing education class on the basics of civil process; and one that she wasn't sure how to understand: Sudden In-Custody Death Syndrome.

Just how sudden?

"What are you looking at?" Max came out of her bedroom, rubbing his wet head with a towel.

Without a shirt.

His clean jeans hung low on his waist, and she knew she shouldn't be looking, but her gaze flitted over his torso and arrested on a mean-looking scar that curled the width of his muscled stomach.

Her gaze then moved to the red tattoo on his upper arm. She noticed it as he draped the towel around his neck, gripping both ends. "You have a tattoo," she said dumbly.

He glanced at it. "Yep. No idea where that came from."

She went over to him and studied it. "I've never seen anything like this. It looks like a phoenix holding two arrows."

"Are you a tattoo specialist?"

"No, but I have a friend who knows her tats inside and out." She looked at him. "You have no memory at all how you got this?"

"Nothing."

She stepped away from him. "Put your shirt on, Max. We're going on a little field trip."

✳ ✳ ✳

Stacey Dale, tattoo artist extraordinaire and proprietor of Happy Tats, worked out of a small shop in Uptown, banked on one side by a hair salon called the Scissor Shack. PJ stopped in at the salon and waved to her friend and former client Dally Morrison, who was elbow-deep in lather, her raven black hair now shorn close to her head, dressed in a short-sleeved black shirt and a pair of jeans with a row of horizontal rips held together with safety pins. She nodded toward PJ. "Hey, Me, you still solving crimes?"

PJ grinned. "Hey, Me—yep, I'm still on the job."

Max caught her eye, frowning.

She explained, "I spent two long, hot weeks in August as Dally, while Jeremy kept her under wraps, in close protection."

"Not too close," Dally said. Her gaze lingered a second on Max, then back to PJ, a question in her eyes.

"He's a client."

Dally made a round O with her mouth, then wrapped her customer's head in a towel and propped her up. She directed her attention to Max. "You're in good hands. She's why I'm alive today."

Max glanced at her with a look that made PJ warm. "Okay—not entirely true. Is Stacey over at Happy Tats?"

"All true. And I think so."

PJ stepped next door and found Stacey seated on a stool next to a padded chair that looked like something out of a dentist's office. A client's arm extended across a winged pad, and she bent over it with a tattoo iron, grinding a tribal symbol into his arm. He looked about eighteen, fresh out of school, with a pimply face and not much facial hair. Probably the tat acted as some sort of rite of passage.

Stacey wiped away a gathering of blood with her purple-gloved hand and looked at PJ. "Hey, Sherlock, what's up?" Stacey had helped complete PJ's transformation into Dally's look-alike by painting on Dally's various tattoos. In washable ink.

"I see you're working on dreds," PJ said, noting Stacey's longer, red, now-tangled hair.

"No more softball. It's time for my winter look." Indeed, instead of the usual skull-and-crossbones tanks and low-cut jeans, Stacey wore a pair of paint-stained overalls and an orange tee. She'd gotten another piercing in her eyebrow, too. "But what happened to you? You move to the suburbs, turn into a soccer mom?"

PJ looked at her outfit—a pair of jeans, a plain brown T-shirt, a jean jacket. She *was* wearing her high-top patch-work Converse. "It's easier to blend if I don't look like I'm about to knife somebody."

Stacey grinned. "Yeah, I s'pose. Who's the hottie?"

Max shifted behind her. PJ turned and hooked him around the arm. "He's my show-and-tell. I show—you tell." She urged him toward Stacey. "Ever seen a tat like this before?" She turned Max, who took off his jacket and hiked up his sleeve.

Stacey removed her safety goggles. Peered at it. "It's a phoenix."

"Right."

"Well, that means rebirth. And the arrows—I've seen those on soldiers who earn medals. They don't wear them, so they get them tattooed." She replaced her glasses. "I have a guy you should talk to. He's sort of my mentor. Jinx Jenkins runs a shop near the U in Dinkytown. Tell him I sent you." She gave PJ the address and turned back to her client. "You know, that offer of free ink—a real tat—is still open. Maybe make a little flower or something to cover up the one you already have?"

Out of the corner of her eye, PJ saw Max's eyes flicker to her, and she suddenly wanted to put up her hand to cover— or protect?—Boone's scripted name on her arm. Thankfully, she wore a jacket. But she dredged up a breezy smile. "Nah. I'm not ready for that yet."

"Really," Stacey said, knowledge in her voice. "You come back to me when you are."

Max waited until they were out on the street before he spoke. "You have a tattoo?"

PJ unlocked the Vic lounging against the curb. "I have a memory."

He muttered something about her being the lucky one as they climbed into the car and headed for Dinkytown.

Big Ten Tattoos looked like a place that catered to the college set, with many of their designs featuring local fraternities or sororities. Jinx—or Marlon Jenkins, whose name PJ read off the certificate by the front door—came from the back, looking like a man who knew his trade.

Every inch of him was marked. An epic medieval battle

played out in his vibrant sleeves all the way down his wrists, and even the back of his hand bore a black-and-white emblem, something Celtic-looking. A maroon baseball hat bearing a Minnesota gopher capped what looked like a bald head, and she supposed he might even have a tat under there. He set down a tray of instruments—a gun, some ink, a package of black surgical gloves. "Are you my three o'clock?"

"Nope. Stacey over at Happy Tats sent us. My friend here has a tat that we're trying to figure out the meaning of."

He glanced at Max. "What—you don't know what you got?"

"He doesn't remember getting it."

Jinx frowned. "Were you drunk? on shore leave?"

"Do I look like a soldier to you?"

Jinx sat down on the stool, crossing his colorful arms so the thick muscles bulged. "Yep."

Max glanced at PJ and she nodded. "Will you take a look at it?"

Jinx gestured him over. Max again removed his coat, pulled up his shirtsleeve.

Jinx studied it a moment. "Do I know you?"

Max looked at him. "I don't know—do you?"

Even from three feet away, PJ could sense Max's quickening heartbeat, his intake of breath, the hope on his face.

"I've seen this tat before. I inked it on a guy a few years back."

"Was it me?"

Jinx seemed to be searching Max's face. "Nah, it wasn't you. But I do have a picture of the tat."

He reached under the counter and pulled out a three-ring binder, flipping through it until he found a Polaroid of a man's shoulder, including a shot of his torso.

"Fine piece of artistry, if you ask me."

"Is there a name with it?"

"Nope. I only keep records back for a year."

Max stared at it. PJ leaned over his arm. "That's not you, my friend. Sorry."

"How do you know?"

She pointed to the picture. "It's different from yours— it's missing the fire yours has around the phoenix. This one is more plain." She glanced at Jinx. "But still very artistic."

Jinx studied Max's arm for a moment. "You're right. It looks like the work of a friend of mine. He had a shop down the street. I do remember quite a few soldiers coming by at the time."

"Do you have his name?" Max asked.

"Yep. But it's not going to help you." He closed the book. "Guy was killed in a bar fight about a year ago."

PJ could feel Max's hope deflate beside her.

Jinx focused on Max's face as if probing for guile. "You really don't remember getting this?"

"I wish I did."

"Well, soldier, maybe you shouldn't. I've seen variations of this tat around on a few men. They all have one thing in common."

"What's that?" PJ didn't know why, but her hand found its way to Max's forearm as if to steady him.

Good thing, too, because as soon as the words left Jinx's mouth, Max stiffened and inhaled hard.

"Guys that have these usually survived being prisoners of war."

Chapter NINE

"He was a POW?"

Boone couldn't erase the note of surprise—PJ would even label it admiration—from his voice as they sat overlooking the veranda at Sunsets Supper Club. The night hovered beyond the splash of setting sun on the waves, and a family of Canadian honkers had stopped and bedded down on the beach on their journey south.

"That's what the tattoo guy said. And that probably accounts for the scar on his chest. And two more—one on his calf and the other under his jaw—that he showed me when we returned to the house." PJ finally took a bite of cold steak. She chased it with her Diet Coke.

"Stop right there. That's too much information for me, PJ. Even if we aren't dating."

Inside the supper club, she knew a few eyes had turned

on them as they walked in—and what girl wouldn't enjoy the prestige of dining out with Detective Boone Buckam, dressed to kill in a green button-down shirt and a pair of jeans. But she wasn't Boone's girl anymore, even if that left her feeling a little like Dog next to him, homeless and without a clear identity.

At least she didn't look like a vagrant, thanks to Connie's jacket and a white dress shirt. Connie had been stirring up a batch of brownies, Davy seated at the counter licking the wooden spoon, when PJ stopped by.

"Auntie PJ!" He flung himself into her arms, and she gave him an extra twirl, not caring that he smeared her jacket with brownie goo.

She wiped it off with a sponge and stayed to visit for a while, snagging a couple of late-afternoon brownies on her way out.

Which probably accounted for why she was swimming her flank steak through the mushroom sauce, replaying Max's reaction to Jinx's proclamation. She'd called Jeremy and left a message, asking him to send Max's picture to his contacts in the military.

"That's some pretty good legwork," Boone said, finishing off the last bite of his salmon.

"See, I am a private investigator."

"Oh, I've never doubted your ability to uncover the truth." Boone smiled over his glass. "Just the wisdom of it." He set down his glass. "Which reminds me . . ." He reached into his suit coat and pulled out an envelope. Set it on the table.

"What's this?" PJ reached for the envelope. It contained two sheets of paper.

"One is a copy of the police report on the night Max washed up onshore. I'll sum it up for you." Boone signaled to the waiter. "The Kellogg hobo found Max Smith around midnight four years ago in October. He was floating in the water, and the hobo pulled him ashore. The report lists the statement and Max's injuries."

"I can't believe the Kellogg hobo is still around. He's been homeless in Kellogg since . . . well, since we were kids. But I did see him recently—he actually gave me a handkerchief a couple months ago." The night Connie had thrown her out on the street, to be exact.

"His name's Murph, by the way. At least, that's what he calls himself. He's still homeless, although believe me, efforts have been made to get him into a shelter. He always seems to bounce out—as if he doesn't want the help. Then he disappears for a while, only to pop up again after a couple months. I think he must make a circuit around the lake. The good news is that I saw him not long ago, camped out under the Maximilian Bay Bridge, not far from where he pulled Max out of the water."

"Maybe I could talk to him, see what he remembers."

Boone winced. "I'm not sure that's the best idea. Besides, what is he going to remember?"

"I don't know—but shouldn't I follow up every lead?"

The waiter came over, and Boone gestured to PJ's plate. "Her dinner is cold—can you reheat it?"

The waiter picked it up. "Right away, sir." He took it away as PJ tried to catch up.

"How'd you know my steak was cold?"

Boone shot her an I-know-you; don't-be-stupid look. "The only thing you eat cold is pizza. And you've been pushing your food around your plate for a half hour. What are you thinking about?"

"Max. And Joy Kellogg. And a guy named Hugh. And this strange locket Max found."

"Who's Hugh?"

"I don't know. His name was on the back of a picture in the locket."

Boone wiped his mouth. "Which brings me to the next page." He reached over and tugged out the bottom sheet. "I wrote up a little summary of the police report on Joy."

PJ stared at his hand-scrawled summary. "You did this for me?"

"The case files belong to the Kellogg police. And although the file is cold, it's still open. I can't take it out of the station. I only took Max's because he's given his tacit permission."

PJ tried to scan the page, but Boone curled his hand over the top, folding it. "Here's the gist—Joy Kellogg was trouble. She ran away from home when she was a teenager, and when she returned, she had a baby girl with her. Then, suddenly, she married Clay—you know, his father owned the sailboat place? Things weren't always pretty between Clay and Joy. According to the maid's account, they fought a lot and especially the night she went missing. Apparently Joy and Clay got into a ringer, and she stormed out of the house. They found her the next morning, face-down in the pond. Clay was at home all night—he has an alibi, verified by the maid. And there was no real sign of foul play. It could have been an accident—"

"I thought you said she was murdered?"

"Rumors around the station. But nothing was ever proven. So?" He lifted a shoulder.

PJ put the summary in the envelope just as her plate of food returned. She dug into it. "I want to go talk to the hobo after dinner. Do you think we can find him?"

Boone pressed his lips together. "Peej—we need to talk."

Her appetite left her, despite the sizzling steak. Now he would ask her to reconsider their breakup, and he'd do it by smiling softly, that tease in his blue eyes that could make her brain turn to mush. And if he took her hand while he did it, ran his thumb over the top if it, then she just might say—

"I met someone."

She stilled, her fork unmoving in her grip. He gave her a grim smile. "She works for the paper, someone I've been friends with for a while. We saw each other again at the Harvest Festival, and . . . well, I just wanted you to know before . . ." He swallowed. "Before you saw us around town or something."

Which she easily read as a thinly veiled reference to the fact that he'd walked straight in on her and Jeremy in a lip-lock. The thought of Boone pulling another woman into his arms . . .

Yes, she'd definitely lost her appetite. She set down her fork, put her hands in her lap. Breathed. Smiled.

"Oh. That's. Nice." That wasn't really her voice, was it? She sounded pitiful. She tried again. "I . . . I'm happy for you."

She should just give up now. But Boone was buying it—or at least acting like it—because he sighed, something like relief washing over his face. "I'm glad. I wanted us to be friends, but I wasn't sure how, and I think this is a good place to begin. Like a fresh start for both of us. You with . . . Jeremy, and me with Lindy."

Lindy? As in Lindy the photographer? Perfect.

She forced a smile through her teeth, trying oh so hard to unclench them. Connie's words came back to her. So maybe this was what it looked like to be friends with Boone. She'd just breathe through it. "Yes . . . good for us. Or you. I'm not exactly with Jeremy."

He leaned forward. "Really? Is everything okay?" His move didn't seem proprietary as much as something, indeed, a friend might say to another friend. Like two mature adults.

Her eyes burned. She was so not talking to her ex-flame about her confusing non–love life with the mysterious Jeremy Kane, when she right now had the overwhelming urge to grab his hand, force him to race with her out to his Mustang, and head for the border.

And what was that? Leftover pride? The remains of their affection?

She took a breath as she stared at her food.

"PJ, are you really okay?"

She closed her eyes. Oh, please, please, she didn't want to

cry. She broke up with Boone for good reasons, like the fact that he couldn't see the woman she wanted to become, or that they had both vastly changed since high school. But . . .

She got up, feeling a little woozy.

"PJ?"

"I need some air." She pasted something that might have been a smile on her face, strode through the restaurant, and pushed straight out into the cool night. The rich fragrance of fall, the stirring of the wind in the trees trickling leaves at her feet and sweeping the waves onto the shore—it all jolted her, and she gulped in a breath. Another.

But she needed more than air. She needed her brain clear, her heart free.

A fresh start.

But—and the truth lunged at her, took hold even as she stalked out to the beach—she didn't want one. She did like being Nothing but Trouble, the girl for whom Boone had pined ten years. She wanted him to carry a torch for her. She loved the thought of falling effortlessly back into his arms.

Perhaps she wasn't quite ready to give up trouble.

As if reading her mind, Boone came up behind her and slipped his hands onto her shoulders. "You sure you're okay?"

She couldn't help it; she leaned back against him, and his arms went around her shoulders, holding her tight, his chin balanced on the top of her head. He breathed with her a long moment.

She waited for him to say the words—*It doesn't have to be this way; we could get back together.* But he didn't. And she didn't know if she should be grateful or hurt.

Hooking her hands onto his strong arms, she sighed hard. "I'm sorry, Boone. I know you always thought of us together. I did too. I don't know why it doesn't work now."

He loosened his arms. "Me neither. But I've had a lot of time to think since we broke up, and I think you're right. I always saw myself as the guy who got PJ into trouble. I'm not sure I'd know how to be anything else."

The guy who got PJ into trouble. So he had his own haunting voice, his own brand from the past. PJ nodded. "Me neither."

"Maybe it's time we both figured that out."

PJ took his hand and stood beside him. He clutched hers as they watched the sunset dip finally into the horizon, leaving only the milky sheen of the emerging moon upon the waters.

"As a start . . . could you be my bodyguard while we go and talk to the Kellogg hobo?" *Please, Boone, don't pull away.*

He didn't. And when she looked at him, she was surprised to see a smile.

"I think I could do that."

✳ ✳ ✳

"How does someone become homeless?" PJ let Boone take her hand as they walked through the short, October-crisp grass that edged the beach around the Maximilian Bay Bridge. They'd passed the mushroom house on the way, and from this vantage point, nearly across the bay, it appeared forlorn and miserable, its dark eyes peering out over the water.

"A lot of homeless people are mentally ill. And the ones who aren't . . . well, maybe they're victims of a moment in time when everything collapsed," Boone answered.

"But where are their people? the ones they're supposed to turn to? What happened to them?"

"What happened to yours? I recall that up until two days ago, you were living on a sofa. Or worse, in your car."

"I had people. But I had pride, too."

"I think that might be a bigger part of the equation for a lot of people. No one likes to admit they're beat."

"You should know, by the way, there was no camping out in the car. Although the Vic *has* come in handy."

"I'm glad you have another Bug. I can't wrap my mind around my PJ in a cop car."

My PJ. The words lingered in the sounds of the night.

"I guess I'm going to have to get used to not saying that."

She swallowed past the clog in her throat. "I can't wait to get it back from Sammy and give the Vic back to Boris. I love the car, especially the moonroof, although it's a bit sticky. Sammy's working on it, as well as replacing the air filter. It feels as though every time I drive down the road, another part dies."

"What do you expect from an old Bug?"

"Vintage, Boone. Vintage."

"Speaking of vintage, how is Gabby the dancing queen?" Boone sounded a smidge too enthusiastic at the change in topic.

"She's thinking about moving into an apartment for the

elderly—although don't get any fast ideas. It's not assisted living. They hold Saturday night dances."

Boone had met PJ's elderly former neighbor, dancer, and B-movie actress during her stint as Dally Morrison. A neighbor who had saved PJ's life with her quick thinking and savvy acting.

"She'll be the belle of the ball, no doubt, entertaining them with her monologues."

The moon had risen into a perfect circle, a spotlight that limed down upon them, marking a beam through the grassy park toward the beach. The scent of smoke tinged the air, and next to Boone, she, too, wasn't immune to the fingers of time reaching out to pull her back. "Do you remember the time the hobo found us on Kellogg Beach?" She looked at Boone, recognized memory in his eyes.

"Yes." He cleared his throat. "That was, uh . . . probably the best thing."

"Scared me to death, though."

"You nearly jumped through the windshield when he rapped on the window. He just wanted a couple bucks."

"I think you gave him everything in your wallet."

"I was seventeen. He scared me, too."

"I remember his bike and his tangled beard. He had sad eyes; I remember that, too."

"He's never caused trouble, never been arrested. Or rather, we've chosen not to arrest him. He seems like a man who's decided to live outside the system, more than anything." Boone pulled her toward the bridge and pointed to a girl's bike, four plastic bags tied to the basket, leaning against the wall of the bridge. Under it, a campfire flickered.

Boone put PJ slightly behind him. She let him.

"Hello?" he called, and she recognized his cop's voice.

A form sat near the fire, and the man looked up as they approached. Years lined his face, embedded in his matted beard, his shoulder-length tangles. He wore a gray stocking cap and a knee-length Army jacket, grimy at the cuffs. A wary recognition sparked in his eyes when he saw Boone, and he climbed to his feet. "Officer—"

"It's okay. We just came to ask a few questions." Boone still had a firm grip on PJ, even as the hobo ran his gaze over her as if not recognizing her.

"What can I do for you?" he finally said.

"You remember the night you pulled a man from the lake? four years ago?"

The hobo narrowed his eyes at him and finally, slowly, nodded.

"Can you tell us more about that?"

He seemed to consider them for a long moment. "I pulled him out from down by the lifeguard stand. He was floating there." He turned to point. His voice emerged low, gravelly, as if not often exercised. "I figure he'd been in the water only a short bit, because it was cold out—he would have died if I hadn't seen him. He was naked as a newborn baby when I yanked him out of the drink."

"Do you remember anyone driving by, maybe throwing him in?" Boone asked, pulling PJ along behind the hobo's trail.

He shook his head. "I was asleep. Although I do wonder

what woke me up. I always thought it was another night-mare, but maybe I heard something."

"Like what?"

He turned and stared, as if seeing beyond them into the past. "122mm rockets. You don't forget the sound of them coming in."

"Like gunshots?"

"Like . . . a scream." He took a breath, fear in his eyes.

PJ stared at the gnarled man. 122mm rockets. The kind a soldier might remember. She tried to peel back time, to see him as a soldier, eyes staring at the sky as artillery pounded him. Tried to hear the whistle of death in his ears and feel the explosions that shook him to his bones.

No wonder he just wanted to be left alone.

"Is there anything else you can remember from that night, Mr. . . . uh . . ." PJ looked at him, hoping he'd fill in his name.

"Murph. And no, there's nothing else."

Boone still had a hold of her hand.

"Thank you for your help, Murph."

Murph's gaze fixed on PJ, now looking at her as if he rec-ognized her. He took a step closer, his hand moving from his side as if he meant to take her hand. "PJ?" His voice sounded young suddenly, seasoned with an unfamiliar hope.

PJ froze.

Boone put his hand out, a barrier.

"How do you know me?"

But Murph only continued to stare at her, tilting his head

to one side. "I didn't mean it, you know. I . . ." His face clouded, his eyes darkening. "I didn't mean it!"

"I think we're done here."

PJ put a hand on his arm. "He knows me."

"He doesn't know you," Boone said softly, his eyes on Murph. "Look at him."

Indeed, Murph clutched his chest, backing away from her, almost afraid. "I didn't mean it." His voice broke, and he turned, stumbling toward the beach.

"Boone—go after him!"

"Let's just back away. He'll be fine."

"He's upset."

"He's mentally ill, PJ. He's seeing something that isn't there."

"It might be a memory. What if he's talking about the PJ from the past—what if he knew her?"

"What PJ?"

"The one—the one in my mother's yearbook."

Boone stared at her. "What are you talking about?"

"I don't know. . . . I found this entry from a PJ in my mother's college yearbook."

"How would he know someone from Wheaton?"

"My father's from Kellogg. Maybe he knew her."

Boone had hooked one arm around her waist now. "I'm taking you back to the restaurant. I'll radio in a cruiser to swing by and check on him."

PJ had no words, watching as Murph collapsed to the sand and covered his face with his hand. She thought his shoulders might be shaking.

Her eyes filled and she whisked the irrational tears away.

Boone drew her in close as they walked to the car. He drove PJ back to the restaurant in silence.

"What do you think was wrong with him?" she asked as they pulled up.

Boone lifted a shoulder. "I don't know. Memory? Regret? Maybe he's caught inside his own grief, unable to move forward. That happens sometimes—people get so tied up in the past, they can't see the future or even the present. They only see what they did or who they were, and it paralyzes them. They can't break free."

Can't break free. Was that what Boone was doing with her? breaking free?

Which meant what—that she was his prison?

"The screaming could have been tires, brakes on the pavement."

PJ found her voice, hating that it shook a little. She probably put too much tease into it. "See, you're curious, too."

"I'm a detective; I'm supposed to be."

"Maybe that's what got us into so much trouble. The combined forces of curiosity."

Boone glanced at her, a smile on his face that resembled affection more than chagrin. "That's one theory."

PJ held out her hand. "Good night, Boone. Thanks for dinner."

Boone took it and, probably out of habit, ran his thumb over the top. "Take care of yourself, PJ."

She wasn't sure why the door closing on the Mustang, the sight of him disappearing into the night, left a pinging sound in her heart.

The mushroom house slumbered as she drove up. Max had left after they'd returned from the tattoo parlor. Now she flicked on the entry light, and then the hall light, letting the glow seep into the main room as she padded through the house and out onto the terrace. She'd have to get the heat working soon; the bite of winter was on the edge of the breeze.

She stood for a moment, arms wrapped around her body, then continued down to the lake. It rolled onto the shore, reaching for her toes, as if hoping to entice her in. She found a stick, wished Dog were here to fetch it. Then she threw it underhand into the water, watching it arch against the inky night. It splashed into the water, the waves already gulping it.

Barking from across the yard jolted her. Dog loped toward her.

"Hey, Skip."

Dog licked her hands, then bounded out to the water.

Max nearly materialized, silent, almost lethal, from the shadows. PJ would have stepped away if it weren't for the expression on his face. As if he'd been hollowed out, left on the street to perish. He stared at her a long time.

"You okay?"

As he moved toward the beach, he patted Dog, who came up, hoping for a stick.

Across the bay, in the lighted picture windows of the magnificent houses facing the lake, she spotted families moving around, getting ready for bed, reading.

Max held out his hands, staring at the scars in the

moonlight. PJ tried not to look, but the chipped, leathery skin drew her eyes.

"How'd I get these?" He didn't seem to be talking to her, really. "Was I tortured?"

PJ winced. "I don't know."

Max shoved his hands into his pockets. "Where have I been? What have I done? Who am I, PJ?"

"You have a name, Max."

"Really?"

PJ stiffened at the edge in his voice.

"What if it's a name I can't live with? a past I can't bear?"

PJ dug her foot into the sand. "We all have a past we can't bear. I think the important part is how we move on."

Across the lake, in the darkness against the bridge, she made out the flicker of a campfire. A man stood before it as if in effigy. Legs planted, arms outstretched to the streak of the Milky Way and the pinprick of stars, he held his hands wide as if trying to catch the universe and hold on.

Chapter TEN

"PJ!" The voice sliced through the shadows, cutting away Davy's face as he splashed through the waves.

PJ kicked through the folds of sleep and opened her eyes.

"PJ, are you here?"

As she sat up, she blinked against the filmy darkness of her room, grasping for her bearings. Oh, the blue room, not Jeremy's couch or even Connie's beautiful eyelet-lace bedroom. Moonlight slanted through her side window, striping the carpet, and a nip in the air prickled the skin on her arms.

The bedroom door slammed open.

PJ screamed. She launched from her bed to the floor, crouched behind it, groping for anything—a ball, a bat . . . a shoe! Her hand closed on her discarded Converse tennis shoe and she let it fly.

"Ow!"

Then the light slapped on, blinding her. She held up a hand, blinking. Through the blotches, she made out Jeremy filling the frame, holding his face.

But he hadn't finished his invasion. "Where are you?"

His eyes found her, and in them boiled a sort of wild-eyed panic that made her lurch to her feet.

"What—?"

He gaped at her as if she'd just clipped the edge of death. She half expected—okay, *hoped*—that he'd chase that look with sweeping her into his arms.

Instead, he held up his hands and spoke to someone other than her. "Okay. This is *not* working."

PJ peered past him into the hall. "Who are you talking—?"

"Are you hurt?"

She closed her mouth. And for some reason looked herself over, just in case. "No . . . no, I seem to be in one piece. Are *you* okay? Are *you* hurt?"

In fact, he did appear wounded; she spotted a red mark on his cheek—oh, that could be from her shoe. But the other eye bore a fresh bruise. What, had he taken up fight club? "You *are* hurt."

"I'm fine. I'm . . . *fine*." He took a breath, then scrubbed a hand down his face. When he looked back at her, it seemed he'd composed himself, at least enough to talk in coherent sentences, though still without his inside voice. "Where were you tonight?"

She blinked at him. Her mouth opened just a little. "Seriously?"

He said nothing, grinding his jaw so hard he could probably make diamonds.

"Last time I checked, you weren't the boss of—"

His eyebrows arched.

"Okay, you *are* the boss of me. At least some of the time. But I was on official private eye business, tracking down leads for Max."

His lips remained pinched as if holding in words.

"Fine, I was with Boone. Doing PI work. Did I mention that?"

Visible relief washed over him. Transformed him from Attila the bodyguard to a human being she recognized.

"Jeremy, what is the matter?"

He rebounded fast out of relief and apparently landed straight into anger, his voice clipped. "The matter is your new handyman could be a car thief—or worse, a murderer!"

"Have you been hit on the head?" PJ grabbed a shirt and pulled it over her tank top. She'd have to make do in her Superman pants—it wasn't like he hadn't seen those before. "C'mon, maybe you need some fresh air."

She walked over to him and touched his arm. She could have been trying to pull the statue of *David* off its marble post for all the good it did.

Especially when he curled his hands around her upper arms. And sighed.

It was the sigh that stopped her, a heavy, burdened release that also uncoiled the knot inside her that had formed from being nearly thrown from her bed in the middle of the night.

She looked at him, and the sudden gentleness, almost worry in his eyes caught her breath. He pressed his forehead to hers. "Don't do that to me again," he said in a near whisper.

His hands on her arms shot tingles through her, everything inside her suddenly very alive. His breath on her skin, the smell of him seeping into her, the strength that poured off him drawing her in . . . When she touched his chest, she felt his heart hammering beneath the spread of her fingers. "Do what?" she managed, just above a breath.

He closed his eyes. "I am in way over my head here." Then he sighed again and slowly let her go.

She stood there, her heart banging to be set free, her legs ropy. "Jer—"

He slipped his hand into hers, pulled her into the kitchen, turned on a light. He looked rougher than she'd realized—a raw scrape along his jaw added to his blackened eye, as if he'd banged the front door in with his chin.

Hey . . . "How did you get in?"

He turned to her, an accusing expression on his face. "I would like to say I picked the lock, but you left the back porch unlocked. Anyone could get in here, attack you—"

"In the middle of the night, in my own bed? Yeah, *that* could happen." She folded her arms, still feeling his grip around them.

He didn't even have the decency to look sheepish. "Where's your phone?"

"In my bag."

"Where's your bag?"

She thought for a moment. "I think it could be on the terrace outside?" She made a face. "Why?"

He turned, stalking out through the porch, along the side of the house. She followed, the stone glacial on her bare feet. Jeremy retrieved her giant canvas bag, turned, and hooked her by the arm. She stubbed her foot on the stone and cried out.

"Sorry." He swung her up into his arms.

Okay.

She looped her arm around his neck and studied him for a moment. He seemed truly upset, a steely set to his whiskered jaw, an almost-desperate tinge to his expression. He carried her to the kitchen, set her on the counter, and plopped the bag in her lap. "Find your phone."

"Bossy." But she dug through her purse. Located the phone.

Oops. Twelve calls from Jeremy over the past two hours.

She looked at the screen, then at him. "Sorry. But please tell me, what is so urgent?"

"You promise me you'll never scare me again?" His voice still contained a raw, tremulous edge.

"Jeremy, what is going on here? You are completely over-reacting. I was fine. So I didn't answer my phone at two o'clock in the morning! I was *asleep*."

"You could have been laying here, bleeding to death, or with your house on fire, you burning alive."

"Oh, that's a lovely picture. Between that and the ghosts of Kellogg Manor, are you trying to drive me back to your sofa?

"Maybe."

What? *Maybe?*

She slid off the counter. "How can I possibly understand if you don't tell me anything?"

Jeremy pulled her against him, so close she had no choice but to put her arms around him. He pressed a kiss to her head. "I wish . . . PJ, the fact is, I don't know what to do here. You . . . unhinge me."

She touched his face. "I don't understand."

"I know." He looked down, tracing her cheekbone with his fingers. "You're so beautiful."

PJ stilled.

"You don't know it. But you are. And sometimes when I see you, all I see is what could happen to you. It wasn't like that at first. I'm not sure when it started . . . maybe after the Dally assignment, when you nearly got killed. Or maybe it just snuck up on me one day at a time. But all of a sudden, I realized that every assignment I give you could hurt or even kill you."

Oh no. She knew exactly when it had started. Or at least when he'd realized it. "Please tell me that you're not buying into what Boone said. I'm not going to get—"

Jeremy put his hand over her lips. "He was just confirming something I already knew. But don't panic. I'm not going to tell you that you can't be a PI. I know you're going to be a great PI. You have amazing instincts. And even though you're not weapons trained, you do have stellar aim."

PJ touched his cheek, where a welt was beginning to form. Right along with a hint of a smile.

"The fact is, I don't trust Max." He reached into his jacket pocket, pulling out a couple pages of paper. "I found two articles in the newspaper archives about the night Max showed up here in Kellogg, crimes I think might be related to him."

He laid the copies on the counter. "This one's a story about a guy busted for car theft and reckless driving. He was picked up just down the road at the Maximilian Bay Bridge right about the time Max was found floating in the water."

PJ read the article—a quick police report. "Is he still around?"

"I have a last known address. We can check it out tomorrow. In *daylight*." He flashed her a grin, one she recognized. One that made warmth curl through her. It seemed her Jeremy might be returning. His shoulder rubbed against hers, and his words replayed in her head. *"You're so beautiful. . . ."*

"What's this one?" *Woman Killed, House Burned in Apparent Robbery.* It included a grainy black-and-white photo of the victim, Bekka Layton. She looked about twenty-five.

"That's the story about a woman whose house was broken into while she was home. She was shot, the house torched, and the culprit got away. She died of her burns."

"And you thought of Max's hands."

Jeremy nodded. "I've got a loose theory. I think Max was in on the robbery, and something went south. It's not uncommon for an arsonist to get caught in his crime—at the very least they hang around, watching. Maybe Max got cold feet or had a bout of conscience and tried to pull her out of the fire. And maybe his accomplice didn't want to risk him going to the cops, so he knocked him out, threw him over the bridge. I think Max might be good for the murder of this woman."

With every word, the coil around her chest tightened until her breath caught, trapped inside. "No."

"Why not? Just because he can fix electricity and connect a few pipes doesn't make him a hero." He met her eyes. "Does it?"

"He's not a murderer."

"And you know this because . . ."

PJ compressed her lips. "My instincts tell me there's more to Max. His tattoo, for one."

"Tattoo? You saw his tattoo?"

"Yeah, after he showered—"

"He *showered* here?"

"You're shouting again. For pete's sake, he was crawling around in the mud. What was I going to do?"

"Send him home to his own shower!"

"What if he doesn't have a shower? What if he's homeless?"

"Are you taking in strays now?"

"I have a soft spot for strays." She tried to manufacture a dark look to equal his. "Being one myself."

"You're not a stray." He let his anger slide out in a long breath, then said quietly, "You just haven't quite figured that out yet."

That took the gust out of her anger. "The tattoo is on his left shoulder. And it's of a phoenix clutching arrows. Jinx—a tattoo artist in Dinkytown—"

"I know Jinx. He did my ink."

Oh yeah, Jeremy's Celtic symbol on his arm. Another mystery from her cryptic boss.

"Jinx said it's usually worn by soldiers who are former POWs."

"Which makes sense. Maybe he was a POW who snapped when he got stateside. The stress was too much."

PJ rubbed her hands on her arms, the chill from outside spilling into the room.

"I really don't want him here unless I'm here." He folded up the articles, then stuck them in his jacket pocket. "The fact is, it's . . ." His jaw tightened and he swallowed, looking away. "I already lost someone once. Someone I loved very much."

He'd already lost someone? PJ cupped her hand to his cheek and turned his face to her, ignoring the quiver inside. "Who?"

"My fiancée."

PJ blinked at him. "Your . . . *fiancée*." She said the word just to confirm, and it razored through her. His fiancée. No wonder the guy had giant black holes he lost himself inside.

"Her name was Lori. She worked as a drug counselor downtown at a rehab place. One of her clients went berserk and took her hostage . . . and . . ." Jeremy looked beyond her. "I wasn't there. I was in Iraq at the time."

"It wasn't your fault."

He flinched at her words. She held in the rest. And she didn't reach out to him because she knew this look—the kind that said, *Please don't, because if you touch me, it'll only get worse.* Indeed, he seemed to be collecting himself. "I really haven't ever . . . Well, I figure it's not an easy thing to find that one person who gets you and understands you and puts up with your issues and . . ." He cleared his throat. "Someone you might want to spend the rest of your life with."

The rest of his life?

But he wasn't talking about her. She knew that. Knew that the dream had died with Lori. Still, his pain spiraled inside, coiling around her heart. Her eyes burned watching him press his hand hard to his mouth and turn away from her.

After a moment, she touched his back, right between his shoulder blades. Walked around to face him.

He found her eyes then, met them, held them with more than she'd expected. "The thing is, when I'm with you, I forget. I forget about Lori and that dark place that took me. I feel . . . *hope.* Maybe that's the word. I hope again." He reached up to push her hair back. "Most of all, I want to deserve you. I want to be the kind of guy that buys you a dog and fixes your electricity and keeps you from getting hurt."

Jeremy caught her red hair between two fingers, ran his fingers down the length of it. "But you send out confusing signals, Princess. Boone, me . . . I am not sure if I'm stealing you—or if you're being stolen from me."

His hand moved behind her neck, and he seemed to be searching her face as if asking for something.

Yes.

His gaze finally settled on her lips, and she longed to move toward him, to let herself sink into his embrace. But there it went again, the sharp, bullet pain pinging inside as Boone drove away.

No! She wasn't checking over her shoulder, not really. She just needed a moment to gather her heart, point it again in the right direction. But apparently Jeremy could see the imprint of Boone's memory on her face because before she could answer, he set her away from him.

"I'm not sure whether to fight for you or let you go."

Fight. The word pulsed inside her, nearly made it out.

But he shook his head and sighed. "I wish I knew. But the fact is, Princess, there are simply some mysteries that only you can solve."

✳ ✳ ✳

Didn't anyone sleep anymore?

The banging resumed, and then a voice needled into the last veils of sleep. "PJ! Are you in there?"

Nope. She pulled the sleeping bag over her head, pressed the pillow to her ear.

"PJ!" More banging, and then the bark of a dog.

Dog. Max. PJ sat up, her heart pounding. She had stared at the ceiling too long after Jeremy left last night, rolling his accusations about Max around in her head, trying to see danger and malice in Max's lopsided, nearly shy grin or in the look of horror he'd worn when Jinx guessed that he'd been a POW. As though the idea of war might actually be repulsive to him.

He was no more a killer than she was a . . . princess? Oh, she didn't know what to believe about anyone anymore.

Especially herself. Because even as she had longed to run after Jeremy, to give him an answer, a part of her knew his words resonated with truth. What had seemed so clear two days ago now made her heart clench.

It just wasn't so easy to forget someone who had been like a piece of yourself. Sometimes the memories simply swallowed her whole.

But maybe Jeremy understood that, too.

A rap on the window shook her nearly out of her skin and she leaped from the bed. Max!

Max peered in her window, his hand cupped over his eyes as he pressed against the glass. "It's nearly 9 a.m.!"

PJ got up, wrapping the sleeping bag around her. She'd have to start sleeping in her jeans and T-shirts instead of her tank tops and Superman pants if men and dogs intended to start invading her house at all hours of the night. Or, er, *morning*. She opened the window, shivering at the rush of fall air. "What are you doing?"

Max held a cup of coffee in his yellow-gloved hands, looking ready for work in a padded vest, which he wore over a flannel shirt. "I've been sitting outside for two hours, waiting for you to open the door. I was getting worried."

"You've been here since 7 a.m.?"

"I usually start work at six, but I thought I'd let you sleep in."

"What kind of crazy person starts work at six?"

"The kind that is going to fix your plumbing?" He

grinned at her. Dog ran around behind him, sniffing. Frost licked the grass, and the morning sun reflected off glassy, frozen dips in the driveway.

No wonder she was shivering. "I don't suppose you could get the heat working, could you?"

"One problem at a time, missy. Besides, it's a beautiful day."

"You'd better be saying that with coffee for me in your hand."

He lifted a cup toward her. "I'll share."

"I'll let you in the front—just give me a second."

She shut the window on him, reaching for her discarded sweatshirt. However, Jeremy's warning simmered inside her as she slipped her bare feet into her Converse and scuffed to the front door. She still wore her sleeping bag like a cape around her shoulders.

"Who are you, Supergirl?" Max asked, moving inside when she opened the door. Dog ran in, nearly taking her feet out from under her.

"Hey there, Speedy!"

Dog didn't brake.

"I attempted Duke this morning. Not even an eyebrow twitch."

"Were you serious about sharing?"

Max lifted his cup, something cheap he'd gotten at a nearby convenience store. She recognized the label. "Hazelnut cappuccino. I'm willing to share if you'd like, but FYI, it's cold."

She didn't care if it was glacial. "People actually pay for cold coffee, you know. But that's okay. Jeremy said he'd be by this morning. He'll bring me my fix of the good stuff." In fact, she could hardly believe he wasn't camped out on her front lawn after his tirade last night.

She didn't exactly know why she added that little tidbit about Jeremy—just, well, a guy should know that they were onto him, should he have something nefarious in mind. She pulled the sleeping bag around her shoulders and followed Max as he tapped on the wall as if reorienting himself to yesterday's find.

"I have bad news."

"You're out of coffee?"

Max sipped his cup and smiled at her. "Not that bad. We need to find the source of your leak. Which means getting into the room upstairs."

"The room where Agatha Kellogg died? the *locked* room?"

He gave her a slow nod. "If there is a leak, then it could be coming down the walls. Which would account for why they're still soggy."

Max opened his toolbox, producing a screwdriver and a hammer.

"What's that for?"

"We may have to take the door off the hinges."

"Hold on there, handyman. I think I have an easier way."

She left him there and returned to her room, grabbed her jeans, caught her hair into a ponytail, then brushed the Velcro off her teeth. Finally she grabbed her bottomless purse, hauling it over her shoulder as she fished around in the depths.

Max was sitting on the stairs, one hand scratching Dog's

head. She plopped down next to him and opened the bag. Ah, a bottle of vitamins. She opened it and pocketed one to take later (in hopes Jeremy might deliver promised coffee). Then she unearthed a pair of socks she'd taken off to walk the beach with Boone—how long ago had that been? She slipped off her Converse and pulled them on. She cleaned out a half-crushed bag of peanut butter crackers and a slightly bruised apple she'd swiped from Connie's, set those together on the step, then—

"I hate to interrupt, but are we making camp for the night?"

"Listen, I do have a point." She dove back in, opening her bag to the light. There, on the bottom, where Jeremy had tossed it after breaking into her mother's house—

"Is that a lock pick set?"

"Yep." She piled the food into her bag. At least she had breakfast. But oh, she could use more coffee. Like a couple gallons. And really, they were in no hurry to get into that room, right?

"Why are we still sitting here?"

She wrinkled her nose at him. "It's creepy. She died in there."

Max gave her a long, slow smile. "Are you afraid there's a ghost?"

"No, of course not. I just . . . It feels like we're invading her privacy."

"She's not there anymore. She doesn't care."

PJ turned the lock pick set over in her hand, running her thumb over the smooth case. "But she did care, because she left me this house. Who leaves a house, their entire legacy, to a complete stranger?"

Max rubbed Dog behind his ears and said nothing for a moment. "She must've known something about you—something that apparently you haven't figured out for yourself."

PJ glanced at him. "Now who's the detective?"

"Just learning from the master."

"Right." PJ got up and climbed the stairs. Stopping briefly at the library, she let her imagination linger over the shelves, picturing a lazy morning in an overstuffed chair. Someday.

"Now you're just procrastinating." Max braced his hand on the doorframe above her. "Do you want me to do it?"

"Can you pick a lock?"

He didn't answer, and she turned to study his face. His gaze seemed to land not on her, or even beyond her, but inside, to a place known only to himself.

"Max?"

"Actually . . . I think maybe I can."

She handed him the lock pick kit. "Knock yourself out."

He took it and pulled out the pins. Then, to her astonishment, he had the lock on the door picked in less than twenty seconds.

Okay, that freaked her out. And made her just a smidge jealous.

The ease with which he'd picked the lock seemed to unnerve Max, too, because he turned and handed her the lock pick set without a word and with a paler cast to his face.

So maybe he had been a burglar . . . and thus, a murderer?

She took the kit and dropped it into her bag.

"Ladies first," Max said, stepping back from the door.

"Oh no, you picked the lock; you go in first."

Max pressed his lips together. Took a breath. Put his hand on the doorknob and turned it.

PJ peeked over his shoulder as he eased the heavy oak door open.

The room smelled of years passing, only revered years instead of the kind covered in dust and grime. It seemed that the entire room had held its breath, trapping the air inside, like one might hold time in a bottle. Two grand windows overlooked the backyard, a magnificent view of the lake, and a front window looked down on the ivy twining along the cedar roof.

A pink and brown wool rug, worn along the edges, held stacks of boxes leading up to a grand mahogany four-poster, flanked by books and books and more dusty books. A picture of a family hung over the bed, sepia toned, solemn except for the sparkle of a smile from the young daughter seated on the lap of the mother, dressed in a low-waisted dress of the 1920s. PJ guessed it might be Aggie Kellogg smirking at the camera.

She was probably smirking right now, too, at the ghosts PJ had conjured inside her head.

Not that she'd admit that to Max. Or Jeremy.

PJ moved into the room, drawn inside by some magic to trail her finger over the boxes, to pick up a book, blow off the dust—*Moby Dick*? She set it aside when her gaze landed on a floral box on the floor beside the bed.

No, it couldn't be. . . .

She knelt in front of it, staring at the lid. Max had moved into the bathroom off the bedroom, the one done up in pink tile, inspecting the damage. Now he came out, probably startled by her sudden intake of breath.

"What? There's nothing dead out here, is there?"

PJ couldn't answer. Just ran her fingers over the box, over the nine padded letters cut out from pink flannel. Tiny red beads outlined the first two letters, each glued precisely to the next to form two huge, triumphant initials. Initials that identified the box as belonging to . . . PJ Kellogg.

Chapter ELEVEN

"Whatya got there, Princess?"

PJ looked up at the voice, and warmth slicked through her at the sight of Jeremy, holding a cup of coffee from the Kellogg Koffee Hut. Mr. Dangerous at her service in his black Converse shoes, a pair of jeans, and a dark leather jacket. He sauntered through the main room, where she sprawled in the middle of the floor unloading the box of goodies of one PJ Kellogg.

He crouched in front of her, handed her the coffee. Leveled her a sweet smile.

"I'm not sure whether to fight for you or let you go." She took a sip. "Vanilla latte."

"Of course." He picked up a small notebook with the word *Diary* cut out of pink felt and glued to the front. "What's all this?"

Around her lay two Wheaton College yearbooks; a John Denver album cover, in which she'd discovered a Doobie Brothers record; a well-worn copy of *Are You There, God? It's Me, Margaret*; and a pair of fluffy blue pom-poms with bells. A fat blue envelope held a stack of photos, which she still had to go through.

"It's the personal effects of someone named PJ Kellogg." PJ reached for a yearbook, paged to about the middle, and held it out to Jeremy. "Third row down, right-hand side."

"Carl Sugar?"

"It's my dad. He knew PJ." She flipped the book to the back. "Here's his inscription to his friend, PJ. Signed, Carl Sugar."

Jeremy read it, but PJ already knew it by heart. *"All the best to my wild friend."*

"This was PJ's freshman year at college. My father was a junior." She turned over a couple pages. "And here's my mother." She pointed to a black-and-white picture. "My parents were already dating then. But I did find an inscription in her yearbook. Look: 'To PJ, from Lizzy, may you find your dreams.' My mother has a note in her yearbook. It's from PJ, something about them being best friends." She leaned back on her hands, her stomach growling. "Here's the strange part. I've been through this entire yearbook. There is no PJ Kellogg listed. Not even a mention of a Kellogg."

"No Kellogg at all?"

She shook her head.

"Then who is PJ Kellogg?"

PJ began to pile the loot together. "I don't know. But I intend to find out."

Jeremy picked up the blue envelope and started pulling out pictures. He handed them one by one to PJ.

"This house is in a few of these." She flipped over a square black-and-white snapshot of a group of people in shorts holding tented drinks. No names, no date. Another with a shot of a snowman in the front yard of the mushroom house. A few larger color shots of what looked like the backyard.

"Check this one out." Jeremy handed it to her. A woman in a printed green one-piece bathing suit and cap lounged on the beach, her hand on the back of a little girl who sat with a bucket, her shovel in the sand. PJ couldn't make out the adult's face, but the little girl looked at the camera, beaming.

"Turn it over, babe."

PJ read the scrawled print. Blinked. Read it again. "Prudence Joy and Sunny, Kellogg Beach, 1966."

Jeremy touched her arm. "Seems like a coincidence, doesn't it? Prudence Joy?"

PJ cupped her hand over his. "You're right—Joy Kellogg. That was the woman who drowned in the lagoon. Prudence Joy Kellogg . . . oh, wait, no: Prudence Joy *Barton*. Barton—that was Clay's last name. Barton Dock Works—the sailboat place. Of course! This is her."

Jeremy was staring at her, a frown on his face.

"That's why I got together with Boone last night—he summarized the facts for me. She had a fight with her husband, and then the next morning, she showed up dead in the lagoon." She started to get up, but Jeremy stopped her, tightening his grip on her arm.

"That's not the coincidence I was talking about here. Prudence Joy. *PJ.* You don't see the connection?"

PJ looked at his hand, looked up at him, and sank back down. "Uh, I . . . It's a bigger coincidence than you know, Jer. Because . . . well . . ." She took a breath, wrinkled her nose. "I really didn't want to tell you this, but Prudence is my first name."

"Prudence? Your name is Prudence?"

"If I hear one nasty joke—"

He held up his hands. "I much prefer PJ."

"Hence, why I changed it. At age six."

"And what about Joy?"

"No. *J* does not stand for Joy."

He seemed to be waiting for more, judging by his eyebrows-up expression.

"I'm not telling you what the *J* stands for."

"Jessica? Jasmine? Just Joking?"

"Stop."

"Maybe I will call you Prudy—"

"Don't do that. Really. Don't do that. PJ. That's my name."

He tapped the box. "You're not the only one."

"Wait—in my mother's yearbook, there is a Sunny Barton. This toddler is the same Sunny! And Joy is her *mom*."

"Then who is PJ? Because this box contains memorabilia from the seventies—when Sunny would have been a teenager. But is it Sunny's or her mother's?" He tapped the box.

PJ ran her thumb over the picture. She looked closer at it,

able to make out the Kellogg pier, the lifeguard buoy floating beyond the high-dive platform. "I think the box is PJ's—Joy's—but maybe Sunny kept it after her mother died."

Outside, Dog barked, chasing ducks probably. Upstairs, Max had begun some sort of ominous pounding.

Jeremy took the picture from her and placed it back in the envelope. "Let's solve one mystery at a time." He pointed toward the banging overhead. "Has he behaved himself today?"

"If you're asking if he's tried to murder me and steal my money and assault me, well, just that one time, but I gave him the old PJ flip, and he learned his lesson."

He shook his head, caught between a grin and a glare. "Of course you did. That's my girl."

As soon as the words left his mouth, his smile dimmed. He made a face as if wishing to take back his words.

PJ sorta wanted to reach out and grab them, pull them close.

He held out his hand to pull her to her feet. "Actually, I have a surprise for you."

"Other than coffee."

"A thousand times better than coffee." He put his hand on the small of her back, led her to the front door, and opened it. "Ta-da!"

"My Bug!" Sitting in the driveway, shined up as bright as the blue October sky, sat her vintage 1960s Bug with a convertible moonroof. "When did Sammy finish it?"

"He left a message on my machine. He brought it over this morning. I thought you'd enjoy having it back."

PJ turned to him and laid her hand on his cheek, patting it. "You're a good boss."

"Yeah, well, the Vic gives me the creeps. Give it back to Boris. He needs the wheels."

"What about you? You said it was the perfect stake-out car."

"It is. But I have my own wheels."

"Your Harley? C'mon—it's getting colder out."

"Don't worry about me, Princess. Let's grab your plumber–slash–former soldier–slash–could-be murderer and take a field trip over to Hopkins, see if we can't jog his memory about that night he ended up in the drink."

"Who's in Hopkins?"

"It's the last known address of Lyle Fisher—the speed racer the cops picked up that night. I'm hoping if we start showing Max's face around, we'll get a hit."

"Did you know Max can pick a lock?"

Jeremy's mouth tightened into a grim line. "Let's just get this over with."

PJ stopped in the doorway to the upstairs bathroom and pressed a hand to her stomach. "This I didn't need to see."

Max stood over the bathtub, pulling a long metal drain snake from the pipe. His flannel shirt lay over the pedestal sink, his phoenix tattoo visible on his bare arm. Years— maybe centuries—of disgusting black goo lay in dribbles and soggy piles on the pink subway tile floor.

"I think I'm going to be sick."

"Welcome to your relic. This tub was probably installed in the forties, at best. But the plumbing dates to the early

1900s. The pipe in the tub is plugged, and that's why the overflow didn't work. My theory of old Aggie Kellogg falling asleep waiting for her tub to fill may have been correct because the floor was completely flooded, as evidenced by the water damage along the baseboards. The pool found the edges of the bathroom and ran down inside the wall, which is why the wall downstairs is destroyed. There's major cosmetic damage—all your plaster has to be replaced. And in this house, it's lath and plaster, so we'll have to rip it all out and put up Sheetrock."

PJ braced her hand on the doorframe, waiting for her knees to buckle. Anytime now . . . "How much is that going to cost me?"

"Labor? Nothing. Sheetrock runs about $10 a sheet. But you might have some structural damage. I won't be sure until I get in there. But that's not your biggest problem."

Of course not.

"I need to get into the wall and replace the entire drainpipe." He was winding the snake back up. "It's an old house; the plumbing is probably rusted through. I was snaking it out, and I'm pretty sure I poked a hole in the drainpipe."

"When you say *drainpipe*—"

"The one that runs from the tub through the wall to the drain in the basement. I have to rip down the wall on the first floor to get to the pipe. Otherwise you'll have a swamp in the basement. Sorry."

"I'll give you sorry." Jeremy said it so softly, it seemed that Max hadn't heard it, the way he bent over, putting his tools away.

PJ glanced at him. "It's not Max's fault the place is a wreck."

Jeremy just hardened his mouth to a tight line.

"I guess I have to replace the wall anyway. . . ." She closed her eyes, doing the math.

"I'll loan you the money to get started," Jeremy said.

"Since when do you have money?"

He smiled, something darkly cryptic inside it. "I don't sit around all day waiting for lost people to fall into my lap, Sugar."

She opened her mouth, closed it. "I'll find Bix. I will."

"I know." Jeremy slipped a hand into hers, squeezing just a little. He turned to Max. "You can get started on it when we get back."

"Get back from where?" Max closed the toolbox and stood. He'd removed his stocking cap, and in full-out revolt, his hair couldn't make up its mind which way it wanted to go.

"We found a lead on the night you went over the bridge. A speeder got picked up right around the time you were found on the beach. We think he might have a connection to you. He's gone missing, but we do have a last known address. We're going to go talk to his landlord. Tag along, and let's see if anyone recognizes you."

PJ glanced at Jeremy, at the dark expression on his face as he spoke. He hadn't removed his hand from her shoulder.

Max grabbed his flannel shirt and nodded. "I'll get Dog."

The smell of fall gripped the air—the fragrance of old leaves, apples, and pumpkins—as PJ, Jeremy, Max, and Dog climbed into her VW Bug.

"Okay, I take it back; I already miss the Vic," Jeremy said. "I feel like a pretzel."

"You're the one who told me to give it to Boris. You should have heard him on the phone—he's probably sprinting over here."

Behind them, Max was trying to wrestle Dog onto his lap. "We should have taken my car."

Jeremy flicked him a look, which PJ didn't require translation to read. He had no intention of trusting the guy, even enough to drive.

The town of Hopkins always charmed PJ. The tiny bungalows with their quaint attic rooms, wide sidewalks edging groomed yards filled with rows of hosta, cedar bushes, clipped hedges.

However, the charm had died at Lyle Fisher's last known residence. The duplex, a converted Cape Cod covered in stucco, bore the stamp of afterthought architecture. A dormer addition ran the length of the back, and another smaller one capped the front, with long, narrow windows like two hooded eyes peeking up from the roof. Leaves peppered the yard and stuffed the edges of a cracked paved driveway. A snarled rosebush grew between the two sets of cement steps leading to the separate residences. Only a white impression, outlined with grime, remained of the former metal numbers signifying Lyle's address.

The place betrayed all the earmarks of desertion.

"I hadn't held out too much hope, I guess," Max said quietly from the backseat.

PJ opened her car door. "There's still someone living here, maybe next door."

"How do you know?"

"The garbage is out." She pointed to the rubber can at the end of the driveway.

Jeremy pried himself out of the car, followed by Max, who shoved Dog back into the car while PJ cracked the window. "We'll be right back . . . Jake."

Dog looked at her with what seemed disgust and flopped down on the seat.

"Please don't eat my vinyl. I just got it fixed."

PJ kicked a few leaves along the cracked sidewalk, letting them catch in the air. She stopped to peer inside the duplex window. Vacant, with shiny oak floors and a floral wallpaper border in the orange kitchen. She'd lived in too many places like it over the past ten years.

From a duplex to a mansion. It seemed as if her résumé had a few logical gaps.

Jeremy mounted the steps of the next unit, already ringing the bell when PJ stepped up beside him, in front of Max, and smiled widely for whomever might be peering from behind the wispy curtain at the window.

An elderly woman eased the oak door open. Her tidy, graying hair was short and curly around her timid blue eyes, and she shoved her face into the crack between the door and the frame. "I'm already a Christian woman; I don't want to hear about the end times or why I need the Book of Mormon."

PJ hid a smile. "We're actually looking for someone.

A former tenant in the other unit. Have you lived here long?"

The woman glanced at Jeremy, then back to PJ. "I own the place. Who are you looking for?" Before PJ could answer, the older woman's gaze drifted to Max. Her face screwed up. "Do I know you?"

Max's entire body stiffened. "I don't know; do you?"

The woman's mouth tightened into a tiny knot as she peered at him. Then she reached into her housecoat and pulled out a pair of round, bottle lenses. Propped them on her nose. "No. Sorry. It's hard to tell without the hair. I guess you all look alike."

"Are you talking about Lyle Fisher?" PJ glanced at Max. He looked like he should sit down.

"That's right. Fisher. He up and disappeared four years ago—taking his rent for the month with him, thank you very much, I haven't seen him since. But I do have a box of his stuff." She slipped her gaze over to Max again. "Something about you seems familiar, though. Are you sure you don't know Lyle?"

"I don't—," Max started.

"He's his cousin," Jeremy said. "Lyle sent him to get his stuff."

"Well, then maybe he can pay me the last month's rent, too."

Oh, good one, Jeremy.

"How about part of it?" Max reached into his pocket. "I have about a hundred here."

There went the little knot in the old woman's mouth

again as she considered Max's offer. "Fine." She swiped the bills from his hand and disappeared.

"You'd better hope she's coming back," Jeremy said quietly.

PJ shoved her hands into her jacket pockets and glanced at Max. He was using his X-ray vision to stare through the door.

The woman returned with a printer box, the top secured with packing tape. She opened the storm door with her hip and held out the box. "It's all yours. The rest I donated to Goodwill."

On the side, the name Lyle Fisher was written in black block letters.

She gave Max a last look. "Next time you see him, you tell your cousin I want the rest of my rent. Two years of putting up with his odd disappearances and strange friends, and this is the thanks I get."

Max nodded, as if yes, indeed, he'd do that very thing.

She closed the door on them.

Max carried his treasure out to the Bug and balanced the box on the hood, then stepped away from it, considering the box as though it might contain national secrets. Or perhaps a bomb.

Jeremy produced a pocketknife. Max took it from him without a glance.

PJ watched Jeremy's face, his eyes scrutinizing Max as he ran the knife under the tape and loosened the top. He tried to hide it, but she sensed his relief when Max closed the knife and handed it back.

Inside the car, Dog woke up and began to bark, shoving his nose out the window. Leaves, swept up by the wind, became a whirling dervish, caught in her hair.

Max stared at the box. "Okay." He took a breath. Wiggled the top open.

A manila envelope full of mail lay on top. Max picked it up, riffled through it. "Junk mail, all of it. All addressed to Lyle Fisher."

PJ picked up a dusty black calculator. "It's dead."

Under the envelope lay a belt, a Maglite without the batteries, a plastic canteen, a pair of warped aviator sunglasses, and finally, a watch.

Max took the watch out, ran his thumb over the black band, the raised dial face.

"That's a military watch. The kind special ops uses," Jeremy said.

"You can buy these off the Internet, can't you?" PJ asked as Max handed her the watch.

"They're pretty pricey, but yeah." Jeremy leaned over her and took the watch from her hands. He worked the dials. "It's the waterproof kind that SEALs wear."

And he would know. She saw Jeremy pause as if scrolling through memory. Then he shook himself out of it. Handed the watch back to Max. "Why would Lyle leave this behind?"

"Or these." Max riffled through the envelopes. "Hey, look at this. It's a picture." He tugged out a four-by-six snapshot, staring at it. His chest rose and fell with heavy breaths.

"Max?"

He flipped it over, shook his head, then handed the picture to her without a word.

A picture of a threesome. Two men sat on a bench, with a woman in the middle. One man had long blond hair, tied back, bronzed and muscled in a sleeveless shirt. The other, his brown hair also long, sat bare-chested, his arm curled around the back of the woman. Her eyes twinkled as she laughed into the camera; the wind had caught her hair and dragged it across her face. Both men grinned, but only one had a dimple pressing into his cheek. From this vantage point, PJ couldn't make out a tattoo. Yet, despite the hippie hair, PJ easily recognized her new plumber, although in this picture, his eyes appeared brighter, his smile without the tinge of sadness.

More importantly, she also recognized the woman in the middle. She'd seen her in grainy black-and-white next to a news article about a fire at her complex.

"This is the woman who died in the fire the night Max went missing."

✳ ✳ ✳

"I'm not sure I want to know."

"Calm down, Max. We don't know for sure that you had anything to do with that fire or that woman's death."

Max paced another tight circle in PJ's empty living room as PJ sat on the floor, searching for clues in the picture.

Telling him about the fire—and Bekka Layton's death—might *not* have been the smartest move. He'd braced his arm on the car, breathing in hard a few times—something she'd seen Jeremy do on occasion. Like when he'd discovered that she'd nearly been killed by an assassin or by a rogue FBI agent.

Or discovered one more connection to the idea that her new client could be a murderer. Jeremy stood just a few feet away, watching Max pace, stop, stare out the window, pace again.

"What if I *did* do those things? What if I was the guy that broke into that woman's house and . . . and killed her? Am I the kind of person who could murder someone?" He wore such a stricken look that PJ couldn't find words.

"I just . . . I can't bear that idea. I don't want to be that guy. Maybe we should stop looking." He held up his hand as if pushing away the news. "I have a good life and a dog . . ."

"You started this because you wanted to know if you have family or friends," PJ said.

"I obviously killed them!"

"Calm down, Max." This from Jeremy, who walked over to join PJ. Or hover over her, depending on the point of view. "You're making giant leaps here. You don't know what connection you have to this woman."

Max seemed nonplussed by Jeremy's tone. "Something about her seems familiar. I can't place it. What if she was my girlfriend?" He picked up the picture. "What if this Lyle guy *is* my cousin? or my brother?" He held up his scarred hands. "Is that fire how I got these?"

"Maybe you were trying to save her," PJ offered. "Maybe you were walking by and saw the fire—"

"Now you're just reaching because you don't want to face the truth."

"Which is?"

"I'm a criminal. A murderer. Maybe an arsonist. I think we need to just stop the investigation right now."

"But what about justice?" Jeremy said in a clipped tone. "Maybe you need to find out so you can own up to what you did."

PJ shot him an are-you-crazy? look that he rebounded with one of his own.

Maybe. She found her feet, turned to Jeremy, and pitched her voice low. "Listen, maybe Max is right. Without more evidence, he could be arrested and dragged through the court system. He's probably innocent, and we'll be tearing his life apart. I have a little experience about how this feels, and trust me—we need to tread carefully before we start handing information over to the cops."

Jeremy attempted his best lethal-silence glare.

She ignored him. "Don't you think people deserve a chance to prove themselves innocent?"

That got him. "I do believe in letting people prove themselves. I'm even a wholehearted believer in second chances," he said tightly. "You know that. But some people *can't* change."

She matched his tone. "Are you saying that once someone is trouble they're *always* trouble?"

"Sometimes. I think for some people, it's in their blood. Or it gets in there after seeing so much horror."

"What do you mean?"

He hooked her around the arm and drew her closer to

himself, then bent over so it was just his breath in her ear, hot and urgent. "There's something about him. He carries himself like he isn't afraid. Like he's been trained in self-defense. And the POW tattoo—where'd he get that? The only POWs I know are in Iraq. Was he in the war?"

"Maybe," she hissed. "What if he came home to start over and something went wrong?"

"Or maybe he came home to find his girlfriend sleeping with his best buddy and tried to kill them both. And something went wrong, and he's the one who got dumped in the drink." He raised his voice. "Where he should have stayed."

"Jeremy."

"Wake up from happily-ever-after land, PJ. Everything points to him being someone dangerous." He took a breath, scrubbing one hand down his face.

Max's mouth tightened. He'd probably heard every word—their voices echoed like they stood in the Sistine Chapel.

PJ walked over to him. "Max, listen. I have instincts. And mine are telling me that you didn't do this. You aren't a murderer."

Max's expression suggested he was trying on that idea for size. Or maybe grasping like a dying man.

"Maybe Jeremy is right. People *don't* change . . . which means that the guy who crawled around in my creepy basement and dug gunk out of my drain, the guy who adopted the homeless dog and won't call him anything but his real name, *that* guy didn't murder anyone. Because he's not a criminal and never has been."

"Your instincts tell you that?"

"My *PI* instincts." She gave him a slow smile.

Max's gaze tracked past her to Jeremy and back. He sighed. "I don't know."

"Don't you want to know who you are? how you ended up here?"

"What if it's ugly?"

"I think we all have a little bit of ugly in our past. But I do believe in fresh starts. Even if some people in the room don't."

"That's not what I said," Jeremy growled.

She held up her hand to silence him. "Listen, Jeremy and I are going to see what we can learn about this woman. Maybe dig up something on you. We'll take the picture, flash it around—"

"I want to go too."

"You're staying here," Jeremy said in his boss voice. "Sorry, but if you suddenly show up in the flesh, especially if PJ is *wrong* and you *were* involved in this murder, your showing up back from the dead might make everyone clam up. Let's see what we can find, and we'll bring it back here and take a good look-see before we decide what to do."

His words seemed more a line in the sand, daring Max to protest. Or worse, a suggestion to leave now, while he still had the chance.

But Max simply gave them both a small nod.

Jeremy cupped his hand around PJ's elbow as he escorted her out, as if he might be her bodyguard.

"Max is innocent, Jeremy, and I'm going to prove it to you, no matter what it takes."

"That's what I'm afraid of."

Chapter *TWELVE*

"I do believe in fresh starts," Jeremy said quietly as they walked down the sidewalk in the neighborhood where Bekka Layton had died. Not a hit so far from the neighbors surrounding the now-rebuilt town house. So far, of the three tenants who agreed to talk to them, no one remembered Bekka, and none showed even a glimmer of recognition of Lyle Fisher or Max.

Overhead the sky had turned crabby, as if a storm might be rolling in. PJ stuck her hands in her pockets, trying not to step on any cracks.

"In fact, I'm the recipient of my own fresh start."

PJ waited for more, leaning into his words, hoping.

He must have seen her expression. "I just . . . When I came home from Iraq, I was tired. Mentally and physically."

"Being in combat could do that, I'd bet."

"I never thought I'd leave the teams. But things changed." He hooked her arm, stopping her. "I have no problem with someone wanting to erase their past and begin again. But the truth is, a person has to live with their choices; there's no getting around that."

PJ looked at the picture of the couple, the smiling, deceased Bekka Layton. "What about grace? waking up to a new day, another chance? How do you balance living with our choices with the fact that God forgives us over and over?"

He sighed. "Okay, I give you that. Both are true."

"I just don't want to believe that there's no escape from the past. You have no idea what it's like to be labeled trouble, to have to haul it around with you everywhere you go, branded into your skin."

She saw Jeremy's gaze travel to her shoulder.

"Yes, that brand, too. Boone is a part of that trouble label. It's one reason why I kept moving for ten years. Everywhere I went, I became a new person. No baggage. No labels. Just a clean slate. But not in Kellogg. There, I'm a troublemaker, and it's not only the country club. Now that I'm a PI—"

"*Almost* a PI."

"*Going to be* a PI . . . it's like I *specialize* in trouble. I'm a professional troublemaker."

"You're not a troublemaker."

"I want to believe that, but how do you leave your past behind when it's all you've ever been? How do you start over? And what do I call myself now?"

"Oh, PJ." Jeremy caught her hand and his eyes met hers, held them. "You've come so far since the day I found you impersonating a lawn girl. But you keep dragging your past around with you, calling yourself trouble."

He pushed a wild, blowing hair away from her face. "Remember how after Peter betrayed Jesus, he returned to fishing? He panicked . . . and despite all the change God had done in him, all he'd learned about Jesus, the Messiah, he went back to what he knew—the simple life of a fisherman. He only saw himself as a fisherman.

"But he wasn't supposed to be there, and Jesus went after him. He called him back from his past, forgave him, reminded him that He had a new life for him, and then empowered him to go be that person."

Jeremy hiked up the collar on her jacket. "You've been forgiven and renamed, PJ. Don't slip into your default mode and start thinking of yourself as only trouble. You're going to have to start thinking of yourself as someone else."

"Okay, who?"

He grinned at her, his eyes sweet in hers. "How about the Kellogg heiress?"

"You have too vivid an imagination."

"No, I just call it as I see it."

She let herself hang on to those words, his touch lingering on her cheek, warm in the parched, windy air as they crossed the street.

Inside the next two-story, cream-colored town house, a dog began to bark, high yips that suggested a terrier or a Chihuahua.

The door opened to reveal a middle-aged woman, her hair up in a towel, wearing a bathrobe. She carried a Chihuahua under one arm. "I already have my phone book. I don't need another." She had the basement tones of a lifelong smoker.

"We're friends of Bekka Layton," Jeremy said. "Did you know her?"

PJ handed her the picture.

The woman took it, scrutinizing the faces. "Yeah, I saw her sometimes. We talked a few times. Nice girl. She was living here while her man was overseas, waiting for him to come home. A military man, although I don't know what branch. I think he was the baby's daddy."

Baby?

"She had a child?" Jeremy asked, taking the picture back.

"Yeah. About a year old, maybe more. Cute little boy. Curly brown hair. His name was . . . Tyler, I think. I didn't see him at the fire. I was just getting home from night shift and saw the fire trucks and the ambulance."

"What about the father? This soldier. What was his name?"

"Don't know. I think he came home a week or so before she died. I saw someone pull up in a taxi. Could have been a soldier. I remember his duffel bag, although it was dark— I didn't get a good look. And then, the day she died, they had a huge fight right on the front yard."

"Were either of these men him?" PJ handed her the picture again.

She gave it another once-over. "It's hard to say. He wore a baseball cap, but I remember thinking how odd it was that he was in the military, because with his long hair, he looked more like a redneck. Oh, I do remember something—he had a tattoo on his arm. A big one. Red." She handed back the picture. "Like an eagle or something."

"A phoenix?"

"Is that a bird?"

"You didn't see him the night of the fire?" Jeremy asked.

"No—but I left for work in the afternoon." She seemed to be looking past them, as if peeling back the layers of that night. "I wish I could remember. It was chaos—so many fire trucks and cops. I couldn't even get into my driveway. I had to park down the street. Then they were cleaning the streets the next day, and I got a ticket from the city of Bloomington. A girl can't get a break."

She gave the yipping dog a one-finger smack on the snout. "Enough, Spike."

PJ inadvertently put a hand to her nose. Ouch. But Spike, hmm. PJ would have to try that one on Dog. "What happened to the little boy?"

"I don't know. He might have had family, or maybe it was just a day care provider. Every once in a while, I'd see a car parked in the driveway, and one time I saw an older woman carrying the little boy to her car. Might have been Bekka's mom. She said her mom was moving here from someplace out West."

"You don't have a name or address?"

"Nope. Listen, I gotta get to work." She hung on the door for a second. "I do hope you find out who set the fire. She was really nice. I know she was hoping it would work out between her and her man. But then again, who doesn't?"

They stood in silence on the steps after the door closed.

"What if—?"

"That's a pretty big leap." Jeremy led the way back down the sidewalk. What, now the man could read her mind?

"It's not such a big leap. Max has brown hair—and she said, specifically, curly brown hair. What if Max was in the military and the little boy is Max's son?" PJ said. "It would account for why he was never around."

"Which means he came home and murdered them." Jeremy turned and gave her a that's-the-only-logical-answer look.

"Why would he do that? That's a crazy accusation."

"Not so crazy—you heard Spike's mama back there. He and Bekka were seen fighting."

"It might not have been Max. Jinx said there was another soldier he'd given the same tat to—what if it was this other guy in the picture?"

"Can you hear yourself? You're so desperate to believe Max is innocent, you're creating a soap opera in your head. It's simply a case of a jilted soldier—he probably came home and found his woman had stepped out on him."

"Now *you* listen to yourself! The woman said that Bekka was pining after her man—"

"She didn't say *pining*."

"Okay, *waiting* for him to come back to her."

"It didn't mean that she didn't go looking for some-one else."

"Wow, are you Mr. Doom. I don't know why you're read-ing so far into this."

He stood before her, jaw tight, nearly vibrating, his hands

hard balls buried deep in his pockets. His chest rose and fell as he stared at her.

And then she got it. The fact that when he'd come home, there hadn't been anyone waiting for him. That, possibly like Max, he'd returned to heartache.

Yeah, suddenly this mystery had punched Jeremy right in the chest.

"Listen," she said quietly, her heart in her throat, "not everything is black-and-white. Some things are complicated. And Max certainly didn't throw himself into the lake—"

"Unless he was trying to get away and Lyle Fisher tracked him down. Maybe him ending up in the bay was a little vigilante justice." Jeremy's eyes darkened. "Think about it, PJ. He has a tattoo. His hands are burned. Bekka was fighting with a tattooed soldier just hours before her death in a fire. Max goes missing that night. Why is it so hard for you to believe that Max could be a killer?"

"Because I feel it right here!" She palmed her chest, over her heart.

"The PJ Sugar method of investigation—follow your heart?"

"Yes, that's right. Sometimes that's the only thing you can do."

"I swear, PJ, you could drive a man . . ." He held up his hands as if in surrender. "Do you have a thing for him, too?"

PJ's mouth opened, and Jeremy winced. "Wait—forget I said that."

Oh, sure. She stared at him, watched his face tighten, saw him look away. "That's it, isn't it? You're jealous of Max."

"Don't be ridiculous."

"I'm sorry, but did you not stand in my kitchen just last night, or rather this morning, and claim that you didn't know where you fit into my life? whether you should fight for me or let me go?"

His mouth tightened to an unforgiving line. "That has more to do with you than me, PJ. And probably Boone, doesn't it?"

PJ stared at him a moment, just to make sure her indignation came from the right place. Yes. "This is not about Boone. Boone and I are over. And there isn't anything between Max and me either, so don't go there."

A muscle pulsed in his jaw. "I'm sorry. I just hate that you're defending Max. I can read the evidence, PJ. The guy shouldn't be trusted!"

"Because he's trouble!"

"Yes!"

"You're wrong. And frankly, I'm not sure why you're getting worked up. You can't be jealous of what's not there. And it's not like you've even made one move in my dir—"

And just like that, he caught her around the waist and kissed her. It wasn't a gentle kiss, either, like his last one. Not at first. His lips moved against hers as if wanting to silence her, as if he had something to prove. Strong. Demanding. The desperation in it shook her until, suddenly, his touch softened. He slowed his kiss, gentled it, and she felt him relax even as he wound his fingers into her hair.

By then, she'd forgotten the fury that coiled inside her,

the way he could drive her to her last nerve, and even the look of hurt that had flashed across his face and let herself kiss him back. He tasted of coffee, smelled of aftershave, and in his touch remained just a hint of hunger.

Jeremy. Yes, he confused her, annoyed her, forced her to see herself differently. But he also sorta fought for her or perhaps for the woman she wanted to be.

And that's why she loved—

Wait. No. Not yet. Boone's outline in her life had barely faded. She couldn't . . . *love* Jeremy. Right?

He moved away, meeting her eyes. "That was in your direction."

"Mmm-hmm." She licked her lips. "So are you fighting for me now?" She managed the barest of smiles.

Emotion rose to his eyes, something she couldn't place. Desire, maybe. Or challenge. "I'm not sure. I'm hoping you'll help me figure that out."

She smiled. "Oh, then I think I'm going to need another clue."

✳ ✳ ✳

"What is this called again?" PJ bent over, feet flat to the floor, hands palmed on the mat, stretching like the pregnant woman on the video explained it, slowly walking her feet forward. "Oh, that hurts."

"Downward dog, and you'll get used to it." Connie, of course, moved like a ballet dancer up the mat, rising to a standing position, her arms over her head.

"I was born for contact sports." PJ finally just stood up, shooting her arms in the air. "This really makes you feel better?"

"For those of us who don't have the attention span of a three-year-old, yes, it's very relaxing." Connie finished her stretch, put her arms down, and breathed in through her nose, out through her mouth. A regular yoga master.

"Enough of this. Do you have ice cream?"

Connie opened one eye. Made a face that looked a lot like guilt.

"You cleaned yourself out of all the junk food?"

"I'm thinking I need to pace myself. I have seven months to go."

PJ grabbed her bag, walked over to the kitchen, opened the fridge, and found the milk. Boris was in the screened porch with long strips of plastic, laying them out on the floor, measuring them with a retractable tape measure. "What on earth?"

Connie continued to breathe in deep, lung-filling breaths, although the pretty, flexible woman on the screen had stopped and was now promoting her line of yoga videos for expectant mothers. "He is covering the porch with plastic." She said it in a tone that sounded relatively normal.

PJ poured herself a cup of milk. "With *plastic*."

Connie gave a final, long exhale. Then opened her eyes. "Yes, for winter. It's how they do it in the old country." She rolled her *r* on the last word.

"They know you *designed* the porch that way, right? With the holes to let the air in, yet too small for the mosquitoes?"

Connie shrugged. "I've abdicated my role of housekeeper to Vera and Boris. First it was the potato field in the backyard, and then the homemade vodka—no, don't worry, we're not actually making moonshine. They've simply decided to add to their store-bought vodka the neighbor's unused plums from the formerly ornamental tree next door." She nodded, a wide smile on her face. "That was fun to explain when they came home to find Boris entangled in their tree with a bucket. Good thing I'm a lawyer."

"Please tell me he was wearing clothing."

"It was after 10 a.m. He was *mostly* clothed. But brace yourself—he's thinking of starting a polar bear club here. Says we're not healthy enough."

"I swear to you I will never jump naked into the lake at the height of winter."

"Turning over a new leaf?"

"I have limits, you know." PJ dug into her bag, laying her hand on the diary she'd found in the floral box.

Connie rolled up her yoga mat. "I'm just glad I felt well enough to do a little work at home today. But I'm not sure I'm going to survive my pregnancy with Vera in the house. I can't voice possible baby names—because, you know, that's bad luck—and I shouldn't cut my hair for nine months, because it could do dangerous things to the baby."

"At least she cares."

"Between Boris and Vera, I think there is a significant amount of overcaring happening in this house." She deposited the mat in a basket near the door, next to her running shoes. "What are you reading?"

"The journal of Prudence Joy Kellogg Barton."

Connie's mouth opened just enough for PJ's satisfaction. "You're kidding."

"Nope. I found it today mixed in with her daughter Sunny's possessions . . . in a box marked with a *P* and a *J*."

Connie slid onto a stool. "No, seriously? PJ?"

"I never kid about mysteries. And this is a good one. The box is rich with paraphernalia from the past—mostly the 1970s. But there are pictures that go back further, and one in particular is labeled with the names Sunny and Prudence Joy."

"Weird. Especially since your name is Prude—"

PJ held up a finger. "You made a promise."

"And you're expecting me to keep it now? Oh, brother. Fine. Do you think there'll be any clues in the diary as to who killed her?"

"Or maybe why her mother left me a giant mansion? I hope so."

"You do have a knack for finding mysteries."

"If people would stop leaving me houses in their wills . . ."

"So how is the beloved mushroom house?" Connie took the diary and paged through it.

"The plumbing overflowed in the upstairs bathroom and took out a wall and turned my basement into a sewer."

"Oh—"

"Not to worry, because Max is helping me repair everything."

"So he's working out? He seemed like such a nice guy when I called."

"I think he is, but . . . did you know that he has amnesia?"

"Really? Like he can't remember *anything*?"

"Jeremy and I have been trying to figure out his identity. However, it seems that the more we uncover, the more sinister Max gets, and now Jeremy probably has him under the bright lights, doing some sort of extreme torture therapy for memory recovery."

Connie returned the diary, then folded her hands on the counter. "So . . . Jeremy thinks Max is dangerous?"

Oops. Connie wore her attorney face.

"He's not dangerous. Max is a great guy. He wouldn't hurt anyone."

Connie raised an eyebrow.

"Really. And I'm going to prove it."

"What does Boone think about all this?"

"Boone and I broke up."

"Maybe I shouldn't tell you then that I saw Boone out with Lindy Halston at Hal's today at lunchtime. And the way he leaned over the table, the look in his eye . . . Let me tell you, he was not interrogating her. At least not on police business."

Oh. PJ knew it would be coming, should have expected the fist inside that snatched her breath. But he'd warned her, and the sharp pain eased after a moment, leaving only a dull throb. She nodded. "He told me he was going to date her."

"And you're okay with it?"

PJ shrugged. "I don't know. According to Jeremy, I'm not over Boone. He says that he feels like he's *stealing* me from Boone."

"Is he?"

"No. I'm over Boone—or at least over thinking we should be together. And clearly he is too, if he's out with someone else."

"Maybe he's trying to rewrite his future, just like you." Connie finished off PJ's milk.

PJ drew her finger through the condensation on the countertop. "And how do I do that?"

Connie set the glass in the sink. "Do what?"

"Rewrite my future. The truth is, Boone was my first love. It's not so easy to let go of those feelings. I know we aren't right for each other anymore. But I'm having a hard time being me without him."

"That's just silly. You were you without him for ten years."

"No, in my head, I was always with Boone. I'm having a hard time getting my footing without him. And Jeremy is reading that as regret. Or even a divided heart. But I'm just trying to get used to a life without him in every sentence."

Connie opened her freezer, pulling out a pan of lasagna. She hefted it to the counter. "I know. I remember the day Burke died. I came home from the funeral, and although he'd cheated on me and died with his mistress, I floundered without him. I wrapped myself in his wool coat and went to our study and sat in the dark trying to figure out what to do next. I had my life mapped out with this one person, and I couldn't see beyond that moment. I refused to call myself a widow. It was awful. So . . . I moved out of the condo and bought a house. Being in a new place meant that I could rewrite my life. I had to tell myself I was going to be okay. . . . until I was."

"Is that why you took tae kwon do?"

"You have to admit, Sergei is unexpected. No one—not even I—would have guessed that Sergei, with his accent and amazing shoulders and gentle smile and dream of owning his own fitness club, would be the perfect man for me. But he is. And it's because I dared to believe I could be someone different."

PJ glanced at Boris, now tacking plastic to the inside of the screened porch. "I'll bet you didn't imagine the accoutrements."

Connie lifted a shoulder. "Part of the unexpected fun." She ran her hand over PJ's arm. "You know what I think? Boone is a habit. He's part of the old PJ package. The question is, now that you're without him, who do *you* want to be?

Maybe . . . no longer trouble.

"Princess, there are simply some mysteries that only you can solve. . . ."

Storm clouds blackened the sky, the air leaden with incoming rain as PJ drove back to the mushroom house. She'd hung around, waiting for Davy to ask her to read to him, finally landing a gig as Horton and Maisy, too.

How she missed the hubbub of Connie's house.

She'd sort of like to have a hubbub someday. She could see little dark-haired SEAL wannabes running around the house. . . .

She stopped at the bottom of the drive, opened the gate, and puttered her Bug through to the house. Rain had begun to dribble from the sky, a fog rolling in from the lake. Max had closed up shop and left the place gloomy. She wished Dog would launch from the bushes, greeting her sloppily as she let herself into her quiet, dark mansion.

Cold seeped in, holed up in the corners, and radiated off the tile floor as she padded to her room, finally finding the light in the kitchen.

A crumpled bag of bagels from the deli near Jeremy's office lay on the counter. She looked inside. Two poppy seed and one cinnamon.

Good man. He'd obviously stopped by to check on Max. She half expected him to step out of her bedroom. Waited for it, even. Nothing but the gurgle and hum of the hungry fridge, the whisk of wind ushering in the storm over the lake.

No Jeremy.

Well, perhaps it boded well for a quiet evening. Just PJ and Joy, reliving old times.

Solving whatever mysteries they could.

Chapter *THIRTEEN*

June 1959

I always knew it would be Hugh
I would love. Even from the days
when I would see him walking home
from school on the railroad tracks,
swinging his lunch pail, he'd
look up at me, whizzing by in my
father's Roadmaster, and I'd see it
in his eyes. So tonight, when Hugh
told me he didn't want me to finish
my sixteen years without being
kissed, I let him.

PJ lay on top of her bed, bundled in her Superman pants, a sweatshirt, and a pair of nubby wool socks, reading by only the splash of a bedside lamp she'd unearthed in the belongings on the other side of the house—which, with the rain pinging against the windows and the wind trying to whittle its way inside, felt like it might be in the next county. She had shut her door to conserve heat while diving into Joy's diary.

> He played me our song afterward. Betty and Chuck went out to the lagoon, probably to kiss, and Hugh put on the Flamingos' "I Only Have Eyes for You." We were dancing and almost didn't hear my parents come home. Luckily, Hugh got out through the service entrance. One of these days my mother will hear the door squeal and know. I lay in bed for a long time after he left, still feeling Hugh's lips on mine. . . .

His lips on hers. PJ rolled over on her back, staring at the ceiling, at the ornate crown molding around the hanging milk-glass light fixture.

Boone had also kissed her at sixteen. Stopped his motorcycle at Kellogg Park, sat sideways on the seat, and pulled her close. She could still remember the expression on his face—so few times did she actually see him nervous, but the question in his eyes as he tugged on her hand, then lowered his face to hers, made her entire body tingle. When he'd kissed her, she slipped into his arms as easily as the waves on the sand, and with that one touch, he'd reached right down to her soul, wrapped his fingers around it, and taken it into his hands.

No wonder she struggled to see herself without him. But maybe she was just learning to disentangle herself from his grip. Because she could only taste Jeremy on her lips, his last kiss sweet and filled with teasing. Jeremy turned her body electric, his kisses intoxicating and mysterious. And with one touch, he too could touch her soul. Yet he stirred it to life.

Jeremy had awakened a PJ that she wanted to be, a PJ she would someday recognize.

September 1959

My mother came in and informed me that she spoke with Hugh's mother on my account. She told her that Hugh wasn't to see me anymore. She sat there in her Chanel suit, fingering her pearls, fresh from the symphony, telling me that Hugh wasn't the "right kind

*of boy" for me. She says he looks
like trouble, a rebel without a cause,
with his jeans and his leather jacket,
his slicked-back hair. I think she
only sees his father driving his milk
truck in from their dairy farm.
She doesn't know Hugh like I do.
I don't think she knows me, either.*

Outside the door, in the bowels of the house, something thumped. Heavy and loud, making the entire house tremble.

PJ sat up, set the diary on her bedside table. She held her breath, trying to listen over the thunder of her heart.

Clearly the expanse of the house, and reading a dead woman's diary, had—

Another thump. Then a slow, mournful squeal.

She caught her breath.

A door—opening?

Okay, it might be Jeremy, coming back to check on her. He had a tendency to let himself in. She picked up her phone and checked it for messages. Nothing. She hit his speed dial.

He picked up on the second ring, sounding sleepy. "What's up, Princess?"

"You're not sneaking through my house, are you?" she asked in a tight whisper.

"What?" She could imagine him sitting up, turning on

the light. "Did you say that someone's in your house? Hang up and call the police this second. No, forget it; get out of there. I'll call the cops—"

"It's raining out."

"Are you kidding me? You're not going to melt, Sugar. Oh, *why* isn't there a lock on your door? Why didn't I put one on? Okay, I'm coming over there. Just *get out*."

Another high-pitched squeal. This one short, followed by a voice or something that sounded like muffled talking. "I think there's more than one of them—"

"Get out of the house!"

"But who would break in? It's not like I have anything of value."

"You're freaking me out here—ow! Where'd I put my shoes? Just, please, get out! I'm on my way over."

"Jer—"

But he'd hung up.

Fine. She blew out a breath, then turned off her light. Maybe she should leave, but that would require a trip through the kitchen and into the gale-force storm outside.

She slipped out of bed, crawled to her bedroom door, and cracked it open.

On the other side of the kitchen, near the basement, light strobed across the bottom crack in the door.

Her heart climbed to her mouth. Okay, maybe running wasn't such a bad idea.

She groped around in the dark, found one shoe, shoved it on over her woolen sock. She had the other in her hand when she heard footsteps . . . coming closer.

Blocking her exit.

Hide . . . *hide* . . . maybe the bathroom? She brailled her way across the carpet, banging her face on the doorframe. "Ow!" Her hand found the door; she pushed it open. Too hard. It slammed into the wall next to the tub.

Resounding through the house.

She'd have to hone her stealthy-hiding techniques. Scrabbling into the bathroom, across the tile floor, she found the tub, dove inside, and pulled the curtain with a swish.

She held her breath. And maybe she should hold her heart, too, because it made enough racket to betray her in the middle of a sold-out Vikings game.

She closed her eyes, listening.

Low voices. Coming from the . . . kitchen?

Then someone cracking open her bedroom door. Her light flicked on, flooding the adjoining bathroom, melting through the flimsy shower curtain. She reached for the soap, nearly a full bar, and pulled off her sock. Shoving the soap inside, she found her feet and slowly stood.

She held her breath. Gripped the sock by the end.

Steps into the bathroom. PJ's pulse drowned her hearing.

The curtain drew back. "Are you in here, P—"

PJ slung the sock weapon with everything she had, connecting with the jaw of her attacker.

"Ow! PJ, what in the world?"

Boone. Oh . . . Boone! She braced her hand on the wall, her breath huffing out. Her legs just might collapse on her. "Haven't you ever heard of knocking? Or how about calling first? Since when do you let yourself into my house?"

"I didn't," he growled. She'd left a welt on his unshaven chin. He gave her a look of annoyance, and she matched it.

She stepped out of the tub, the tile cold on her bare foot, the other overheated and crammed into her tennis shoe. "I'm confused. Are you in my house or not?"

Boone cast a look over his shoulder.

Max stood in the bedroom, holding a flashlight like he might bean someone atop the head with it. "Hi."

Oh, good grief, was she operating an all-night café? "What are *you* doing here?"

"I found a secret passageway when I was down in your basement yesterday. I wanted to see where it ended, so tonight, after work, Dog and I went exploring," Max said, flipping on the bathroom light.

Boone turned to examine his chin in the mirror. "Sheesh, PJ, you pack a wallop."

That's right she did. No apology here.

"I didn't see your car here when I came back."

"I went to Detective Buckam after I discovered the secret passageway to the carriage house."

"A secret passage? Oh, puh-*leeze*. Was it behind the bookshelf in the library? Did you have to say the secret password and click your heels three times?"

"No," Max said, his tone clipped, a spark of annoyance in his dark eyes. "It was in the basement. The door which, by the way, you so lovingly referred to as Capone's Vault."

"Hey, it had an epic look about it, like I should call Geraldo."

"Just one hour inside your brain would fuel Stephen King

for a year," Boone said, touching his jaw where it had begun to swell.

"There is a secret passageway, and more, if you're interested," Max said. "We parked there and followed it up."

"And it couldn't wait until the morning?" PJ came close to Boone, reaching out to touch the welt. "Want some ice?"

"No, it couldn't, if you'd just let us explain!" Boone pulled away. "And yes, I think I need ice."

She shook the soap bar from the sock and dropped it into the sink. "I need pizza."

"Did you learn the soap trick during your stint at Sing Sing?" Boone asked, trailing behind her.

"That and other tricks, smarty-pants. It worked, didn't it?" She toed off her one shoe, then pulled her sock back on.

Max had already opened the freezer. "No ice." He opened the fridge and retrieved the carry-home box from Hal's. "The pizza fairy will need to stock us up soon."

Uh-oh. The pizza fairy was probably on his way over at the speed of sound. Oops.

"I should call Jeremy." PJ found the phone on her bedroom floor. The call flipped to voice mail. "I'm fine. You don't have to come over," she said to his cell phone, which would probably be lodged in his back pocket during the chilly ride on the bike from Minneapolis.

Clearly her midnight fun and games had only started.

She pulled out a slice of pepperoni and faced her sulking intruders. "So tell me again why you emerged from my basement like a couple of moles?"

"Remember that cellar you fell into a few days ago?"

Boone said, picking up a piece of pizza, then making a face of disgust and dropping it. "It was a midpoint entrance to the tunnel."

"What tunnel?"

Max had no such reservations about the pizza. "Like I said, I opened the door, then followed the passageway. It's a brick tunnel with a rock floor and thick black electrical wires attached to the walls that light ancient bulbs about every ten feet, encased in these old metal cages. It did, by the way, feel very Al Capone."

"See?" PJ angled Boone a look. Nodded in triumph.

"There's more," Boone said, folding his arms over his chest.

"So," Max said, finishing off his piece of pizza, "I followed it all the way to the end and came out inside the carriage house."

"I've been inside that house—where?"

"In the entryway. It's made to look like a closet, but there are stairs that go down, under the house, and then up to the big house."

"But that's not the troubling part," Boone said. He braced his hands on the counter. "Someone's been living in the carriage house. We found blankets and food wrappers and bottles and evidence of the fireplace being used. We did a search through the house, and I think it's all clear, but I'm not comfortable with you staying here."

PJ put down her pizza, no longer hungry. "Are you telling me that someone, besides you guys, could get into *my* house?"

"There's no lock on the servant's door. So yes, if they

knew where the tunnel was. But you'd have to actually lock your door, PJ, if you wanted people to stay out. You're entirely too trusting." He chased his words with a little shake of his head.

PJ leaned against the counter. The wind moaned outside. Lightning flashed, revealing the vines clasping the window, like fingers trying to pry their way in.

"Maybe that's how Joy was murdered. I found a bunch of memorabilia, and in it was Joy's diary. What if someone got into the . . . Hey, what if it was Hugh? her old boyfriend?"

"Are you still on that? I thought we agreed you'd drop it."

"Did we?"

"It's a cold case."

"Not to me. But listen, what is glaringly important here is that someone could have gotten in or *out* of the house anytime that night that she ended up in the lagoon. Didn't you say that her husband claimed he never left the house all night? Well, no one saw him leave the house . . . but what if he did? Through the service entrance!"

Boone drew a breath. "Okay, that's about enough excitement for one night. What *I* see that is *glaringly* important here is that you aren't staying in this house one more second."

"What? This is my house—"

"I couldn't agree more," Max said.

"I'm *not* moving out of my house because of a pile of clothes and a few empty bottles. They could have been left there months ago. Talk about overreacting. I'll just lock all my doors."

"Oh, sweetheart, I haven't begun to overreact with you. You attract trouble like bees to nectar. It's like trouble can smell you." Boone moved closer to her as if he might grab her and make a run for it. Something he claimed he'd wanted to do most of her life. "You can't get away from it."

"Yes, I can! I'm *not* trouble anymore." She inched away from him.

"I don't want to disagree, but there are so many places for me to begin to argue, I have a hard time choosing. The bottom line is, I'm not letting you stay here."

"You're not *letting* me stay?" PJ closed the pizza box on Max's hand. "Get out, both of you."

Boone glared at her. Max frowned, yanking his hand back.

"You heard her." Jeremy materialized from the screened porch, Glock first. Water dripped down his face, soaked through a black sweatshirt. His hard eyes took in the situation in one swoop, finally landing on PJ, and he lowered his weapon. "What's Boone doing here? Did you call him, too?"

Ouch. "No—I called *you*. Boone is my intruder. Shoot him."

Jeremy tucked his gun away. He turned to Max. "What are you doing here?"

"We weren't really intruding. It just felt that way," Boone said.

"You snuck into my house!"

"To keep you safe," Boone growled. He stepped between Jeremy and Max. "There's a person squatting in the carriage house. And Max found a tunnel leading practically to PJ's bedroom."

"Oh, brother. I'm perfectly safe. I have my cell phone, and—"

"Your lethal sock ball?" Boone pointed to the wound on his face. "She made a weapon out of a sock and a bar of soap."

"It worked on you, didn't it?"

Jeremy moved over to her. His feet squished on the tile floor. He shot a look behind him, then bent close to her ear and cut his voice low. "Are you okay, Princess?"

"Hungry, but yes, otherwise. I'm fine."

"She won't be fine if she stays here. Not until we at least get a lock on the door."

PJ peeked out at him. "Stop being so paranoid, Boone."

Jeremy stepped back and gently took her hand as if trying to infuse some of his legendary calm.

Boone, however, had reached a ragged edge. "I'm not paranoid; I'm realistic! I see people all the time who think they're perfectly safe—"

"He does have a point," Jeremy said quietly.

"What?"

"You have to be careful. Especially when you're chasing down old mysteries and dangerous secrets."

"What kind of dangerous secrets?"

Jeremy, whether he meant to or not, glanced at Max.

Max's eyes widened. "Hey."

"I'm not accusing you of anything, but you have to admit, Max, the last twenty-four hours haven't looked so good for you." Jeremy said it without apology in his voice.

Boone glanced at Max. "How is that?"

Max's jaw tightened. "Thanks a lot." His gaze landed on PJ, though, and she picked up his defense.

"I told you, Jer, Max is innocent—"

"Innocent of what?" Boone said.

Jeremy lowered his voice just for her. "You have to stop investigating with your hopes and dreams and take a look at the truth."

"What *truth*?" Boone thundered.

Jeremy closed his mouth, raised a dark eyebrow. PJ sucked in a breath and turned to Boone, trying to figure out where to start.

Max opened his mouth first. "I might have killed some woman and set fire to her house."

Silence pulsed in the room, a beat of shock, inside which PJ realized she was doomed. Boone looked murderous, glancing first at Max, then at Jeremy, and finally his stare landed straight on PJ. "Come *again*?"

"It's just speculation," PJ said, slipping over to stand in front of Max, a sort of shield between him and the two men who both suddenly turned into a couple of alpha male wolves, fur up, eyes slitted. A shard of pity shot through her for Max. "We tracked down someone who had a picture of a couple of guys—one who looks like Max—and a woman who died in a suspicious fire. But today, we followed the lead on this woman, and she might be Max's girlfriend, so I seriously doubt that—"

"What?" Max stepped around her. His eyes bright. "My girlfriend?"

PJ glanced at Jeremy. "I thought you told him when you stopped by here today."

"He was gone."

"I was crawling around under your house," Max said, his eyes never leaving PJ's.

PJ put a hand on his arm. "We talked to a neighbor who said the woman who died—Bekka Layton—was seen arguing with a guy who had a tattoo . . . not unlike yours. And there's more. She had . . . a son."

PJ half hoped this information might trigger something—light that new fuse he'd mentioned. Max just went very, very still. She heard him breathing, hard. Saw his jaw tighten.

"A son."

PJ nodded slowly.

"Did he . . . oh . . ." He put his hand to his chest, breathing as if he might actually be in pain. "The little boy—he didn't die?"

"No. They think he's living with a relative. Bekka's mother."

He looked away, blinked. "Is he . . . related . . . to—"

"Maybe. I think he could be your son."

Max moved away from her, bracing himself against the counter. She wanted to put her arms around him, to pull him close, maybe reassure him. But, oh yes, *that* would send the right message to the two hulks behind her. Instead, "We'll figure it out, Max."

He said nothing.

Jeremy and Boone had also gone quiet.

Outside, the rain continued to lash the house, thunder groaning in the distance.

Max finally seemed to rouse out of whatever dark place he'd run to. He turned and slowly shook his head.

"What?"

"I want you to stop searching for me. I don't want to know anymore." He glanced at Jeremy. "I'm *not* afraid of paying the price for my crimes. But I can't live with the fact that I could have been that person and done those things. What kind of man kills the mother of his . . ." He winced, his voice emerging tight, raspy. "His own kid. I feel sick just thinking about it."

"Max, it wasn't you."

"You don't know that! And I agree with Jeremy. You gotta stop believing in me. I might be exactly that monster."

"You're not."

"Maybe I am." He tightened his fist, released it. "Sometimes I feel it. A rage, like a coal inside me. Burning." He took in a long breath, his jaw tight as he looked at the floor, shaking his head. "The truth is, it scares me. I can't escape it, and if I put a name on it, then it'll consume me. Maybe it's better to keep running. To not know."

"Or maybe that fire is something else," PJ said, despite the fact that Jeremy slid his hand over her shoulder, tugging her back. "Maybe it's the burn of injustice. Or grief. Maybe it's the pain of watching someone you love die."

Max lifted his gaze to her, and it made her want to weep. "Then I don't want to know that, either."

"Max—"

"No, PJ. Knowing isn't better. It's just terrifying." Max turned and walked away.

Jeremy's hand squeezed her shoulder. "I know you don't want to leave. I'll sleep outside tonight, and we'll get a better look at this in the light of day. How's that sound?"

"I'll give Max a ride home. Call me if . . ." Boone's gaze shot to PJ.

PJ was no fool. Apparently Boone and Jeremy had silently worked out some two-pronged defense system, because beside her, Jeremy gave a small, approving nod.

Good grief. Even if she did attract trouble, it hadn't a prayer of getting past her guard wolves.

She watched Boone follow Max out, the darkness swallowing them before their footsteps faded away.

"You sure you're okay?" Jeremy asked. He turned her, cupped her face with one hand. "You're shaking a little."

He drew her close, his arms enclosing her. She put her arms around his waist. Despite his sodden, cold clothes, his body radiated heat. Still, she shivered.

Maybe, right here, right now . . . yes, she might be okay.

✳ ✳ ✳

"Are you sure you don't need a blanket? or a tent?"

Jeremy stood in the kitchen, a towel around his neck, wearing one of her oversize Disneyland sweatshirts.

"You're kind of cute as Goofy."

"Don't go there. And no, I don't need a blanket. I have one in my car."

"Your car? You have a car?"

"I couldn't rightly drive the bike in the rain, could I?"

"So do I get to see it?"

He smiled, something scallywag in it. "Hmm. I think you're finding out way too much about me these days. A guy has to have a few secrets."

"About what kind of *car* you drive?"

He made a face. "Well, okay, I don't just drive it. Sometimes I sleep in it."

"For pete's sake, are all the men in my life homeless?"

"No, I still have my loft downtown. But sometimes when I'm on a stakeout or up late, I just . . . Well, maybe you should see what I'm driving."

"Most definitely."

The rain had died to a hazy drizzle, the air murky and wet as she stepped out onto the front stoop. Jeremy flipped on the outside light, then walked out behind her, closing her castle door. "So what do you think?"

A candy apple red, split-window VW camper bus sat in the middle of the drive. "You're kidding me. This is your car? It's amazing. My dream wheels!"

He grinned. "I figured."

"When did you get it? Is it a real camper bus?"

"I've had it since I got out of the military. And yes, the backseat folds down into a bed, and there's a little fridge and stove. I keep it in storage in my loft garage in the summer. It comes in handy in the winter, especially if I have to sit for long hours. There's a little heater, too."

"It's not exactly inconspicuous."

"No, but I have some tricks. And it doesn't scream *Cops* like your Vic."

"Hey, I have my Bug, too—"

"Which, I have to admit, is one reason I sort of like you."

He *sort of* liked her? He sort of *liked* her? What was that, another clue?

"It's a thing of joy and beauty." She walked over to the bus and opened the side door. Sure enough, inside, the compact kitchen looked clean and in working order. And a rolled-up Army sleeping bag on the backseat suggested that yes, he might be just fine out here.

"Jealous, aren't you?"

"Completely." She climbed inside and crawled to the backseat. Ran her hands over the vinyl. Sighed.

Jeremy levered himself in and sat beside her. "What?"

"Max. How can I watch his life unravel without stepping in to stop it? If I don't keep investigating, get to the bottom of this, for the rest of Max's life he'll think he's a murderer."

"Maybe he is."

"Don't."

"I'm saying, maybe this time we give him a free pass. For the record, I don't hate the man. I just don't necessarily trust him."

"With me."

"*Especially* with you." He wore that pirate smile again. Leaned near her. Something about this night had unleashed all his overprotective instincts, from the way he searched the house, room by room, to the way he stormed into the kitchen after securing the house and pulled her to his chest, holding her for a very long moment.

She'd let him, listening to his heartbeat, steady, solid.

Now he drew an S on her leg, tracing the Superman symbol. "I love these pants, you know. And I miss you sleeping at the office."

"You said it was a good thing," she said softly as he raised his beautiful eyes.

"It is," he whispered. Then he leaned in and touched his lips to hers. She couldn't help but hold her breath, his kiss was so sweet, so perfect. He didn't move to hold her, just touched her cheek ever so lightly with his fingertips. Then he backed away, smiling. "Most definitely, it is."

Heat rose to her face, and she found herself grinning.

Jeremy took her hand. "Listen. Max doesn't want to know his past. And maybe that's for the best."

PJ wove her fingers into his. "Maybe you're right. I keep thinking of that word Max used—*terrifying*. I think I know what he means."

Jeremy didn't speak.

"The more I dig into Joy and Sunny's past, the more I have this knot inside me. I know it doesn't turn out well for Joy, and Sunny's vanished off the planet. And the fact that my mother has left the continent is altogether inconvenient. I have a few questions for her. Somewhere in all this I can't help thinking that maybe I'm a Kellogg or at least connected to the Kelloggs. And I think my mother might know it."

"Why?"

"Well, my mother went to school with Sunny—there is a picture of them together in my mother's yearbook. And apparently Connie saw my mother and Agatha Kellogg fighting not long after I left town ten years ago. She seemed to think that it might have something to do with me. Like Agatha might be angry at my mother. Maybe for letting me go . . . I don't know. I'm probably letting my overactive imagination—" she shot him a soft grin—"have its way with me. I'm not related to the Kelloggs."

"Would that be so bad?"

"It seems that the more I probe around the Kelloggs' history, the more I see a legacy of pain. What if that's why I can never get out of trouble? Because I'm a Kellogg and it's in my genes? What if Boone is right—I just attract it?"

"Boone's not right."

"Why not? It's true. I gravitate to danger and chaos. I mean, no wonder you ran through a storm to get here. No wonder Boone doesn't want me to be a PI. You guys are constantly having to rescue me."

"I didn't rescue you. You rescued yourself. With *soap*. Which I find slightly ingenious."

"I could have just as easily slipped on that very soap and ended up cracking my head open. Because . . . that's the kind of person I am. Trouble. No wonder Matthew broke up with me."

"Matthew? Who's Matthew?"

"An old boyfriend who said I wasn't pastor's wife material."

Jeremy wore a sad look. "Can I have his full name, please,

so I can run a search on him and beat him to death with your soap sock?"

PJ ran her hand down his whiskered face. Shook her head. "He was right. And I've known since I was a kid. Sometimes I would look at Connie and wonder why it was so easy for her to be a Sugar. Perfect and beautiful and smart—"

"PJ, you are all of those things."

"I'm not, Boone!"

Jeremy blinked at her. Stiffened.

She swallowed. "Uh, Jeremy. I'm not . . . those things."

He took a breath, then slid his hand out from hers. Nodded. "Yes, you are. But you can't hear that from me, can you?"

Tears burned her eyes. "I didn't mean that. Boone and I are over."

"Maybe you are. But you're not over the imprint he made on your life. Nothing but Trouble. I'm so tired of hearing that. It's like he branded it on your soul. And the worst part is, it's not Boone calling you trouble anymore—it's you!"

"I don't like being trouble."

"Sure you do. Because if you're trouble, then no one can hurt you."

"What on earth are you talking about?"

"I'm talking about your being your own worst enemy. If you label yourself as trouble, then it's easy to tell yourself that people won't love you. Can't love you. You forgive them for rejecting you before they have a chance to hurt you. Like Peter, running back to fishing instead of facing what he thought was God's rejection. Don't you get it, PJ? You are holding *yourself* captive. But it doesn't matter what I say, does it? Because if you can't see it, if you can't hear it, if you can't believe it, then you'll always go back to fishing."

His voice gentled. "Princess, I can fight Boone for you, but I don't know how to fight *you* for your own heart." He put his hand on her cheek. "No matter how much I want to."

She leaned into his hand, her eyes blurry. "You do want to fight for me?" Another tear dripped down her chin. "Why?"

Jeremy brushed her tear away with his thumb. "Oh, PJ, are you serious? Because you're the furthest thing from trouble. You're smart and brave and funny, and you're incredibly cute, and you take my breath away nearly every day. You are *my fresh start.*"

PJ closed her eyes. "I've never been anyone's fresh start."

"Yeah. I was kind of hoping I might yours, too. But a guy only has so much fight in him."

She opened her mouth, hoping to protest, but he put his finger over her lips. "Go to bed, PJ. We'll solve more mysteries in the morning."

Chapter *FOURTEEN*

Someday, PJ would have her own PI shop, with her own one-room office, located on the second floor of a small office building in Dinkytown, carpeted with manila files. Only, she'd take better care of the thirsty spider plant in the window, and she'd never leave cold coffee perched inches from the computer, daring someone to knock it over onto the keyboard.

Tracking down Bekka Layton's mother might be a trick, but she had two bagels, a tall vanilla latte, and enough frustration in her to fuel her for a week.

"It's not Boone calling you trouble anymore—it's you!" Not anymore. Jeremy's words had looped through PJ's mind for the better part of the night until she finally wrapped her fingers around one solid truth. She had to actually *solve* a case, not stumble upon the answer or let it creep up on her

only to figure it out after finding herself—and various family members—held at gunpoint.

Trouble created messes. PJ Sugar, PI, cleaned them up.

No more being held captive by her own low expectations. By calling herself names from the past.

And it didn't so much matter if Max didn't want the details of his past. This wasn't Max's case. Not anymore. Because PJ Sugar didn't quit. Not when the game was afoot.

She'd dig up the truth, then give him the choice of hearing it.

While she booted up Jeremy's computer, she tasted her coffee. It needed sweetener. Outside, the rain had cleansed the sky to a radiant blue. She had gotten up early enough to see the sun rise, thanks to Jeremy's other comment.

"You are my fresh start."

It still sent a curl of heat through her. She'd never been anyone's fresh start.

Logging in to the PI search database as Jeremy and entering his ID and password, PJ ran a credit header search, cross-referencing Bekka's last known address. A Social Security number popped up from her rental application.

PJ added some sweetener to her latte as the Social Security search ran. The neighbor had mentioned someplace out West, and sure enough, four addresses down, PJ found a former residence listing in Portland.

Running a check on the ownership of the records at the Portland address, she bingoed on another name—Flora Layton.

See, that's what Jeremy might call a fresh lead.

She ran a credit header check on Flora, at that address, and landed pages of hits. Thankfully, Flora wasn't a popular name, and it spit out a Social Security number.

Halfway through her second bagel, PJ found Flora listed near Minneapolis. She'd moved twice since her daughter's death, finally landing in Brooklyn Park.

She had her jacket half-on, holding half of the bagel in her mouth, as Jeremy walked in the door.

"Good morning," His eyes, however, spoke reserve. As if he'd been recently kicked in the teeth and didn't want round two.

"Morning," she said, hating that she'd done the kicking.

He blocked her path with his foot. "Where are you going?"

She stopped in the doorway. Took the bagel from her mouth. "Uh, just . . ."

His eyes darkened, the wounded look replaced by the tight pull of his jaw. "You're still looking for Max, aren't you?"

Why was it that she could take on nearly any undercover identity and let lies flow out of her like syrup, but in her own skin, talking to her boss—and the guy that considered her his *fresh start*—she had nothing more intelligent than "Uh . . ."?

"You've tracked down the victim's mother, haven't you?"

She took a bite.

"I thought so." He pushed her out the door, following her down the stairs.

She swallowed. "I can do this alone, Jer."

"Humor me. How did you find her?"

PJ outlined her investigation methods as she unlocked her Bug. Jeremy slid into the passenger seat. "Okay, I'm impressed."

"See, I can be a real PI. And I didn't even cheat and use my instincts. This was pure brainpower."

"I can feel the energy waves from here." Jeremy sipped his coffee, looking at her from over the rim of his cup. He wore his black baseball cap today, a grey button-down shirt, untucked over a pair of dark jeans. He braced his cup on his knee as she motored them through Dinkytown and out of the city toward Brooklyn Park.

"Max didn't show up for work this morning," she said. Not that he'd know, because when she looked out her bedroom window at the crack of dawn, the red bus had vanished.

"No Max. No Dog. I left the door unlocked, just in case."

"You seriously think he's coming back?" Jeremy shook his head, not looking at her.

"He has a job to finish. My living room looks like the Hulk plowed through it—half the wall is torn up, and there's plaster from one end of the room to the other. And he left half of Home Depot in my front room—an air compressor, a nail gun, a couple sheets of drywall."

"If he doesn't show, I'll find a new handyman. Or maybe I'll track him down, make him clean it up. While I stand watch; don't worry."

Which, of course, worried her.

"What's our cover, boss?" he asked, taking another sip of coffee.

"I like that. Keep it up."

Jeremy smirked, leaned down, and flicked on the radio. Drive-time KQ92 was headlining the news.

"No cover. We're just going to go in straight. PIs on the hunt."

"Babe, maybe your instincts are misfiring today, but remember, there is a child involved. The grandmother is going to be suspicious if we flash the old picture around. We know that the kid's dad was a soldier, so let's play the Army benefit card. We're insurance investigators looking for Bekka's beneficiaries."

PJ sighed.

"What?"

"I'm tired of always being someone else. Lying. It feels wrong. I'd just like to be me, asking the questions, helping someone find answers."

Jeremy said nothing, just looked away from her, out the window.

Flora Layton rented a duplex right on Brooklyn Boulevard, facing the street, a nondescript brown house with a carved pumpkin on the stoop and a cheerful row of red chrysanthemums flanking the front step. A blue tricycle lay tipped on its side in the yard.

PJ rang the doorbell.

Jeremy had left his cap in the car and now ran his hand over his hair as if to groom it. Smiled.

He resembled a panther, grinning at his dinner.

"Let me do the talking," she said.

A woman came to the door. Bone-thin, in a pair of khaki

pants and a patterned sweatshirt, with bottle-black hair and saggy cheeks that stripped the youth from her face, she looked them over with suspicious, tired eyes. "I get my Christmas wreath from the Shop and Save," she said through the door.

PJ grabbed on to Jeremy's cover story. "We're insurance investigators looking for the relatives of Bekka Layton."

Something sparked in the woman's eyes. "I'm her mother, Flora."

"Can we come in?"

Flora nodded, although her gaze shot to Jeremy.

"Stop smiling," PJ whispered as they followed Flora inside. "You're scaring her."

They'd entered through a time portal to the eighties: faded mauve carpet, a green and blue plaid sofa, a blue chair, and toys strewn across the family room. A small, round pine table separated the kitchen from the family room.

"I'm Jake Davis and this is Rose Parkins. We're just finishing up our investigations for the death benefit from the Army," Jeremy said smoothly.

Rose? She looked like a Rose? PJ smiled, stuck out her hand.

Flora shook it. "The Army? You mean they found Owen's body?"

Jeremy shot PJ a look. "Yes . . . that's right."

"Finally. Only took the military four years." She lowered herself onto the sofa chair. Sighed. "When he went MIA, I knew he was dead. Bekka refused to believe he was gone, right up to the end, said she knew he'd come back to her. But

I knew he was into something dangerous." Her eyes welled up, and she covered her mouth with her hand. "I kept telling Bekka that she should move on, not wait for him."

"Did Bekka have someone else in her life?"

"Oh no, she adored Owen. I just thought the entire thing was so fast; they dated less than three months. Frankly, I didn't trust him. Of course, he shipped out before I had a chance to really get to know him. It's hard to know someone over the telephone."

"You never met your daughter's . . . uh . . . boyfriend?"

"Is that what he put on his forms? that they weren't married?" Her eyes sparked. "I knew it was a line, his wanting her to keep her maiden name. Like there aren't a hundred McManns in the phone book."

"What do you mean?"

"Oh, they were married all right. A whirlwind romance. They met in a burn unit—he'd hurt his hands in a grease fire or something. Bekka was a nurse, you know. But he wooed her, and then suddenly they were getting married and moving to Minneapolis. I thought it was strange that he asked her to keep her name. For her own protection, he said. The man was paranoid. Wouldn't even let her keep a picture of them in the house. Said he was afraid they'd bring the fight stateside."

"Bring the fight stateside?" Jeremy didn't spare PJ a glance. But she wanted to leap off the sofa and pump her fist into the air. Because, yes, she'd known he wasn't a killer. That's right. Another point for her stellar instincts.

"You know, because he was Special Forces. Maybe it was

true. My house was broken into after Bekka's funeral—they tore it apart as if they were looking for something. I had taken Tyler to visit relatives, and we came back . . ." She pressed her hand to her mouth. "I thought it was a fluke—dismissed it as being in a bad neighborhood. That's why I moved. . . . But do you think it had something to do with Owen's job?"

"I don't know," Jeremy said, but a quick look at him told PJ that Max had moved from former soldier to black ops operative in Jeremy's head. Perfect.

PJ schooled her voice. "Do you have any pictures of Bekka and Owen's wedding? I'm sure we have a marriage certificate on file, but it would help to verify their relationship."

"The Army loses everything. I can't believe it. It took you a month after Bekka died—*two* months after Owen went missing—to get his belongings to us. His last package didn't show up until a month after she died either. And even that was nothing. "

Jeremy had rid himself of the smile. "You're right, ma'am, and we're very sorry about that."

Flora's mouth tightened in a thin line of disgust.

PJ couldn't look at the woman, sure her face would betray her. An eight-by-ten picture of the five-year-old, with his short curly brown hair, brown eyes, and a dimple on his pudgy cheek, hung on the wall next to a picture of Bekka.

The little boy had Max Smith written all over his cute little face.

"What was in the package?" PJ asked.

"A teddy bear. Just a cheap trinket he picked up in some

airport, probably. But Tyler carries it everywhere, never sleeps without it." She shifted in her seat. "I'll try to find some pictures Bekka might have; they eloped, so I don't have any of the wedding. And all her boxes are in my storage unit. I packed everything away when I moved. . . . It was just too difficult. But I could look."

PJ dug into her bag for the picture of Bekka and Max they'd unearthed in the box of Lyle Fisher's possessions. She handed it over. "We found this in Owen's belongings. Can you identify the people in it for us? It's just a formality."

Flora took it. Her hands shook. "Well, that's Bekka and Lyle. And his friend of course. I remember him from the funeral. His hair was much shorter then, but still so blond."

"So Lyle is the one with the dark hair?"

"Of course."

"We thought it might be Lyle; we just wanted to confirm," Jeremy said, unfazed.

"Oh, that's Lyle, for sure. Bekka told me how they went to Valleyfair together." She pointed to the rides behind them. "Some photographer took their picture—you know, for money. Bekka sent for it later, after he left. And I recognize Lyle's dimples. He did have such a nice smile." She handed back the picture with a sigh. "Lyle visited Bekka for a couple weeks, maybe six months before she died. Tyler was about seven months old."

"How did Bekka know Lyle?" PJ asked.

"Lyle was Owen's cousin. He served with him, and Owen sent him home with gifts and letters for Bekka—sort of like proxy, I think." She leaned in. "Personally, I think he was checking up on her, if you know what I mean."

PJ took the picture again. Stared hard. If Max was Lyle Fisher, then who was Owen? Who exactly ended up in the lake, minus his memory, and emerged as Max Smith?

And who had been arrested as Lyle Fisher that night?

"Do you know the man with the blond hair? the one who came to the funeral?"

"Yes . . . he told me that if I ever needed anything, I could call him." She stood and went to the kitchen, where she opened a drawer and fished around. PJ watched as she whisked a hand over her cheek. "Oh, I can't find his number. But I remember he used to skydive at an airport around here. St. Cloud, or . . . oh, I can't remember. He called himself a . . . sky bum."

"A sky bum?"

Jeremy leaned toward her. "Like a ski bum. Only instead of ski resorts, they hang around jump schools."

"Do you remember this guy's name?"

"Something like *snow* or *breeze* . . . Wait, I remember . . . *chill*. That's it—Windchill."

"I'm sorry for your loss, Mrs. Layton. It's so good of you to take in Tyler."

"Oh, I love my grandson. He's my entire life. I just hope they get the man who killed Bekka."

"Do the police have any leads?"

Flora's eyes hardened. "No, but *I* do. I talked to her neighbor, and she told me it was that soldier with the nasty tattoo. I remember Bekka telling me to look out for him. Owen

was always paranoid—even made Bekka scared. This soldier showed up a few hours before the fire and had a terrible
fight with my Bekka, right there in the street. Bekka was
scared, and she packed up Tyler and came right over. I told
her not to go back, but she said she had to—that he was
waiting. Of course he was waiting—to kill her!"

Everything emptied inside PJ as she listened to Flora's
story. "Did Bekka tell you the man's name?"

Flora shook her head. "No. I'm sorry. Maybe that
Windchill fella can help you."

PJ stood. "Thank you, Mrs. Layton. If you find those
pictures, could you give me a call?" She rattled off her
number.

"You don't have a card?" Flora wrote it down.

"Not today," Jeremy said.

"You're not with an insurance agency, are you?" Flora
tacked the paper to the fridge, then turned and gave them
a narrow-eyed look.

PJ put her hand on Jeremy's arm, holding him in place.
"No." He frowned at her, but she ignored him. "But we're
better than insurance agents. We're PIs and we're going to
find your daughter's killer."

A beat pulsed as Flora considered them, and Jeremy tried
to incinerate PJ with a glare out of his peripheral vision.

"Well, why didn't you say so in the first place?" Flora
came forward and took PJ's hands in her own. "I just knew
that God would send someone to uncover the truth. Thank
you." She pancaked PJ's cheeks between her hands. "What's
your real name, honey?"

"Oh, I'm PJ Sugar. And this—" she patted Jeremy's arm—"is my assistant, Jeremy Kane."

✳ ✳ ✳

"You enjoyed that, didn't you?"

Jeremy had stalked straight out to the car, to the driver's side, and held out his hand.

Just this once, PJ dropped her keys into it and slid into the passenger seat. "I did, ever so much." She leaned back, put on her sunglasses. "Okay, so what do we have?"

"A mess," Jeremy said, working the gear into place and pulling away from the curb. "Who is this Max guy—Owen or Lyle?"

"Bekka's mom says he's Lyle . . . and I agree; the guy in the picture looked just like Max. But if Owen is Tyler's dad . . . well, that little boy looks a lot like Max too."

"She said Owen and Lyle were cousins—it could be a family resemblance. But what I want to know is how Max, as Lyle, could be getting arrested right around the same time that Max, formerly Owen, was washing up onshore. He can't be in two places at the same time."

PJ pulled on her seat belt. "I want to check out this Windchill guy, see if he knows anything about Max."

"Over my cold, dead body. What if he was the guy that dumped Max off the Maximilian Bay Bridge? No way. Forget it. If anyone is checking him out, it'll be me, thanks."

"Now who has the vivid imagination? What's he going to do—push me out of a plane?"

Jeremy glanced at her, his expression suggesting that very thought. "I'm getting a headache from the entire thing. I'm telling you, PJ, we should drop this case and run away."

"Why?"

"It's not going to be a pretty ending. I can feel it in my gut. Either Max killed this woman, or he was involved in some way. Maybe Bekka was even killed *because* of him. Any way it turns out, it's going to destroy him."

PJ shook her head. "I know Max is innocent, and if he is, he is going to want to know who did this."

"No, he's not! Trust me on this. Leave it, PJ."

The thought nudged PJ that perhaps they weren't talking about Max anymore.

They turned onto the freeway, on their way back to the city.

She schooled her voice, not looking at him. "What do you mean, Jeremy?"

He pulled a long breath, then another. Finally, "Knowing means you have to live with it. Live with your own imagination running like a movie in your head, including the sound track of her screams. You have to live with the anger like a hot coal—just like Max said—inside your chest. And you have to live with what you do about that."

He didn't look at her with those last words. Just inhaled, then reached out and turned on the stereo.

PJ listened for a moment before turning it off. "'Do about that'?" she said softly.

"I'm just saying that sometimes *not* knowing is better, okay? You can forgive easier that way. You don't have a face to put your hatred toward, and maybe, someday it dissipates. I wish . . ." He shook his head, something tortured in his expression.

Jeremy had known the identity of his fiancée's killer. She could see it on his face as clearly as if he had tattooed it.

And just maybe, he'd let his hatred spiral in, take control. She touched his arm, and he sucked in a breath, as if, for a moment, he'd been someplace else, and her touch brought him back.

"What happened?" she asked.

He glanced at her, then shook his head again, quick, short.

Oh, Jeremy. She sighed, then leaned over and touched her forehead to his arm. "You can trust me, you know."

He put his hand on her head, weaving his fingers into her hair. She barely heard him when he said, "You have no idea how much I want to believe that."

She sat up. "You don't have to be alone in this. I'm your fresh start, remember?"

"I remember. There are just some places I can't take you."

"Is that why you won't let me in on your field trips?"

Oh, there went the poker face.

"Because my eyes do work, and I'm not blind to the fresh scrape on your chin. Is that where you went this morning after you left my house at the crack of dawn? taking out bad guys?"

Jeremy drove without speaking.

"You know, you could invite me along when you apprehend your dangerous bail skippers. I might learn something."

"You're not going to learn anything from these guys."

"I was thinking I might learn something from *you*, Rocky. After all, you *are* the pro."

A muscle pulsed in Jeremy's jaw. "I don't want you to learn this. I especially don't want you to see it."

There he went again, receding into the enigma of his dark side. And for a second there, she'd seen a glimmer of light. *Don't run, Jeremy!*

"I'm not so easily spooked. You should know that by now."

His breath rose and fell in his chest as he drove, all humor gone from his expression.

"If you want us to be partners, Jer—really partners— then you don't get to make all the rules. You can't just come out and play when you want to. It goes both ways. You're going to have to learn to trust me."

"I do trust you."

"No, you trust me with what you want me to know. Not with all of you."

"Why do you have to know it all? Isn't what I give you enough?"

"Because it's who you are—"

"No it's not." He turned to her, his eyes hot. "It's the furthest thing from who I am."

She could hear the sirens, the warning bells pinging, but his heat had ignited her own. "Maybe it's not who you want to be, but it *is* you. We all have dark places, and the fact is, it's part of the Jeremy package. I know it, and I'm *not* scared of it."

He hit the brakes, shifting down a little too quickly as he took their exit from the highway. "Maybe you should be. Maybe you shouldn't be so drawn to people like Max . . . and me. People who have a place inside them that is ugly, and . . ." He took a deep breath, blew it out. "Where can I drop you?"

"Are you serious? That's it? Conversation over? Cha-*ching*, the wall goes up?"

"What do you want from me, a full confession? a list of my crimes?" He looked away from her as if hiding.

"No, I don't need that." In fact, suddenly she didn't want that at all. "The last thing I want you to do is relive your pain. But I wouldn't mind understanding why it's so difficult for you to let me close, to let me know that shadowy part of you."

"Because I don't want you to see that part of me!" he roared. "There's a reason I don't talk about my life as a SEAL. I know that I'll always be that man, but I don't have to like it. And I especially don't want you to know that man."

PJ stared at him, at his reddened eyes, at his fast breathing, and she didn't recognize him. The Jeremy she knew was full of teasing, controlled, always had an answer. Her Jeremy could make her laugh and turn her to liquid with a smile. This Jeremy appeared unraveled . . . broken, even.

And it made everything inside her shatter, tiny pieces of her heart embedding in her lungs, her soul. She couldn't breathe without a spear of pain.

She took her hand off his arm. "I want to be your partner, Jer. But I can't be unless you trust me. You say I make my own prison, that I call myself trouble to protect myself. But you do the same thing. You've separated yourself into two parts—the pretty part and the part you don't think I can love."

Jeremy's hand whitened on the steering wheel.

"That's why you don't like Max, isn't it? Because he reminds you of that part of yourself. And you're furious with the thought of him not paying the consequences for his crimes."

He refused to look at her, and her eyes burned. "By the way, you're driving my car, so feel free to let yourself off anytime." PJ looked away, wiping her cheeks, shaking.

They rode in silence all the way to the office, and when he finally pulled up, he left the motor running and got out, saying nothing as he slammed the door behind him.

Halfway down the sidewalk, though, he turned and stalked back to where she still sat in the passenger seat. She rolled the window down.

But he didn't have apology on his mind. "The consequence of my crimes is that I know who I really am. What I'm capable of. Unlike you, I know where I came from. I can't break free of it, and it terrifies me, just like Max said. The only difference is, unlike Max, I know my past; I *know* why I need to be afraid."

He backed away, hands up in surrender. "You can psychoanalyze me all you want, PJ, but the bottom line is, you can't fix me. And I can only offer you the good part of me. The part that wants to start fresh. The other part—there's nothing for you there. Take it or leave it." He closed his mouth, his eyes daring her to speak.

She willed herself not to cry. But any words she had were glued to her throat.

"Fine," he said to her silence and stalked away.

Chapter FIFTEEN

"I'm a total idiot, Connie. I just let a perfectly good man—one I think I could even love—walk out of my life." PJ walked the length of the sidewalk and back again, the wind chapping her cheeks, herding leaves down the gutter. The sub shop pumped out the heady fragrance of baking bread, and not far-off, a radio hip-hopped out the hood.

She just wanted to get into her car and drive. She didn't care where. Just anywhere to fill the thrumming ache inside. *"Take it or leave it."*

"He didn't mean it." Connie had resurrected her lawyer tone, and PJ pictured her in her high-rise office, just over the river, downtown, staring out on Nicollet Avenue, even though she was probably sitting on her enclosed porch in a pair of yoga pants.

"He *did* mean it. He's got black holes in his life so big he could get lost for a year inside them."

"He was angry. You were angry."

"No, I was heartbroken because, the fact is, I truly understand what it feels like to walk around under the specter of your past. And for all his 'fresh start' talk, he has no idea what it means."

On the other end, Connie said nothing.

"What?"

"I'm just wondering if you do, either."

PJ let her sister's words find her pores, sink in, even after she hung up and went in search of lunch. Finding Windchill took her the space of half a meatball sub. The display ad, right in the middle of the yellow pages, read, *Windchill Skydiving, Flying That Will Take Your Breath Away.*

Right now, her breath was so heavy in her chest, she needed something to scrape it away.

A fresh lead.

A call to the spunky receptionist confirmed that Windchill was in, and PJ headed out to the Windchill Skydiving base west of the Twin Cities.

If she ever had an inclination to throw herself from unimaginable heights—which she didn't—she might do it from one of those shiny red and white Cessnas parked in front of the domed, metal hangar of Windchill Skydiving. The sun smiled off the metal, and in the distance, airplanes puttered along the tarmac, lining up for takeoff. A ten-foot painted sign with a cheesy picture of a parachute hung over a side door.

PJ entered the small, paneled office with a ratty sofa and a rack of jumpsuits, the walls covered in cheap photos of skydivers,. A girl who looked like she might be blown hither by the first big gust filed her nails behind the counter, her blonde hair in two neat braids.

"Hey," she said, looking up at PJ. "Do you have an appointment?"

"I called earlier—I'm looking for a guy named Windchill?"

"He's just coming in from a flight. You wanna book a jump?"

PJ considered the pictures on the wall, blue and yellow parachutes unfurled like kites against a greater blue canopy. "I'll wait for Windchill."

The girl gestured to a long hallway. "You can wait back in the equipment room if you want."

PJ wandered down the paneled hallway, checking out pictures, searching for any faces that resembled Max. Mostly happy skydivers giving a thumbs-up to the photographer. But no happy Max.

Backpacks, shoes and jackets, open soda bottles, and chip bags littered the so-called equipment room. The picture windows overlooked the expansive landing field off in the distance, and PJ watched a red canopy, no larger than a pinprick, drift from the sky. It looked at once lazy and exhilarating and terrifying.

"Makes you want to try it, doesn't it?"

She turned, and a man in a blue jumpsuit, carrying an orange and yellow unfurled chute over one arm and a silver helmet in the other, stepped inside the room, shrugged out of a small backpack, set the entire mess on the sofa, and grabbed an open can of soda.

257

"I don't know. It looks . . . Yes, there's a small part of me that wonders what it might be like. But the truth is, I'm terrified of heights, so—"

"Don't let that stop you. You never know what you can do if you look beyond your fears. Might find a whole new you."

"Right now, I'm just looking for a guy named Windchill."

"You found him." He lifted his soda at her, smiling. "Wayne Chillard. But my friends—" he added a wink behind the word—"call me Windchill."

Windchill screamed military head to toe, from his short, razor-cut blond hair and clean-shaven skin to the solid shoulders and lean build outlined by the jumpsuit, unzipped and peeled off his shoulders to his waist. Even the way he carried himself branded him as a soldier thanks to the aura of confidence she'd begun to expect from the other various former military men in her life, without, perhaps, the tortured look in his eyes.

And without the smile on his face in the picture with Lyle and Bekka.

He took another swig of his drink, then set it down on a shelf and picked up his chute, shaking it out with precise, mechanical movements. "What can I do for you?"

"My name's PJ Sugar." She extended her hand, and he took it, met her eyes for a moment with a cryptic smile. Then she glanced at his biceps and the absence of a tattoo leaking from his shirtsleeve. Shoot. She had clung to the flimsy hope that Windchill might have been the man arguing in the street the day of Bekka's death. "I'm trying to track down friends of Owen McMann."

Windchill's smile faded, and a ripple of something she might call fear threaded through her. So maybe she *should* have waited for Jeremy.

No, she could do this. No more leaning on her boss for help. She'd managed to traverse the country for years and even nab a few bad guys over the past several months without Jeremy's help. She could talk to Windchill.

"Why do you want to find Owen?" He had a low voice, and she rubbed her prickled arms where it rumbled under her skin.

"Actually, I think he might have found me. Showed up on my doorstep a couple days ago."

He had stretched his chute out on the floor; now he stood, concern evident in his knit brow. "You're the one who put his picture in the paper."

Owen's picture? So now Max *was* Owen? She swallowed back any surprise from her expression. Maybe she'd scrub any mention of Lyle Fisher. "Uh, yes." She couldn't believe that he'd seen the ad after only one day.

Windchill stepped closer. "Have you lost your mind?"

She blinked at him. Wow, she had to look way, way up. When had she shrunk? "I . . . am not sure how to answer that question."

He raised one eyebrow.

"Perhaps we should start over. I'm actually on Max's side—"

"Who's Max?"

"I mean . . . Owen." She made a face as he stared at her. "Listen, your pal Owen lost his memory."

"He lost his *memory*?"

"Someone tried to kill him four years ago, and we're trying to figure out who that might be. We have a couple leads, but . . . well, Owen's a bit sketchy on his past."

"I wondered why he let his picture go in the paper. It's because of you. Good job. They'll be back to finish what they started."

Finish what they . . . "What are you talking about?"

His mouth tightened into a line of quiet anger. Then, "Is he going to get his memory back?"

"We're . . . hopeful."

Windchill looked past her, out the window. "Have you ever been flying?"

PJ glanced at the chute. "Is that a prerequisite to my getting to question you?"

"It sure is, honey. You want to talk to me about Owen, we'll do it in the air."

The air. "You can't be serious."

"Do you want answers?" Windchill picked up the nylon edge of his chute, tucked it under his chin, and began to straighten the lines extending from the chute to the harness.

"Yes, but . . . can't we do it without jumping?"

He folded the chute in half, then spread it out on the long table. He folded it in half again. "Not if you want to know who's after Owen and why it might have been a lousy idea to announce to the world he was still alive."

Uh . . .

"I have time for one jump; then I have places to be."

"Fine. Only if you promise I'll live through this."

"You'll more than live." He gave her a smile.

She watched as he took the lines of the chute, folded them back and forth, and laid them onto the nylon. Then he folded the rest of the chute accordion style into a tiny box and set the entire thing inside the pack. He glanced at her. "Well, go grab a jumpsuit. We're leaving in five."

"You do promise to tell me what you know about Owen, right?"

"Scout's honor," Windchill said, pointing to the rack.

PJ grabbed a jumpsuit and climbed in. "You're not going to let me jump alone, are you?"

"Why? You scared to jump alone?"

PJ swallowed. "No. . . . Okay, that's a lie. I'm terrified."

He grinned. "Honesty. I like it. Don't worry; I'll hook you up to me. We'll jump tandem." He walked over to her, holding a harness, and held it out while she climbed in it, balancing herself with a hand on his shoulder.

She must've lost her mind. Or left it inside the hangar, because as she followed him out to the plane buzzing on the tarmac, something foreign stirred inside her. A breathlessness. Perhaps a longing.

She climbed into the plane. The seats had been removed. Windchill nodded to the pilot. She sat on the floor, in front of Windchill, letting him pull her to himself. She felt him behind her, hooking on clips to her harness. "You're not going to drop me, are you?"

"No promises."

She looked back at him. He wasn't smiling. "I really am a friend of Owen's."

"I believe you." He handed her a helmet.

The plane lifted off. PJ watched out the window as the landing strip shrank. They rose above the outlying houses, which turned into Monopoly buildings, the cars into Matchbox. Fields patchworked the ground, the road became a thread, and she could taste her stomach. Still they climbed.

Okay, seriously, she'd taken this investigation thing a bit too far. What would Jeremy have done? "What do you know about Owen?"

"We jump first."

"What if I don't want to?"

"Fear is not an option."

"Thank you, Arnold."

"You ready?" Windchill reached over, opened the door. The wind took her hair, her breath, her thoughts.

"I don't know." She fisted her hands around the harness straps.

"When we jump out, I want you to put your arms out like you're flying. Then, after we fall for a bit, you'll pull them in and I'll open the chute. Then we'll talk."

Talk? She'd have a hard enough time breathing.

He moved her to the edge and she tiptoed her foot to the doorway. Below her the ground looked surreal, so far. A sort of crazy adrenaline raced through her stomach, and even as she stared out at the nothing but space between her and the ground, the fear left her. Simply zipped away, like she'd already pulled the cord and let it rip free.

"Ready?"

She nodded.

And then she was flying. The wind battered her ears and sucked away her breath, cold and angry. But she drank it in, her arms out.

Flying. Like Supergirl.

She put her legs together, spread her arms, barely aware of Windchill over her, his own arms spread wide. She might have screamed, might have whooped, but the wind ate the sound as they hurtled toward the earth. She gulped in the freedom, the exhilaration sweet on her lips.

Flying.

And for the space of seven seconds, she forgot who she was, who she'd been. Forgot Boone and Jeremy and Max and why she'd hurled herself from a plane. Forgot the mushroom house and Prudence Joy and even Aggie Kellogg and her mysterious benevolence.

Flying.

It scooped her out whole and filled her with a new breath, tingling in every pore. Tears whisked her eyes, and inside she heard a voice.

Princess.

It may have been Jeremy, or perhaps her own memory, but as Windchill curled her arms around her to pull the chute, the word sang inside her.

Princess.

The chute jerked hard, and they soared to the heavens, leaving most of her stomach below. "Wow!"

Then everything hushed. The rushing had stopped,

leaving only the whisper behind. Windchill held the parachute toggles and steered them as they descended.

"Hang on a second." She felt him fiddling with her clips. "You're not going to drop me, right?"

While she waited for a laugh, she looked up at him. He reassured her with a smile even as she felt her lower clips give and she dropped further into his lap. "Just trying to make it more comfortable."

"Did you know that Owen had a son?"

"Yeah. He talked about him a little."

"So sad. He has nothing left of his father—oh, except this teddy bear, but even that came after he disappeared."

He grabbed the toggles again. "Did you see the kid?"

"No, but I saw pictures. So cute. And the grandmother says he never goes anywhere without that teddy bear. So you served with Owen?"

He steered them through the sky, toward a grassy patch that appeared not more than a splotch of color. "We were both involved in missions I can't talk about, but a few years ago, before he disappeared, we went into Sierra Leone during the last days of the UN peacekeepers. We were there to train locals in minesweeping. It was supposed to be a low-key event, until a mine exploded. Four of our guys were hurt—Owen was one of them. He had a head injury, was flown out to Germany. They weren't sure he was going to make it. Everything was on the down low—I think they even listed him as MIA. He'd already done a tour, even did some time in an Iraqi POW camp during the beginning of the war on terror, so they shipped him home, medical leave. Only something happened. Right after he got home, his wife was killed, and he went missing. Rumor had him as good for it, but I never believed it."

"Why not?" The ground hurtled toward them, houses growing chimneys, yards widening. Already, the taste of joy had begun to fade.

"Because there were rumors of our guys taking something more than souvenirs."

"Like what?"

"Like diamonds. Sierra Leone is one of the biggest diamond producers—and hotbeds for smugglers—in Africa."

"So you're saying maybe Owen took the diamonds?"

"I don't know. But if he didn't, he knew who did and was being shut up or even set up."

"What do you mean?"

"The smugglers had to get the diamonds into the States, and the military isn't exactly loosey-goosey on security. A guy headed stateside makes a pretty good transport. Maybe he brought something home."

The wind took his voice. Or maybe she just sensed him waiting, as if she might fill in the gaps. She shook her head. "Not that I know of. Do you really think Owen was in on it?"

"No . . . or at least I didn't. You get to know guys when you trust them with your life, but then again, look at Owen and Ratchet—they went through the fire and they hated each other."

"Ratchet?"

"Yeah. Ratchet was on our squad, but he and Owen didn't get along."

"Why?"

"They knew each other from before . . . from Iraq. When they were both POWs. Something happened that neither one of them would talk about. After Owen disappeared, Ratchet dropped off the map too. I think he was hanging around, trying to figure out how Owen might have gotten those diamonds home . . . Okay, we're going to come in soft, so hold your feet up, and we'll land."

He pulled on the chute, and she felt a hiccup, then a silky landing as she skidded onto the soft grass.

Windchill wrapped one arm around her as the chute settled with a soft puff around them. He didn't let go of her, kept his voice soft in her ear. Still, she felt the edge of warning. "You didn't hear any of this from me. But you watch your back, and you tell Owen—or Max or whoever—to keep an eye out for Ratchet because I have a feeling this isn't over."

*** * ****

"Jeremy Kane, leave a message."

Hmm.

"Hey, Jeremy, I think I have a lead."

Um . . .

"Jeremy, I know you're probably still angry . . ."

Well . . .

"It's me. . . . Are you still mad?"

Okay . . .

"Where are you? You better not be lying dead in an alley."

So . . .

"Did I mention I went skydiving today?"

Fine.

"I'm going back to my house. See you there."

PJ hung up her cell phone, tossed it onto the other bucket seat, then reached out to make sure it stayed where she could get to it, just in case one of her messages actually prompted Jeremy to call back. The sun hovered over the horizon, a simmer of hot red against a pellet gray sky. She had the radio cranked up high, the windows cracked, as her Bug pulsed its way through Minneapolis toward Kellogg.

She felt invincible. The millisecond her feet—or rather backside—touched the ground, she wanted to fly again, every cell in her body vibrating with power.

And she had a new lead. Windchill had given her Ratchet's real name—Randy Simonson—and she'd raced back to the office. It had taken a number of traces—apparently Randy Simonson liked to move across the tristate area. From Sioux Falls, to Des Moines, to Fargo, and finally back to Minneapolis, landing at the Golden Valley Tire and Lube.

She'd probably wait for Jeremy for the next little chat, although the invincible feeling had her wanting to pull into the place and ask for an oil change.

She turned off the highway and onto Old Mill Road, the one that wound around the lake, over Maximilian Bay Bridge. The lake was choppy, foam piling on shore. She passed mansions set back from the lake, long front lawns. From this entry, she could make out the backyard of the mushroom house, the lawn gristly and wild, leaves papering the yard. Hopefully Max and Dog had returned, and Max hadn't simply run, again.

Jeremy's words hung in her mind. *"Knowing means you have to live with it."*

Max had used the word *terrifying*. Yes, perhaps if she found out that she'd killed someone she loved, she might find her past terrifying. . . .

Maybe it was time to let Max fade into his future.

But it didn't mean she would give up.

Not on Bekka. Not on Joy. Not on herself.

And not on Jeremy.

Not when she could still hear the voice.

Or maybe it sounded more like a song.

Princess.

Soaring across the sky, the earth's breath swelling her lungs.

Princess.

The smell of the leaves stirred by the wind.

Princess.

The word tasted like a McIntosh apple, crisp and alive in her mouth.

Princess.

Maybe this was what it felt like, that fresh start. Not wiping out the past, but getting a view of everything from above and seeing it with a new perspective. The perspective of joy, of invincibility, with a new breath, a new taste in your mouth. A new name—

Something bumped her from behind. Her head jerked forward. "Hey!" She glared in the rearview mirror.

A white Pontiac nearly climbed up her backside. She hit her horn.

The car banged her again, and she fought the wheel, gunning it. "What—knock it off!"

She couldn't make out the driver behind his visor. He came at her again, and she floored it, coming up fast on the car ahead of her. "Sorry!" But she couldn't pass—not with oncoming traffic. The approaching car passed, and the lane looked open, so she gunned it out into the opposite lane, shooting past a red Honda.

How about that. She'd left the Pontiac a car length behind. She scooped up her phone, debated for a second, then speed-dialed Boone.

At the moment, he was the only one still talking to her.

He picked up on the second ring. "PJ?"

"I'm being followed. White Pontiac. It's too dark to see the plates. I'm on Old Mill Road, about a mile from the bridge—"

"Someone is following you?"

"They've bumped me twice."

"What? Just keep driving; don't panic—"

"I'm not panicking—oh, wait . . ." The Pontiac passed the Honda and moved in behind her.

"What?"

"Okay, now I'm panicking—it's on my tail again."

She could hear him yelling something to Rosie. "Where are you now?"

"I'm coming up to the bridge. I can see—"

The Pontiac bumped her again, a neck-jarring smack

that carried her forward. "Boone, it's pushing me—" She dropped the phone, grabbed the steering wheel, her adrenaline like fire in her body. "Stop!"

She slammed her brakes and heard squealing, lifted her own voice in a scream. Burning rubber fouled the air. They topped the bridge, the guardrail too close.

Suddenly the Pontiac veered into the opposite lane.

It nudged her on the outside—*Brakes!* PJ heard the impact at the same instant it surged through her. She slammed her feet on the clutch, the brake pedal, grinding it into the floorboards.

The Pontiac smacked her hard against the back fender. As though it had wings, the little car lurched forward, then bounced against the rail. Metal screamed as the rail tore at the Bug. PJ fought to control the wheel, to get out ahead, but the Pontiac had pinned her, pushing her . . . over . . . into the lake?

No! PJ gunned it, but the Pontiac moved abreast of her, sideswiping her. The guardrail whined, then surrendered with a rending scream.

"No!" She slapped the window. "Help!"

Her seat belt strap strangled her as the VW slipped over the rim of the bridge, the steel rail like teeth, raking the short length of her Bug.

The vehicle teetered, rocking, a pendulum ticking off the seconds toward fate. Below, the lake's frothy tongues lapped at her, ready to slurp her in. The cell phone bounced on the floorboard. "Help, help!"

And then, with a final, deadly screech, the railing opened

its mouth. PJ threw out her hands, feeling them hit the windshield as she splashed, bobbed like a buoy. Then the lake drank her in with a triumphant gurgle.

"No, no, no!" The water spilled in through her open window. Maybe if she could open it wider—

She grabbed the crank handle, fought it. But the Pontiac had crumpled the door, and the window didn't budge. Water rose from the floorboards, freezing, needles creeping up her ankles, her calves.

She unbuckled her seat belt as the water climbed to her thighs. She pounded on the window. "Help!" Her hand found the door handle, and she wrestled with it, throwing her shoulder against the door.

Nothing. The water crept to her chest. She launched herself at the other door. That, too, had been crushed.

The water already engulfed the backseat, the heavy engine nosing the car up. Water climbed up her back, ripping at her breath as she banged on the side windows. *Kick them out!* But she had no leverage, not with the water now to her shoulders.

No—no—oh, please, God, no. I'm not ready . . . "No—" The moan of her own fear shook her as she pressed her mouth up to the vinyl-covered ceiling. *Please, not like this.* Not when she hadn't said good-bye, not when she'd left things so badly with Jeremy.

As the water reached her chin, she took a final breath. Then the water closed over her nose and she went under.

Chapter *SIXTEEN*

PJ had been fourteen the first time she dipped her toes in the ocean. She'd watched the water for hours first as it curled onto the shore like a giant fist, reaching with foamy, weedy fingers, then dragging pieces of shell, sand, crabs, and the occasional sand toy back to the depths. Over and over. Tireless.

The fingers were cool and even gritty on her skin when she finally slipped her foot into the waves. Her mother read a book onshore; her father collected seashells. Connie lay on a blanket, already brown to PJ's reddened skin.

A wave slid over her ankles, jostling her bare feet as they sank into the watery sand. Pulling away from shore, the wave tugged at her, an invitation to the depths.

Again. And again. Until the waves seduced her in up to her chest. She consented to float, lifting her feet off her moorings, letting her body undulate in the rhythm of the sea. From shore, Connie waved and yelled something, but PJ couldn't make out the words. She held out her feet but couldn't see them, the sand like a cloud, a layer of grit on her skin.

Connie was still waving.

She waved back and Connie shook her head, pointing.

She turned in time to see a wall of water twice her height, dangerously silent as it rolled toward her. She caught her breath—probably the intake that saved her—and raised her arms, trying to protect herself.

The wall crashed on her. Knocked her from her feet. Like a tentacle, the wave wrapped around her, spun her. She gulped briny water; her eyes burned with salt, the horizon turning milky.

Her toes scraped the bottom once, twice. Her fingers clawed against seashells; her shoulder scrubbed the seafloor.

Then hands reached down and caught her upper arms. Pulled her free from the ocean's grasp, into the hot, full sunlight.

Her father stood, breathing hard, still in his T-shirt, his eyes reflecting her own fear.

"Just stand up," he said. "If you get tossed by the waves and turned around, if you're blind and can't figure out how to get your footing, just calm down, find the bottom, and *stand up.*"

Stand up.

Black dotted her eyes as her breath began to leak out.

Stand up.

She pounded the Bug's ceiling, frantic, hit fabric.

The ragtop. Maybe the water had bowed it back, loosened it. She was already crammed against the roof. She groped for the handle. *Please, God, let this work.* She wrestled with it. It didn't budge. *No!* She hit it once, again. More. *C'mon!*

It popped free. Yes—air—

She reached up to pull herself through, burping as the last of her breath leaked out. *Don't breathe in; don't—*

Oh, she had to breathe!

Hands grabbed hers and yanked her through the roof. She tried to kick, but she had no energy, no . . .

A mouth covered hers and blew in air. Light strobed in her brain as she gulped it in, trying to hold it.

Then they burst to the surface.

Air. Sweet—she gasped.

"You're okay . . ."

She coughed, tried to breathe, choked on the water in her lungs.

"Just keep breathing," said a voice, husky, ragged, as her rescuer dragged her toward shore.

Everything inside her burned—her throat, her arms, her legs, her belly. She gulped in more air, and it razored down her throat.

Breathe.

Her feet touched ground, but she had no strength, became a rag doll. His hand wrapped around her waist, and then he simply lifted her into his arms and walked to shore.

Her body wracked as she coughed, but still he held her. Water dripped into her eyes, shivered over her skin.

"You're okay, PJ; you're okay." He set her down on the sandy shore, kneeling next to her.

Jeremy. His curly brown hair was slicked to his head, and his eyes betrayed how close she'd come to drowning. His breath came fast, tumbling out with his words as he ran his hands down her arms. "Are you okay?"

She leaned over and coughed up lake water from her lungs.

Sirens in the distance and more voices. The sun had nearly deserted them, and long shadows pressed into the beach, over the gurgling, hungry water.

Jeremy sat behind her, wrapped two arms around her, and pulled her tight to his chest. His heartbeat thundered, banging inside him, a bullet against her back, and he shook. He had his face buried in her neck. "What if I hadn't made it?"

She hooked her hands over his arms, let him pull her tighter. Floodlights scraped the shore as red lights splashed against the sky. Then came an outline in the darkness, and Boone burst across the grassy park.

"PJ!"

Jeremy raised one hand. "Here. We're here. She's okay—right? You *are* okay?"

Boone didn't stop at the shore, came right to her, dropping to his knees before her. "Are you kidding me? I thought I was going to find you trapped in your car, dead." He sank back on his haunches and scraped a hand over his face, bracing himself with the other on the sand. "You are going to kill me one of these days. I swear it."

"Or get herself killed," Jeremy said, his voice still wrecked. "Please tell me you're on this guy's tail. I saw his car—late model white Pontiac GT convertible. I didn't get the plates."

"How'd you get here so fast?" Boone seemed to be checking her over.

"Believe me, after the thirty or so messages she left on my phone, and especially the last one, I had to track her down. I heard the accident as I came onto the bridge. I spotted the Bug right before she . . . went over." Jeremy sucked in a watery breath and let her go.

PJ watched as he got up and stalked away from her. He became a silhouette of agony in the darkness as he braced himself against a tree, then bent over the nearby garbage can.

She turned back to Boone, who tore his eyes from Jeremy, shaking his head. "I feel like doing the same thing. Who was it, do you know?"

Her teeth clacked together. "Not a clue. Although I have a sick feeling it has something to do with Max. Have you seen him today?"

"No." Boone took off his jacket, draped it around her shoulders, then turned at the sound of another approaching siren. An ambulance pulled up.

"Really, I'm fine, Boone."

"Good, because after they confirm that, they can shoot me with a couple of sedatives." But for the first time, he gave her a soft smile. Reached out and touched her cheek. "I hate to admit it, but I'm glad Jeremy is in your life."

"PJ!" A dog barked as Max tried to wrestle past a couple police officers.

Boone waved him over and the officers freed him. Max tore down the grass, his flannel shirt flapping, Dog leading the way.

The animal launched into her arms, and she caught him as he slathered her face. "I love you too, Butch."

Dog danced away, past her, unfazed. When Max caught up, he looked from Boone to PJ. "Was that you who went into the water? I was at the house and saw the entire thing through the back windows. I couldn't believe it when I saw your Bug go in. Are you okay?"

Jeremy had returned, treading up silently in the sand behind her. "Were you really at the house?" he asked, his voice calm. Deadly calm.

Max glanced at him. Silence bulged between them until finally Max gave a small shake of his head and crouched before her. "Do you know who did it?"

"Someone who didn't want her sniffing around . . . *someone*," Jeremy said, now kneeling beside PJ. His hand went to the back of her neck, wiping away her sodden hair.

Max ignored him, worry in his eyes. Yes, little Tyler had to be his son.

"I met a guy today who said you needed to watch your back. He knows you."

Max appeared dazed, as if he was clearing water from his brain. "He knows me?"

"At least, he said he recognized the picture we put in the paper." She couldn't help a slight wince at that. "That's a good thing, right?"

"Not if they're trying to kill you," Jeremy said with an edge to his tone.

PJ put a hand on Jeremy's arm. "That might not have been the smartest move, because apparently, someone else—someone you might have needed to hide from—might have also recognized you."

"Someone I needed to hide from?"

"You may have been mixed up in something overseas." She couldn't look at Jeremy for the next part. "Apparently you were some sort of special ops soldier and you were in Sierra Leone, helping de-mine the country. But you were wounded, a head injury of some sort."

"I have scars." His hand went to his head. "I wondered what happened. I thought maybe it was related to that night."

"No, Windchill—"

"Windchill?" Max asked.

"My jumpmaster."

Boone didn't move. "Did you say *jumpmaster*?"

"Oh yeah. Probably I shouldn't tell you that I went sky-diving today."

"Yes, I'm going to be ill." Boone shot another look at Jeremy.

Jeremy's mouth tightened into a granite line.

"Hey—it could be worse. I didn't go and talk to Ratchet on my own."

"I'm not even going to ask."

"Windchill said you were shipped stateside, but when you got here, your wife was murdered, and your son—"

"So he is mine?" Max sat back with a thump on the sand, pressing a hand to his chest. He looked like he might be the one who needed the oxygen.

PJ glanced at Jeremy, who closed his eyes, almost in a wince. She turned to face Max. "He has your dimples."

"Okay, yeah, he's probably yours," Jeremy said. "Although right now, you're the best guess to be the murderer, so I wouldn't go knocking on his door just yet."

"I told you, I'm willing to pay for my crimes," Max said, his voice solemn. "I'm just hoping that . . . I'm not that guy."

Oh, see, this was why she needed to prove it wasn't him—that look of sheer torture on his face, in his eyes. "You're *not* that guy, Max. I think you may have had information about some diamond heist in Sierra Leone, where you were injured. And apparently you already had a paranoia meter—so much so that your wife didn't even tell her mother you were home. But there might have been someone who knew—a guy named Ratchet came looking for you. You and he were POWs together in Iraq a few years back." She pointed to his arm. "Ratchet might have been the guy the landlady saw, the one with your tattoo."

Silence. The murmur of spectators and car engines entwined with the lake still raking the shore, the wind shivering the trees.

"He has my tattoo?"

"He was a POW in Iraq. So he might be the guy Jinx

was talking about. The bad news is that Ratchet is still out there, and Windchill thinks that the picture in the newspaper may have resurrected ghosts from your past."

"Why would Ratchet want to kill him?" Jeremy asked, his hand still on her neck, warm on her skin.

"Windchill seems to think that Owen was involved in diamond smuggling—maybe even smuggled the diamonds home for Ratchet. I'm wondering if Ratchet showed up later on Owen's doorstep, armed with a little 'Tell me where they are or else,' and Owen and he got into a fight. Maybe Ratchet even killed Bekka to get Owen to talk, except I keep thinking about the fact that Owen was injured. What if Owen didn't have anything to do with the diamonds—what if they sent the package home, not expecting him to recover? He wouldn't even have known what they were talking about. And Windchill did say that he and Ratchet had some bad blood between them. Maybe Ratchet came over to get the package, and Owen surprised him."

Jeremy sucked in a breath, and she heard his words in her brain: *"You have to stop investigating with your hopes and dreams and take a look at the truth."*

But for some reason, her words *felt* like the truth. Max, as Owen, couldn't be a diamond smuggler. "I'm wondering if Ratchet thought Owen might be dead—or close to it—when he dumped him into the bay. And then there's always arson as a cover-up for murder evidence."

"Do you think this Ratchet guy might have been at the wheel tonight?" Boone asked.

"Could be, although I don't know how he found me. Unless he was watching Windchill."

"This just gets worse," Max said, shaking his head. "Why did I ever decide to track down my past?"

Boone shifted in the sand, watching the chaos on the bridge.

"Because . . . it matters." Jeremy glanced away, the edges of his mouth tight as if his words had leaked out beyond his control. "Because knowing who you are gives every choice you make relevance." He stared at PJ, tenderness in his eyes. "Because if you know what you've been through— the things you've done, both good and bad—the choices you make today have merit. Resonance." He touched her face, ran a thumb down her cheek. "Not knowing your past steals meaning from your future."

Then he nodded as if in answer to some lingering question. "A fresh start has no meaning unless you understand what you left behind."

The paramedics hit the beach, one carrying his medical kit, the other with a blanket.

"I'm fine," PJ said, raising a hand toward them.

"Humor us," Boone said, towering over her, his arms akimbo.

An hour later, she sat wrapped in a blanket in the back of the ambulance. Other than a bruise on her sternum where the seat belt garroted her and the raw burn of her lungs from the icy water, she'd suffered no lasting effects. They'd given her a tetanus shot and some antibiotics all the same. She'd refused an overnight stay at the hospital.

"Let's go home." Jeremy stood just outside the ring of light slanting from the open doors of the ambulance. He'd turned eerily quiet as the paramedics took her vitals, checked her for bleeding.

Boone harassed the crime scene team, having blocked off the bridge, their spotlights glaring on the jagged metal.

The wind cut through her sodden clothes as she returned the blanket and slid out of the ambulance.

Boone crossed the grassy park toward them. "Listen, I think she needs to sleep at her sister's tonight. I've already called. Connie is waiting for her."

PJ opened her mouth to protest but let it die before it could gather speed. Yes, a night at Connie's might help her sleep.

Jeremy turned to him. "I hate to ask, but it's too cold to ride home on the bike."

"I know. I'll drive it to Connie's place. I have a guy waiting to take you to Connie's." Boone gestured to a cop leaning against his rig in the lot.

"You'll stop by the house?" Jeremy asked.

Boone nodded.

PJ sensed more in that question than she could currently sort through.

"Where'd Max run off to?" PJ asked as Jeremy led her to the parking lot.

"He's cleaning up the house and moving on," Jeremy said quietly.

"But I want to ask him more about Ratchet, see if we get any electrical jolts."

"Stop!" Jeremy held up his hand. It shook, and the emotion in his eyes rattled clear through her. "Just stop, already." He took off his jacket and curled it around her, holding on to the lapels. "I should have driven the bus. . . ."

"Jeremy." She caught his wrists. "Jeremy, I'm *okay*."

"You might not have been!" He closed his eyes, notching his voice down. "Someone tried to kill you and nearly succeeded."

"But they didn't."

But her words were lost on him and he turned away.

She put a hand to his back, felt his muscle pulse. "I'm sorry we fought," she mumbled.

"What if I had lost you?" He turned, his eyes red as he stared at her as if not seeing her.

She had no words.

"The worst part about all this is that I never thought I'd feel this way about someone again. It's like I'm watching it happen all over, with the nightmare getting closer and closer, and I can't do anything to stop it."

Then, before she knew what to say, he stepped close, slid his hand around her waist, and kissed her. He tasted of the lake, and it seemed her entire body remembered his lips on hers, breathing life into her as they'd risen to the surface. Every part of her tingled, and somehow, she tasted salt.

Could it be her own tears? Because even as he held her, she knew the truth. Trouble. It didn't matter who did the name-calling—Boone or Jeremy or even herself. Or even the voice she'd heard as she'd flown through the sky. She couldn't hide from the truth. Not when it was written in every dripping pore of her body. She couldn't escape it. And just like Jeremy couldn't bring her into his past, she couldn't keep him away from hers.

She put her hands on his chest and pushed. He broke away and buried his face in the crook of her neck. His lips moved as if he were breathing her in. His soggy shirt made her shiver, but he held her so tight, she couldn't quite let him go.

Tomorrow. She swallowed and her throat burned. She'd let him go tomorrow. Because together, they were headed for broken hearts and disaster.

Finally he pressed his forehead to hers. "Did you say you went skydiving today?"

She wiped her tears with a quick swipe of her hand, fighting for a smile. "I think I'll wait to answer that until I have a pizza and dry clothes."

* * *

She'd seen the Pontiac before. PJ stared at the ceiling of her old bedroom in Connie's house, tracing the moonbeams slatted on the white chenille bedspread, finally able to feel her toes, and trying to erase the feel of Jeremy's hands on her, holding her. She kept replaying the accident—she refused to call it attempted murder, thank you—through her mind, second by terrifying millisecond.

Yes, she'd seen that car before. But where? The image burned into her brain, knotted her into the covers.

Okay, she should surrender to the inevitable, get out

of bed, pad downstairs to where Jeremy slept in the guest bedroom/office—thanks to Connie's generosity and keen lawyerly recognition of a man on the edge—and wake him. Together they could log on to her computer, maybe access the DMV database . . .

Except that would only drag him deeper into her world.

Her tangled, suffocating, near-death-experience world. No, she'd stirred the hornet's nest. She'd have to extricate him before anyone else got hurt.

She flattened the covers on either side of herself and stared at the ceiling. The front headlights of the GT bored into her like eyes, the malevolent grin of the grille—

That was about enough of that. She skimmed the covers off and flicked on the side lamp. Light puddled over her. They'd stopped by the mushroom house on their way to Connie's—not pausing to survey the wreckage of her walls—and picked up her belongings, as well as Joy's diary. It lay on top of her duffel, and she swiped it up, nesting it into the covers as she flipped it open.

Clearly, she and Prudence Joy had more in common than she wanted to admit in the wee, grainy hours.

September 1960

A new life. That's what Hugh
promised me, and I believed him.
I believed his smile and the way he
held me, the way he told me that
he would never leave me. But now

what? I suppose we'll be okay; he says it and I hold on to it. But while the rest of my friends were boating and making their college plans, I stood out in the hot North Carolina sun, my body expanding, not even able to wear the thin ring he gave me, and watched Hugh in his brilliant new uniform. He is brave and strong, and the baby moves inside me, and all I can think is . . . yes, a new life. God, I pray it's true.

April 1961

Sunny is beautiful. She has her father's green eyes, and they light up when he comes into the room after his long days, and sometimes nights, of training. The Army is more difficult than he anticipated. Hugh is changing. I expected his joy, and instead, he treats me with a sort of fear. He asked me to write home to my mother, to tell her where we are, but I can't.

He doesn't know that my mother already found me. Sent me a telegram, telling me that unless I return home, there is no forgiveness waiting in Kellogg. I threw it away. I have Sunny. And Hugh.

March 1962

I think I will die if I don't hear from Hugh. Nine months is too long to wait for a letter, a note, a call. And worse, they won't tell me where they sent him. I know he's not safe, and at night, the fear chills me. Sunny had her first birthday, her first tooth, calls me Mama. He is missing his child's life, and the ache burns in me with every silent day. My mother wrote again. I have her letter in my bureau next to the bed.

February 1963

It's been three weeks. Three weeks since the knock on the door. MIA.

*I know he isn't dead—I would
feel it.
    Come home to us, Hugh.*

A thump on the stairs. PJ stilled, her pulse ratcheting high.

Another thump and squeak.

PJ put her thumb in the diary, then pushed the covers back and stepped lightly on the floor.

She eased the door open. The moon turned the hall milky from the tiny window over the stairs. Tiptoeing out, she closed the door behind her and crept down the stairs.

Connie stood bathed in the cold light of the open refrigerator. PJ watched her sister take out the orange juice, pour herself a glass, and then sit down at the table with a magazine.

"What are you reading?" PJ whispered.

Connie jerked, spilling her orange juice down the front of her. "What are you doing? Are you stalking me? Good grief." She swiped up a couple napkins and dabbed the front of her pink silk bathrobe. "Now I'm all sticky."

"Sorry. I didn't want to wake Jeremy." She pointed to the closed door of the office.

"If he's even sleeping. From the look on his face when you went upstairs to bed, I half expected him to be sitting on the bottom step or pacing the hallway."

"Maybe he's taking a break."

"Poor guy. It's not easy to be in love with PJ Sugar." Connie winked at her.

PJ slid into a chair at the table. "He's not in love with me. I'm more like his worst nightmare."

"I disagree. He never took his eyes off you all night." She sighed. "Boone never looked at you like that."

"What do you mean?"

"Oh, Boone always had a half smirk on his face—well, when he didn't look like he wanted to strangle you. There was a sort of amusement there. But Jeremy—he looks completely undone when he sees you. As if you scare him to death, but with a sort of confusing admiration. Like the way he stood at the bottom of the stairs and just watched the empty space after you left as if he might be waiting for you to materialize."

"I do scare him to death. Especially after tonight. "

"You scare all of us. Hence, why I'm up in the middle of the night—"

"Reading a baby magazine?" PJ flipped the pages to the front cover. "*Baby Today*?"

"Hey, it's the only time I get to read the contraband."

"Contraband?"

"It is according to Vera and her silly superstitions. I'm not allowed to buy myself anything for the baby until after it's born. The entire layette—we'll have to stop off at Babies and Baubles on the way home from the hospital."

"Why?"

"She says we don't want to tempt fate."

"That's completely morbid." PJ reached over and took a sip of Connie's juice.

"Well, not if you think about their sketchy medical care

over there. Anything they can do to give their baby a fighting chance for survival. I can't cut my hair, sit in a draft, eat spicy foods . . ." She lowered her face into the crease of her magazine. "I'm losing my mind."

PJ rubbed her sister's neck. "It'll be worth it. At least you don't live with our mother."

Connie turned her cheek on the magazine. "Who called, by the way, and said she'd be back tomorrow night. She said she has a surprise for us."

"Shirts that say, 'My mother went on an awesome cruise without telling me and all I got was this lousy T-shirt'?"

Connie grinned. Sat up, began paging through the magazine. "So what are *you* reading?" She gestured to the book in PJ's hand.

"The journal of Prudence Joy Barton."

"Oh, let me at it. That sounds much better than *Baby Today*."

PJ handed it over. "It is. Joy ran away with Hugh because she was pregnant. He joined the Army—I think he must have been in special forces or something, because they didn't tell her where he went, although I have a feeling it might have been Vietnam."

Connie paged through the journal. "I read an article about how there were Green Berets training the South Vietnamese long before Kennedy sent troops in. There were MIAs and POWs before we even admitted to being there. "

"I think maybe Hugh turned out to be one of them. He went MIA in 1963."

"So what happened? Did Hugh die?"

"Probably. I haven't gotten that far."

"That's so sad."

"Yeah. That could be why she came home and married Clayton Barton. She needed a father for her child."

Connie read an entry. "Do you think she still carried a torch for Hugh? Maybe Clayton got jealous."

"Of a dead man?"

"Oh, believe me, dead men have more power than you think. Just ask Sergei. He could look at Davy and see Burke if he chose to. But he doesn't—he sees a little boy that belongs to me. He sees the boy that's becoming his son."

"So your previous marriage never bothered him?"

"There were questions. But we decided we could have something much better. Knowing the betrayal I'd had before made him want to heal that for me. He wanted me to see that this time, it could be different. He proves that to me every day." She ran a hand over her tiny belly. "But some people just can't figure that out."

PJ nodded. "Maybe Clayton couldn't move on."

"Or Joy couldn't. Not everyone is able to recover from their first love."

PJ sank her chin into her hands on the table. "Jeremy thinks I can't move on either. He believes Boone and I are over but I can't let go of the past. He thinks I'm holding on to the name Trouble because it makes me feel safe. That if I'm trouble, then I can't expect anything more from myself."

"Hmm, sounds like something someone *wise* might say to you."

"I remember, Connie; you get full credit."

"Well, your Jeremy is a good PI to figure it out too."

"It's a good thing one of us is . . . because I think all my supersleuthing just might get Max killed. If someone from his past tried to kill me tonight, then he *is* in danger. And I caused it. What Jeremy doesn't get is, any way you look at it, I *am* trouble. It's not a brand; it's a fact. And one of these days, someone is going to get hurt."

Connie took a long breath. "You're not trouble. But I do live in fear. I wish you'd drop this."

"I have to finish it. Find out if someone is after Max, and stop them."

"I think you should leave that to Boone."

"No—I've dragged him and Jeremy and even you and your family too far into my world. I gotta fix this."

"You're starting to scare me. I'm waiting for an 'and then what?'"

PJ sighed. Closed her eyes. And then maybe it was time to leave town and take trouble with her. Away from the people she loved. She lifted a shoulder. "It would be better for Jeremy if I wasn't here. All I do is remind him of his greatest fears—seeing someone he loves get hurt, even killed."

Connie wrapped her hand over PJ's arm. "What does Jeremy have to say about that?"

PJ drummed her fingers on the counter. Behind her, she heard a creak, the groan of the wood floor under shifting weight.

Jeremy stood in the foyer, wearing a pair of Sergei's

running pants and a gray T-shirt. "I just wanted to make sure you were okay. . . ."

Perfect. "Jeremy—"

He held up a hand. "Listen, I didn't mean to eavesdrop. I'll see you in the morning."

He moved into the office, closing the door softly behind him.

Chapter SEVENTEEN

"What do you think you're doing?"

PJ had been asking herself that for the better part of ten years. Usually at the beginning of every crazy job she'd landed, from the time she spent the summer scrubbing pots in a Russian-language immersion camp, to her gig as a large-animal feeder at the San Diego Zoo, to her longest job—a two-year stint learning how to jump out of flaming buildings. She'd been a bicycle delivery girl—well, a delivery girl of all sorts, really: pizza, newspapers, flowers—and a waitress, and of course, she'd managed a gig at a gym, handing out keys.

Which came in handy when faking a lost health club pass.

"What does it look like I'm doing?" PJ yanked her wrist from Jeremy's grip as he bent down by the pool, after grabbing her between laps. "Swimming. I should ask the same thing about you. What have you been up to? I woke up at Connie's and you'd split. Not even a note."

"I had things to do, Princess." He gave her a splash. Smiled as if he hadn't been standing in the hallway last night, overhearing her comment about their doomed future. And how she planned on doing her own split, right out of his life.

"Since when do you swim laps?" He took off his sunglasses, and already a line of sweat trickled down his face from the heat of the indoor pool. Leaves tapped against the bank of windows behind him, trying to get their attention.

PJ shot a look across the pool, through the wall of glass, to the workout room, where Randy Simonson, aka Ratchet, hoisted free weights onto his shoulders, now doing squats. "Since the guy I've been tailing all day works out at the weight room and pool. Good thing I still had some clothes in the Vic or I would have had to swim naked."

"I don't want to speculate on whether you would have gone that far." Jeremy glanced at the weight lifter. Ratchet packed the muscle into a sculpted package, all curves and sinew.

"Does he have a tattoo?"

"Yep. Just like Max's. I think this guy might be the Lyle Fisher we're looking for."

"Wait a second—I thought Max was Lyle. At least Bekka's mother says so."

"No, Max is Owen . . . or . . ." She shook her head. "Okay, yes, I don't know who Max is. But put a baseball cap over his red hair and Ratchet certainly could have been the one outside arguing with Bekka before she died."

"Then who rented the house in Hopkins and threw Max into the lake?"

"Ratchet—as Lyle Fisher."

"Then who's the Lyle in the picture? *That* Lyle looks just like Max. Are there two Lyle Fishers?"

"Okay!" She held up her hand. "Point taken. We're just missing something."

"Yeah, like someone with a memory of who he is. I hate this case." He reached out a hand and she took it, letting him haul her from the water. "When I got your message to meet me here, I have to admit, I thought maybe you'd decided to live on the edge, attend an aerobics class. I couldn't believe it when I saw you in here doing laps. Have you been following this guy all day?"

She walked over to her towel and began drying herself off. "Started at his garage, watched him work on high-end imports, then over to his apartment in St. Louis Park, then here. I wanted to see if he had that tattoo and maybe get close enough to ask him a few questions. Pry his past from him."

"I don't even want to know how you planned to do that."

PJ gave him a smile, all teeth. His mouth tightened to a disapproving scowl.

"I'm just trying to get some answers and do my job."

"And what *job* is that?" Jeremy said, purposely running his gaze down her body and her one-piece swimsuit.

She hooked her finger under his jaw to raise his gaze back to her eyes. "The one that will prove that Max is innocent and figure out who tried to kill me last night. And the person who tried to kill Max and possibly killed Bekka. The someone who is still after Max, I think."

"I know. I heard you last night."

She didn't want to ask what else he'd heard. "So have you been out saving the world? You don't *look* like you've been in a brawl." She gave him a mock pout. "What? No knock-down-drag-outs for breakfast? You must be heartbroken."

"I could work one in now if you're interested." He gave her a smirk that suggested he'd like nothing better at the moment.

"Hah."

"I'm a little surprised to see you in a pool today, after what happened yesterday." He gentled his voice. "You okay?"

PJ pressed the towel to her face. Yeah, diving into that water had nearly sucked away her breath, made her launch to the surface with a scream.

But it also made her feel . . . less like a victim. "I've decided that swimming is a lot like skydiving."

Jeremy sat on the diving board, twirling his glasses between his fingers. "How's that?"

"The weightlessness. And diving in is a lot like throwing yourself from an airplane. Breathtaking."

Wow, he had beautiful eyes, and they seemed to twinkle now. "Yeah. I guess it is. Breathtaking."

The way he said it made her wonder if he wasn't exactly talking about skydiving or swimming. But she'd just have to learn to be immune to that devastating smile, the way he looked at her as if she might be a mystery he'd like to solve. They had too many empty, black holes between them and a happy ending. Holes in his life that he didn't want her to see, holes in hers that he could too easily trip in and get hurt.

She wouldn't look at his strong hands or remember the way he'd held her last night. Or pay attention to the way that now, even from three feet away, she could smell his skin, his after-workout soap.

Nope, not a good idea.

"You left Google open on the computer. I saw that you did a little research on Sierra Leone."

Thank you, Jeremy, for always focusing on the job.

"Oh. Yeah, Sierra Leone happens to be a diamond smuggler's paradise. They have illegal mines, and they're smuggling diamonds over the border. And it's not just Sierra Leone, but Angola and Zambia and Zimbabwe. I don't know, but it's possible that Max knew the smuggler."

"Or was mixed up in, maybe even the leader of, said smuggling operation, one that Ratchet was also involved in—exactly what Windchill said."

PJ said nothing.

"You know it could be true, PJ. Not everyone is who they seem. You have to stop leading with your instincts."

She ran the towel around her waist and hooked it like a wrap skirt.

"Listen to logic, PJ. Why would Ratchet come after him if he wasn't involved? My bet is that he had the diamonds, and Ratchet wanted them. Still wants them."

"Okay, then how did Max get the diamonds back into the

country? He was wounded, right? I still say he didn't know. Ratchet surprised him."

Jeremy held up his hands. "I know; I know. He's innocent . . . you feel it."

"Listen—"

"Jump ahead with me for a second. Regardless of who is in charge, how would the smuggler get the diamonds home?"

Beyond the glass, Ratchet finished his squats, wiped his face with a towel, then flung it over his shoulder.

"I don't know. But you'd better head into the showers and keep an eye on him," PJ said, slipping on her flip-flops.

Jeremy glanced over his shoulder. "*Now* you need me?"

She couldn't help herself. "I always need you."

His face lost its smile and left only an enigmatic look before he headed off to the locker room.

PJ changed quickly, running her hair under the dryer, and shoved her wet towel and suit into a duffel bag. How *would* Max/Owen/Lyle/Ratchet get diamonds home?

And could Max really be a smuggler?

Jeremy leaned against the edge of a giant planter in the brick lobby of the club, arms and ankles crossed. He picked up her stride. "He's showering."

"That's all I need to know."

Jeremy grinned. "I have to admit, I wondered how you would get around today. Since your wheels are at the bottom of Maximilian Bay."

"I borrowed the Vic from Boris."

"A large vessel which may have come in handy yesterday."

Relief flushed through her at his easy humor, the way

he obviously tried to push the horror out of his mind. See? Maybe they'd both survive without any long-term injuries.

"Your place or mine?" Jeremy said, gesturing to the red minibus parked at the other edge of the lot.

"Yours. Just because I miss my Bug."

He put on his sunglasses. "It's a crying shame how you go through cars, Your Highness." He unlocked her door, and wasn't it sweet the way he held her elbow, helping her into the creamy white vinyl seat? "Have you eaten today?"

"Are you thinking of cooking up a pizza in your camper oven?"

"I keep a ready supply just in case you need immediate pizza therapy."

Oh, she'd miss his teasing. Because in the back of her mind, she'd already packed the Vic. Already laid out her journey to the next stop. This time she'd head east, to Chicago. Maybe find another PI. An overweight gumshoe without dark, steamy eyes and the ability to make her see more of herself than was good for her.

Yes, she'd be a PI. Because, really, why waste all these superb troublemaking skills?

"Here he comes."

"He's not driving a white Pontiac," Jeremy said as Ratchet walked down the sidewalk, wearing a baseball hat and a black mechanic's jacket, a duffel bag over his shoulder. He passed a Silverado pickup and went straight for the older model black-and-white restored job in the corner of the lot.

"Chevy El Camino. I should have guessed."

"It's a pretty ride, I have to agree," PJ said. It sort of reminded her of Boone and his '67 Mustang. And the hours he spent under the hood. Strange, but the memory didn't pinch quite so much.

Ratchet opened the back door and tossed his duffel inside. Then shut it and got in the driver's seat.

"I'm hoping he goes to a sports bar or something. I could use a basket of chili fries."

"PJ, I think maybe I should take it from—"

The explosion rocked the bus. PJ held her head as Jeremy leaped toward her, knocking her down into the seat. Another rolling explosion. He tightened his hold on her, pulling her head to his chest. He had one hand braced over her, on the door, the other around her back, tucking her into himself.

She stayed in that cocoon, listening to metal fly off the El Camino, slam into nearby cars.

And, okay, she dug her fingers into his shirt. Reflex, that's all.

When Jeremy lifted his head, he scoured her face with his eyes. "You okay?"

She nodded. Looked past him, shaking. "Ratchet."

Jeremy eased away from her, his hand tight on hers as he stared at the flaming wreckage of Ratchet and his car and the three cars around it.

He reached for the door handle.

"What are you doing?"

"Maybe he's—"

Another explosion. PJ ducked, Jeremy's body shielding hers.

Ratchet's car flipped, landing upside down.

Jeremy's face tightened, his jaw stiff as he pulled out his cell phone.

He didn't let go of her hand while he called 911.

The flames curled around the top of the car, a plume of black, toxic smoke billowing into the sky. Crazy tears escaped her eyes. "He seemed like an okay guy. Worked on cars all day. Laughed with the other guys working out in the gym. Not like a guy who would kill people, despite what Windchill said."

Jeremy turned to her, his eyes narrowing for a second. "Did you see Max today?"

"What? No. Did you?"

Jeremy shook his head. "But if anyone would know how to plant a car bomb in a jiffy, it would be an ex–special operations soldier."

PJ opened her mouth. Closed it. Then, "Max doesn't even remember his own name! How on earth could he remember how to do that?"

Although picking a lock had come right back to him, almost on reflex, hadn't it? And he said he somehow knew Arabic. She pushed away the thought.

Jeremy had his eyes on her. "Maybe Max isn't exactly what he seems. What if he's been using you this entire time to flush out Ratchet and throw suspicion off himself?"

"Then he's doing a terrible job, because guess what—it's not working!" The screaming probably didn't help, but she added an emphatic get-your-hands-off-me gesture as she tore her hand from his grip.

Jeremy held his hands up in surrender, but he wore nothing less than a lethal expression. "Okay, we're going to solve this once and for all." He climbed into the driver's seat and fired up the bus.

"Let me out!"

"Not on your life—what if *your* car is rigged?"

"Oh, sure, Max is going to take out the one person who believes in him? who is on his side?" She reached for the handle. "No wonder I can't get trouble out of my head—you see it even when it's not there!"

Jeremy put a hand on her arm. "Stop. Please."

It was the *please* that stilled her.

"I admit that perhaps I'm reading into things here, but there is a car *on fire* on the other side of the lot, with a dead man in it. A man connected to Max. Like you are connected to Max. And you nearly *died* last night. Am I getting through?"

As if directed by his words, PJ looked at the burning car. Sirens whined in the distance. For a second, she tasted the freezing water, pulling her under, stealing her breath, gulp by burning gulp.

"Maybe Max isn't the connection. Maybe it's me. Maybe *I'm* the one who brought this on Max, on Ratchet—"

"What?"

"Maybe it's not even related to Max. What if it's . . . I dunno, Bix?"

Jeremy's mouth opened a moment before he repeated her name.

"Yes—she knows I'm after her, knows that I'm going to bring her in."

"Bix is trying to kill you?" The way he said it, it did sound ridiculous. But he didn't appear to be humored.

"Okay, you're right. That's silly." She rubbed her arms. "Let's go over to Ratchet's place before the cops can figure it out, see if we can track down a connection to him and Max and maybe someone *else* who might want both of them— and me—out of the picture."

Jeremy closed his hands over the steering wheel and stared ahead. "Everything inside me says I should drive to Kellogg, call Boone, and have him put you in protective custody."

"I can still get out of the car."

"I can still stop you."

So rarely did he use his SEAL tone, it sent a tremor through her.

He pulled the bus out of the lot as the fire trucks pulled in.

Ratchet lived in a small one-bedroom apartment in St. Louis Park, on the second story. PJ played cable girl until someone buzzed her in.

Jeremy picked the lock, and before slipping into the apart-ment, he handed her a pair of purple rubber gloves.

"We're getting very CSI."

"The guy is toast. The cops won't take long getting over here."

PJ put on her gloves.

They could conduct surgery inside his small apartment. A lemony disinfectant odor permeated the clean counters, the round pine table, the dustless end table that flanked a crisp black sofa. It all pointed toward a wall-size flat screen with a slew of electronics stacked beneath.

"It looks like a safe house. Not a picture on the wall," PJ said.

"You watch too much television. A safe house would never have a sliding-glass door this size," Jeremy said, pulling the drapes and hitting the lights.

"He's gotta have something." PJ went into the bedroom, staring for a moment at the frameless double bed, the second-hand dresser drawers. "Doesn't the Army pay people?"

"Special forces get paid by rank, just like everyone else. People don't go into it for the cash."

Jeremy pushed past her, opened a dresser drawer, another. "He still folds his underwear; Army training runs deep."

PJ moved over to the night table. A Robert Ludlum book lay dog-eared and worn next to a glass of water. He'd even made his bed.

"This is depressing me. He had no one—no girlfriend pictures, no little black book—"

"Keep looking for the little black book. Nobody is this clean without having something to hide." Jeremy had his hand under the bed, searching.

PJ turned on the bedside light, then followed the cord to the socket, three feet from the table. "Maybe he put it between the box spring and the mattress."

She moved the mattress. Nothing. Except . . . "There's another socket here, hidden behind the bed."

"So?"

"Why would he plug his lamp into that one if this one is closer?"

Jeremy came over, pushed the mattress away. "Because it's not real." He knelt on the bed, pulled out his knife, and screwed the cover off the outlet.

And voilà, a compartment behind it revealed Ratchet's equivalent of a little black book—a notebook, passports, and an envelope rubber-banded together.

"Good job, PI," Jeremy said, flashing her a look of approval.

"How'd you know he even had a book?"

"It pays to remember names, dates, and phone numbers of the people in your life that share your secrets."

Okay, she sorta wanted a look at *his* little black book. In the hope that her name might be in it. In ink.

He replaced the outlet cover and pushed the mattress against the wall. "Let's get out of here."

They closed the door behind them, left the apartment, and were in the bus by the time a cruiser pulled into the lot.

"I feel like I did in high school, hiding from the cops in the back of the parking lot."

"I don't want to know what you were doing."

A blush burned PJ's cheeks. "What's in the book?"

"Names, dates, phone numbers, e-mail addresses." He flipped through the passports. "He had a few different identities."

She watched Jeremy process the information as though none of it came as a surprise. "How many identities did you have?"

He looked at her. Considered her for a moment. "Four."

Oh.

"At least, the ones that I maintained. I had others, but only short-term."

"How many languages do you speak?"

"Just three, fluently."

Oh. Just three. *Fluently.*

He gave her a little smile, then handed her the envelope. "See if you get any hits off that."

Receipts, a boarding pass. A newspaper article. She unfolded it—a cutout from the *Star Tribune. Two Minnesotans Survive POW Camp.* And next to the story, a picture of Ratchet and a man named . . . Lyle Fisher.

A man who looked painfully like Max Smith, who also seemed to be Owen McMann.

PJ handed Jeremy the article. "I'm so confused."

"Me too."

She put the newspaper clipping back in the envelope, then reached for the stack of passports. Ratchet's face on an American passport, an Israeli passport, a French passport, and—

She put her hand on Jeremy's arm. "Look at this." She held out the British passport. Pointed at the name. "Lyle Fisher."

"Lyle Fisher. With Ratchet's face."

"If Ratchet is Lyle, then why did Bekka's mother say that Max was Lyle?"

Jeremy was shaking his head, a wince forming on his face. "Oh . . . I can't believe I didn't see this. When I was a . . . working in my former profession, a bunch of us used a similar cover when we were on leave. It sort of confused our trail and kept anyone who was following us off track. If Max was involved in anything black-ops related, he would have had numerous aliases. He may have used one for this newspaper report . . . and even to come home, under the radar, to see his baby son and his wife."

"Then why tell Bekka's mother—"

"Maybe they were trying to protect her." Jeremy closed the passport. "What if Lyle Fisher was a . . . community alias? We sometimes did that—traded names so we were harder to track. So people who might want to hurt our families couldn't find them."

"So . . . Owen was Lyle. And Ratchet was Lyle," PJ said slowly. "The Lyle Fisher who took Bekka to Valleyfair— that was Owen. And the Lyle Fisher who rented the house in Hopkins and threw Max from the bridge . . . was Ratchet?"

"And the Lyle Fisher who just blew Ratchet to tiny bits," Jeremy said, "is back to Owen. Aka Max Smith."

"Wait—we don't really know that. There could be more Lyle Fishers out there."

Jeremy closed his eyes and ran his finger and thumb into them. "PJ, no one else knew that we'd found Ratchet. It makes perfect sense. No wonder Max took off last night— he knows we're onto him. I think Ratchet did come over that night Max went into the lake. He was met by Max, who wasn't interested in sharing his loot. They fought— maybe Bekka got in the middle and was killed, and maybe Max tried to get away, and Ratchet took off after him.

Who knows—maybe there's a collection of cars under the Maximilian bridge. Max washed up on the beach and cooked up this amnesia story as a way to lie low until he could track Ratchet down. Through us. He may have been playing us all along, hoping we could find him."

"You're crazy! Max had no idea who Ratchet was. And you remember his reaction when we told him he had a son."

"So maybe he *did* have memory loss. But his memory has certainly kicked in now."

"Are you saying Max is a diamond smuggler?"

"Maybe, yes."

"Then where are the diamonds?"

"I don't know—at the bottom of the lake? Maybe Max has been sitting on them until he could find Ratchet and kill him. It doesn't matter—Max is a killer. I want you to head back to Connie's house. I'm going to call Boone and ask him to—"

"Babysit?"

"Sugar-sit." Jeremy was packing up the passports, bunching them together, and securing them with the rubber band.

"Not on your life! You're wrong about Max. He's in danger—"

"PJ! He. *Is*. The. Danger." Jeremy said the words slowly, every one enunciated as if she had difficulty comprehending. She could actually feel him receding into the black hole of himself. But she couldn't stop herself from going after him, yanking him back into the light.

"Don't do this, Jer. Max is *not* the criminal here. He's innocent, and I know it."

"Then you are wrong." He didn't shout it, didn't even raise his voice. No, he was so lethally quiet that his tone slipped right under her skin and turned her cold. "Buckle up."

She stared at him, at the gulf widening between them. "You don't get it, do you? It's not even your decision. It's *my* case—"

"You work for me."

She shut her mouth and shook her head. "And that's the end of the sentence, isn't it? Once Jeremy Kane makes up his mind, then it doesn't matter what the truth is."

"The truth is, you're wrong." He reached over to snap her buckle. She held up her hands, letting him.

"If you want us to be partners—or even more—you're going to have to trust me a little. I'm not just a trouble-maker. I actually can solve crimes."

"Of course you can. You're the one who figured this out." Except his tone and the way he was peeling out of the lot didn't match his words. "But this is where you get off."

"That's right—I figured out that he's *innocent*."

He turned to her. "Guess what? I actually have my PI license. Because I'm actually a PI."

"And I'm what?"

"Right now? Overzealous."

"Overzealous? Was I overzealous when I ferreted out an assassin? How about when I tracked down Dally's stalker?"

"You were lucky."

She turned away. Lucky. Probably he was right about

that. But he used to say she had great instincts. "Please, Jeremy, let me go with you."

"No."

Just *no*. She wanted to swear or maybe hit him. Instead she fisted her hands in her lap, looked at them. "Because I might get in the way?"

"Yes!" He slammed his hand on the wheel. "Listen—what is so wrong with my trying to protect you?" He shook his head. "Sheesh. Now I know why you drove Boone crazy."

Her eyes widened. She opened her mouth, but no words emerged.

Oh. *Oh*. She turned away, hating the rush of emotion into her eyes.

On the opposite side of the car, Jeremy had gone silent. He took a turn too fast, ground the gears, then finally slammed the stick shift into place. "I didn't mean it that way."

"Yes, you did," she said, her voice sounding too much like it might be on the outside of her body. "I figured you out, by the way. You like being the dark hero. You like fading into the night. You're this highly trained warrior who's been wounded unthinkably, and you go after all those guys that are the prototype of the guy who killed your fiancée. I understand that. I know it kills you that you weren't there to protect her. I know you can't help your feelings of panic. But here's a news flash: *I'm not her.*"

"I know that." He didn't look at her as the bus rumbled down the road. He obviously wasn't taking her back to the health club where her Vic waited.

"No, you don't. You don't because you're still trying to

fix the past. But you can't, Jeremy. You have to stop believing everyone is the villain. I understand why it's so hard for you to believe that Max might be innocent—you don't *want* him to be innocent."

"That's not true—"

"It is! You don't like Max because . . . it's simply not fair. He doesn't have to live with the nightmares because he doesn't remember them! And like you said, he should have to pay for his crimes. Just like you do, every day."

She let the tear trail down her check; she didn't care anymore. "You say you want a fresh start, but frankly, I don't think you do. The past gives you an out. Makes you feel powerful. Like there's a reason and a place to put your anger. But you'll never be truly free until you let it go. Forgive yourself. Forgive *her*, for dying. Forgive the world for making you hurt."

She put a hand on his arm. "Forgive God."

He stared at her, a warning look in his dark eyes.

But she couldn't stop. "Jeremy, you can't change the past. And you can't control the future. So you're just going to have to live in the middle like everyone else."

"What does that mean?"

She closed her eyes. "It boils down to this: do you want me to be your partner or not?"

He said nothing, his jaw so tight that she thought he might break something.

"Jeremy?"

He glanced at her, his eyes hard. "No. I guess not."

Chapter *EIGHTEEN*

No, *I guess not.*

No, I guess *not.*

No, I guess not.

The words reverberated through her even as she piled all her belongings into her duffel bag. *I guess not.*

She'd been an idiot not to see that coming. A PI with a few of her self-touted instincts should have been able to predict that Jeremy had no real room for her in his life.

From the first day she climbed into his beater pizza delivery car, he had kept her a thousand miles from his real self, from his heart. Even the first time he kissed her, he'd done it reluctantly, with a sort of agonized frustration.

Yeah, that boded well for a long-term relationship.

And yet, she'd practically sprinted into his not-so-open arms, trying to pry her way inside.

No, a partner was the last thing Jeremy Kane, enigma, bossy PI, wanted.

"Now I know why you drove Boone crazy."

PJ ran the meat of her hand over her eyes. Maybe she had driven Boone crazy. But he'd driven her crazy right back. He simply couldn't see her the way Jeremy . . . no—wait— the way she *thought* Jeremy saw her.

But apparently, he only saw in her his fears.

"PJ? Are you here?"

Connie's voice lifted from the bottom of the stairs. She heard steps and steeled herself, stuffing the last of her belongings into her duffel.

"What are you doing?" Connie stood in the hallway, a frown on her face. She wore a fuzzy pink bathrobe over a pair of jeans, and her leather slippers. She clutched a book to her chest. "I thought I heard you come in."

"I did—but I'm taking off." PJ tried to keep the words breezy. But they tore through her, and she had to look away, put a hand on her duffel to steady herself. "I have some things to do."

Connie stood silent, watching her until PJ looked up.

Fury, or perhaps disbelief, ringed Connie's green eyes. Her jaw tightened as she shook her head, so very slowly. "I'm not an idiot. You're *leaving.*"

PJ leaned over, smoothing the made bed. "Thank you for letting me stay." She picked up the duffel, but Connie moved to stand in front of her.

"You're leaving?"

PJ bit the inside of her mouth to stop herself from crying.

She had to close her eyes to keep from watching as she tore her life apart, piece by piece. "Yes. I'm leaving. I'm not . . . Things aren't working out here at all."

"What happened?" Connie said in her soft, sister voice, and PJ pursed her lips. She would not cry. She would not—

Shoot. "I made a wreckage of things here, Connie." PJ opened her eyes, hating that she could barely see Connie through the film of tears. "I can't be a PI. I'm a total joke. At least Jeremy thinks so. He's who knows where, tracking down Max, whose hope for a new life is about to be ground into dust. I live in a house that's as big as a football field and is practically caving in on itself—frankly, it's a good metaphor for my entire life. Which is in shambles."

"Your life isn't in shambles."

"It is. My car is at the bottom of Lake Minnetonka—and the only good part about that situation is that I still have the Vic, which I'm moving into tonight."

"You can stay here—"

"*No!* See, that's the thing. Everybody keeps taking care of me, rescuing me from myself. You were right—I do like trouble. Because it's all I expect. Maybe I need to get completely away from the old me to find a new one. Like Max—forget my past, start with a blank slate."

"What happened with Jeremy?" Connie put a hand on her arm and squeezed.

PJ muscled past her. "Jeremy doesn't want me."

"That can't be true." Connie was hot on her trail.

"It is—he told me himself. He doesn't want a partner."

"He doesn't want a partner, or he doesn't want *you*?"

PJ paused. Something about Connie's words . . . "Both?"

Connie shook her head the way she might at Davy when he told a lie. "He wants you, PJ. He's just out of practice trusting someone."

PJ sighed. "It doesn't matter, really. Like I said last night, I'm sort of his worst nightmare." She thumped her bag down the stairs.

Connie followed her out to the front porch. "Where are you going to go?"

"I don't know. East this time, I guess. I was thinking that Chicago has bad guys. Or maybe I'll just keep going. I've always wanted to see North Carolina."

Connie's eyes had already filled, and now her breath caught. "Please, PJ. Don't do this. Don't go. I know it's what's easiest for you—but it's devastating for us. Davy needs you, and I need you—my baby needs you. Even Boone needs you. And most of all, Jeremy needs you too."

"Jeremy is going to have a party when I'm gone."

Connie's eyes flashed. "Yeah, well, you'd like that, wouldn't you?"

PJ snapped her gaze to Connie. "What?"

"Yeah. You'd like that. Because then you'd confirm everything you believe. Jeremy will be happy to be rid of the troublemaker in his life—"

"Hey—"

"You know, the fact is, you *are* a troublemaker."

"What?"

"You stir up a person's hopes, make them love you, and

then, when you think you let someone down, when it gets a little rocky, instead of facing it, you run. You go right back to the life you've always known—living out of your car and suitcase. Completely ignoring the people waving at you from behind, their lives in shambles."

PJ stared at Connie, her flushed face, her red-rimmed eyes, and heard Jeremy. *"Like Peter, running back to fishing instead of facing what he thought was God's rejection. . . . But it doesn't matter what I say, does it? Because if you can't see it, if you can't hear it, if you can't believe it, then you'll always go back to fishing."*

PJ dropped her duffel. She couldn't hear it . . . or could she?

She walked over, sat down on the wicker chair on the porch, and the anger flushed out of her as she stared out at the twilit neighborhood, shaded in jeweled tones of lavender and rose. Across the street, a pool of lamplight spotlighted a stuffed scarecrow on the front porch. A decorative wind sock blew in the breeze.

". . . for you are a chosen people. You are royal priests, a holy nation, God's very own possession. As a result, you can show others the goodness of God, for he called you out of the darkness into his wonderful light."

Maybe it was time for a new name.

Chosen. Royal. A possession of God.

Heiress.

Beloved.

The word thumped inside her. She leaned her head back,

feeling again the rush of wind against her face, losing her breath, then finding it again.

Beloved daughter of God.

Indeed, a . . . princess.

She looked at Connie, who stood in the doorway, backlit by the glow of the house. "It's time to come inside, PJ. Where you belong."

* * *

"Did you unpack?" Connie lay on the sofa with a blanket over her, puffs of Kleenex like snowballs on the green knitted afghan, her eyes red.

"For now. Until I find Jeremy."

"So where is he?"

"Probably trying to find Max. He's not answering his cell phone." PJ entered Connie's now snow- and ice-tight screened porch, pacing to the edge and back. "He probably stopped by the police station to get Boone, where they loaded up their six-guns and got on their white horses and tracked down the current Lyle Fisher to hang from the nearest poplar at first light."

"You're making me seasick, PJ. Sit down. Are you sure you don't want a banana? They're really tasty before bed."

PJ sat in a teakwood chair. "I can't eat."

"Oh, me neither."

PJ looked at the litter of banana peels, half a box of crackers, and a cup of tea. All since dinner—deep-fried chicken à la Vera. "I can see that. What's with the Kleenex?"

"It's this diary. It's so sad. "

"Is that Joy's diary?"

"Yeah. I stayed up too late reading it last night, and now I can't get it out of my head. Thanks a lot." She sighed. "Poor Hugh."

"Poor Hugh?"

"Haven't you read any of this?"

"I got as far as Hugh MIA."

Connie gave her a disgusted look.

"I've been busy!"

Connie put the diary down. "You missed the best part. Hugh didn't die."

Hugh didn't—"What?"

"Two years after he went MIA, he walked out of the jungle, wounded, angry, and in need of help. He went to a vet hospital and then came straight back to Kellogg."

"He came back to Joy."

Connie nodded as she grabbed a Kleenex. "Oh, these hormones. I've just been blubbering all day."

"Why?"

"Because Joy had already come back to Kellogg and married Clayton. His dad ran the Barton Dock Works. They fixed sailboats—remember the place?"

"Yes, I remember. Right by the beach. Big gray building. Didn't they turn it into a restaurant?"

"Yeah. They tore it down a few years ago, when old man Barton died. But Joy met Clayton right after she got back, at a picnic. She even admits that her grief changed her, that maybe her feelings weren't real, but she fell in love with

Clayton—as much as she could—and married him five months later."

PJ tried to imagine the overwhelming grief of losing someone she loved. Yeah, that could change someone. Make them marry someone they might not have expected. She reached for an unused Kleenex. "What happened when Hugh showed up?"

"Baby Sunny was four years old, and the only daddy she knew was Clayton. Joy fought with herself for weeks and finally told Hugh she wouldn't leave Clayton."

"Poor Hugh."

"Yeah, well, he left town."

"Did he go back to Vietnam?"

Connie shook her head. "I don't think so. But he was never heard from again."

"Never?"

Connie sat up. "Well, maybe not *never*. I started thinking. We had this case a few years ago, a local woman who was moving to a nursing home. My firm handled it—the wills and estates department. I remember one of the associates talking about it because she was from Kellogg—lived on that big acreage to the west of town. I called into the office today and they did some checking of records. Her name was Janet Murphy. And she had a son named Hugh."

"Hugh? *Joy's* Hugh?"

"I think so. Mrs. Murphy was signing over her acreage to the nursing home in return for her stay there, but she didn't want to give up her house. Apparently she said her son would take it over when she moved out."

"Did she know where he was?

"No—no one had seen him. As far as anyone knew, he'd vanished, no forwarding address. Some attempt was made to find the son—according to the notes on the case, they spent about a month searching marriage records, property owner-ship, death records . . . and military records. According to the Army, Hugh Murphy was a deserter."

"A deserter."

"Yep. Went from special forces to a deserter. That's a pretty big leap."

"He'd spent two years surviving in the jungle, doing and eating who knows what, only to come home and find out the very reason he'd stayed alive had vanished." PJ wiped her eyes. Good grief. She wasn't even pregnant.

"But Joy thought he was dead," Connie said, throwing out one Kleenex only to grab another.

"I'm not blaming Joy," PJ said. "It's just . . . horrible. They loved each other so much, and life just threw them off course."

"It does that. But here's the important part: Joy really did begin to love Clayton. Listen to this—it's on their fifth anniversary."

July 1968

We picnicked at the beach today for the celebration. Clayton took our picture with his new Olympus. Then we walked the

beach. Sometimes, when I look at
Clayton, I'm amazed at my life,
at the way it turned out. I don't
love him the same way I loved Hugh.
I love him better. Stronger. He is the
face of God's grace to me. The face
of mercy and compassion. Yes,
I loved Hugh—loved the wildness,
the freshness, the hope of it. But
Clay took that hope and gave it
depth and commitment. He nursed
me through my grief; he helped
me find my way back to Sunny,
to myself. Clayton is my happy
ending. Five years. I hope for
fifty.

Connie pressed a Kleenex to her face and blew her nose.

"He helped me find my way back to myself." PJ stared out the window to the blackness outside. Thankfully, Boris hadn't covered the ceiling, and she looked through it to the stars. *"He is the face of God's grace to me."*

For a while, Jeremy had made her believe that he saw the real PJ Sugar, the woman she wanted to be. He'd been the face of mercy, of compassion. The face of hope.

With Boone, she'd never seen herself as anything but trouble.

But Jeremy had set her free from that. Jeremy believed she could be more . . . or at least she thought he did.

Princess.

"PJ?"

"I'm fine. Just realizing that some stories don't have happy endings." She wiped her eyes. "So Hugh never came back—"

"Oh no, that's what I was trying to say. He did. His mother said that he'd returned to Kellogg in 1977, when the draft dodgers were pardoned by Jimmy Carter. But no one ever saw him or even mentioned him. Except . . ."

"Joy."

"Yes. There're a number of sketchy entries around that time, and then listen to this:

March 1978

If he wanted to destroy our lives, why did he choose now? Seventeen years—as if he knew how I would feel, remembering the night he kissed me, on the eve of my own seventeenth birthday. Poor Sunny didn't even know him—of course she didn't know him. I found him in the kitchen, at the door of her bedroom, watching her. He'd even brought her a gift—diamond earrings. Tears ran down his face, and he shook as I let him take me in his arms. We still had our daughter between us, and I couldn't begrudge him that. He left on his terms, but if he must return, it will be on mine. Of course I will make room for him. Clayton disagrees, and we had a terrible argument after Hugh left. He is so angry. Not at me, but at Hugh. He doesn't want Sunny to know. I don't know what to do. Of course she should know Hugh is her real father, and I was wrong to hide her past from her. But I feared she'd never see the life she'd been given with Clayton. Maybe I was wrong; maybe I should have let her see her legacy. Hugh was such a good man, before . . . If only I knew how to help Hugh let go of his nightmares. If only I wasn't the one who caused them.

"'If only I wasn't the one who caused them.' Is that the last entry?"

Connie shut the book. "Yes."

"And no one ever saw Hugh again?"

Connie rubbed her hand on the book. "Nope. He probably took off again for Canada or wherever he'd gone during those deserting years."

"Is his mother still alive?"

"No, she passed about a year ago."

Davy came down to the kitchen, his curly dark hair still dripping, his pajamas stuck to his wet skin. "Hey, Auntie PJ!" He bounced toward her, leaping onto her lap. "See my new *lapa*?"

He shoved a long-eared stuffed dog onto her lap.

"Lapa?"

"It's Russian for teddy bear or something like that." Connie said, closing the diary.

Sergei entered the room, looking half-soaked.

"Did you bathe too?" Connie asked, laughing.

He leaned down to kiss her, then lifted her legs and sat under them, replacing them on his lap. Connie ran her fingers into his dark hair. "You know, Davy *could* use a towel."

"Ah, *nyet*. Khe vants his own vay." Sergei glanced at Davy and gave him a wink.

"See, my *lapa* talks to me!" Davy pressed the dog's floppy ear, and PJ heard the voice of Sergei emerge, in Russian, *"Ya tebya lublu."*

I love you. "How'd you do that?"

"He went to Babies and Baubles. They let you make your own stuffed animals there and add your own recorded message."

Davy hugged the dog to his chest.

As PJ watched him, Flora's words rushed back to her. *"A teddy bear. Just a cheap trinket he picked up in some airport, probably. But Tyler carries it everywhere."*

The last package Owen had ever sent home.

"How would the smuggler get the diamonds home?" PJ touched the *lapa*'s ear, heard the voice play again.

What if the diamonds were inside the teddy bear?

But had Max sent them . . . or someone else?

He'd been wounded, sent to Germany . . . recovering from a head injury.

One that probably necessitated shaving his head . . .

The Kellogg hobo had said that Max had arrived onshore naked as a baby. Had he also meant bald?

Which meant Max *couldn't* have been the long-haired, tattooed soldier standing on the driveway yelling at Bekka. She'd been right—it had to be Ratchet. And when Bekka said to her mother that she "had to get back to him," she must have meant Owen—wounded, hurt Owen.

Owen, who probably never even *knew* about the package since he was busy recovering from a head injury . . . one so damaging that a fall into the bay easily knocked the memory out of him.

Ratchet *had* been there that day . . . and maybe he'd come back that night, even dumped Owen.

But . . . it still didn't feel right. They'd been POWs together in Iraq. If she spent time suffering with someone, they'd probably have a lifelong bond. They'd even brand it on their arms.

Her hand went to the tattoo on her shoulder, the one with Boone's name. She too had a lifelong bond. With Boone, just like he had with her. And yes, like Owen's, it was based in suffering, even if it wasn't quite as deep as wartime pain. And despite their wounds, she and Boone would never really be enemies.

In fact, their friendship might even be the kind that went so deep he'd risk his life for her. And vice versa. At the very least, warn her of trouble.

Except, according to Windchill, Ratchet and Owen were enemies . . .

PJ sat up. "I can't believe I didn't see it."

Connie took her hand from Sergei's hair. "What?"

"If Ratchet was planning on killing Owen, or even demanding the diamonds from him, he wouldn't have had an argument with Bekka out in the street for the entire neighborhood to see. If he was any kind of special ops soldier—especially a black ops soldier—he'd know to stay under the radar. If anything, Jeremy's taught me that. And they were fellow survivors. Not enemies like Windchill said. They had a lifelong bond to protect each other." She wanted to scream or at least grab someone—Jeremy—by the lapels. "I'll bet that Ratchet went to *warn* Bekka!"

Connie gave her a long look. "Should I take notes?"

She pressed her palms to her head. "I'll bet Windchill showed up, and Max, being the hero he is, got into a fight with him—and Bekka maybe got in the way. So he had to make it look like Max killed his wife. But then why did Windchill go to the funeral?"

"Davy, go get Mommy a pen, please," Connie said.

"Of course, he went to find Ratchet! But Ratchet probably knew Windchill was after him, so he went into hiding. And Windchill's best option was to lie low and wait, hoping nothing surfaced to tie him to the smuggling or Owen's murder. Then I put Max in the paper this week. Suddenly Windchill realized that Owen wasn't dead." She wanted to bang her head against something. "Windchill told me about Ratchet so that I would *track him down*. He needed to cut off any final threads to Max's disappearance and Bekka's murder. And when I showed up, he realized that I would eventually figure it out—wait! What if Windchill was the one who rented the house? What if he's another Lyle Fisher?"

"I feel like we need CliffsNotes of some sort." Connie said.

She turned to them. "I think Windchill was the one who burned down the house, killed Bekka, dumped Owen's body, and then killed Ratchet today." She stood, hands up. "What if Windchill was the one who pushed me off the road?"

Had she seen the GT at the jump school? Oh, why couldn't she remember?

"Why didn't he just unhook me in the air?"

Sergei and Connie were staring at her as if they might be watching a teenage horror movie, mouths agape.

"Because if you're gone, how would he find Max?" Connie asked, suddenly finding her lawyer face.

"Connie, you do have sleuthing genes! Good question."

PJ stared at her sister. "So maybe he wasn't the driver—maybe he just wanted to use me to find Ratchet, then track me back to Max."

"Why would he want that?"

"Oh no. I'll bet he *was* going to unhook me—because I was a liability—until I opened my big mouth and told him about the teddy bear."

"Why would he care about the teddy bear?"

"Because . . . *Windchill never got the diamonds*! Because the package hadn't arrived yet, only maybe he didn't know it. He tossed the house, and when he didn't find them, he set it on fire—to cover his tracks. I knew it!"

"Diamonds?" Sergei asked.

"Maybe he thought they'd never surface, and he didn't want to raise suspicions . . . until, of course, I told him that yes, the package *did* arrive. . . . *Oh no!* Windchill asked me if Max was going to get his memory back, and I said *maybe*! He's going to finish what he started with Max and then find that teddy bear—"

Davy ran back into the room with the pen and handed it to Connie. *"Ya tebya lublu,"* she said, tousling his hair.

PJ patted Davy's head. "I gotta go, little man."

"Are you coming back?" Connie asked, a flare of panic in her eyes.

PJ grabbed her keys, tugged on her Chucky T's. "Oh, I certainly hope so."

Chapter *NINETEEN*

It would really help a PI catch her villain if her cell phone weren't waterlogged at the bottom of Maximilian Bay.

So, well, what was a girl to do? PJ drove to the Kellogg Police Department.

"Detective Buckam's not here," said the night clerk, a woman PJ didn't know, but who knew her based on the way she looked her over with cool eyes.

Perfect. He was probably out on a date with . . . what's her name. Thankfully, this time the thought didn't plunge like a knife straight into the center of PJ's chest.

Not that she was ready to do wild cartwheels or anything.

PJ stood outside the police department, smelling the crisp, loamy October air, and wondered where Max would go.

What did she know about Max? He was a survivor . . .

he'd managed to live through Iraq and a head injury. He was a rescuer . . . he'd taken in Dog. And somewhere deep inside, he was loyal. With everything inside her, PJ knew that Max had gone looking for his child. She'd seen the look on his face when he thought Tyler might be his.

Longing.

So where did a loyal, rescuing, survivor-type go . . . a guy who wanted to make amends?

Was it too much to ask—the mushroom house? After the destruction he'd wrought, she'd bet he was still attempting a rescue of her plumbing, because he'd promised. Because he wanted to put things right.

PJ climbed into the Vic.

An eerie white moon dangled half-full over the lake, winking. Stars needled the cover of night, and the air breathed the watery scent of rain.

Please, God, let Max be at my house. With any providence, Jeremy wouldn't have found him yet; it would give her space to explain the truth to Max. Convince him that he wasn't a murderer, but a survivor.

She knew it, and that knowledge swelled inside her.

She almost rear-ended Boone's Mustang, parked in her circle drive. Her headlights flashed across the fender and then scraped across Jeremy's microbus in front of it.

And Max's Cutlass in front of that.

Oh no. In her head, she saw the scenario—Jeremy had called Boone after tracking down Max. Boone had arrived, and who knows what sort of altercation had gone down behind her unassuming dark windows.

In fact, the house looked lifeless, the only movement her dead hanging plant, its spindly arms tangling in the breeze as she approached the house.

Dog barked, running to her, his voice carried away in the breeze. She knelt and rubbed her hands over his neck. "Hey there, Bruce."

Dog gave her a lick, jumped on her, knocking her back, then bounded away. PJ pushed herself up, dusting off her hands, wet from . . . She held them up in the moonlight.

Something dark and sticky smeared them. She smelled it. Recoiled.

Blood?

She wiped her hands on her pants. "Dog?" He hadn't appeared wounded.

The door creaked open, nudged by the breeze. PJ stilled, staring at it, a fist closing over her heart. Something felt . . . off.

She eased, whisper silent, to the door and edged it open. For once, it decided not to whine, and she slipped inside. She paused, listening to her heartbeat swish in her ears.

Then she heard it: cursing, a thump, people grunting.

"Why do you always have to be a hero, Owen?"

And then a roar, a sound that grabbed her insides and squeezed.

She ran to the front room, stopped, crouched by the door. In the dim light cast by the night into the main room, she saw Max on the floor, Windchill on top, his hands wrapped around Max's neck.

Squeezing.

"Why can't you just stay dead!"

Max's legs kicked up, wrapped around Windchill's neck. Jerked him away.

Behind him—no, no! Boone lay on the floor, handcuffed, bleeding from his shoulder.

Max grabbed his throat, sucked a breath, then pounced on Windchill just as he found his feet. They slammed into a wall.

PJ averted her eyes as they pummeled each other. *Do something.*

She needed a weapon—if she dove into the fight, Max would only try to protect her and get hurt in the process. She'd learned that much about the heroes in her life.

And then she saw him—the dark form of Jeremy collapsed and unmoving beside the open doorway. And lying in the center of the room, what looked like a gun.

PJ pressed a hand to her stomach. *Breathe. Just . . . breathe.*

"You killed my wife!" Max's fist slammed into Windchill's chin.

"You killed her by trying to stop me!" Windchill grabbed Max around the waist, tackling him to the ground. They wrestled, and PJ winced at the grunts of pain.

Oh, see, someone should listen to her—and her instincts! She knew Max wasn't a smuggler.

Windchill found Max's neck again. Max's face whitened as Windchill's fingers dug into his throat.

Jeremy stirred.

Windchill turned at the movement. Max threw him off. Scrambled for the gun.

Windchill tackled him. The two slammed into the French doors. Glass shattered, littering the floor.

PJ scanned the room for a weapon. Soggy lath and plaster littered the floor, none of it weapon-worthy.

She spied Max's toolbox across the room. His tool belt lay on the floor. But what was she going to do—throw a hammer? She'd hit Max or Boone or even Jeremy.

The two men hung on to each other's throats, dead-locked.

Oh . . . oh . . . God, please! Help me think!

Max's grip fell from Windchill's neck. He fought Windchill's stranglehold.

PJ launched herself to a spot behind the compressor still set up in the middle of the family room debris field. Gun— the *nail gun*! She snaked her hand down the hose, fumbled for the gun.

Please, let it still be loaded. Please . . .

She pointed at Windchill, hoping it worked like one of the weapons Boone had taught her to use, and pulled the trigger.

A nail shot out, ricocheting off the fireplace.

She fought the recoil, pulled again.

This time, it might have chipped something—hopefully skin—off Windchill. He whirled around with a roar. Max lay on the floor, barely moving.

She ducked behind the compressor, hands over her head

as he scooped up the gun and popped off a couple shots. The sound shook through the empty house.

Dog exploded through the front door, and Jeremy erupted from the floor. Crashing, grunts, roars of fury. Boone shouting. Glass shattering.

Two more shots.

She heard more scuffling, then a shout—

Jeremy skidded to his knees in front of her.

She dropped the gun and launched herself at him.

He grabbed her shoulders, stopping her. His gaze raked over her. "Are you okay?"

"Are *you* okay?" She caught his face in her hands.

"You're going to kill me one of these days."

"I hope not. Oh, I hope not."

Shots popped off, outside.

"Max!"

Jeremy put her away from him, met her eyes, and she nodded.

He scrambled out the back after Max. Outside, a motor kicked up in the wind.

Boone lay in the middle of the room, eyes closed, face a little white.

"Boone?"

"I'm okay," he said in a voice that most definitely did not sound okay.

She sprinted to the kitchen, grabbed one of her new towels, returned, and pressed it to his wound. He turned his face away.

"Get a knife—you need to cut through the flexi-cuffs

he put on me." Boone grunted, rolling to his side, revealing plastic zip-tie handcuffs.

He was still breathing through his mouth, long, controlled breaths.

Outside, more shots popped off. One crashed through the window, splattering glass across her floor.

She crouched, zagging to the kitchen, yanking open drawers.

Another shot, and—

Boom! The wall exploded in, splinters flying, a fireball hurtling into the great room. The force rocketed PJ back. She slammed against the wall, hitting her head.

Fire plumed into the room, hot, black, acrid smoke fogging the ceiling. Her eyes watered; her head hammered. She wanted to retch with the pain. Rolling onto her stomach, she tried to find her feet.

Then, like a hand over her eyes, everything went dark.

✳ ✳ ✳

"Wake up. Wake up!"

A hand on her face, slapping, and not gently either. PJ roused, then bent over, coughing.

Smoke blackened the house, filling every corner. She couldn't breathe, couldn't see. Except for a flicker of light from the flames.

And in the flicker she saw a face.

She screamed.

The roar of the fire ate it. "C'mon, soldier, let's move it."

Hands around her collar, pulling her by the scruff of her jacket. Pushing her close to the floor as she obeyed. Next to her the man crawled as if in a combat zone. They reached the stairs to the basement, and he yanked open the door.

"Down!"

She found her feet, but he kept his grip on her shoulder as she stumbled to the basement, her hand dragging down the side for balance. Light buzzed in cages, illuminating the underground passage past the service door.

"Move it; move it!"

"What about Boone?"

"Not now, PJ."

PJ turned. In the wan light, she saw the Kellogg hobo, Murph, gaping at her. Brown teeth against a beard tangled like seaweed. His grimy stocking cap pulled low. And blue eyes, that seemed, at this moment, clear and bright. "Get moving!"

Then he pushed her down the passage.

PJ half ran, half stumbled in front of him. The musty smell of the tunnel pressed against her as they tripped into the darkness.

Halfway in, Murph hooked her arm. "Up! We go up!"

And sure enough, a door in the wall opened out and emptied into the little room she'd fallen into that first day. The gaping hole opened to the glowing sky.

"How do we get out?"

He bent down, hooked his fingers together, and she stepped into the web. He hoisted her up, hard, and she found herself airborne as if he'd actually tossed her from the pit. She landed on her stomach, her breath whooshing out.

Ten feet away, Boone stood with a group of EMTs, hands on his knees, bent over, coughing, spitting out something from his mouth. One man kept trying to give him oxygen even as he pushed it away and stared at the house.

"Boone!"

His eyes landed on her, some sort of disbelief on his face. "She's here! Jeremy, she's here!"

From out of nowhere, Jeremy came at her without stopping, a crazed expression on his face, in his eyes. He grabbed her forearms and yanked her off the ground. "How'd you get out? I thought you were still in there. I thought . . ." He looked unable to breathe as he pulled her to himself.

He didn't even bother, it seemed, to hide his emotions. Just let them shake out of him, his arms so tight around her, his breath erratic as he picked her up and carried her away from the tunnel.

"Where's Max?"

"He's hauling Windchill out of the lake."

She looked over his shoulder, and her stomach lurched at the flames curling like tongues over the house.

Her mushroom house.

"My house . . ." She sucked in a tremulous breath. Shook her head, her hand over her mouth. "Oh . . . my house."

A fire engine had already arrived, firemen in full gear,

running with hoses inside her front door. She heard a yell over the din: "We found her!"

Jeremy set her down but kept ahold of her and now took her face in his hands, forcing her to look at him. Tears pooled in his eyes despite his ferocious expression. "Are you kidding me? You're worried about your house? I thought you were burning alive. I tried to get back in—"

"I'm okay. The—" She looked past him, at a fireman now hauling Murph from the cellar opening. "Murph . . . saved me."

Jeremy wore a strange expression, that information registering as something besides shock. "He's the one who's been squatting in the carriage house. Boone had a little chat with him last night after I brought you home. Apparently he knows the way into the house."

PJ considered Jeremy, the way he didn't quite meet her eyes, the way he ran his hands down her arms, the way he looked like—

"You know something."

He clenched his jaw. "I'm just glad you're okay." He pulled her again to him.

Okay. PJ wrapped her arms around his shoulders. Pushed her face into the well above his collarbone. He smelled of smoke and sweat, his breathing still too fast.

"How did Windchill get the drop on you?" PJ stepped away, knotting her fingers into his shirt.

"He had already shot Boone when I showed up. He came in by boat, so I didn't see his car and was waiting for Max. . . . Like you said, he got the drop on me." Frustration flickered over Jeremy's face. "I walked through the door, and Windchill must have heard me coming because the next thing I knew, I was waking up, and Max and Windchill were killing each other. I don't know when Max came in. But then you shot them."

He smiled. "I underestimated your sharpshooter abilities with a nail gun." Then his smile dimmed. "Actually, I think I underestimated you in general." A tenderness, almost a fear, touched his expression.

"I do make a good partner, don't I?"

He ran his hand over her hair. Nodded. Then he wrapped his hand around her neck and kissed her. Just dove right in as if . . . she belonged to him. As if he wanted to belong to her, too. PJ molded herself to him, kissing him back. When he pulled away, he didn't let her go, just kissed her cheekbone, then her neck, her nose.

"Jer—"

He leaned back and took her face in his hands. "I'm sorry for what I said. I didn't mean it."

"I know."

"No, listen. I know you're not Lori. I *know* that. But sometimes, those feelings—helplessness, panic . . . I'm just back there, and I hate it. I see the person I was, what I did."

What he did? Her intake of breath voiced her question. "You didn't . . . hurt the person who killed Lori?"

"No. But, oh, I wanted to. I lay in bed at night and conjured up ways I could take the guy apart. I let my anger seep through me like tar, take over my thoughts, my lungs, my soul. Worse, it took everything good I'd done as a SEAL and twisted it. Along with knowing how to defend my country, I realized I knew a hundred ways to kill this guy with my bare hands. I . . . plotted to kill him, PJ."

"Why . . . why didn't you?" She let the question trickle out, slowly, gently.

"Because God stopped me. He gave me a glimpse of myself, and I saw a killer instead of a hero. I managed to stumble my way into a church, into forgiveness. That's when I got my tattoo. It's the Christian symbol of the Trinity with a circle. I wanted it to remind me of grace and how to find my balance."

"You still see yourself as a killer?"

He blew out a breath. "Not when I'm with you." He squeezed her hands, almost too hard. "But when I go back to that place . . . it sucks me in. I feel the shame and the anger. I see that I could so easily be the person I don't want to be." His eyes burned into hers when he looked up. "I think I've been holding on to that anger. It does give me a sense of power. Maybe you're right—I don't want a fresh start . . ."

PJ loosened her hands from his and cupped his face. "Jeremy. You do want one. And I want to help you find it. Maybe you just don't know what it looks like."

"And you do?" He said it softly, without rancor.

"I . . . think so. I think it's standing up and seeing life from a new place. Like when I went skydiving and I saw the big picture. I can't explain it except it felt—"

"Breathtaking. You told me, remember?"

"Yeah, breathtaking. I think that's what a fresh start is all about. Not ignoring the past, but seeing it through the eyes of God, through the eyes of grace. Knowing where we've been and where we're going. A fresh start isn't about forgetting; it's about perspective."

She watched another hose attack the blaze from the front. Water misted in the night air. Steam rose into the sky.

"You're the one who said it: 'A fresh start has no meaning unless you understand what you left behind.' Jer, we can be each other's fresh start. We'll point out the grace, give truth to the past, and help each other recognize the future. We'll be mercy and compassion to each other. That's our fresh start."

As Jeremy took a breath, he touched his forehead to hers. "You know why I love you?"

"You love me?"

"For months now, Princess. It's because somehow you always figure it out. And you take me with you."

"Is that a good thing?"

"An amazing thing." He managed a smile, his eyes sweet and light.

She rose on her tiptoes and kissed him. Slowly. Gently. The blanket fell to the pavement. He seemed to hold his breath, collect himself, and then he returned the kiss, leaning forward, reaching out for her, kissing her with a sort of hunger that made her wrap her arms around his neck.

"Are you two about finished?" Boone stepped up. He looked like he'd survived a bombing, his face blackened, blood on his lips, his eyes red and still watering. He held a pack to his shoulder, where he'd been hit. "We need a statement from you when you're ready, but I'm headed to the hospital."

"Are you going to be okay? That looks pretty bad."

His smile was slow. "I think my tattoo might have been destroyed, but other than that, I'm going to pull through." He gave her a half smile but trailed it with a wink.

His tattoo of her name. Obliterated. Maybe it was time for hers to go too.

She couldn't help but smile back.

"Am I going to have to relive your relationship with Boone every time I see him?" Jeremy spoke into her neck.

"The important part is, it's in the past."

The front yard resembled a convention for emergency services. Two more fire trucks, three police cruisers, and an ambulance had arrived. Moisture hung in the air, spray drifting over PJ's hair, landing like icicles on her body. The flames had diminished to a few die-hard tongues, and even those disappeared as another plume of water spilled over the house. The air smelled of creosote and ash.

"My poor house. I don't even know if I have insurance." Now what? Back to her car? Back to Connie's house? She stood there for a long moment.

PJ's glance went to Murph, slumped on the side of the cellar hill, his hands over his face. Through the smoke, she could see his shoulders shaking. "Is he crying?"

Jeremy glanced over, then took her hand. "Yeah, I think that's a good guess."

She edged toward the weeping man, but Jeremy stopped her.

"He might need to be alone, Princess."

"Why?"

"Because the woman he loved lived in this house. He's probably reliving the night she died."

PJ looked at him. "I don't understand."

Jeremy slipped his hand around her waist. "That's Hugh Murphy, PJ. The guy that Joy Kellogg ran away with so many years ago."

"Hugh Murphy? Murph was Joy's husband? But I thought he vanished."

"How'd you know that?"

"Connie and I read Joy's diary. She did some sleuthing of her own."

"It's in the genes."

PJ smiled at him. "Something like that. But how do you know he's Hugh?"

"I've been doing some extracurricular investigating. I took the name from the locket, Hugh, and I did a trace on anyone with that first name from Kellogg. It shot back a Hugh Murphy. From there, I found out that he was MIA and then deserted in 1965."

"Weren't the draft dodgers pardoned by Carter?"

"Yes—but Murphy was a deserter. It's a different situation."

"So could he still be arrested?"

Jeremy's mouth closed to a tight line. "At this point, Hugh Murphy the deserter no longer exists, as far as the military is concerned. But Hugh Murphy the man who loved Joy is sitting over there, remembering the grief he brought to his wife."

"I don't understand."

"After we found out that someone was squatting in the carriage house, I went through his belongings. I found an old picture of a farmhouse, asked around, and someone at the library said it looked like the old Murphy house. I discovered the woman had died, so I went to the grave of Murphy's mother and found evidence that someone had left flowers. I left a camera there and when I checked on it, I discovered that Hugh had made a cameo. I tracked him down, sobered him up, and had a little chat."

"So that's what you were doing this morning."

"Yeah. Hugh is from Kellogg. He returned on his daughter's seventeenth birthday. He thought he was pardoned, see, and it was only when he fled to his mother's house after the drowning that he realized he might never be pardoned—and I'm not talking about the law."

"Did he kill Joy?"

"No. But he did try sneaking into their house to talk her into leaving with him. According to him, he was waiting in the carriage house, hoping she'd change her mind. He saw her come outside, saw her walk around the grounds. He said he knew something was wrong and went out to talk to her, but she was drunk. Sitting on the end of the pier. She told him to let her go. To start over. He told her he couldn't . . . but she told him to leave, and he did."

"You don't think he's lying?"

"No, he's broken. I saw it in his eyes. And he's never left. I think Joy's death was an accident, PJ. Not murder."

PJ watched Murph's shoulders shake, an outline of grief amid the haze of the night. A picture of a man stuck on the outside, unable to move into grace.

"That's not all, Princess. . . ."

Chapter TWENTY

"In my defense, I was trying to help." Jeremy placed a large pepperoni pizza on the granite countertop of Connie's kitchen—a peace offering, if she read his posture correctly. Even showered, his hair wet, he still reeked of smoke. PJ did too, probably.

PJ opened the lid and slid out a piece.

"As a lawyer, I want to suggest not qualifying your statements. Just lay it out there." Connie sat at the table, wrapped in her fuzzy robe, wearing her game face. PJ had a feeling Connie had invited everyone over just so she could get a handle on where to put her emotions after seeing PJ, disheveled and grimy, nursing a softball-size bump on the side of her head. Which still throbbed, despite the shower, the pizza, and the fact that everyone survived the fire.

Even Dog. Who lounged at Sergei's feet, having been

washed of Boone's blood. PJ had agreed to dog-sit while Max went to the police station to give a statement.

Windchill hadn't exactly confessed, but a trace on his fingerprints had turned up—surprise, surprise—Lyle Fisher. The same Lyle Fisher who had been arrested for speeding the night of Max's disappearance . . . shortly after throwing his body off the bridge. And the same Lyle Fisher who had gypped his Hopkins landlord out of her last month's rent. Figured.

PJ would probably live a long and happy life if she never heard that name again.

And maybe tomorrow, they'd head over to Flora's house. Introduce Max to his son. For once it didn't matter that he didn't remember. Tyler didn't know him, either. It seemed like a good place to start.

"Okay, fine. Here's the bottom line," Jeremy said, handing Connie a piece of pizza. "Ever since PJ moved back, she's believed she brings trouble with her."

PJ made a face at him.

"I would agree that perhaps she has a knack for finding mysteries . . . but I never saw her as trouble." His eyes softened. "I overheard something Connie said—about her and Sergei wanting to have something better than they had before. That knowing her past gave him the chance to prove that he loved her better. To heal her wounds." Jeremy dragged his hand around the back of his neck. Never had she seen him quite so nervous.

She had to admit, it suited him in a way. Just like his role as her boss. And current hero. Okay, so she loved all sides of Jeremy Kane.

Yes, loved. He was the face of God's grace to her, just like Clayton had been to Prudence Joy. And although Boone would always be in her past, she loved Jeremy better.

All the way to the happy ending. Or at least she hoped there'd be one. Because with her house still smoking and her front lawn shredded and her bathroom plumbing in pieces and her Bug at the bottom of the lake and Dog still nameless at her feet and her PI license three years in the future, a happy ending seemed a little like Davy's Jell-O cubes—wiggly and oozing between her fingers. Impossible to hold.

Still, she knew what she wanted to reach for.

Jeremy closed in on her. "I wanted to do that for you— to prove to you that whatever was in your past, it didn't matter to me. That you weren't trouble, whether it was in your blood or in your upbringing. I didn't mean to dig quite so deep."

PJ glanced at Connie, who lifted a shoulder.

Jeremy took her hand. "So I took the name you found in your mother's yearbook—PJ—and added Barton to it. Sunny Barton popped up in my Google search—class of 1978, East Minneapolis High. The reason she didn't show up in the senior yearbook from Kellogg was because she and her father, Clayton, moved away after Joy died."

Connie put her hand on the journal. PJ had filled her in on the rest of Joy's story while Jeremy showered.

"She went to Wheaton—she knew your father from

when she attended school here, and she made friends with his girlfriend, Elizabeth Mulligan. Your mom. That's why she's in your mother's yearbook. She changed her name, at least socially, to PJ, which incidentally are the initials of her middle names—Prudence Jewel, the maiden name of Hugh's mother."

PJ's eyes widened. Uh-oh.

Jeremy smiled. "Jewel? Of course. I would have guessed that eventually." He winked at her, then took a breath. "I didn't expect there to be an audience for this."

"It's okay—whatever you have to say, Connie can hear it."

Jeremy glanced at her. "I wanted to see if she was alive, so I . . . found her father. Clayton Barton. And I went over there."

PJ went very still.

"He had a picture of you, PJ."

She stepped back from him, a tremor snaking through her. "Uh . . ."

"Right next to a picture of his daughter, Sunny."

Connie suddenly decided to abdicate her place at the table. As she stood, she folded her hands over her chest.

"I don't understand," PJ said softly. "What are you saying?"

Connie walked over to PJ. Kissed her on the cheek. "I think he's saying you're a Kellogg, honey."

PJ didn't move. Couldn't move. "Are you saying that Sunny Barton is my *mother*?"

"We can petition the court for records, but . . . you look just like her, Princess. She has your incredible green eyes. And your *blonde* hair—don't think I don't know the truth. Although I think you're amazing as a redhead."

"So Sunny gave birth to me and then, what, handed me over to the Sugars?"

"Basically. Yes."

"What about this Clayton Barton? my . . . grandfather? or stepgrandfather? How does he know about me?"

"Your mother told him."

"My mother . . . Sunny?"

"No, your mother Elizabeth Sugar. She sent him letters and pictures. She told him that you were an amazing person."

And he'd told Agatha Kellogg.

Who had attended PJ's play because she wanted to see her great-granddaughter.

"Why did Sunny give me up for adoption? And where is she today?"

"According to Clayton, she got pregnant in college. He said she couldn't raise you. She wasn't married, and after the grief she'd had losing her mother, she wanted you to have a family. So she chose her friend Carl Sugar and his new wife, Elizabeth." He touched her hair. "I'm sorry; I did ask where she was. Clayton hasn't spoken to her in over twenty years."

"She's lost?"

"Or maybe she doesn't want to be found. Maybe she discovered her own fresh start. After she gave you yours."

"I *am* a Kellogg."

"And a Sugar," Connie said. "You're both."

Jeremy ran his fingers into her hair. "See? You're not locked into trouble. When Sunny gave you up for adoption, you got a chance to start over. To reset the Kellogg line."

"Don't forget that when God gave you to our family, He changed our line, too." Connie touched her sister's arm. "Made us better. Definitely more curious."

"Aka trouble?"

"Nah—let's call it . . . adding spice to the Sugar line."

"So why did Aggie give me the house?"

"Maybe because you would know what to do with it," Jeremy said.

PJ sagged into her chair. "Yeah, blow it up."

"You couldn't help that Windchill shot the propane tank on the grill."

"It's such a shame. I loved that house. It was the fairy tale, the dream come true."

Jeremy hooked a finger under her chin and drew her gaze to his. "And it's because you know that, Princess, that Aggie Kellogg gave it to you."

Or better yet, God had given it to her. Her legacy, her fairy tale, her hopes of a happy ending. *". . . you can show others the goodness of God, for he called you out of the darkness into his wonderful light."*

"Aggie Kellogg wrote in her note to me, 'Know that the blessings of your inheritance are also your destiny.' I think I figured it out." She pressed her hands to Jeremy's face, gave him a quick kiss. "I know what I'm going to do."

"Oh, good, everyone is here!" Elizabeth Sugar swept into the foyer and gestured to the man behind her—probably her taxi driver, carrying in her bags. She dropped a quilted bag onto the floor, clapped her hands, and held her arms open for Davy.

He dropped off his stool. "Grandma!"

Connie followed behind him. "Mother, where have you been? We've been so worried!"

We? Hello, how many messages had Connie left?

"Oh, Constance, I'm fine." Her mother kissed Connie's cheek. Indeed, she looked radiant—tan, wearing a pair of linen pants and a loose silk top, a coral necklace at her throat. World traveler Elizabeth Sugar. "I had a wonderful vacation." She glanced behind her at the driver.

PJ gave him a quick once-over. He was royal-boned and dashing even in his late sixties, judging by his powder-white hair, and he also glowed with the look of the sun-soaked—especially against his pressed pink oxford and a pair of white pants, matching patent shoes. A gold chain at his neck, a matching stud in his ear solved the mystery—her mother had brought home the cruise ship lounge singer.

Or maybe not, because he smiled at her mother as if he knew her.

The kind of smile Jeremy might give PJ. An indulgent, knowing, affectionate smile.

"Hello," he said, holding out his hand to Connie. He had an accent—British, PJ would guess. "Cornelius Bacon."

Connie, bound by Sugar courtesy, shook his hand, her curious expression glancing off her mother, then PJ, and landing on him with a smile.

Elizabeth sidled up to PJ, hooked her by the arm, then caught Connie. "Girls, I'm so excited to introduce you to . . . my new husband."

Epilogue

"I've always thought you were a big turkey." Jeremy straightened the multicolored felt collar, then her feathered hat.

"Don't talk to me. Can't you see I'm working?"

He pressed a cold-lipped kiss to her mouth. "Go get 'em, gobbler."

PJ pushed him away, slapping her mittened wings together and stamping her feet. Her breath outlined her impatience in the brisk air.

Jeremy rebounded, kissing her on the nose. "Can we keep the costume?"

"You know, being the parade Turkey is considered an honor."

"Oh, I know. Not everyone can pull off being a turkey like you can. You have a special talent."

"Funny."

"Listen, I don't want all this gobbling going to your head. Just because you donated your old house—"

"We call it the mushroom house, thank you."

"—to the city doesn't make you the mayor or anything."

PJ moved to avoid a row of Girl Scouts–turned–elves chasing each other through the jammed grocery store parking lot. "I know. But I could be. Did you see the picture of me in the paper this week? I got to officiate at the ceremony for the start of work on the new historical library."

All those donated books, plus the city's historical documents from the basement of the county library would have a home. Thankfully, Agatha's insurance hadn't lapsed— which meant the historical society had plenty of funds to renovate. She wished the Kellogg women—Aggie, Joy, and Sunny—could have seen the plans for the Kellogg family memorial room. Aggie would love seeing all the beautiful things she'd hoarded finally displayed.

Although PJ did pick out just a few for herself.

"Yes. At this rate, maybe I *will* have to start calling you Ms. Mayor," Jeremy said.

She liked Princess the best, thanks.

And these days, she did feel a bit like royalty, living in the gardener's house across the road from the big house. Her little one-bedroom house had the quaint aura of Snow White's cottage, with a tiny orchard of shiny crab-apple trees to match. And this morning, a stencil of lacy frost on the windows.

"It's better than prisoner 13789 down at the poorhouse. The

property taxes on the final appraisal alone would have put me on the street. Now at least both Hugh and I have homes."

"He still making campfires on your beach?"

"Not as much. Most of the time, I see smoke trickling from his chimney in the carriage house. And he lets me invite him over for dinner sometimes, although I'm not sure he likes Chinese food."

"One of these days, you might have to learn to cook."

"Did you know that Clayton is a cook? He's bringing sweet potatoes to Thanksgiving dinner. I still can't believe my mother invited him. Someday perhaps he and Hugh can be together in the same room."

"Maybe. It's not easy to be around a guy your girl once loved. But it can be done." He winked at her. "I'm going to go find a place next to the theater, with Max and Tyler."

"It's his weekend?"

"For now. The courts still have to decide. You have to cut Flora some slack for holding on tightly to the little guy—she doesn't even know Max."

Nor did Max, who still hadn't regained his memory. But maybe that was a piece of grace. A new beginning for the former Max Smith, aka Owen McMann, now going by Max McMann. The contractor slated to repair and restore the mushroom house.

"Connie said that my testimony and Boone's report cleared up any question the Army had about his disappearance and involvement in the diamond smuggling. Especially when they recovered the diamonds in Tyler's bear. Apparently the Army was investigating the diamond-smuggling operation, but of course, they won't confirm any record of Owen McMann in special forces."

"Of course not. I could have told you that." Jeremy took her hand. "Still—instincts, baby. You got 'em."

"Enough to get my license?"

He squeezed her hand. "License for trouble, maybe."

"Jeremy! You watch who you're calling trouble."

"I'm not calling you trouble, Princess." He smiled at her, pulling away.

"Say hi to Sergei and Connie—I'll be sure and find them after the parade. Oh, and you'd better duck if you see my mother. She's still on the rampage about your 'find PJ's heritage' mission."

The little scene, not long after Elizabeth had announced her nuptials—a declaration eclipsed by PJ's story—ran through Jeremy's eyes. He winced. "Yeah. We've got some ground to make up."

"I think she wanted to be the one to tell me."

"You think? I think I know where you learned your turn-a-man-to-ashes look. How are she and Cornelius doing?"

PJ shook her head, still clearing away the vestiges of shock. Apparently her mother had met Cornelius on an Internet bridge site and dated him for a year without telling her daughters. They'd been planning their cruise wedding for months—Elizabeth even going so far as to have monogrammed bathrobes made for her and her new husband. "I can't believe they actually eloped."

"Hey, I think that's the Sugar thing to do, don't you?" He winked again.

She stilled. "Uh . . ."

"Auntie PJ!" Davy ran up, dressed as a large orange pumpkin, a green cap perched on his head. He attempted to fling himself into her arms, but both of them had acquired an unfamiliar girth, thanks to their costumes. They bounced off each other, and Davy landed on his bottom on the sidewalk, laughing.

"I'll see you two menu items after the parade." Jeremy kissed her before she could grab him with her wing and wheedle out the meaning of his comment.

"I think that's the Sugar thing to do."

Elope?

He wasn't asking . . . ?

"C'mon now, David," Mrs. Nicholson, the director of Fellows Academy, said, coming up behind him. PJ forced her mouth closed. No, *no*, she would not laugh at giant Mrs. Nicholson in her state-fair-winning-pumpkin costume.

"Morning, Miss Sugar," Mrs. Nicholson said, memory sparking in her gulag-guard eyes. Apparently she well remembered PJ as the irresponsible aunt who got Davy kicked out of Fellows over the summer.

Not anymore. Now, she was the Town Turkey.

Er, in the best sense of the word.

"Good morning," she said, grinning as Davy skipped away.

She heard a whistle, and then the parade organizer motioned her over. She would follow the Fellows Pumpkins, walking in front of the Kellogg High band.

Davy turned and waved at her from his flatbed truck. She flapped at him.

Another car pulled in behind it—a yellow convertible Pontiac GT.

PJ stared at it, and for a second, in memory, she hung on the bridge, watching a white car of the same make and model push her over.

Just as the band began playing "Up on the Rooftop" (apparently forgetting they were here to celebrate Thanksgiving) signaling the start of the parade, and the pom-pom girls edged up on her, PJ placed it.

Babies and Baubles.

A white Pontiac GT had been parked outside the baby store while she was hunting for Bix.

The white car that pushed her over would have been damaged and possibly repainted. But it couldn't be the same car, could it?

Maybe. Because after all, a person didn't rush to part with a convertible. Boone still had his vintage '67 Mustang, despite all the memories he might or might not want to keep.

PJ stared at the car, trying to identify the occupants. Sure enough, seated at the wheel: Miss Deena Hayes. Best friend of Meredith Bixby through thick and thin and even betrayal. Of course. Boone had taught her that move too. And next to one of the chunky gourds in the backseat of the open car—Bix's daughter, former Tinker Bell, currently Miss Junior Kellogg.

If Bix wasn't here to watch her daughter's debut as a

beauty pageant queen, then PJ was a bigger turkey than she appeared.

If only she could get Jeremy's attention . . .

The Fellows Pumpkins and Deena's car rolled forward. The parade was only seven blocks long—the length of Main.

Seven blocks to locate Bix.

PJ pasted on a smile as she waddled along, waving to the crowds, scanning every face, first one side of the street, then the other. If she could locate Bix and get a message to Jeremy, he'd pick her up without causing a scene.

Because that's how partners did it.

And lately, he'd let her into his world, toe by toe, foot by foot, teaching her surveillance, weapons training, even the murky Sudden In-Custody Death Syndrome. And he'd written up recommendations of her successful investigations, including the case of Max and the missing diamonds.

Bix wasn't hiding by the bank or by the row of beachwear boutiques or on the streetside veranda of Sunsets Supper Club. Occasionally PJ shot a glance at her daughter, checking out—

There. Tinker Bell had even climbed up to stand on the seat, waving in a manner unbecoming a beauty queen. "Mommy!"

PJ followed her gaze.

Gotcha. Bix hid just behind a man holding a Mylar balloon, her hair hidden by a baseball cap and her eyes by dark glasses.

Anyone else may not have recognized her, but PJ well remembered those sinister raccoon eyes.

After all, she knew how to spot a criminal.

She kept marching. Thinking. Once Tinker Bell had passed, Bix would take off.

Vanish.

Not again.

PJ sprang out of line, straight for Bix.

For a moment, the sight of the Kellogg Turkey bursting out of line and running toward the onlooking crowd stunned even Bix into silence. Her mouth opened slightly.

Then she bolted.

"Bix!" PJ banged through the crowd. "Make a hole!"

Most seemed so horrified to see a hundred-plus-pound turkey lunging at them that they scattered. A few bumped off her costume, but she wasn't trying to negotiate the bottom of a hot dog bun this time. No sirree, she had her running legs and Converse on and she lit out after Bix like a gobbler escaping a farmer.

Bix ran into the parade, checking a few Girl Scouts into a float, bowling over a handful of others. She scooped up a couple aluminum cans from the Recycle for Life bins and chucked them at PJ.

Oh, please. She'd had real killers after her. With real bullets.

"Bix, it won't do you any good!"

Bix didn't look back, just rounded the edge of the Meyer Brothers Dairy float and barreled down the other side.

PJ sprinted down the opposite side of the road, eyes on

Bix. She dodged an elf, another, finally flattened a third as Santa's float rumbled toward her.

"PJ, what are you doing?" Boone's fake bowlful-of-jelly tummy bounced as he took to his feet.

"It's Bix!" PJ pointed at the woman, now running without glasses or hat.

Boone pulled off his beard, and the crowd gasped as he jumped off the float.

But PJ was already past it, running flat out for Iwo Jima. The VFW float had won the award for best detail, and yes, it certainly had all the elements of the rocky knoll where the World War II soldiers had staked their victory. She half bounced, half scrabbled up the side, glad they'd reinforced it with some sort of chicken wire, then hit the top.

Bix looked up, a sort of horror in her eyes.

And why not? A turkey on top of a mountain, ready to leap upon her, might make any hardened criminal trip, stumble, cry out—

PJ leaped from the top of Iwo Jima in a perfect all-state tackle that even Boone would have been proud of.

They rolled, hard, into the gutter. Thank goodness for extra stuffing, because the costume cushioned her fall.

Bix, however, lay on the street, groaning.

"You got 'er, PJ!" A gravelly voice hollered from the flatbed behind, where the veterans sat on their folding chairs. PJ didn't have to look up to recognize Hugh's voice. Not when he lived right across the street from her in the carriage house. Benefits from the sale of his mother's estate—supervised by

Connie and doled out to him monthly—meant that Hugh could live the rest of his years off the streets.

Good old Kellogg—despite his dishonorable discharge from the military, the veterans decided to let him aboard their float.

But Bix wasn't done. As PJ grabbed her jacket, she rammed her elbow into PJ's face, and a cry went up from the crowd. PJ scrabbled after her, grabbing Bix's foot as Bix rolled to her knees.

She kicked at PJ. "Get away from me!"

"You pushed me into the lake!"

Bix kicked at her again, a seesaw effect with PJ at the other end. "I did not—"

"Give it up, Bix. I bet if I run the plates, I'll find out it's your GT Deena is driving. I saw the Kellogg High tassel hanging from your mirror. You need to get over the past and start living in the now. High school is *over!*"

Then she launched herself again at Bix, flattening her to the ground.

Not necessarily a practiced move, but a good PI improvised, too.

And in case she needed help, Dog ran up, barking wildly, slurping them both on the face.

"Get away from me, you mutt!"

"He's not a mutt!" PJ said even as she flattened one arm into Bix's neck, twisting her hand into a submission hold.

"Ow!"

Thank you, Jeremy Kane school of martial arts.

PJ looked at the dog. "You're your own breed, aren't you, Killer?"

Dog slurped her again on the face. Sat down. Wagged his tail.

Killer?

No . . .

"PJ!" Boone ran up. "What on earth?"

"I'm making a citizen's arrest—attempted murder and bail fugitive!"

Boone stared at her with a look of half horror. Then a smile grew on his face. "Well, I guess you could say Turkey Lurkey got her girl." Boone motioned to a couple cops working crowd control, then leaned over and cuffed the now-cursing Bix. Two cops came over and hauled her to her feet. PJ struggled to find hers.

"Oh, funny. You could move faster, you know, Santa." She let him pull her up.

Jeremy came running over, out of breath. "Hey, that's my girl you got there!"

"And thank goodness." Boone let her go even as he gave her a little wink. "Okay, everybody back now. There's nothing to see."

"Nothing to see?" Jeremy said, dusting off her feathers, straightening her collar. His dark eyes shone, a message in them that went clear to her stuffing. "Oh, I think they haven't seen anything yet."

I am adopted. It's never been an issue for me. Whether because I had amazing adoptive parents who loved me, or perhaps because of my makeup as a person, it's never been an open wound in my life. Still, growing up, the fact that I was different from my parents (especially in appearance— I had blonde hair; they were both dark-haired) didn't escape me. Nor the fact that my personality seemed to be so much more out-of-the-box than my parents might have expected. As you can imagine, they put up with a lot of daydreaming! I always wondered if perhaps my birth mother was like me— someone who liked to laugh and embrace life and have fun with friends and live large and sometimes messy.

For a long time, I only focused on the differences . . . until a friend spoke truth into my life. She said, "God changed the lineage and the makeup of your adoptive family line by putting you in it. It was meant for their good, as well as yours."

So in other words, God intended for my messy, exuberant, sometimes-creative personality to infuse a blessing into my adoptive family's lives. As if God, knowing who I was and would be, added molasses to a batch of chocolate chip cookies. (Try it—nummy!)

I love this idea.

I have great respect for my birth mother. Having my own children, I now understand how it takes such selflessness and courage to give your child into the arms of another. I wanted to convey this idea through the Kellogg family—by giving PJ to the Sugars, they were giving her a new life and an opportunity to be a blessing to the Sugar line. But her personality was still Kellogg born, and while she'd been given a new name, she could be a unique mix of both.

As I began book three, I also saw PJ wanting to become more than she was and yet unsure of how to get there, sometimes feeling trapped by the person she'd been, not sure how to synthesize the two.

I think that Christians, despite the transforming power of God in our lives, can be trapped by who we were, the identities of our past. What does it look like to be adopted by God and then live today, with that new identity, in this world? It's just not that easy.

And if we're adopted by God, what does it mean to be coheirs with Christ?

If you'll indulge me for a moment, I believe the answers are found through a journey of looking at who Christ is, a look at His Sonship. Throughout the Gospels, Jesus points out that He and the Father have a unique relationship. The Son and the Father are in close communion, so much so that if you've seen Jesus, you've seen God. God empowered Christ to do miracles, to obey, to live sacrificially. More than that, because of their relationship, God's love for us poured out through Jesus, so much so that our entire destiny was changed.

See, when Jesus appeared to Mary that third day, after rising from the dead, He passed on to us His unique and mind-blowing relationship with God, the Father. (John 20:17). We were no longer outsiders, but brought into the Kingdom, into the family. When we become Christians, our adoption changes us fundamentally. We are given a new identity as children of the King, with all that entails—access to our Father, all the Kingdom power on our side, God's love transforming our lives so much that we could also impact our world. This is what it means to be a coheir; this is our earthly inheritance.

The bottom line is, God gave PJ her inheritance not just for her but for the Sugars and Jeremy and Boone and Kellogg at large. What's more, like Jeremy says, looking back into the past gave her life today meaning. She saw more clearly God's mercy and grace and love. And she passed that on to those around her.

If you have accepted Jesus' payment for your sins and joined the family of God, then you've been given a new identity. You don't belong to the past anymore. Let that new perspective change you, and may you spill out "a little sugar" into the world.

IN HIS GRACE,
Susan May Warren

About the Author

Susan May Warren is a former missionary to Russia, the mother of four children, and the wife of a guy who wooed her onto the back of his motorcycle for the adventure of a lifetime. The award-winning author of over twenty-five books, Susan loves to write and teach writing. She speaks at women's events around the country about God's amazing grace in our lives. Susan is active in her church and small community and makes her home on the north shore of Minnesota, where her husband runs a hotel.

Visit her Web site at **www.susanmaywarren.com.**

THE DEEP HAVEN SERIES

Romance, suspense, and adventure on Minnesota's North Shore . . .

THE TEAM HOPE SERIES

Meet Team Hope—members of an elite search-and-rescue team who run to the edge of danger to bring others back. Unfortunately, they can't seem to stay out of trouble. . . .

have you visited
tyndalefiction.com
lately?

Only there can you find:

→ books hot off the press

→ first chapter excerpts

→ inside scoops on your favorite authors

→ author interviews

→ contests

→ fun facts

→ and much more!

Sign up for your **free** newsletter!

Visit us today at: tyndalefiction.com

Tyndale fiction does more than entertain.

→ *It touches the heart.*

→ *It stirs the soul.*

→ *It changes lives.*

That's why Tyndale is so committed to being first in fiction!

TYNDALE FICTION